# Winterspelt

*Alfred Andersch*

# WINTERSPELT

*Translated from the German
by Richard and Clara Winston*

PETER OWEN · LONDON

ISBN 0 7206 0550 4

Translated from the German *Winterspelt*

This book has been published with financial
assistance from the Arts Council of Great
Britain

PETER OWEN LIMITED
73 Kenway Road London SW5 0RE

First published in Great Britain 1980
© 1974 by Diogenes Verlag AG Zürich
Translation © 1978 by Doubleday and Company Inc

Printed and bound in Great Britain
by Redwood Burn Limited Trowbridge & Esher

*Dedicated to the person,*
*mentioned on page 24,*
*"known to the author as*
*extremely reliable."*

# Contents

# HOW ONE WOMAN BECAME A PARTISAN 175

# ORDERLY ROOM INCIDENTS 243

# CAPTAIN KIMBROUGH 307

# DOCUMENTS, DREAMS, AND FOOTNOTES ON MAJOR DINCKLAGE'S TREASON 371

# SAFE-CONDUCT 401

# CASUALTY FIGURES 463

# CONTENTS

The quotations on pages 215 and 399, given without sources are from Karl Marx and Jean-Paul Sartre respectively.

The description of the behavior of an injured owl in captivity is based on an account in *Paläoanthropologie* by Rudolf Bilz (Frankfurt am Main, 1971).

The painting *Polyphonically Bounded White* by Paul Klee has never been in the possession of the Städel Institute in Frankfurt am Main. It belongs to the Paul Klee Foundation in Bern.

The author wishes to express his gratitude for invaluable help in finding and obtaining materials to: Herr Georg Michaelis, Jr., Gerolstein (Eifel), Mme. Beverly Gordey (Paris), and Mrs. Kate Medina (New York); also to the Zürich Observatory.

Berzona (Valle Onsernone), 1972–74        A. A.

It was cold and raining and blowing half a gale, and ahead of us was the dark forest wall of the Schnee Eifel range where the dragon lived . . .

Ernest Hemingway
*By-Line Ernest Hemingway*


The past is never dead; it isn't even past.

William Faulkner, according to
a newspaper story

*Enemy Position, Military*

## All Quiet on the Western Front

The western theater of war / Military activities between September 2 and October 9, 1944 / Only local engagements took place in the vicinity of Aachen, but these mounted in intensity; in the Eifel and on the Moselle front quiet prevailed. (*Kriegstagebuch* [daily log] of the High Command of the German Armed Forces, abbreviated KTB, written up by Helmuth Greiner and Percy Ernst Schramm of the Armed Forces Operations Staff, Volume IV, p. 400.)

## Hitler, or Inadequate Depth

The Führer was counting on the autumnal weather to ground the enemy air force periodically, and thereby reduce the enemy's superiority. The Führer considered an operational advance advisable if only because the French must not be given the opportunity to expand their formations; for in his view the seventy formations that the English and Americans could be expected to field were not strong enough for a front 700 kilometers long. Hence our object must be to create a front line along which our forces were massed in such numbers that in the area of the offensive they would be superior to the enemy. Initially, the Burgundian Gate and the area of Holland were considered as the base for launching the offensive. To this end, in the middle of the fourth week in September the Armed Forces Operations Staff undertook the requisite calculations of forces.

What was now being planned, however, was no longer an operation initiated on an ad hoc basis to exploit gaps in the enemy front or flank weaknesses, but an offensive from a fixed front subject to continual enemy air reconnaissance. This attack, moreover, would have to pierce a front that the enemy had meanwhile had time to consolidate. Obviously, such an operation required long preparation. And since the western army was in a state of extreme battle-weariness, forces for such an operation could be obtained only by extensive rest and recuperation and new recruitment. Ultimately, more time was needed than had been originally assumed; from the enunciation of the first plans to the last order before the attack some two and a half months passed.

During this period the direction of the operation remained entirely in the Führer's hand. He made the suggestions and the decisions; what is more, he looked into all details, balancing the preparations for the offensive against the defensive battles that meanwhile had to be waged on the western front.

By the end of September the front to the east of Liège had been delimited as the area suitable for a breakthrough. Since a breakthrough had been achieved there before, in May 1940, reports on the operations of the Sixth and Fourth Armies on that occasion were requested from the archives, which had been stored in Liegnitz. These documents were dispatched on October 5. Unfortunately the records were not complete; essential files had been lost in a fire in 1941. However, useful notes were found, in particular a terrain analysis of January 1941 which had determined that an advance in Luxembourg and southern Belgium was preferable to one in the Netherlands, since the number of successive lines of fortifications and obstacles athwart the direction of attack was smaller and both the terrain and traffic arteries more favorable than in the northern part of the Ardennes.

The following conditions were regarded as prerequisites to the planned operation:

1) Maintenance of the western position, inclusive of the Netherlands, and the West Scheldt.

2) A situation in the east that does not place excessive demands upon the forces of the Commander of the Reserve Army.

3) Continued reinforcement of the West in both personnel and matériel.

4) Onset of a period of bad weather lasting ten days to two weeks, to compensate for the lack of air support.

5) Swift destruction of the enemy on the front, to make up for the inadequate depth. (KTB, Volume IV, Part I, Section 4)

## Bradley, or Five Miles

For a period we had a total of only three divisions on a front of some seventy-five miles between Trier and Monschau and were never able to place more than four in that region. While my own staff kept in closest possible touch with this situation, I personally conferred with Bradley about it at various times. Our conclusion was that in the Ardennes region we were running a definite risk but we believed it to be a mistaken policy to suspend our attacks all along the front merely to make ourselves safe until all reinforcements arriving from the United States could bring us up to peak strength.

In discussing the problem, Bradley specifically outlined to me the factors that, on his front, he considered favorable to continuing the offensives. With all of these I emphatically agreed. First he pointed out the tremendous relative gains we were realizing in the matter of casualties. The daily average of enemy losses was double our own. Next, he believed that the only place in which the enemy could attempt a serious counterattack was in the Ardennes region. The two points at which we had concentrated troops of the Twelfth Army Group for offensive action lay immediately on the flanks of this area. One, under Hodges, was just to the northward, the other, under Patton, was just to the south. Bradley felt, therefore, that we were in the best possible position to concentrate against the flanks of any attack in the Ardennes area that might be attempted by the Germans. He further estimated that if the enemy should deliver a surprise attack in the Ardennes he would have great difficulty in supply if he tried to advance as far as the line of the Meuse. Unless the enemy could overrun our large supply dumps, he would soon find himself in trouble, particularly in any period when our air forces could operate efficiently. Bradley traced out on the map the line he estimated the German spearheads could possibly reach, and his estimates later proved to be remarkably accurate, with a maximum error of five miles at any one point. In the area which he believed the enemy might overrun by surprise attack he placed very few supply installations. We had large depots at Liège and Verdun but he was confident that neither of these could be reached by the enemy.

Dwight D. Eisenhower
*Crusade in Europe*
Garden City, N.Y.: Doubleday & Company, Inc., 1948, p. 338.

## Poor General Middleton

It is not surprising that the four weak infantry divisions strung out thinly over the seventy-five miles of the Ardennes front were overwhelmed by the weight of enemy attack. They were, they thought, in spite of the heavy barrage preceding the attack, which many of them believed "friendly," in a quiet sector, almost a rest and rehabilitation area where green troops might become accustomed to the discomforts of the "front line" without too much danger. Of the three infantry divisions of the U.S. VIII Corps under General Middleton, two, the 4th and 28th, had sustained severe hammerings and suffered heavy casualties in the grim autumn battles farther north. They were dog weary and plagued by trench foot, bronchial troubles, and other minor disorders. The third infantry division, the 106th, had relieved the second division in the line four days earlier after an exhausting truck journey in biting cold across France and Belgium. They were a "green" division. Attached to the 106th, the 14th Cavalry Group patrolled an eight-mile-wide gap between the VIII and V Corps. It was a dangerously weak "seam." The right flanking infantry division of the V Corps, the 99th, completed the picture. It was an inexperienced, but well-trained division. It proved itself. (R. W. Thompson, *Montgomery, the Field Marshal* [New York: Charles Scribner's Sons, 1970, p. 243f.])

*Phases of a Changeover from Documentary to Fiction*

1.

Whether the German 416th Infantry Division also proved its mettle could not be determined. No mention is made of this division in the roster of military formations (KTB, Ellis, von Manteuffel) which were readied for the Ardennes offensive. Probably it was withdrawn from the front before the attack began and replaced by a fully mobile division.

It is pure assumption that in October 1944 it was located in the sector of the front which was the scene of the events hereafter described; assumption also that among its battalion commanders was one named Joseph Dincklage.

Consequently, the 416th need not feel itself implicated in the present narrative. On the other hand, an account such as this one requires just such a division as the 416th. An armored division, an elite formation like the 2nd or the 9th, would not do. Nor would any of the "grenadier militia" divisions—which, however bravely they may have fought, are consigned by their very name to the lowest ranks of the army organization. In such divisions, the events summed up in "confidential file Dincklage"—which is not to be found in any military archive—would be incredible from the outset. But under certain circumstances these events are conceivable in an ordinary infantry division. In 1944 the simple name *infantry* conferred on a body of troops a note of rarity and antiquity. Hence the ghostly appearance and disappearance of such a division within the area of the CiC West (Commander-in-Chief in the West) seems eminently appropriate.

2.

What was said above applies, however, not only to the 416th Infantry Division. In the entire German armed forces, neither in 1944 nor before nor after, did there exist an officer who entertained such plans as are here attributed to Major Dincklage. Consequently, the German Army as a whole need not feel implicated in this narrative.

3.

For the above-mentioned reasons this story could be presented in only one form: as fiction.

## Georgia on My Mind

The 106th American Infantry Division will have to forgive the present reporter for having it appear at the front as early as the end of September. As is well known (see Thompson and other sources), it moved into its positions only four days before the start of the Ardennes offensive, that is to say, on December 12. But the statement that its third regiment (precise designation: 424th Regiment) formed the right wing, that is, was positioned to the southeast of Saint-Vith, is historical fact. Military history does not inform us that the C Company of one battalion of this regiment secured the Maspelt sector and established its quarters in that village; but the possibility exists. On the other hand, ascribing to it a company commander named Captain John Kimbrough is simon-pure fiction. Heaven only knows why he grew up in the South, in the small Georgia town of Fargo, which is surrounded on three sides by Okefenokee Swamp. Most of the soldiers of the 106th—this again is factual—came from Montana.

## Feeble Correction

A person known to the author as extremely reliable, who lived in the west Eifel region from 1941 to 1945, wishes to persuade him to revise his assertion in Part 2 of the section entitled *Phases of a Changeover from Documentary to Fiction*. She maintains that she frequently listened in on conversations among German officers in which plans were discussed resembling those entertained by Major Dincklage. But when asked whether at any time and in any way such plans were not only considered but carried out, or at least moved into the initial stage of execution, she has had to concede that such was not the case.

## Sand Table

History relates what happened.
Fiction plays out a possibility.

# *Enemy Position, Morale*

*Von Rundstedt, Model, Blaskowitz, von Manteuffel, Guderian,*
*Balck, Hauser, Schulz, Thomale, etc.*

On the other hand it must be remembered that the commanders had no alternatives; they had to "keep going." In spite of
their inadequate information on the situation as a whole, they
knew enough to realize that given the close ties between the
Western Powers and the USSR there could be no question of a
separate armistice. Only total surrender would be accepted. But
that would mean asking the three and a half million men stationed in the East to walk voluntarily into Russian prisoner-of-war
camps. That was one of the considerations that also painfully
troubled the consciences of the July 20 conspirators. For a commander who was not one of their number the only alternative was
to continue the war with the vague hope that some "miracle"
might still occur—and that meant: to go on obeying as he had
done before. (KTB, Introduction: The Role of the Commanders
of Army Groups and Armies)

### Churchill

P.M. [the Prime Minister] not in his usual form and on the
flat side. However, his fighting spirit was the same as usual and he
said that if he was a German he would get his small daughter to
put a bomb under some British bed; he would instruct his wife to
wait till some American was bending over his basin washing to
strike him on the neck with a chopper, whilst he himself sniped at
Americans and British indiscriminately. (Arthur Bryant, *Triumph
in the West*, A History of the War Years Based on the Diaries of

26

Field-Marshal Lord Alanbrooke, Chief of the General Staff [Garden City, N.Y.: Doubleday & Company, Inc., 1959], Volume 2, p. 241)

## Red Army

Did Major Dincklage share the concerns of the army group and army commanders, or the painfully troubled consciences of the July 20 conspirators with respect to asking German soldiers in the east to walk into Russian prisoner-of-war camps? That can no longer be determined; the answer to the question has been lost in the slight obscurity that already surrounds many aspects of this problematical character. What is certain is that he was never at the front in the east and moved heaven and earth to keep from being sent to Russia. He managed this by referring to the arthrosis of his right hip joint, which had developed since 1942, and by supplying the proper medical certifications. This was all the odder because Dincklage otherwise made a point of having his illness ignored. Perhaps such conduct suggests a fundamental trait of Dincklage's, an innate disposition to show himself in a mysterious and contradictory light—the trait that, for example, emerged in his fateful encounter with Schefold. Perhaps political and historical convictions underlay this conduct; or perhaps he felt a purely temperamental distaste for life as a soldier in the east. The question cannot be settled. Possibly all three motives played a part.

He encountered the Red Army for the first time after he reached Winterspelt, and even there only at so early an hour that he could not see very clearly, for it was still dark when the Russians came down the village street. Dincklage observed them almost every morning after his own arrival in Winterspelt. He stood, leaning on his cane, at the window of the orderly room, in which because of blackout regulations he could not switch on the light. Since he regularly awoke at four o'clock and could not go back to sleep because of the pain in his hip joint, it became part of his technique for whiling away the time, until the battalion staff headquarters came to life, to watch the Russians as they went to their work on the farms. Guarded by two militia soldiers, old men with slung rifles, the Russians appeared in the form of a tolerably straight column at Dincklage's upper right, in the section of the road that led down into the village from a height named Held. Two at a time they would peel off into the farms on the right and left, so that the column steadily diminished in size. When they reached the Thelen farm, which was directly across the village street from the house in which the battalion staff was quartered, only ten men were left. The Russians were not deported civilians but regular prisoners of war. They were housed in a barn on the Held. Dincklage had observed that they wore no shoes, only wooden clogs and foot rags fastened with string. They seemed to have no overcoats. Dincklage asked himself how they would last out the coming winter in such outfits. A thought like this contained the implication that the war would last out the coming winter.

The two who were assigned to Thelen went toward the farmhouse. When they opened the door and entered, the light in the house became visible for a moment. Immediately thereafter it reappeared briefly because either Thelen's own daughters or one of them with Käthe Lenk came out of the house and busied themselves in the yard, rattling milk cans, pumping water.

Staff Sergeant Kammerer, who stood beside him one morning and likewise looked out of the window, had explained the procedure to him. "Now the Russkies are having breakfast," he'd said, "and the girls are keeping watch. If a guard comes by to check, one of the girls delays him while the other runs into the house and warns the men to scurry over to the barn."

"I see." Involuntarily, Dincklage laughed.

"The farmers are forbidden to give the Russians any additional rations," Kammerer explained, "but none of them obeys the order." He seemed to disapprove of Dincklage's laughter. "The Russians get the same food the farmers themselves eat."

"Well, Kammerer," Dincklage said, "can't you imagine the

kind of garbage they're getting in their shed up there? And they're supposed to do heavy work all day long on that? The farmers have to keep up their morale."

"Sir," the top sergeant said unyieldingly, "those Russkies are eating stuff our soldiers hardly see any more. Eggs, bacon, butter."

"Still and all," Dincklage replied, "in this matter no report is to be made, Kammerer."

"I wasn't even thinking of doing that, sir," Kammerer said.

Dincklage treated the staff sergeant in a vigorous but friendly manner. There was never any friction between them. The main thing was to react quickly when the man relapsed into the presumable madman's way of thinking. Kammerer was a Party member, but in 1944 he no longer seemed to be acting accordingly.

### Soldiers and Farmers

Dincklage alone lived in the staff headquarters building itself. The other members of the staff had been quartered with the farmers. Kammerer was a pretty sharp observer. After only three days in the Eifel region he remarked to Dincklage: "The farmers here don't like us." As evidence for this statement, he quoted what old Thelen had said when Kammerer in some connection or other had addressed him: "You as a German farmer . . ." Thelen interposed quickly: "I'm not a German farmer, I'm an Eifel farmer."

Dincklage, who came from Emsland in the northwest, looked sharply at this Protestant Thuringian from whose tunic the Party badge had vanished some time during the summer in Denmark. He considered delivering a little lecture on certain peculiarities of deeply Catholic peasant regions, but decided not to bother. Instead, to head off any inclination Kammerer might have for denunciation, he remarked: "Oh well, as long as the old fellow says that only to you, he isn't sticking his neck out." For he knew quite well that he could rely on Kammerer's bent for subordination. Kammerer would never do anything that he suspected did not suit his immediate superior, whoever that happened to be at the moment.

### Secrecy

"But I hope you won't rely on him where your plan is concerned," Käthe Lenk once said to Major Dincklage, "because there his obedience will stop, you know. If you drop so much as a hint to Kammerer, you're sunk."

Dincklage, who was not used to receiving tactical advice from women, replied tersely: "If everything works out, Kammerer will be just as surprised by the operation as the rest of the battalion."

Accordingly, Kammerer will scarcely play any further part in this narrative, aside from an episode in the section *Orderly Room Incidents*. Of all the members of the 4th Battalion of the 3rd Regiment of the 416th Infantry Division ("Dincklage's men"), only Corporal Reidel will have some inkling of what was afoot.

### West of the Limes

In any comparison between Major Dincklage and Captain Kimbrough it is noteworthy that some of the characteristics of the former cannot be determined as exactly as the corresponding characteristics of the latter. Vagueness persists. For example, Kimbrough's divisional number—the number of the division he did not belong to—can be legitimately given. In Dincklage's case the same number is a pure assumption. The situation is similar in regard to some of the views held by the two officers. No amount of research has been able to establish what Dincklage thought about the problem of surrender in the east—and that is typical of the obscurities surrounding Dincklage. On the other hand, there is no doubt whatsoever that Kimbrough, had he known what Churchill would have done if he had been a German, would only have shaken his head. Looking up from reading the note made by Field Marshal Viscount Alanbrooke, he would have said to Bob Wheeler, the regimental G-2: "So if Churchill were a German he would do exactly what Hitler expects him to do!"

Wheeler's (imaginary) answer would be: "I suspect that the Nazis can be beaten only by someone who is able to put himself into their way of thinking. If it can be called thinking."

"That's not how I see it," Kimbrough would have answered. "They can be beaten only if their thinking is rejected on principle." And with typical incisiveness—in civilian life he was a lawyer—he would have added: "Anyhow, the British are not the ones who are beating the Germans, but we and the Russians."

In continuing this conversation, the conditional forms can be dropped, for it actually took place. Kimbrough himself reported on it; he did so in that conversation with Schefold in which he was forced to admit that Regiment, after querying Division, refused to have any part of Dincklage's plan. "You know, of course, that I am friendly with Major Wheeler. He went in with me to see the colonel. When we came out again, he said to me: 'Listen, John, you're making a mistake. You imagine we're here to free the Germans or somebody from that monster.' He started expounding the view that we Americans are not in Europe just because some European nation chose dictatorship as its form of government. I interrupted him and said that had never been my idea either. He was rather surprised and asked me why I thought we were here. I said: 'Because we're in the mood to wage a war.' 'Of course that's nonsense,' he said. And once more he proved himself a professor of medieval German literature. 'We're here because we are the Romans of the twentieth century,' he said. 'We aren't as refined, aren't as cultivated as the Greeks whom we're defending, but we are unquestionably setting up a *limes*.' I asked him who the barbarians were against whom he was planning to build his *limes*, and he said promptly: 'The Russians.'

"This gives me one more reason for feeling we shouldn't have come over here," Kimbrough said to Schefold.

### Applause from the Wrong Side

"A consistent thinker, this American professor," Hainstock said when Schefold told him—the very next day—about his conversation with Kimbrough. "He thinks in the categories of the superstructure, of course. Intellectual history, they call it. But all the same . . ."

It was characteristic of the old Marxist Wenzel Hainstock that he referred back to Wheeler, whereas he simply ignored Kimbrough's remark about the mood to wage a war, so that he did not repeat it to Käthe Lenk who—this may be assumed—would instantly have agreed with the man from Georgia.

### Adverb and Adjective

From the conversation Wenzel Hainstock had with Käthe Lenk: After he had outlined the theory of imperialism to her, she objected: "But there's something wrong about that. The capitalist countries have now joined in an alliance with the Soviet Union to defeat Hitler. So the lineup is monopoly capitalism with socialism against fascism, which you say is nothing but the form of government the monopolies grasp at when faced with an economic crisis."

"This war," Hainstock said, "is the war of a sick brain. Hitler

32

has become insupportable for capitalism. He discredits the bourgeois social order; he exposes its foundations too blatantly."

She was a teacher of German, had last taught at the Régino Gymnasium in Prüm. The word *insupportable* bothered her.

"You mean *intolerable*," she said.

"I don't care," he said, irritated.

"There's a great difference," she went on, "between thinking somebody insupportable and feeling that he's intolerable. To my father, for example, Hitler was simply intolerable."

Her father had even managed to keep her out of the Bund Deutscher Mädel, and had later advised her on how to avoid entering the National Socialist Student League. He had been a salesman of machine tools, and so professionally obliged to keep his ears open and to adjust to all sorts of people, not just to pretend cordiality. Yet he had not really been broad-minded. Käthe rather remembered him as stern, dry, and skeptical. Perhaps he had not always been an agreeable husband for her mother; he threw a sharp shadow as he moved through their house on Hanielweg, stooped, with the hint of a hunched back, a newspaper in hand, looking for the cigar he had left somewhere in one of the house's many ashtrays. Her mother had been slim, dark, pretty, always ready to laugh.

When she remembered her parents, Käthe found it impossible to believe that the actions of the monster reflected the fundamentals of bourgeois thought.

### Strategic Study

"In any case," Hainstock remarked after he had listened to Schefold's report of Kimbrough's conversation with Wheeler—or did he use this phrase to end his discussion with Käthe on Lenin's theory of imperialism?—"in any case the Americans entered the war only because they could not afford to let the Russians defeat Hitler all alone."

## Others' Chestnuts from the Fire

Kimbrough had no personal reasons for instinctively rejecting Churchill's fantasy about how he would behave if he had been a German. Kimbrough had no German forebears. He knew little about German history and culture or anti-culture. His name would indicate Scottish origins.

The small town of Fargo is situated, as has already been mentioned, in the southern part of the state of Georgia. The state of Georgia is one of the Southern states of the United States of America. Kimbrough had given his Southern birth as his grounds for saying that the Americans "should not have come over here." "We Southerners think the USA should not have let itself be dragged into the world's quarrels," he once said to Schefold. "We're isolationists. I don't know exactly why we are isolationists. Maybe just because the Yankees are anti-isolationists.

"Besides, we're Democrats," he went on. "I come from an old Democratic family. Everybody in Fargo voted for Roosevelt. Now we're peeved because Roosevelt got us mixed up in this war."

"I am not peeved," Schefold said. "If it weren't for Roosevelt, Hitler would live to be ninety."

"Get your Hitler off your backs yourselves!" Kimbrough said, not rudely, but with judicial coldness.

Schefold puzzled over why this isolationist of all the Americans was ready to take a chance on Dincklage's plan, whereas his superior officers, army men who were probably altogether in accord with Roosevelt's war aims, flatly turned down the major's proposal.

34

*Apropos of Schefold?*

The Battle of the Ardennes was won, and a heavy defeat inflicted upon the enemy, by fine generalship supported by able commanders in the field, by heroic defensive actions, notably at Saint-Vith and Bastogne, and by the swift and skillful creation and deployment of reserves. All these deeds have been "sung" and will live in military annals, but the disruption of the enemy plan and the imposition of delays from which it was impossible to recover was brought about by anonymous men, anonymous groups, often of stragglers of no fixed intention, whose deeds will never be known. (R. W. Thompson, *Montgomery, the Field Marshal*, p. 244)

# *Major Dincklage*

## Biogram

Joseph Dincklage, born 1910 in Meppen (Emsland), only son of the owner of a brickmaking plant named Joseph Dincklage and his wife Amalie, née Windhorst, Catholic, graduated (1929) from the Salesian Gymnasium in Meppen, attended the universities of Heidelberg, Berlin, and Oxford (studying political economy and languages), brief intermezzo in industry acquiring practical experience in plant management in Duisburg. Because of the building boom resulting from the construction of the Westwall line of fortifications, Dincklage senior was able to keep his son abreast of the preparations for war. After long talks with his father, Joseph Dincklage, then twenty-eight, decided on an army career, in order, as he put it, "to come through National Socialism with halfway clean hands." (Dincklage senior, a strict communicant, advised against that course. "Go back to Oxford instead," he said. "Or even better to the USA. I know how to protect myself so they won't be able to ride me because of it." But the son did not act on this advice.) After 1938 a variety of military academies; at the outbreak of the war officer candidate, by spring of 1940 second lieutenant (Upper Rhine front), 1941–42 first lieutenant and captain (Africa), 1943 Knight's Cross and promotion to major (Sicily), from autumn 1943 to autumn 1944 in the occupation forces in Paris and Denmark.

Unmarried, but chiefly from lack of opportunity, the consequence of too frequent changes of location. At seventeen he had begun an affair, which continued over three summer vacations, with a woman five years older than himself, a farmer's wife in Bentheim County. The recollection of that made it more difficult for him to strike up the usual relationships with fellow students during his early university years. He had some casual encounters

38

with these girls, occasionally a serious one, but none developed into a lasting interest.

Dincklage was 5'7½", just short of medium height, with the kind of leanness that comes from never putting on an ounce of fat ("wiry"). Dark-blond, straight hair, gray eyes, straight nose with broad bridge, but narrow at the base, wide mouth; eyes, nose, and mouth well placed in the thin, evenly tanned face. Not much concerned about food, inclined to strictly ration his drinking and smoking (cigarettes).

### Factors

The gentle slope of the meadows down to the Thames. The afternoons reading in the Bodleian Library. Discussions on the genesis of the "social product." The loud arguments about Keynes in Professor Talboy's seminar while the lights outside the windows of Merton College changed from gray-green to blue-gray. If he were to return to Oxford, the British would intern him for a while at the outbreak of the war, later release him. He could then peacefully complete his research on the altered role of money in the sixteenth century. Stillness, the rustle of paper, soundless thinking, the chimes above High Street.

He could imagine it all. He could not imagine it for himself. From the window of the office where he was talking with his father, looking out at the cluster of brick furnaces, he said: "I'd rather be an army officer," and, giving the matter a semblance of logic: "If I've got to be a soldier, better to be an officer than an ordinary mud-hog."

Eight years later, in Winterspelt, Käthe Lenk said to him that she wanted to go to Lincolnshire. The simple and decisive way she made this remark suddenly prompted him to see his renunciation of England as the greatest mistake of his life. She did not say why it had to be Lincolnshire of all places; she merely told him how she had come across the name of this English county. Since he had once taken an outing to Lincolnshire, he began describing the region to her, but stopped when he realized that his account did not interest her.

"I should have settled down in Lincolnshire and waited for you there," he had said then. "You would have come."

She said nothing, in no way manifested a wish to have met him there.

But if I had stayed in England, he argued with himself, lapsing into logic, I would not have met Käthe Lenk. For the moment, these coincidences seemed to him, quite contrary to his usual viewpoint, entirely fated.

He had noticed that although Käthe hated the war, she was nevertheless impressed by his Knight's Cross, and so he began telling her: "Northwest of Syracuse the Americans attacked with a single strong tank formation. I was once again on the left wing." He added: "I always find myself on the left wing. The left wing hounds me. Anyhow, the tank formation was so strong that the only thing to do was to sound retreat and make yourself scarce. But a machine-gun platoon in my company simply stayed in their holes and decimated the infantry the tanks were escorting, so that the tanks suddenly stopped and then turned back. Actually, the Knight's Cross should have gone to the leader of that platoon, Master Sergeant Bender. I didn't reach the platoon's position until the worst was already over. All I could do was congratulate Bender. But in our outfit it's always some superior gets the reward. When I put in for a medal for Bender, the battalion commander just waved that aside wearily. 'In the operative framework,' he said superciliously, 'your left wing fended off this dangerous breakthrough, Herr Dincklage.' So that's how I came by this piece of tin," Dincklage concluded his story. "You civilians have some pretty mistaken ideas about decorations. Every three months so and so many Iron Crosses are assigned to me for the battalion, and of course I distribute them primarily among the noncoms because I have to keep up their morale. That's how a mess sergeant becomes a wearer of the Iron Cross, First Class."

"This civilian," Käthe said, "would much rather see decorations going to cooks than to marksmen."

It was a source of never-ending amazement to him that the left wing always came his way—as was now the case in Winterspelt also. Even as a boy in the gang battles for which the terrain of the brick plant was so ideal, he had always been made the leader of the left section of "his" gang—after all, he had to be made a leader because he provided the theater of war—with his father's approval and after hours. And he recalled how he had always slunk along the walls of the furnaces and sheds on the left, followed by boys armed with laths and sticks, trying to curb their heavy breathing. Behind the corners of the left quadrant formed by drying or already burned bricks they had lain in wait for the enemy. The light had always been twilight streaming from the translucent sky above the Emsland moors into lanes framed by clay yellow and brick red, falling into dusky zones of brick dust. Because of this light the gang wars went off fairly mildly; the light converted the fights into feints, shadow-boxing. Father's warning not to get too rough proved unnecessary.

In politics Dincklage had never caught himself edging to the left. During his stay in Oxford he had avoided discussions of the Spanish Civil War, which was then at its height (in the winter of 1936–37), as far as he was able. He was so little leftist that he even defended the Soviet Union when British students denounced it for not intervening militarily in Spain, as Germany and Italy were doing, and instead only supplying weapons. "The Russians think in longer time spans," he said. He realized that this was an apology for half-heartedness, but accepted the onus of that.

Apropos Emsland—of course Dincklage was electrified when Käthe mentioned that on her journey to the west she had become acquainted with Emsland for the first time, had even "padded around," as she put it, in the Bourtang Moor.

"Were you in Meppen also, Fräulein Lenk?" he asked. (This was at a very early stage of their acquaintance, when they were still formal with each other.)

She nodded. "I imagine so; I went everywhere," she said.

"If you went into the moor from Meppen you must have noticed the big brick factories. On the road to Wesuwe."

She shrugged. Perhaps she had taken another road.

"They're my father's," he said. "Too bad that we did not know each other sooner. You could have visited my parents, stayed with them."

She did not know what to reply. If she understood it correctly, she was receiving a proposal of marriage, the first of the two proposals Dincklage made to her, as she was later to realize. The first had come too soon, the second too late.

"Meppen is a pretty town," he said. "Did you see the Town Hall and the church? One of the finest architectural ensembles in all of North Germany."

She could not bring herself to tell him that places like Meppen and all the other stops of her journey meant nothing more to her than meatballs composed of vegetable leftovers, gruel, bread with turnip tops, beer, ersatz coffee, the rancid smell of rooms whose walls were painted brown or green, and speechless nights of going to bed too early.

But she was able to tell him about the curious areas into whose range she had stumbled in the Emsland moors. There she would run into armed patrols who would check her identification and without saying why would order her back along the road she had come by. When she told Major Dincklage about the use being made of his native region, he recited a litany. "Börger Moor," he said, "Esterwegen, Aschendorfer Moor, Neusustrum." And he actually finished with the word *amen*, but it exploded from his lips like a curse.

Africa, Sicily, Paris confused him. Inevitably he gathered impressions, but strictly forbade himself to act the tourist. He took no part in officers' outings to Cyrenaica, Segesta, or Chartres, preferred staying back in the tent or dugout, would rise abruptly and stalk out when the talk turned to archaeological matters or art history, did not even curl his lips at the ever staler taste of jokes about "joining the army and seeing the world." He concentrated fully on his duties. As his battalion commander in Africa once said, after watching him in the course of an evening at the officers' club: "Apparently, Lieutenant Dincklage, you don't care much for the finer things in life."

After a skirmish at Beghazi (on February 5, 1941; he'd noted the date) he started to laugh when several men of his company who were stretched out on the desert sand, showered with dust by the maneuvering tanks, did not at once stand up and brush the sand out of their uniforms. He did not realize what he had done until he noticed the soldiers standing near him staring at him in dismay: they assumed he was laughing at the casualties. That skirmish was by no means his baptism by fire; he had long since grown accustomed to the sight of the dead. Rather, he had been overcome by a sense of unreality. Later attacks of this kind were touched off by more innocuous causes, and were usually accompanied by déjà-vu sensations. For example, for ten weird minutes the tents under the palms of Martubah took on the filmy cast of fantasies; but what was more, he had seen them once before, only he did not know when. Or a village street in the vicinity of Ragusa that consisted not of crumbling Sicilian houses but of some ethereal stuff—this happened while he was heading a combat patrol combing the village—reminded him of that same street, though he had never previously set foot on it, not even in a dream. He examined his philosophical outlook, decided that he had never had any traffic with the idealistic and romantic view of existing things as illusion. He had always been a realist.

In Paris he consulted a medico who was said to have had psychiatric training. The doctor, cautious in view of Dincklage's Knight's Cross, sounded him out for a while before risking any opinion. "Of course you have a little neurosis, Herr Kamerad," he said. "But nowadays that's more a sign of health. I'm really worried about the officers who have none because they regard whatever they're experiencing as quite normal. The traumas that are in store for them—no thanks!"

Dincklage understood: the doctor was implying that he was suffering from a collective neurosis. Arrangements were made for another appointment, but he did not return because the doctor had said to him in parting: "If I may give you a piece of advice meanwhile: find yourself a nice girl-friend if you haven't already done so." That was really making too light of his case, Dincklage thought. He did not know that Dr. K. had entered on the file card after Dincklage's departure: "Schizophrenic interludes since 1941." Probably a faulty diagnosis. The hallucinations Dincklage had reported were not symptoms of an incipient splitting of consciousness. Dincklage was not schizophrenic but schizothymic, that is, merely highly sensitive.

For the Cox arthrosis, which had also come on in Africa, Dincklage had been taking a new corticoid drug that Dr. H., the division medical captain, was trying out on him. He avoided taking his medicine in the battalion orderly room, or having a glass of water brought to him, although he did not fool himself; the top sergeant and the clerk noticed when he went to the kitchen himself to fill a glass of water and then continued on to the upstairs room where he'd had his army cot placed.

Whenever he downed his tablets at eleven o'clock in the morning, the roar of planes could no longer be ignored. Dincklage would step to the window and open it. The wing was flying eastward at great height. Usually Dincklage tried to calculate how many squadrons of interceptors would be needed to scatter bomber formations of such strength. If we had any fighters left, he thought, they would have to intercept the Americans over Belgium. Instead, the Americans are free to fly without fighter escorts. Dincklage was no longer perturbed by these conditions in the sky because he had already experienced them in 1943 in Sicily and at the beginning of this present year in France. He only wondered that phrases like *if we had any fighters left* or names like *Hermann Göring* could still not cross his mind without causing him bitterness. When I should rather be pleased about the mess, he thought. Even the little word *we* is wrong. What I should by rights be thinking, quite as a matter of course, is: *they* have no fighters left.

Contemplating the sky over Winterspelt, before he closed the window, he wished he were back in Denmark. In Denmark the

44

sky had been empty. The drills on the Randers heath had proceeded as smoothly as poems. He could suggest to company commanders that marches should be terminated at bathing beaches
on quiet Baltic sounds. Meanwhile he himself would stroll along
a lane and could even fancy that he would be spending the rest
of the war looking at thatched houses and phlox in bloom.

The phlox was past its prime, but not even news of July 20
wrenched Dincklage entirely out of his dreams, even tough Colonel Hoffmann subsequently became more and more unbearable.
(The division commander, General von C., in his address to the
officers, had carefully skirted the word *traitor*. He had merely
spoken of *irresponsible elements*, using a tone that in no way
differed from criticisms of a maneuver.) Reveries, phantoms. The
416th Infantry Division, to which Dincklage had been transferred
from Paris in the spring, was not a division destined to be forgotten in Denmark.

The citified villa, smoothly stuccoed and characterless in the
midst of the whitewashed farmhouses and rough stone barns of
Winterspelt village, had already been requisitioned for a staff
headquarters by the unit they had replaced. This unit, which
belonged to the 18th Motorized Division, had participated in the
entire retreat through northern France and Belgium until at the
beginning of September it came to a halt literally in the first German village behind the frontier. For obscure reasons the Americans had not pressed on. "I suspect they are having supply difficulties," said the major whom Dincklage relieved. "They could have
chased us all the way to the Rhine, all the way to the Rhine without any trouble, that's how done in we were." And he had begun
telling stories of the Falaise pocket, from which the 18th Motorized had barely escaped.

This major had been in the dumps; he expected his formation
would be sent to Russia, although of course he had no hard information. He had congratulated Dincklage. "Around here it's like
the autumn of 1939. Where were you then?"

"On the Upper Rhine."

"Well, then, of course you know the story. A little patrolling, a
few popguns shot off now and again, but that was about the size
of it. An odd sort of war back then, wasn't it?"

Dincklage agreed.

"I wouldn't be surprised if the war were to end on the same note as it began," Major L. said. "If you're lucky, Herr Kamerad, you'll see in the armistice right here."

The war, Dincklage thought, was a breeding ground for every kind of lunacy. He changed the subject. "I don't imagine you'll be going to Russia," he said. "So far as I know your division is staying with the Fifty-third Army Corps."

He was only guessing; he wanted to cheer up the man. When his words proved true and the 18th Motorized was sent not to Russia but to Koblenz (preparatory to the operation, at that time still camouflaged by the code name *Watch on the Rhine*), Major L. for several days considered reporting Dincklage for irresponsibly revealing an operational order he must have been privy to (infraction of Führer's Order on secrecy 002252/42, which had just been reissued). Major L. finally forbore, first because he was afraid Dincklage might retaliate by quoting what he had so thoughtlessly said about a forthcoming armistice, and also because he was an easygoing fellow.

In talking to other officers Dincklage occasionally spoke of his men—"my men need better rations," and such phrases—the possessive pronoun always sounding as if it were inside verbal quotation marks. His regimental commander, Colonel Hoffmann, alert to such nuances, once bawled him out for that. ("I will not have this tone, Herr Dincklage"—"Yes, sir!"—"Those men are really your men. You'd better realize that."—"I'll do my best, sir.")

"If I were married," he once said to Käthe, "I would be very reluctant to use the expression *my wife*."

"Of course that impressed you," Hainstock said when Käthe quoted this remark to him. "He knows exactly how to impress you." As a rule Hainstock managed not to let his jealousy show.

Dincklage used the word *enemy* with as much circumspection as the possessive pronouns. He rather admired the way Colonel Hoffmann never spoke of the enemy, but always of the other side,

except when there was no avoiding such technical expressions as
*enemy position*. For example, when Major Dincklage criticized
the Luftwaffe he would say: "It's enough for you to know the
enemy position right in front of you. Your men are holding the
eastern heights above the valley of the Our, the Americans
the western heights. Nothing prevents you from determining the
other side's strength and exact position. I must insist that you
keep your men up to snuff in this respect."

Precisely in this respect Dincklage was not keeping "his" men
up to snuff. Given his frontline position (with the lines separated
by a river), he regarded patrols to reconnoiter the other side's activity as foolishly risky, a pointless playing Indian. Sometimes he
dispatched a patrol into the murky forested valley used by
Schefold when he wanted to get behind the German lines.

"Wouldn't it make sense to blow up the viaduct at Hemmeres,
sir?" he asked.

"I suggested that to Division," Hoffmann said. "There is an explicit order from Corps not to. The thing is to stand."

"Aha," Dincklage replied. He could venture the mocking, even
contemptuous intonation he gave to the two vowels separated by
an aspirate because the tone in which the colonel had spoken left
no doubt of his own opinion of the operational idea behind this.
But Hoffmann quickly braked the process of their harmonious
agreement. "Sometimes you seem to forget that you are forbidden
to draw conclusions, Herr Dincklage," he said. He turned away.
"Besides," he added, "at this point I'm glad for every bridge that
remains standing."

Concerning Dincklage's infraction of discipline, to which Colonel Hoffmann had alluded: On command of the Chief of Staff to
the CiC West, Corporal Rudolf Dreyer of the tactical group of
the CiC West was assigned to provide clerical assistance for certain tasks. Corporal Dreyer was strongly reminded to speak to no
one about what he would hear and write, also to draw no conclusions from the materials heard or written. (Lieutenant Colonel of
General Staff W. Schaufelberger, *Secrecy, Deception and Cam-*

*ouflage illustrated by the German Ardennes Offensive of 1944*
[Zürich, 1969], p. 30)

"I have reports," Dincklage said, "that some Americans are coming down to the Our and fishing for trout there."

"Ah!" Hoffmann whirled around and looked sharply at him. "And how are your men behaving?"

"I have the impression that it goes against the grain for them to fire at men who are fishing."

"What a situation!" The colonel actually giggled with indignation. "Herr Dincklage," he said, "the battalion will deliver a few trout to me by day after tomorrow at the latest. And after that this nonsense stops completely, of course!"

"I guarantee it will, sir," Dincklage said.

The fishing actually did irritate him. Sometimes he seriously considered going on radio to bawl out the American officer who was permitting this slackness to creep in among his men. (The regiment had a signal platoon that was constantly engaged in monitoring the frequencies the Americans were using. But in October '44 strict radio silence had been imposed on the entire western front.)

"There you have it," Hainstock said when Käthe told him about Dincklage's impulse to establish contact with the American commander opposite him. "This fellow is still dreaming about a war waged among officers and gentlemen." But he found it odd that Dincklage would talk about military problems with a woman. Perhaps, he thought, it was one of his tricks for getting to Käthe. The Our was a fabulous trout stream. Apparently the war had done wonders for the trout in the Our. The anglers of C Company—most of the soldiers in the 106th Infantry Division came from Montana and were used to sparkling mountain streams—had made some sensational catches. Kimbrough had envied them. Though a country boy himself, Kimbrough was no angler; it had been a disappointment to his father when he found he could not teach the boy fishing.

When the anglers in his company finally did come under fire,

Kimbrough almost felt pleased. He called a muster of the company and forbade anyone to set foot again in the no-man's-land of the Our valley, except for such military operations as he ordered. In addition he had to take care that word of this fishing business did not get around. Major Carter, the battalion commander, would chew him out, holding him responsible for the men's having come under fire because of a slackness that he, Kimbrough, should have prevented in the first place. Since nobody had been hit, he might be able to hush up the matter.

Reidel felt affronted when he was not allowed to join the squad assigned to drive the American anglers from the bank of the Our. He had volunteered and been rejected. Whereupon he had complained. Sergeant Wagner had shrugged. "Sorry, Reidel, but this isn't a job for you." And then, to Reidel's amazement, Wagner had selected the worst duffers in the unit (third platoon, second company), all kids—Borek among them—who had never yet had a moving target in front of them. "Training mission for recruits," Wagner had said with a touch of embarrassment. "Direct order from Battalion." When those rookies returned to quarters in the evening Reidel had asked them: "Well, how many did you knock off?" He'd heard the chattering guns from his foxhole, embittered because they weren't letting him take part in this target practice. Instead, those duffers! "We don't know," one of them had answered. From their expressions he could see that all they'd scored were near misses.

Schefold had been glad when the fishing at the Our ceased. He'd come to regard the valley bottom around Hemmeres as a neutral zone—"my neutral territory," as he said to Kimbrough. Hence he'd always regarded with displeasure the GI's standing among the bushes along the shore and fishing only a short distance from the hamlet, like combatants who'd penetrated into some Switzerland, although only to engage in illegal angling. They disturbed his peace. Now they were gone, and the farm and the meadows lay even more deserted than usual under the autumnal sun that fell upon the valley, walled in by shadowy slopes.

The only signs of soldiers were at the tunnel on both sides of the viaduct for the railroad (it had long ago stopped running) from Saint-Vith to Burgreuland. The viaduct spanned the valley to the north, and now and then small figures of uniformed men, in khaki to the left, in gray-green to the right, sometimes appeared at the tunnel entrances like cuckoos from the opening flaps of a cuckoo clock, showed themselves for a moment, and then were automatically drawn back into the blackness again. Flap, Schefold thought when the blackness closed around them. A pity there are no chimes along with the sight, he thought, like the chimes that ring with the knights on the castle tower in Limal.

Major Dincklage showed keen interest when Käthe Lenk told him Wenzel Hainstock was a Marxist. He would like to meet him, he said; but for personal reasons as well as for reasons inherent in the techniques of political underground work, no meeting between Dincklage and Hainstock ever took place. (Hainstock was not exactly delighted to hear that Käthe had mentioned his name to the major. "No link in a chain is permitted to know the name of the next link," he said. "Oh well, you couldn't have known that. How should you know the rules of underground work? If you'd just cleared it with me beforehand . . ." He stopped because he saw Käthe covering her face with her hands.

Since Dincklage's first university years had coincided with the time of the Weimar Republic—not to speak of Oxford—and since he had studied political economy, he had of course looked into Marxism. He regarded Ricardo and Walras as preëminent exponents of capitalism's laws of motion, but thought that Marx had given the clearest account of those laws, had scientifically laid bare their inner workings as clearly as it was possible to do so, for in the nature of things a residue would always remain that could not be explicated. Dincklage found in Pareto a description of that residue—the psychological motive force of economic life, namely the passions. He continually vacillated between Pareto's cynical doctrine of residues and Marx's humanistic concept of man's alienation. He would have liked to believe entirely in the latter, but could not manage to convince himself that alienation would be overcome by a mere change in the ownership of the means of production.

He was not at all in doubt about the interest big entrepreneurs had in the big business of war. (In this respect his father was a rare bird. But the Dincklage factories could not be classified among the industrial giants, that was for sure.) Nevertheless, Dincklage did not think that a war like this one had been intended by the monopolies whose emergence Marx had foretold. (Dincklage had not had time to acquaint himself with the further elaborations of Marx's theory of the accumulation of capital as set forth by Lenin in his theory of imperialism.) Clever though they were, the great industrialists were so simple-minded that they imagined they could have a wartime boom without war. They wanted to eat their cake and have it too. But aside from such subjective flaws in reasoning, the world war did not, Dincklage thought, accord with the interests and tendencies of large-scale capital. Much rather—if you were going to think in Marxist categories—those interests and tendencies aimed at a subtle exploitation of the world, a world culture of exploitation, so to speak, peace in pleasurable slavery accompanied by a high degree of freedom of thought. But not catastrophe.

But if this war had not sprung from economic laws operating more or less mechanically, then what were its origins? Faced with this question, Dincklage withdrew to the minimal position: man was a creature made of determinateness and chance. He was a product of descent, milieu, education, and constitution, as well as of psychic complexes that were part of his birthright. Within this preëxisting set of factors pure chance reigned; indeed, the factors themselves were the results of chance processes. That two hundred years ago a man had met one woman rather than another was chance, but it had influenced the life of a descendant two hundred years later. A social decline or a trauma, both produced by chance incidents, by a currency devaluation or by the sight of a fire, could crucially affect what are generally called "fates" over the course of generations. Even acts seemingly of entirely free will —someone's deciding to climb a mountain or read a book—were conditioned reflexes. But that remained debatable, whereas it was beyond question that a character like Hitler arose out of the exponential accumulation of certain hereditary traits and the blind operations of the sort of accidents that are called world history. But what did one call a state of being in which constant natural laws and pure arbitrariness became intricately involved and darkly interpenetrated? One called it chaos. Dincklage was convinced of the existence of chaos. Chaos alone explained for him why monsters existed.

Of course, even in the midst of chaos and in the face of monsters, ethical decisions remained, choices between good and evil— in short, conscience. Such choices were the last remnant that Dincklage retained of his Catholic education. Probably, he thought mockingly, his conscience, too, was merely a reflex conditioned by Emsland.

The following happened to him one day when he was sitting with a group of other officers at a military conference. With the index finger of his right hand, with which he was clutching the seat of his chair (because he was in pain), he drew some word that had cropped up in the course of the discussion, let's say the word *battalion* (it really did not matter what the word was), on the wood of the chair. He had frequently done that; it had almost become a tic of his to write these invisible words, always in capital letters and without letting others notice the movement of his finger. But this one time he suddenly felt with absolute certainty that this act would not disappear in the course of all the ages and even in a space conceived as infinite. It was inconceivable that every trace of the writing and the energy used in producing it could be extinguished and fall into nothingness. Even during the conference he wrote the date and the time (October 3, 1944, 1120 hours) on a slip of paper, along with the word (*battalion*), and stuck the note into the left breast pocket of his tunic.

The following night he dreamed that he had come to the edge of the marketplace in a very lovely medieval town. Houses of mysterious size and importance rimmed the square, especially toward the side farthest from him. They were half-timber houses with the timbers at odd angles. One dark-brown house was leaning against a white one—so he was dreaming in colors. As he was about to enter the square so that he could examine the houses more closely, two armed men blocked his way with leveled rifles. They were soldiers in the uniforms of a modern army, but one unknown to him. He had to content himself with walking along the edges of the square, where puppeteers had set up their theaters, stages overcrowded with marionettes and tinsel.

On his nightly rounds (which Dincklage never left to his company commanders), accompanied by a noncom and an orderly, he stopped when he came to the ridge of a hill and contemplated the theater of war. The nights were always clear these days, the sky studded with stars. All was quiet in his sector, and in the adjacent area of the neighboring division to the south there was also nothing to be heard or seen. Somewhere in the vicinity two soldiers were talking in low voices from foxhole to foxhole. Nearby to the north, beyond the Ihrenbach valley, where the 416th's front made a bend to the east because the Americans had occupied the Schnee-Eifel ridge—which from the American point of view was a salient—a flare rose high into the air now and then, and went out. On rare occasions a burst of machine-gun fire followed. From farther to the north, far beyond the mountains of the Schnee-Eifel, the rumble of artillery salvos reached all the way to them and they saw lights—fires? searchlights? "Christmas trees" from planes?—that moved along the wall of the sky and dispersed on it into ghostly glows. It was said that an American formation was slowly working its way up to the dam across the Urft valley. Here, where Dincklage and his companions were standing, the trees, the woods they were looking at, still formed bodies of impenetrable black, every night, with no glints of light playing over them. At such moments he felt keenly the night-shrouded confrontation of two vast armies, sometimes silent, sometimes accompanied by the organ tones of artillery. At such moments his own view of patrol activity, which in spite of Colonel Hoffmann's injunction he was conducting very laxly, spread wider and wider. The sum of all the official acts resulting from the war amounted to no more than a gigantic game of playing Indians. Boys' skirmishes in a brick factory—nothing more! He had a vision of the hundreds of thousands of men who were now talking in low voices in the darkness or standing half asleep in their foxholes, climbing out and under the star-spangled sky, breaking into roars of laughter before they set out for home, back to their lessons.

Fantasies! Incidentally, thoughts of this sort did not stop Dincklage, next time he spotted the flame of a match as he approached a sentinel, from giving the fellow a dressing down that (the noncom later remarked appreciatively to the orderly) so stiffened the man that he'd be able to stand his socks up in a corner.

When Dincklage returned to his quarters from such inspection tours, he sometimes went into his office, made sure before he turned on the light that the blackout blinds were lowered over the window, closed the door which bore on the side toward the orderly room a cardboard sign reading *chief*—Staff Sergeant Kammerer had put it there—sat down at the desk, spread out on it the maps, large-scale sheets 107a and 119b of the German Reich, the so-called strategic maps issued by the Reich Survey Office in Berlin, together with a more detailed Belgian plane table sheet (1:10,000) of the area south of Saint-Vith, and with the aid of a flashlight—for the ceiling light was dim—studied for the nth time the position of the battalion he commanded.

Once again he was on the extreme left wing of a divisional sector, which in this case was the sector farthest advanced toward the west, precisely because of that American formation occupying the Schnee-Eifel to the east. The 416th held the territory around the southern wing of the American positions (to the north a militia rifle division connected up with the 416th). Dincklage's battalion lay in a pocket formed by a loop of the Our in the extreme west. It was almost cut off from the division by the densely wooded Ihrenbach valley, which had no roads at all running in the north-south direction; its only link with the division, at any rate, was by couriers and occasional patrols. The link to the adjacent division to the south was also very loose. Each time Dincklage had again convinced himself of the isolated position of his battalion, he let the point of the pencil in his right hand circle, in the cone of light from the flashlight, over the hamlet of Hemmeres, which lay among the slopes of the Our valley. If a strong American formation were to cross the Our, say on the still intact railroad viaduct at Hemmeres, and by way of the village of Elcherath reach the road from Saint-Vith to Pronsfeld, then advance southeast along that road, his battalion could be cut off and destroyed with ease or, if he, Dincklage, permitted it, captured.

During one (or several?) of these nocturnal study sessions in the glow of the flashlight and the dim overhead light, with compulsively rotating pencil and sharp spasms of pain—for bending at the waist over maps aggravated his condition—during one of those sessions Dincklage must have made the decision not only to surrender the battalion without a fight if such an American operation as he had imagined actually took place, but also not to wait for this operation, to go far beyond anything that could be justified by tactical considerations of defensive problems, and to offer of his own accord surrender of the battalion.

Examining the question of how he could transform idea into act, Dincklage came up against two insuperable obstacles:

1. The very simple, honorable (because in keeping with the old rules of warfare) picture of himself as the negotiator crossing the Our accompanied by a noncom bearing a white flag and presenting himself at the American line—that picture had to be banished from all the scenarios from the outset. If he made known any such intention, Staff Sergeant Kammerer, with the aid of the company commander, would have him arrested on the spot, and would put in an immediate call to Regiment. In no time a detachment of MP's would arrive, followed by Colonel Hoffmann in person; out of concern for the regiment's reputation he would feel it his duty to conduct the first interrogation himself and then without delay turn Dincklage over to the appropriate court-martial. (It was only because the 416th, for some reason, probably merely from a shortage of personnel, had no Party political officer assigned to it that a case like Major Dincklage's could ever reach a court-martial.)

2. The idea of entering into a conspiracy with the other side would have to remain purely in the realm of ideas, although it was characteristic of Dincklage that he did not exclude it from his thoughts.

First of all, to take by surprise a battalion of almost battle strength (approximately 1,200 men), even if the action were directed by the battalion's own commanding officer, represented an almost insoluble operative task. Of the battalion's four companies, two (the first and the supply company) were quartered in Winterspelt, the other two in the villages of Wallmerath and Elcherath. From those villages the men went to their posts in a system—worked out by Dincklage with great precision—of two successive lines of defense in depth. On Day X (rather, Night X) Dincklage would have to use some pretext (but what?) to pry most of the units from their quarters and the line and assemble them, with as few weapons as possible, at a single point where they could be easily encircled. Still, it was possible to initiate a surprise night-emergency exercise with subsequent battalion roll call; and since Dincklage had assumed that the Americans must have a feeling for, and some ability at, playing Indians, the plan had a certain chance of success, especially with a bit of luck.

But since Dincklage had no way of getting in touch with the other side, he considered himself blocked.

From the manner in which Dincklage drew this conclusion—he presented his plan to her in the form of a mathematical equation —Käthe Lenk at once recognized that the surrender of the battalion was for him merely an abstract idea. Not that he had not taken it seriously; he treated it as seriously as anyone treats a hypothesis that has become an obsession. Käthe would have been better pleased if his speech had now and again assumed a somewhat uncertain note, a note of excitement, even a touch of derring-do; for after all something of the sort must be involved when an officer of only thirty-four is preparing a military coup. Instead, nothing but this abstract coldness.

"Oh," she said, "if that's the problem, I know someone who is able to get in touch with the Americans. Someone you can completely rely on."

"If this officer," Hainstock said when Käthe outlined Dincklage's strategy to him, "has not the slightest backing among his troops for his plan, he had better drop it. That is exactly what the Party has always meant when it talked about the lack of a mass basis." (Hainstock had formed the habit of speaking of the Communist Party of Czechoslovakia and the Central Committee of the Communist International in the perfect tense, which some exponents of grammar refer to as the tense of completed action in present time.)

Dincklage could not foresee the effect of his idea, if carried out, upon the course of the war. He did not know and did not care whether the Americans would use the frontline gap resulting from the removal of the battalion for a general breakthrough or whether they would merely advance their line across the Our, thereby diminishing the pressure against the flank of their troops on the Schnee-Eifel, whose position Dincklage, like Kimbrough, considered unfavorable. As a result of the almost complete lack of air reconnaissance, Major Dincklage knew very little about the enemy's strength in depth, an ignorance he shared with Division, Army, Army Group, and the entire Western Command.

### Twelve Noon

It may seem as though the disclosure of Dincklage's plan has let the cat out of the story's bag. Nothing of the kind. It is irrelevant to this story whether Major Dincklage succeeded or failed in his plan to surrender an almost battle-strength German battalion to the Americans. Although the story has taken for its scene what was in those days truly a wild west, it has no ambition to become

57

a western. At the end no dark angel will advance toward a meta-physical scoundrel and draw his Smith & Wesson half a second sooner than the other man.

It would be lovely, of course, if the monster, the war, that figure of chaos, should in the end lie dead on the village street of Winterspelt under the astonished eyes of a battalion liberated from its clutches against its will. But as everyone knows, a battalion's surrender to the enemy by its commanding officer never took place during the Second World War, perhaps not in any war, except for those fought by mercenaries. Even in case of failure such an attempt would have become notorious in military history, would have represented an event of such uniqueness that a sizable little library would have been written about it, primarily, in all probability, by the Allied side.

Storytelling cannot push fiction that far. A war game on a sand table suffices for the storyteller.

Perhaps this story would most easily escape from the noose of fiction by stating: because Major Dincklage did not exist, he had to be invented. But the sentence really makes sense only when turned around: because Dincklage was invented, he now exists.

Storytelling is not, after all, a matter of clapping a moral on a situation.

### Specialist's Blinkers

This story will also not undertake to deal with the motives that prompted Major Dincklage to attempt an act against the war. The story will not gather the particles of narrative around one of Dincklage's meditations and transform them into the circular motion of a hurricane, the "eye" being the solitary decision of "this officer" (as Hainstock liked to call him) to do some thinking. In contrast to the nonexistent literature on the Dincklage case, we have a vast literature on the subject of German officers' attempts to revolt against Hitler. The books on this question catalogue in the minutest fashion the considerations, the philosophical motivations, the arguments and emotions of these tragic figures, above all examining the number and intensity of their conscientious scruples. We may draw upon these works to fill in our general picture of the elements underlying Dincklage's project.

In order to know that Dincklage had all possible political, economic, and metaphysical reasons for his conduct, we need only recall that after Käthe Lenk described her experiences in the Bourtanger Moor he replied by listing the concentration camps in Emsland, concluding with an *Amen* that sounded to her like a curse. But primarily he made his decision on professional grounds. It is well known that in the autumn of 1944 most German officers shared Dincklage's view that the war was lost militarily and therefore should be brought to an immediate end. But Dincklage was the only one among them who was prepared to express in the form of concrete action the principles he had derived from his studies in military science and the insights he had drawn from his experiences as a lower-level commander. In the document collection assembled by Lieutenant Colonel W. Schaufelberger of the Swiss General Staff, mention is made of a Corporal Rudolf Dreyer, a clerk in the office of the CiC West, who heard a good deal; but whether or not he disobeyed orders by drawing conclusions is not stated. Dincklage, at any rate, drew conclusions. Possibly his was a case of exceptionally developed professional's obstinacy—that well-known *déformation professionelle* typical of people who have learned a craft and specialized in it.

It is certainly characteristic that there was never any discussion between him and Käthe Lenk on the motives that led to his plan. Those motives were taken for granted, assumed to be perfectly natural.

Only Captain Kimbrough, as a matter of fact, wanted to know precisely what had led Dincklage to come to his decision. Perhaps it was the lawyer in Kimbrough, the defense attorney in criminal cases, which made him take an interest in Dincklage's motives.

"What makes him tick?" was his first question after Schefold passed on to him the astonishing news from the other side.

Schefold shrugged. He did not know. And he had no desire to bore the young American captain with extracts from those voluminous justificatory writings that at that time had not yet been written.

# *Battle Zone*

## Crow's Nest

The point from which Hainstock scanned the area every day was the crown of the height which, toward the north, dropped steeply into his quarry, while to the south, east, and west it formed more or less gentle slopes of dry pasture over a limestone base. The hill was heavily overgrazed, so that no bushes were able to grow up. Weathered limestone ledges frequently showed through. At the top a few pines had taken root and grown tall; their umbrellas protected Hainstock from aerial observation. When he stepped to the edge of the slope, he could see the work area at the bottom of the limestone cliff, and the open shed where blocks of stone were piled. But it was a long time since any work had been done there. In one corner, the framework of a crane base was rusting away, and several flywheels for grindstones. Along the wall leaned a hundred-foot wooden ladder; Hainstock replaced its rungs from time to time. It extended approximately halfway up the face of the quarry. Between the quarry and the road—the unpaved gravel road from Winterspelt to Bleialf—grew a semicircle of dwarf beech; it had almost completely engulfed the construction shack in which Hainstock lived, so that only the ridge of the tar-papered roof was still visible. The radio antenna was a thin rod. Although Hainstock kept as quiet as possible, the daws, lively and attentive birds who had their nests in the upper part of the limestone cliff, were often disturbed by his movements. Fluttering up, they chattered their *kyacka-kyacka-kyack;* their cries were swallowed without reverberation in the depths of autumn.

As owner of the mountain, Hainstock had left its grassy slopes to the township of Winterspelt for use as pasture. He had done this for years, not just since the pastures farther to the west could no longer be grazed because of the military outposts. It was to his interest to keep the slopes with their stone subsurface visible; he did not want them vanishing under shrubbery. Moreover, Hainstock liked the rare flora of limestone pasturage, ground-hugging thistles, the orchis, borage, and Carthusian pinks, which the sheep did not touch, for they kept to the pasture grasses, the bird's foot and the fescue. Whenever Hainstock reached the top of the path he had by now worn along the eastern rim of the quarry, his first act was to determine where the sheep happened to be at the moment—a herd of some one hundred animals. Sometimes he would exchange a few words with the shepherd, who was employed by the township, although he had difficulty understanding the man's local brand of Low German. Hainstock had come to the region in the summer of 1941, but he still had or pretended to have—after nearly three years—difficulties with certain extreme forms of the local dialect.

He now regularly scanned the area around Winterspelt every day from the crown of his quarry. This was a habit he had formed ever since the second half of August, after the news of the Battle of Falaise and the taking of Paris, which he first heard from the Calais military station and then, with a few days' delay, from the Greater Germany Radio Network.

*October 12, 1944 (a Thursday), shortly before 11 A.M.*—Hainstock had taken his binoculars along as he always did (like so much else, like his liberty and the quarry, these were a gift of Matthias Arimond). Today he specially wanted them on the chance that he might be able to observe Schefold emerging from the wooded ridge on the western bank of the Our and descending the slopes which differed from the hill on which Hainstock was standing only by the fact that on them the juniper, hazel, and privet had shot up. But he did not see Schefold; or rather he found confirmation of what he already knew: that the view of the sector in the west, where Schefold must now be if he had followed Hainstock's instructions, was blocked by the southern arm of the Elcherath Forest, a forest of red beech which because of the dry and windless autumn was still wearing its dark-red foliage.

*Ten minutes later*—He did not think it was the decibel count of the triply screaming motors that made him duck. Rather, he crouched—so he thought—because they were coming over so low that it seemed they would smash against the cliff below him. Or at least shave off the pines under which he was standing. Probably he was mistaken; probably it was after all the fortissimo of howling motors which he could not get used to. But whatever the reason, every time they passed he was annoyed because he had once again hunched his head, pressed his arms against his chest, and bent his knees. Perhaps he exposed himself to these assaults on his nervous system only because he hoped that some day he would succeed in standing there erect and calm. He never succeeded. In the ensuing stillness it took a few seconds before he again heard the *kyacka-kyacka-kyack* of the disturbed jackdaws breaking against the once more closed sonic wall of autumn.

Today was the eleventh day since the American fighter-bombers had stopped making use of their guns as they patrolled the local road between Bleialf and Winterspelt, passing by the quarry, turning sharply over Winterspelt, and vanishing southeastward along the road to Pronsfeld. Here and there, with more or less success, they dropped their small bombs, which always landed as surprisingly as shells, sending up gray fountains with white crowns of foam. But the barrels of the machine guns that protruded from their cockpits remained silent. As Hainstock put it all together a few days later, from October 2 on they no longer found any targets.

*October 2, 1944 (a Monday)*—The poorly camouflaged field kitchen in the big barn at the end of the village of Winterspelt disappeared this morning. A sheer miracle that it had never before been attacked by the fighter-bombers. Only the barn itself, a clumsy quadrangle of rubblestone construction with a slate roof, was still there in what had suddenly become a brooding, lonely atmosphere.

The village of Winterspelt was about two kilometers in a direct airline from the quarry, and Hainstock could actually see only this barn, a few bluish-gray roofs, and the top of the church steeple, the rest of Winterspelt being hidden in a hollow.

64

Hainstock had no view of the highway running northwest toward Saint-Vith. It was obscured by the swell of the parallel hilly zone covered with meadows, harvested rye fields, and clumps of trees; in places roads had been carved among the hills. Beyond the highway rose the mountain range; from its ridge, had he been allowed to set foot there, Hainstock could have looked down into the valley of the Our. Defensive positions had been established there and civilians strictly forbidden to enter the terrain. Hainstock could see a considerable part of it, from Auel in the south to where the oblique slope of the Elcherath Forest cut off his line of vision.

The distance from Hainstock's observation point to this slope amounted to between two and a half and four kilometers. His glasses were Hensold Diagon binoculars that provided 15 x magnification. Their only disadvantage was their weight, so that after twenty seconds the viewed objects began to shake, in spite of Hainstock's grip (Käthe Lenk: "Say, those aren't sinews you have in your arms, those are steel cables"). Through the glasses he could see the German soldiers coming up the slope to relieve the sentries in the foxholes, and somewhat later he could observe the relieved men trudging wearily toward their quarters in the villages of Winterspelt, Wallmerath, and Elcherath. They came and went in small groups that could easily be identified.

This morning Hainstock had been unable to see a single one of these groups of figures. From Auel in the south to Elcherath Forest not a trace of movement could be discerned. The slope of the heights above the Our dropped rather shallowly; the gradual incline was covered with a taut skin of tilled and untilled fields and gray-green meadows. It was a long time since Hainstock had seen it lying there quite so without motion, static in the October light.

Below him to the right—*kyacka-kyacka-kyack* and frantic fluttering as he stepped to the rim of the quarry—there was likewise nothing going on. Emptiness.

On the little local road from Winterspelt to Bleialf there was never any heavy military traffic. (The road could be used only as far as Grosslangenfeld because Bleialf was in the hands of the

Americans.) Now and then a command car would turn up, with officers who were visiting the neighboring unit. Or an ammunition truck. Sometimes, and with a certain regularity, a supply column consisting of three horse-drawn covered wagons. (The horses and wagons had been requisitioned from the farmers.) Then for long intervals there would be nothing but a courier on a bicycle.

Today Hainstock had the impression that the area was not just temporarily empty, that it would remain so forever from this point on. The spruce forest beyond the road, from which Schefold sometimes emerged, stood stiffer and darker than ever all the way down to the ravine formed by the brook.

After the patrol of three fighter-bombers had passed, after Hainstock had unlocked his arms, raised his head, forced his knees to straighten out, and shaken off his irritation that once again he had not stood fast, he noticed that today no bushes at the edge of the road were burning, no ammunition trucks were going up in a series of explosions, no car was bursting into flames and rearing into the air before collapsing. There were no screams from wounded men to whom he sometimes administered first aid. No bodies lay in twisted, unnatural positions on the light-colored gravel and broken stone. (It did not help to shake these bodies.) He could leave his car—his old Adler in which he had sometimes taken wounded men to the field station in Winterspelt—standing in the shed across the road, opposite the entrance to the quarry, the entrance that was half overgrown and also barricaded with blocks of stone.

On the other side also, the slope of the Our, there was likewise nothing, none of those prone shadows he could ordinarily see. In spite of fifteen-fold magnification they always looked very small, so that Hainstock recognized them only by the fact that their camouflage jackets were a shade darker than the ground they lay on, and by the way other shadows, upright, gathered around them after the planes had passed.

But nothing of the sort today. Everything was as it had been before Hainstock had begun coming up here every day. All was the same as it had been during the summer, or in the previous autumn. The untilled slopes, the patches of tillage, the gray-green meadows that did not move even when circular portions of them began to shake after twenty seconds. (Only if you knew them as well as Hainstock did were you aware that they were a skin covering a living body.)

Hainstock put down the glasses and gazed after the planes with naked eyes. They pitched sharply upward south of Winterspelt and joined other groups of three to build formations. Only now did he realize that today the consequences of the furious bursts from their machine guns had been missing. These planes had not stitched seams of fire over the landscape.

The formations united into wings in the same quadrant of sky in which they had earlier appeared. The wing had taken off in Malmédy, or possibly even farther to the west. Even when you saw it at this distance and height you couldn't possibly mistake it for a flock of birds, Hainstock thought.

Käthe, who had come out to see him the afternoon of the previous day (Sunday), had informed him that the night before a new unit had replaced the old one.

"We didn't close an eye all night," she said. "All the men quartered on us were changed, but old Thelen worked it so that again nobody was put in the house. You should have seen the way he sat there not even looking at the corporal who was assigning the quarters and said: 'Here there's an old man, three girls, and four rooms.' And Elise, Therese, and I stood around him. But the corporal was polite anyhow. Actually I felt sorry for him. Then Elise showed him around the farm and he assigned four men to the annex next to the barn."

"But Therese had better be careful for a while," Hainstock said.

Käthe nodded. Therese Thelen was having an affair with one of the Russians who worked on the farm.

When Hainstock went to Winterspelt to buy food late in the afternoon of October 3, he noticed, after he had reached the highway, that positions had been set up in the hilly terrain to the left of the road. That is, of course, he did not observe any positions except once when he saw a machine-gun nest halfway up the slope, to one side of a wood road, and later caught a glimpse of another in the shadow of the trees close to the farmer Merfort's haystack. Pretending innocence, he made an attempt to climb up to Merfort's tillage, but was promptly shouted at by a voice whose owner he could not see and ordered to stay on the road. His observation put him in a bad humor. The establishment of a line of defense on the hills east of the road meant that the front had moved closer to him. Some of the positions—next morning he detected them with his glasses—were at most a thousand meters from his mountain. What surprised him most of all was that from his lofty observation post he had not seen any digging.

He already knew about the removal of the field kitchen in the barn at the end (or beginning) of the village, but he had not reckoned with the total emptiness of the village street. Winterspelt was a linear village with a single ashen-gray main street—though now, at twilight, it assumed a brassy coloration. That street, deserted and lifeless—in other words, the way it had always been before the troops were quartered in Winterspelt—ran at a slight incline to the middle of the village, the only area where buildings formed something like a cluster. From this point it rose again, just as empty of movement or noise, only to vanish beyond the common in which the church stood. Hainstock was astonished. All the bustle that Käthe Lenk had once called *Wallenstein's Camp* had been extinguished. (The phrase had transported Hainstock back to his native Bohemia, the setting of Schiller's play by that name.) Ordinarily Wallenstein's camp was particularly lively at this hour because of the evening roll call; groups of soldiers would come from the houses and assemble in the farm implement parking area behind Merfort's farmyard, where there was enough room for a company to draw up. Was it possible that this sanctified military ritual, the evening roll call, had been abolished—this roaring rattling off of names, this straightening of lines forward and to the sides—all that idiotic animal-training of grown men that Hainstock had learned in the Imperial Austrian Army? He could scarcely believe that.

68

In the taproom of Näckel's tavern, which was usually jammed with enlisted men, two corporals stood at the bar. They were eager to tell Hainstock that they had just come from Denmark and how fine everything had been there. "Looks like this is the world's asshole," one of them remarked, peering into his beer glass. Johannes Näckel threw a glance at Hainstock. Hainstock returned the glance, but did not feel that the corporal was altogether wrong. Näckel's taproom, like the rooms in most Eifel taverns, was a place conducive to melancholia. It was dimly lit, with embossed wallpaper the color of liver spots, and unheated.

Hainstock walked along the deserted street to Weinandy's store. Arnold Weinandy, who was able to continue running his business because he'd had a leg shot off in Russia in 1942, jerked his head in the direction of the street. "Surprised, aren't you?" he said.

"What the devil is going on here?" Hainstock asked. "Winterspelt looks dead to the world."

Weinandy, who liked to play knowledgeable about the war, explained that the new commander, a holder of the Knight's Cross, knew how things should be done so close to the front. *Close* to the front is good, Hainstock thought. With a phrase like that they fool themselves about actually being in the front lines. He looked at Weinandy clipping the bread coupons from his ration card. Although there was no one else in the store, Weinandy dropped into a whisper as he said: "If they keep up the camouflage, maybe the village will get through the war in pretty good shape."

If, that is, the new man didn't carry the camouflage so far that he decided to evacuate Winterspelt, Hainstock thought on his way home. In the darkness he heard not a sound from the hills; not once did he detect the clank of arms. In August the Winterspelt farmers had fended off the order to evacuate by declaring to the Party, army, and government that they were willing to go but would have to take their livestock with them. Upon receiving this word, Party, army, and government had not been heard from again. Would the new commander truckle to such peasant cunning? Could that be expected of a man who was capable of abolishing roll call?

At that time, the end of August, Käthe and Hainstock had made up their minds to move once again into the cave by the Apert if the evacuation order were enforced.

As a matter of fact, on October 7 Colonel Hoffmann had asked Major Dincklage whether it wouldn't be advisable to clear the villages in the main line of defense of their civilian populace. An inquiry about this had come from Division, he said.

"Are adequate reception quarters provided for the farmers and their livestock?" Dincklage asked. "Have arrangements been made for trouble-free transportation to these quarters?"

"Herr Dincklage," Hoffmann said, "that is bleeding-heart sentimentality. Besides, it's not our affair. Give me a military argument!"

"Besides, the presence of the populace doesn't disturb me at all," Dincklage said.

"Thanks," Hoffmann said. "That will do."

Next day he answered Division's inquiry in the negative.

By October 7 Major Dincklage already found it quite unthinkable that the evacuation of the civilian populace of Winterspelt would also involve the removal of Käthe Lenk. During his talk with the colonel that one fact had really been uppermost in his mind.

*October 5 (Thursday)*—"With the arrival of the new commander the war here has virtually stopped," Hainstock had remarked to Käthe Lenk the night before.

"His name is Dincklage," she had informed him.

This Major Dincklage had completely changed the character of the war. Or rather, he had not changed its character; he had made the war itself vanish as though by waving a wand. It was a trick. This man Dincklage was a trickster. Hainstock refused to be deceived for a moment. The war had not vanished. It had only become invisible. Something invisible was working beneath the surface now that Dincklage had appeared in the vicinity.

But Hainstock had never dreamed that the invisible something would affect him so personally, so that today would no longer be simply one more of those azure days that were the rule here every year from the end of September until late in October. From the height where he stood he had a beautiful view of the Schnee-Eifel and northwestward into Belgian territory as far as the Hoher Venn. He studied the blue ridge of the Schnee-Eifel with longing, for the Americans had already penetrated to the top there. If the quarry were only five kilometers farther to the north he would not have awaited their arrival in vain on the night of September 17. Bleialf was only a two-hour walk from his shack, and it had been occupied by the Americans at that time. If he lived there, he would already be liberated.

"Today I started to wonder whether it would really be all over if I were only living in Bleialf," he had said, meanwhile keeping an unobtrusive watch on the huge owl because he knew Käthe was afraid of it. "I have a feeling something is cooking, that the worst is yet to come."

He noticed that she was not listening.

"Something has happened between him and me," she said.

"Between you and whom?" Hainstock asked. But he knew whom she meant.

"Dincklage," Käthe said.

"Good Lord, Käthe!" Hainstock said after a pause.

To think he had not even been alerted when Käthe told him that this Major Dincklage might be entirely different from the kind of man he imagined. Probably he was doing all this, she said, only to avoid a dressing down. A phrase like *dressing down*, such officer's language, coming from Käthe's lips! To think he hadn't caught on to that right away. Only now, looking at the dark pine trees at the bottom of the ravine formed by the brook, did he realize that she could only have heard such a phrase from this officer Dincklage himself.

He had walked her as far as the first houses of Winterspelt, as he always did at night; that was particularly necessary now because she had to pass by the new positions along the road. And she had kissed him goodbye as always, except that her kiss last night had not been merely tenderly friendly, as always, but also sad and even despairing, if he were not mistaken.

Hainstock made up his mind to avoid all kissing for the time being.

The arrival of Schefold was welcome because it interrupted his brooding about Käthe Lenk. He had intended in any case to have a serious talk with Schefold. Schefold's bulky figure emerged from the curtain of pines. He glanced first to the right, then to the left —it looked as though he were making two brief bows—and promptly started moving, striding as majestically as ever across the meadow beyond the road and toward the quarry. Hainstock shook his head. Evidently Schefold considered those two brief bows an adequate tribute to the idea of caution.

"You ought to look the situation over before you leave the woods," Hainstock said when they met in front of the shack. "Not after you're already in the open."

"Did I do that?" Schefold asked. "Oh, you know, I always have this instinct as to whether danger is in the offing."

"I'd like to know whether an MP patrol, if one happens to be in the vicinity, would worry about this instinct of yours," Hainstock said.

"I hope your night owl behaves itself," Schefold said before they entered. "It makes me nervous when it starts threshing around."

"It isn't a night owl, it's a tawny owl," Hainstock said. "It won't bother you this time."


The bird had quieted down since he had built a kind of cave tower for it out of piled-up crates, and it was still perched where it had been an hour ago, in the topmost crate, the one turned away from the light. It beat its wings only once when it felt Hainstock's gaze resting on it for a second.

Hainstock had found the owl a few days ago, a grayish-brown bundle of feathers lying beside a milestone; he had been driving back from a visit to the quarries in Lauch. He'd braked abruptly and got out. At first he thought the bird was dead, but when he closed his hand on it he felt its heart beating. Whereupon he drove to Pronsfeld. Dr. Ballmann, the veterinarian there, said that the bird had probably been struck by a car and was suffering from concussion of the brain. Hainstock should tend it for a couple of weeks and then release it.

Hainstock had never known a shyer creature. What so disturbed Schefold and Käthe were nothing more than the bird's continual efforts to hide. At first Hainstock had been perplexed, for the owl had only one thing on its mind, to conceal itself, and since there were no hiding places inside the shack Hainstock was afraid that in its persistent hunt for cover it would sooner or later injure itself. Then two days ago he had hit on the idea of building a hiding place for the bird.

Hainstock stirred up the fire in the small iron cookstove that heated the shack, added two sticks of wood, and slid the stove rings back into place before he let Schefold take over to make the coffee. Engaged in filling his pipe and endeavoring to keep his tone of direct address as stiff as possible, he said: "Herr Doktor Schefold, I urgently advise you and for the last time to return to Hemmeres at once and not to stir from there until it's all over. It would be even better for you to withdraw to Belgium."

Only after this was said did he light his pipe. He watched Schefold, massive and heavy, adroitly handling the enamelled kettle and the stoneware coffee pot. At his third visit Schefold had taken the coffee-making out of his hands. "It's curious, Herr Hainstock," he had said at the time, "although you come from a country that was part of the old Danube monarchy, you haven't the slightest idea how to make coffee." Hainstock had been forced to admit that Schefold's coffee was superior not only to his own but to any other he had ever drunk. Each time he had a cup of it he was sorry that Käthe was not able to share this pleasure. On the other hand, not very long ago she had said to him: "It bothers me that you always have real coffee. I hate myself for always succumbing when you offer me a cup of coffee." Probably the excellence of Schefold's coffee would only have made the temptation worse. But Hainstock had kept her from ever meeting Schefold.

Just in case Schefold were ever arrested, interrogated, tortured, he must know as few people, as few names, as possible. Actually, it was a bad slip on his own part that he had ever told Käthe about Schefold; it violated the rules for protecting someone in the underground. After all, Käthe too was not yet in the clear, was only conditionally safe at the Thelen farm in Winterspelt.

Schefold's eyes were concentrated in a cool, matter-of-fact way on the processes at the stove. Those eyes were blue in his ruddy face, in which a squared-off, close-clipped mustache was set like a gray field between upper lip and nose. Hainstock estimated him at six feet three inches, and weighing close to two hundred and twenty pounds. But he was only built on massive lines; he had no paunch and in contrast to his weight his hands could play lightly with objects. Or rather, not really in contrast to it, for the bulk of his body and the delicacy of his movements did not make an opposition. There was something flowing about Schefold.

He turned back to Hainstock only after he had completed a number of complicated processes of rinsing, warming, and pouring.

"But why," he said, "if what you say is true and there's not a single German Army man on the roads by day? That should mean I can take my walks with much less chance of interference than in the past."

"Things have turned rotten," Hainstock said. "Before they were only sloppy. Now they're rotten."

"I can guess what you mean," Schefold said. "This new battalion keeps out of sight. That makes it more dangerous than the old one." He pondered this. "Of course, that happens," he said. "There are painters who literally hide a color in a painting so that the color will be all the more effective."

"This hasn't anything to do with painting," Hainstock said.

That was stupid, he thought; I've let him irritate me. If he knew Schefold, he would now be in for a quarter-hour lecture proving that the question had a great deal to do with painting. He was surprised and relieved when Schefold kept to the point.

"I don't enter the frontline villages anyhow, never have," he said. "I go to Eigelscheid, Habscheid, Hollnich."

74

That was true. Schefold avoided the main defense line. Instead he went by the densely wooded valley formed by the brook to the east of Hemmeres in order to get behind the German lines. Hainstock had suggested this route, but reluctantly, only after it became clear that Schefold could not be dissuaded from his walks in German territory. Hainstock had shown him on the map the way through the woods, at the margin of which the system of defense posts had been set up. The woods were empty except for occasional patrols that probably went only as far as the point where the red pines ended and the alders began. Whenever Schefold turned up, Hainstock first glanced at the big man's trouser legs to see whether they were wet from the alder woods, but they were always dry; foolhardy as Schefold was, he used the dry floor of the pine woods rather than the secure but wet thickets in the lower valley. In this way he reached the local road to Bleialf, paid a visit to Hainstock, then turned up again in Eigelscheid or Habscheid or even farther back in the hinterland.

"I'm worried about Schefold," Hainstock once said to Käthe, and that was at a time before there was any talk of Dincklage, when the sloppiness of the 18th Motorized still dominated Winterspelt and the vicinity. "As long as things were in flux here, he could run around the neighborhood as he liked, for all I cared. But now, when the fronts are fixed, what he's doing is simply crazy. What's more, he isn't even a spy for the Allies. For that he's much too conspicuous, and too innocent besides. He just goes hiking around for the hell of it."

"He must be a remarkable man," Käthe had replied. "After all, he was already out of it. Properly out of it. Far off in the west."

"Oh well, Belgium isn't that far off in the west," Hainstock said. "It's right next door."

"For me it's far off," she said. "And if I were already that far away, ten horses couldn't bring me back."

"Eigelscheid is no more than three kilometers back of the front," Hainstock told Schefold. "And you have no idea how quickly every change at the front affects the hinterland."

"But the people there know me," Schefold said. "Why should they suddenly treat me differently from the way they have right along?"

Hainstock revolved the cup in his hand. The coffee was excellent, as always, but it seemed a hopeless task to convey to Schefold any concept of the danger, of the invisible network that from now on would be drawing closer around him.

It was characteristic of Schefold that one day, some time during the summer, he had entered Hainstock's shack, introduced himself, and without more ado favored him with the story of his life. Hainstock had looked at the big man and asked: "Whatever gave you the idea of telling me these things?"

"People," Schefold said. "I've heard people talking about you. Incidentally, they don't talk badly about you at all. They talk about you like—how should I put it?—as though you were their ace in the hole."

Hainstock had laughed involuntarily, and that had established trust between them. This was the frankest explanation he had so far had as to the meaning of that influx—not exactly a flood but a trickle—of bags of real coffee beans, packets of butter, tins of tobacco, and bottles of wine that came his way: cards which would be turned face up on the table in the not too distant future when Hainstock's supporting testimony would be needed. For which reason Käthe considered him corruptible because he accepted the stuff.

Of course Hainstock had used other means to assure himself that Schefold was not an informer. *Innocent* was not the right word for Schefold's behavior. Schefold was careless, frivolous, perhaps naïve in the good-hearted way he went about the villages, stopped in taverns, conducted conversations, relied on the papers that he carried around with him, papers that Hainstock regarded as worthless in a crunch; but he was not really innocent. Hainstock could not hit on the word that really fitted Schefold.

He accompanied the big man out to the road, watched him as he tramped off in the direction of Eigelscheid, tossing over his right shoulder the raincoat he always had with him. Hainstock's warning had been useless; the way the man walked off, massive

76

and in a kind of flowing movement, implied that he was enjoying the fine weather, the deserted road, and the fact that the war had vanished.

If he were arrested, it would be essential for Hainstock to find out about it in good time, so he could clear out before Schefold began talking. Hainstock reckoned on three days' grace, for immediately after arrest and as long as he was being held in some police jail in the Prüm district, Schefold would not be tortured. Mistreatment would begin only after he had been transferred to the Gestapo in Cologne.

It did sometimes happen that intellectuals remained silent under torture while steelworkers (or masons) began to talk after the first few blows, but that was not the rule. The rule was that intellectuals could be broken down faster than steelworkers (or masons).

He unwrapped the piece of blood-dripping liver Käthe had brought him from the Thelen farm yesterday and placed it alongside the owl. The bird did not take it, only shifted irritably to one side.

Last night, before their walk as far as the first houses of Winterspelt, Käthe had looked thoughtfully at the tower of crates and said: "Building hiding places is your specialty, Wenzel."

"It seems I have that in common with Major Dincklage," he had replied.

She had meant to refer to the cave by the Apert, that is to say something that was more than just a friendly remark, but the injury she had inflicted on him was still too fresh. In the future he would keep himself under better control.

She had not replied, had not taken his arm on their way to Winterspelt.

He reached for his pipe again, sat down at the table with his back to the semblance of a crannied rock cliff he had created so that the bird could watch him and at the same time feel that it was not itself being watched, took out the newspaper he always fetched from Weinandy now that the letter carrier no longer came all the way out to his shack, read the headline *Heroic De-*

77

*fensive Battles in the Carpathians* and the communiqué below it, from which he gathered that the Red Army would shortly be treading on Czech soil, and let the newspaper drop to his knees.

Only now did he realize how inexplicable it was that last night of all times Käthe, almost immediately after she had informed him of something that she must know was exceptionally painful to him, had reminded him of the cave by the Apert, that forgotten basalt tunnel which in the days after July 20, when they made a (not very virtuous) virtue of necessity, had been their *love nest*—a phrase Hainstock used only in his monologues because he knew that Käthe would flare up if he ever referred to it in those terms.

"I don't love you at all," she had once said to him. "I like you."

Then why, last night, this sudden allusion to the cave? Among the sometimes trying qualities of Käthe was her way of weighing words—the words of others, but also her own.

Hainstock gave up on the matter. It was far more important now to consider everything that followed from the fact that from now on Käthe stood on the opposing side, even though this idea was personally unbearable and politically inconceivable.

In order to be able to think an unbearable and inconceivable thought, it was above all necessary to sweep away all vague phrases (*exceptionally painful—the injury she has inflicted on me*) and precisely define the thing in itself.

Käthe was now involved with this Major Dincklage. She was sleeping (had perhaps already slept, would sleep) with an officer in the fascist army.

She had, in the most concrete possible fashion, gone over to the enemy camp.

Although these sentences left nothing to be desired as far as clarity went, they seemed to Hainstock inadequate. They did not satisfy him the way a good political analysis of a given situation usually satisfied him, and that was not because he didn't like the result of his examination of the question. The analysis of defeats could provide just as much satisfaction as the analysis of victories. Sometimes more. But he had the feeling that in this case he had not considered certain unknown factors.

Or was this feeling only an illusion?

He heard behind him a scratching, jerking, and tossing, and knew that the owl had attacked the piece of liver.

Earlier, he had said to Schefold: "Take the example of this owl. He hides. He sees everything, but he takes care that he himself is not seen."

"Nonsense," Schefold replied. "You see him perfectly well. You only behave in such a way that he can imagine you don't see him."

Whatever lesson Hainstock meant to draw was lost on Schefold. "It wouldn't do at all for me to sit down in the darkest corner of the tavern, not say a word, quietly drink my beer and vanish again."

"Lord knows you don't do that," Hainstock said.

"Certainly not, because that would be sure to attract attention," Schefold said.

Several times in the course of the summer Hainstock had met him in the taverns of Eigelscheid and Habscheid. No, Schefold never sat unobtrusively in a corner; he stood at the bar chatting with the natives, accepting offers of drinks, paying for rounds himself.

"At least you shouldn't hand around American cigarettes in their original packs, no less," Hainstock said.

"Oh, have I done that?" For a moment Schefold had really been taken aback.

"You have," Hainstock said. "I thought I wasn't seeing straight."

If Schefold was getting away even with that, it was only because there was something about him that shielded him from questions.

Was Schefold simply a creature without timidity, and in that respect not at all to be compared with the creature of the wild that was devouring the liver at the back of the room? But that idea was belied by his having settled down in the hamlet of Hemmeres, a perfect owl's lair, inaccessibly situated in the dark river bottoms. Moreover, he must also be fairly alive to the risks he was courting, for otherwise he would not one day have brought that package containing the most precious picture he possessed, and asked Hainstock, who knew so many safe places (as he expressed it), to keep it for him.

Schefold differed from the owl only in the way he displayed a type of conduct rare in nature and among men: he tried to protect himself by exposing himself.

*October 12, 1944*—At any rate surely not in so crazy a way as today. The way he was moving, you couldn't possibly speak of taking cover. And it was really incredible that he, Hainstock, had chosen his spot under the pines today, under the limestone cliff, on the chance that he might be able to observe Schefold emerging from the wooded ridge above the western bank of the Our and descending the untilled slopes which were twin to the eastern bank except for their growth of juniper, hazel, and privet. It was incredible when he considered that on this same day last week, a Thursday, yes, only last Thursday, he had tried to dissuade Schefold from continuing his walks in German territory; rather, had tried to forbid him. Instead, Schefold at this moment was showing himself in the military area—and what is more, he, Hainstock, had put him up to it. Instead of reaching the hinterland by way of the gorge through which the brook ran, sheltered by spruce and alders and relatively safe, today he was giving up all cover and stepping out in front of the first of Major Dincklage's two lines. And the big man was doing this not because he had suddenly gone off his head but on Hainstock's request and following his instructions. It was incredible. I must have gone off my head when I put him up to this, Hainstock thought, and he was almost grateful for the southern arm of Elcherath Forest for being in the way, as he had foreseen, so that he could not catch Schefold in the lenses of his field glasses.

Earlier, while he had been standing in his foxhole waiting for the hedge-hopping planes whose motor roar he had heard in ample time, Corporal Reidel once more came to the conclusion that the position of the foremost line of sentries was all wrong.

Foxholes were not placed halfway up the slope of a hill. Granted, this was a fairly flat slope, but just because it was so flat the attacker could cross it quickly over this dry soil covered with cropped yellow pasture grass. The ground was not even mined. In an attack of company strength, for instance, the foremost line of sentries would be up shit creek in three minutes. They could each shoot down two or three attackers before the enemy reached the line, but that would hardly stem the attack. By rights the foxholes should have been placed up there on the top; then, when the artillery preparation began, you would have to abandon them for a short time, but immediately occupy them again when the artillery fell silent. Reidel imagined he knew what the thinking was at Battalion: the only job for the foremost line was to check the tempo of the enemy attack so that it was slower and more scattered by the time it reached the main line of defense on the ridge of the road, which was spotted with machine-gun nests. The foremost line was expendable. Defense in depth, that was called. Reidel didn't think much of defense in depth. To his mind there were only three kinds of effective defense: 1) Surprising bursts of fire from completely camouflaged positions that no reconnaissance by the enemy could discover. 2) Massed commitment of tanks, even in the defense. 3) Attack. Because he knew, and not just since his arrival on the western front twelve days ago but ever since his service in Russia, that options 2 and 3 were out of the question, he regarded the war as lost. He was not about to let himself be expended. He already knew the technique of withdrawing from front lines of riflemen, including wrongly positioned lines, before things got too hot. For the present he still cherished the hope that nothing would ever happen in this sector, where for twelve days he had been drawing guard duty for four hours twice a day.

The fighter-bombers came closer. If they again fired a few bursts at the slope, this fellow, this spy who lay flattened out on the ground beside him, outside the foxhole, was as good as done for.

Naturally Major Dincklage had given careful consideration to the placement of the foremost line of riflemen and of the main defense line. He reasoned that the Americans in his sector, contrary to their usual habits, would have to undertake a pure infantry attack because they could not bring any tanks up through the dense underbrush and forest of the slopes of the Our. At least not immediately. A massed infantry attack was bound to bog down in the cleft between the heights above the Our and the opposite line of hills. To place the main line of defense on the heights above the Our was out of the question; it would have been too hard to camouflage up there and would have been attacked day after day by hedge-hopping planes. On the other hand, the slopes of the cultivated heights north of Winterspelt, with their many wooded groves, sunken roads, and stone sheds, were splendidly suited to defense. A thinly manned line of sentries on the untilled slopes on this side of the ridge would surprise the Americans, check the initial impetus of their attack; the loss of those sentries had to be accepted. If the Americans should turn up with tanks anyhow, there was nothing to be done. Aside from bazookas, Dincklage had no armor-piercing weapons. Colonel Hoffmann had refused to let him have a single one of the antitank guns in the regimental stocks. "We need those on the Schnee-Eifel sectors," he had said. "When the Americans come down from the Schnee-Eifel, they'll come with tanks." Before he conceived his radical but abstract solution—after repeated nocturnal study of the maps—Dincklage must have made up his mind to order a retreat at once if a sizable tank formation appeared in front of his lines. At any rate it was in just such specific terms that Wenzel Hainstock interpreted a remark of Dincklage's quoted to him by Käthe Lenk. To behave halfway rationally within the military structure was the least he could still do in this war, Dincklage had said to Käthe. He had added that there was little risk in acting that way. "He's right about that," Hainstock had remarked, and explained to Käthe that both Regiment and Division could do no more than register the fact if the commander of a conventionally equipped infantry battalion reported a tank breakthrough.

He had waited tensely to see whether Käthe would comment on that bourgeois drivel in Dincklage's statement about the military structure, halfway rational behavior, and the little that could still be done in this war—he had waited and had not been disappointed.

"Sounds kinda wishy-washy," she said. When she made deprecating remarks, her ordinarily careful speech tended to be a bit careless.

The conversation between Käthe and Dincklage, in the course of which that sentence had occurred, had taken place on Tuesday, October 3. By Friday, October 6, Dincklage made those revelations that neither she nor Hainstock could consider wishy-washy.

Captain Kimbrough would certainly have smiled if he had known that Major Dincklage counted on his attacking him, and what is more making a *massed* attack. The already mentioned intelligence officer at Regiment had informed him that a full battalion, though a badly equipped one, was dug in opposite his company. Schefold confirmed this intelligence because he kept talking about *the battalion over there*. Kimbrough had once tried to sound him out about the location of the positions, but here Schefold had failed him. "Look, Captain," he had said, "in the first place I don't know where they are posted, I really don't know. Of course I could try to scout out the positions for you; it's inconsistent of me not to do it, but I cannot. When I imagine that you would then order artillery fire on those positions or instruct your planes . . ."

"All right," Kimbrough interrupted, "forget it."

He had to distribute the C Company over a frontal sector five miles along. At Regimental Staff HQ in Saint-Vith he listened to the anxious and indignant talk about the fact that there were only three divisions to hold the seventy-five miles of front between Trier and Monschau, and nothing behind them either; the entire area up to the Meuse was without operational reserves. He frequently climbed up to the heights above the Our and in the cover of tall hazelnut bushes peered eastward through his glasses, observing harvested fields, patches of forest, pastures, the ridge of the Schnee-Eifel to the northeast, houses made of squared stone. He could not discern a single position that betrayed the slightest movement on the enemy's part. He saw the C-47 wings flying eastward above his head, under a blue sky that in this country was not bright but rather filled with filtered light from a thin cloud cover. Their motors sang a dark, muted note. A singularly deserted region it seemed, even to Kimbrough who was familiar with the deserted countryside around Fargo and the Okefenokee Swamp. Isolated groves of trees, beeches or oaks, red or yellow, or already leafless, stood immobile in the muted light. Kimbrough considered it imprudent that the division's other two regiments had been pushed forward as far as the Schnee-Eifel. He was glad that the company he commanded still lay behind the Our, still in Belgium. (He had reason to be glad, for in December this regiment escaped Manteuffel's pincers when Colonel R., without waiting for orders, withdrew it to Saint-Vith; the two regiments on the Schnee-Eifel were taken prisoner.)

When he put down his glasses and turned around, he would look down on the slate roofs of the village of Maspelt, which lay in a hollow, and at the gently graded wooded slopes of the Ardennes behind it. He had imagined everything except this almost peacetime operation they were running here. Sentry duty, cleaning weapons, inspection, sports, movies, occupational therapy of all kinds. Since the Germans seemed no longer to have any planes, movements did not even have to be carefully camouflaged. Why didn't they give up, if their air force was done for?

All in all, an empty war. Kimbrough approved of the absent silence of this vacuum.

*September 17–18, 1944.* Incessant peering to the west, as every day for weeks, ever since the news of the Battle of Falaise and the taking of Paris; peering into Belgian territory, sweeping the glasses over the foothills of the Ardennes, across the Our, hunting for the first American tanks. He made bets with himself: they'll come today. No, not till tomorrow.

"Again only our troops," Käthe had said one day when she was standing beside him.

"*Your* troops, Fräulein Lenk?" he had asked.

The slate roofs of Maspelt, over on the Belgian side, looked as though the houses underneath them were holding their breath.

Above, the wall of the forest, a single nucleated shadow, impenetrable, which began to quiver and was suddenly torn open because half a dozen armored vehicles—armored scout cars?—appeared driving rapidly down the road that led from Grufflange to Maspelt. There were white five-pointed stars on their hoods.

This was actually the order of his thoughts: armored scout cars, the Malmédy—Luxembourg highway branches off in Grufflange, the road to Maspelt—all those thoughts came before he thought: Americans.

Not until he removed the glasses from his eyes because the pentagrams inside began to quiver did he think the word *Americans*, but then he said it aloud: "Americans." Up here only the pines could hear what he said.

The armored scout cars drove into Maspelt and did not reappear.

He did not stir. In the afternoon a large formation at last came in sight: trucks filled with soldiers, field artillery detachments, heavy tractor-trailers, tanks. He counted thirty tanks; one after the other appeared in the segment that the narrow white road cut into the almost black wall of the forest. There were no noises; the deployment was taking place in an area that was five to eight kilometers away from his position, and the east wind, which made the day cool and visibility good, carried the rattle of caterpillar treads back in the direction from which they had come. Soundlessly, the columns moved across the round field of his glasses and down into the hollow of Maspelt.

It went on continually. When he could no longer see anything, he walked back down. Night in the shack. He waited. He would have heard if the Americans had driven through the village, in which there was no more than a single platoon of infantrymen, last rearguard of one of the divisions exhausted by its flight through northern France and Belgium; the bulk of the divisions had already vanished toward the east.

He considered whether he ought to go to Winterspelt, plead with Käthe to come to him, but told himself it was pointless. She had set her heart on being present when the Americans arrived.

But they did not arrive. Each time Hainstock stepped outside the shack, the night remained obstinately silent, so unusually silent that from a great distance off to the north artillery fire could be heard, a rumbling that varied between high and low tones, waves of sound rolling up against the limestone wall that shimmered in the light of the half moon and breaking against it.

When daylight came, he went up on the cliff again. He arrived just in time to observe that the Americans were withdrawing. Their tanks, their motorized infantry, their cannon, were moving back down the road over which they had come yesterday. Their vehicles, one after the other, stood out for a moment against the long black surf of the sea of trees and then were swallowed up by it. He told himself at once that this was inevitable: between Maspelt and Winterspelt there was no road through the valley of the Our, only a footpath, really little more than a track, largely overgrown, and that wooden footbridge at the hamlet of Hemmeres, where Schefold lived. Since there was no road, it would have done them no good to have thrown a bridge across the river that formed the frontier.

He realized that. He was boundlessly disappointed. He cursed an unknown American general who hesitated at the border with an armored regiment or whatever it was. Didn't that general know that he could send his force right down the highway from Saint-Vith without any trouble at least as far as Pronsfeld? What was the matter with him that he couldn't act on the basis of his air reconnaissance, which for weeks no German planes had hampered? Bitterly, Hainstock thought of the phrase *coup de main* as he stared at the once more deserted road that led from Maspelt to Grufflange, and which unfortunately was only a dead-end road. A blind alley.

Later he learned—from Schefold—that the American formation had left an infantry company behind in Maspelt. Schefold also informed him that the division to which this company belonged had come directly from the United States and been thrown into position on the west bank of the Our. The men had arrived in Le Havre only at the beginning of September, Schefold remarked, and not even the company commander, a Captain Kimbrough, had any battle experience.

Which could not be said of this Major Dincklage.

*October 12, 1944.* If that American general had ordered a pontoon bridge thrown across the Our at Steinebrück—and nobody would have stopped him—so that he could march his regiments on the state highway as far as Pronsfeld (at least as far as Pronsfeld)—and likewise nobody would have stopped him—then he, Hainstock, would not have had to stand up here today making this useless effort to observe Schefold as he emerged from the crested ridge of the western bank of the Our. Then this creaking, not to say crackbrained, undertaking would never have been attempted—and I have lent my active support to it, Hainstock thought. Schefold, Käthe, he himself, would then already be liberated, already grappling with the problems of life after the fascist dictatorship, not enmeshed in this desperate adventure by a fool of an officer.

Once, when he had pictured to Käthe what everything would have been like if the Americans had advanced more quickly, more resolutely, she had said: "You know, I don't think there is much sense in dealing with historical events in terms of conditional sentences."

It always took him a while to adjust to her habit of linguistic analysis—the schoolmarm's grammatical focus. But as soon as he caught her meaning, he reacted angrily: "That is the most reactionary statement I ever heard," he said. "If we refuse to imagine what might have been, we shut off the chance of imagining any better possibility. Then we are just accepting history as it comes."

"When it has come as it has come, we cannot do anything but accept it," Käthe had replied.

She saw that her answer depressed him, and tried in all sorts of ways to take back what she had said, but he was not fooled. So his many efforts to familiarize her with the Thought that could change the world had been in vain. After all his instruction in the dialectical view of history, she came out for fatalism.

Recalling this conversation as he stared into the rusty backdrop

87

of Elcherath Forest in the static autumnal light, as he stared and at last abandoned trying to observe Schefold, Hainstock suddenly realized that he, an adherent of a theory and practice of changing the world, rejected the reason for Schefold's hike today, did not like it one bit. Whereas Käthe's only objection to it was that Schefold was the person undertaking it. Aside from that, she had been the moving force behind the whole undertaking. There certainly could be no question of fatalism there.

*Biogram*

Wenzel Hainstock, born in Aussergefild (now Kvilda), Bohemia, in 1892, youngest of three children and only son of a master machinist, Franz Hainstock, and his wife Fanny, née Krehan. Baptized Catholic; left the church in the twenties. His father, who with two journeymen ran a needle-making shop, died in 1907, leaving the family without resources. Like almost all proletarian or proletarianized children, young Hainstock stumbled into a vocation more by chance than inclination. From 1908 to 1910 he worked as an apprentice in a quarry at the southeast foot of the Mittagsberg, learning the techniques of quarrying and working stone blocks as well as the procedures of open-pit mining of minerals. After he finished his apprenticeship in stonecutting and masonry, he served his term in an infantry regiment of the Austro-Hungarian Imperial Army in Pilsen. In 1912 the twenty-year-old worker joined the Social Democratic Party of Austria; he read the *Communist Manifesto.* Journeyman years. He worked for various companies, chiefly in Lower Austria, took evening courses in technical schools and (in Vienna) attended lectures by Otto Bauer on (Austrian) Marxism. By the winter of 1913–14 he saved up enough money to enroll as a full-time student for a three-month course in applied geology at the Mining Academy in Leoben. Simultaneously he helped organize the miners to fight for higher wages. Mobilized at the outbreak of the war, he was taken prisoner by the Russians on the Galician front as early as September 1914 and spent the First World War in Siberia. Since he spoke Czech fluently—he had a Czech grandmother on his mother's side—he was urged to enter one of the Czech legions that were being formed in Russia. He refused. In February 1918 he returned to Aussergefild; on the journey from Siberia to Bohemia he did not manage to see anything of the Russian Revolution aside from "disorders." His mother had died during the war. He passed his master's examination. In 1920 he took part in the agitation for the general strike after the police of the newly formed Czechoslovak government occupied the People's House in Prague. In 1922 Hainstock resigned from the Winterberg (now Vimperk) section of the Social Democratic Party and joined the Communist Party of Czechoslovakia. During the following years he continued to work at his trade; he shrank from accepting the seat as a parliamentary deputy which the Party offered him. Although his political views were known to the bosses and he was elected to the shop committee wherever he worked, he nevertheless rose to be manager of a quarry employing many men, located on the Upper Moldau. Unemployed during the worldwide depression (1931–34), he utilized these years for active Party work. After the victory of fascism in Germany (1933), Hainstock noticed with dismay that the discussions of the CP of Czechoslovakia were overly concerned with the nationalities question. When he had business in Party headquarters in the Hiberner-Gasse in Prague, he did not fail to observe that some Czech comrades were hostile even to him because he was a Bohemian of German stock. Up to this time the expression Sudeten German had been foreign to him; in fact he had never heard the term. If asked, he would always have called himself a "border country Bohemian." On the other hand, he fully realized that Hitler would eventually put an end to all possible coexistence between Germans and Czechs. He therefore decided in 1935 to go to Germany to carry on underground political work there. For a short time he served as a courier and instructor for the Central Committee of the Communist Party of Germany, which at that time had its headquarters in Prague. It was a foolish plan, for Hainstock was exceedingly well known in Southwest

Bohemia as a Communist. By his second trip, in the summer of 1935, his cover was blown, and he disappeared into the Oranien-burg concentration camp, from which he emerged again in the spring of 1941 because a director of the Reich Industrial Association for Rock and Minerals pushed through his release. The director in question, who bore the title of Coordinator of Defense Industry, was named Matthias Arimond. Arimond took Hainstock to the west and appointed him overseer of several shut-down quarries that belonged to the Tufa and Basalt Lava Company, Inc. (in other words, Arimond); actually, those quarries contained neither tufa nor basalt lava, but thick strata of dolomite or limestone and marl. Arimond offered him a company apartment in Prüm, but Hainstock took up quarters in the shack at the Winterspelt quarry; the little cabin had both electric light and piped water.

A year after his return from Russia, Hainstock, then twenty-seven, had married the twenty-year-old daughter of a postal worker. They separated two years later because of the girl's insuperable petty-bourgeois dislike for his work as a Communist agitator; she often made scenes about it. They were divorced in 1923; his wife married again. There was a son from the brief marriage; the boy, as she wrote to him in 1943 (the letter stamped for domestic mail; Bohemia was now part of the German Reich), had been missing since the Battle of Stalingrad. Hainstock had last seen his son at fifteen. In 1930 Hainstock formed a relationship with a Czech comrade, a student eighteen years his junior. In 1933 she left for a research stay in Paris and did not return. Happiness came briefly to him; it never lasted. From the time of his release from the concentration camp until his meeting with Käthe Lenk, that is from 1935 to 1944, he had little to do with women. His two sisters were still living in Aussergefild, both with large families; one of them was already widowed. He had already faced the fact that he would have to take care of her when, as he foresaw would happen, she would be expelled from Bohemia next year.

Hainstock was only five feet five. His student girl-friend, who often played chess with him in a café in Prague's Little Quarter, had once remarked that he looked like a small rook. That had been twelve or more years ago; in the meantime Hainstock's hair had turned iron-gray, but he had retained his small, stubby, and solid appearance. His body was hard; perhaps in order to achieve lasting, rather than only momentary happiness it should have been a shade less so. But his musculature, which Käthe Lenk compared to steel cables, had enabled him to survive several torture sessions and a stay in the concentration camp of almost seven years without damage to his health. In the broad planes of his face, cut across by innumerable horizontal wrinkles like the strokes of an etcher's needle, were a pair of small, porcelain-blue eyes. His lips scarcely showed; the mouth, ground thin, ran straight across; his nose was just the opposite, for it was heavy, pear-shaped, the bridge broken (by the fist of an SS man in Oranienburg); that blow had increased its droop and also displaced it somewhat to the right. He had more or less stopped caring about food after he realized that Pálffy dumplings or boiled pork with horse-radish were things of the past. On the other hand, he had formed the habit of drinking two or three glasses of wine in the evening when he sat alone in the shack at the Winterspelt quarry. When a bottle of wine was given to him, he was most grateful if it happened to be a dry Moselle.

## Factors, or Geology and Marxism

One day at the end of July, lying in the grass outside the cave in the Apert, Käthe said: "Tell me how you became a Communist."

Hainstock, who stood at the entrance to the cave looking down at her, smoking his pipe, said: "When I came home from serving in the army in Pilsen, I went back to work in the quarry on the Mittagsberg, which incidentally has the very same kind of rock as the one in Winterspelt. Blue limestone with strata of this slaty marl. I never would have thought I would find anything so similar in this part of the country."

He started again: "I remember it as if it were yesterday. I was working with the broad chisel, rounding off the edge of a window molding." Pause. "If I start up the Winterspelt quarry I'll want to have a working stoneyard. It wouldn't interest me to deal just in raw blocks."

She did not stir. He came to the point.

"Whenever I looked up from the work," he went on, "I looked at the wall of the quarry. I always used to do that, but on this particular day it seemed to me that I had never seen it before. I don't know why. Maybe because I had been in the barracks only a few days before. Anyhow, while I was looking at it I realized more clearly than I ever had before that it belonged to someone, to a person whom I had seen once or twice. He owned it. This stone wall sliced out of a mountain existed, and at the same time there was one person who could do whatever he liked with it. He alone. It was his private property.

"I don't mean to say," he went on, "that this insight descended upon me from heaven, so to speak. I had read socialistic writings; I knew that I was selling the only commodity I owned, my labor power, to the capitalists, who made their profit out of it, and so on. But, I did not join the Social Democratic Party, which at that time, you know, was a revolutionary party, until I realized that the capitalists owned the mineral resources, the raw materials. They owned Nature, do you see?"

When Käthe did not respond, he added: "It made me furious. I looked at that wall of stone, part of a mountain, a piece of the country. At that time I did not yet think that it ought to belong to everyone; my thought was—I remember that clearly—that it should belong to nobody. I imagined that it ought to be free. Free. Free! But it belonged to a Herr Petschek from Budweis."

For a while Käthe said nothing. Then cautiously, as if she were addressing the blue air above her, she said: "Just the way the Winterspelt quarry now belongs to a Herr Hainstock."

"Arimond is to blame for that," Hainstock replied.

On June 5, 1941, a cold day, he was summoned from work on a drainage ditch. Back at the barracks, the suit he had discarded seven years ago and his old shoes were flung at him. The things still fit; his figure had hardly changed. Only his hair, which had been repeatedly shaved, was now growing in iron-gray. He was led to the camp commandant's office. As he paused in the doorway, before he was beckoned up to the desk, he noticed the plump little man seated in an easy chair in the right-hand corner of the room: white-haired, a mane of silky white hair, legs outstretched under a dark-blue duffel coat, a stiff gray hat resting on his legs, hands raised to his face, the palms touching over his mouth and up to the tip of his nose, cheeks a healthy pink.

The stern beckoning motion of the forefinger. Standing with buttocks pinched, thighs and calves tightened, facing the desk.

"If it were up to me, you wouldn't get out of here until you served ten years."

The camp commandant was also small, like the unknown, like Hainstock himself, but lean: a horseman, red-haired, islands of freckles in the sallow face above the black uniform, which was pressed to knife-edge sharpness.

"You are and will remain a Communist swine. What are you, Hainstock?"

"I am a Communist swine."

"Sir." (That was spoken with a patient hiss.)

"Sir."

"All right now, come along, Herr Hainstock," the man in the background said. Perhaps the most incredible thing on this incredible day was that Hainstock immediately relaxed the muscles of his buttocks, thighs, and calves and turned away from the camp commandant's desk because of the tone in which that *All right now, come along, Herr Hainstock* had been spoken. That tone left no doubt that he could risk this relaxation of the muscles and his turning away (actually turning his back on the commandant!). The unknown had already stood up and donned his hat. Small, that is about the same height as Hainstock, plump, rosy-faced, dark-blue, the gray homburg now on his head and covering that white silk mane, he said, "Heil Hitler!" without raising his right arm because he was using it to hold Hainstock's arm and guide him toward the door.

93

"Heil Hitler!" the camp commandant replied, his tone likewise indifferent; he remained sitting behind his desk, already half turned away from them.

In the corridor the small gentleman walked ahead of Hainstock with rapid footsteps. Outside the barracks a black Mercedes was waiting, and a chauffeur in gray livery opened the rear door. The unknown let Hainstock get in first, sat down beside him, and said to the driver, who had appeared at the wheel in a flash, "Now let's get out of here and quick, Baltes."

"Sure thing, boss," the chauffeur said. He was a lean fellow with an anxious face.

As the car drove by the drainage ditch where he had been working only an hour ago, Hainstock leaned back because he did not want the comrades to see him.

They passed through the checkpoint at the camp gate. Outside, trees being tossed by the north wind, and the open country familiar to Hainstock. Houses on the horizon. "If it were up to me, you wouldn't get out of here until you served ten years." So he was not being taken just to an interrogation. Moreover, the little gentleman and the liveried chauffeur argued against any such hypothesis. Nevertheless he made a test; he turned the crank on the car window, dropping the window an inch or two. The cold wind whistled in, so that he promptly closed it again. No one said anything.

Hainstock asked no questions.

After they reached the Greifswald highway and were driving on in the direction of Berlin, the stranger said: "Incredible, absolutely incredible, such treatment!"

Hainstock had to give this remark some thought before it yielded up its meaning to him, for at the moment the only incredible thing was that to a high degree of probability he was a released prisoner, sitting in the back seat of a car and reading a road sign that told him he was entering the village of Birkenwerder.

"That?" he said at last. "But that wasn't anything. We're used to that kind of thing. It runs off us like water off a duck's back."

"It was worse than any of the things I have heard about the

94

camps," the man beside him said. In the shade of the back seat
his face was no longer a healthy pink, but dark red, apoplectic.

It was only at this point that he introduced himself and offered
a cigarette to Hainstock, who refused it, saying that before his arrest he had been a pipe smoker but now he didn't want to start
again.

He looked out of the window, read the road signs as they entered Berlin, noticed the names of districts, Wittenau, Wedding,
Stettin Station, watched people making use of these and other lo-
calities, going for example down Invalidenstrasse to Stettin Station (or standing still and talking to one another or simply standing, putting down suitcases, or standing in front of shop windows,
or turning around, or otherwise changing direction).

"Before you drive to the hotel," the no longer wholly unknown
man said to his chauffeur, "stop at a hat shop, Baltes. Let's see
whether we can dig up a hat for Herr Hainstock."

They found a haberdasher in the northern end of Friedrich-
strasse, and the little man in the dark-blue duffel coat was able to
persuade the shopkeeper to sell the right-size hat without a clothing ration card. For the second time that day Hainstock observed
the quality of irresistibility in Herr Arimond.

"But the strangest moment of the day was still when we drove
by that ditch where I had just been standing, digging the wet
earth," he later told Käthe. "Although I leaned back, all of them
saw me anyhow, all the guys standing in the ditch, `Dietrich,
Sennhauser, Fisher, and the rest. They saw me. Naturally none of
them risked waving to me. The strange thing about it, and it was
really bad, was that I at once felt: I no longer belong to them.
The man who rode past in a car was a completely different person
from the one who had just been standing in the ditch with them.
I didn't think that at the time, of course; I'm having that thought
for the first time today. At that time I only wished to be invisible."

Following Arimond's instructions, Hainstock kept the hat on
while they were standing in the lobby of the Kaiserhof.

95

"Afterwards, when you are installed and come back down again, you can take it off," Arimond had said.

The hotel doormen did not seem to notice anything unusual about him. He was just some whosit tagging along with Herr Arimond, an esteemed guest of the house for many years who was to be surrounded with standard cordiality; the cordiality and politeness became just a shade more intense when Hainstock identified himself with the discharge certificate from Oranienburg concentration camp. That sort of thing had also happened before in the Kaiserhof. Arimond stood impassively beside him. He had seen to everything; Hainstock's room adjoined his, and in it Hainstock found shirts and underclothes, ties, toilet articles, a light-colored raincoat, and a suitcase. Arimond made no bones about the fact that the clothing came from his own wardrobe.

"I received a description of you," he said. "I knew that you were about my size. Except that you haven't put on as much fat as I have." He laughed good-naturedly.

When he took off the dark-blue duffel coat, there was the Golden Party Badge on the lapel of his jacket. Otherwise Arimond looked dressed to the nines, likewise in a dark-blue suit with fine pinstripes over his plump frame, which perhaps was everywhere as pink, as bathed and well tended, as his face. The white silk mane was again revealed, giving him the look of a small, well-brushed lion.

"If you want an impression of Arimond," Hainstock said to Käthe, "I was once invited to his home in Koblenz, and when we were seated at table his wife nodded at him and asked me: 'Doesn't he look like the Little King?' He didn't mind that at all, laughed without being insulted in the least.

"Yes," Hainstock said, "he's a regular little Rhineland Schwittjeh'."

He had learned the expression *Schwittjeh'* only since he had been living in this mountainous region near the Rhine.

At lunch in the Kaiserhof restaurant Arimond informed him of the part that he played in the mining and mineral industry, told him also he would be taking him to the west the next day, and what position awaited him there. There would not be much to do, he said, but he needed somebody, a reliable technician; quarries had to be supervised even when they were shut down. Could Hainstock drive a car? Hainstock said he could. Arimond offered him a salary of 800 marks and free living quarters. They began to talk shop.

"But you aren't eating," Arimond said. "Oh well, I suppose you will have to take some time to adjust."

He handed Hainstock some money, and took his leave, saying that he had meetings for the rest of the afternoon. Hainstock, who in fact had meant to stay in his room, went out nevertheless. He donned his raincoat, put on the hat, and walked down Wilhelmstrasse and Unter den Linden as far as the Opera, turned right, and returned to the hotel by way of Gendarmenmarkt and Mohrenstrasse. At a newsstand in Mohrenstrasse he bought a newspaper and brought it back to his room. When he realized that he stopped reading every time he heard footsteps in the corridor and was listening to see whether they would pause in front of his door, he went down to the lobby and sat reading the newspaper there. He leafed through magazines that lay on the table, observed the guests, observed stuccoed pillars, fine wood, chandeliers. Around six o'clock he went back up, took a bath, shaved, put on one of Arimond's shirts and the tie that matched it best, checked himself in the mirror and was glad that his old suit of gray corduroy with patch pockets still fit.

It was not until they were having their dinner that Arimond explained the enigma. The meal went off much more pleasantly than lunch because Hainstock suddenly had an appetite and devoured with pleasure a wienerschnitzel and fried potatoes. Arimond had ordered a bottle of Rhine wine; he called Hainstock's attention to the vintage and the grower. Then he mentioned that he had visited the Sudetenland in the spring, to look into the matter of coordinating industry there with that of the Reich.

"Whereabouts did you go?" Hainstock asked.

"Reichenstein, Winterberg, Krumau, and a few other god-forsaken holes," Arimond said. "Why?"

"Then you were in the Sumava," Hainstock said. "That's not Sudeten territory at all."

"Sumava?" Arimond asked. "I've never heard the name."

"It's the Czech word for the Bohemian Forest," Hainstock said.

He would have been glad to educate Arimond on the geography and population of Bohemia, but Arimond said: "Sudeten or Sumava, it's all the same to me. In any case, there's where I heard about you."

"About me?" Hainstock asked. "The only people there who might be talking about me would be my sisters, and you certainly didn't run into them."

"You underestimate yourself, my dear fellow," Arimond said. "One evening I was at a restaurant with some business associates, people of my own class, or whatever you want to call them. We were having an excellent dinner—that's fine food you have in Bohemia—and two of my table partners began talking about how much easier it was to run things since certain people were behind bars. Names were mentioned, including yours. 'Hainstock,' one of them said, 'he's been out of the way since '36, hasn't he?' The other man confirmed this. 'He made his big mistake by barging into the Reich,' he said, laughing. 'They know how to deal with that kind of troublemaker.' I intervened and asked who this Hainstock was. 'A first-rate technical man,' I was told, 'but a red son-of-a-bitch.' I made so bold as to say that I would have phrased that in reverse order: a red son-of-a-bitch but a first-rate technical man." Arimond set the wineglass, from which he had been on the point of drinking, vigorously down on the table. "I beg your pardon, Hainstock," he said. "I shouldn't have told you that. You've already had one animal epithet thrown at you today."

When he saw Hainstock's smile, he went on with his story. "My dinner partners were quite embarrassed when I took out a slip of paper, made a note of your name, and said that industry could not afford to go on losing first-rate technical men. They might have bristled, maybe even muttered a few threats, but this thing stops all bigmouths." He indicated the Golden Party Badge. "Defense Industry Coordinator," he said.

"So that's it, and now you are here," he said. "It took a while to find out where the devil they had put you. After that it all went fairly quickly."

He changed the subject, remarking that he had found the Sudetenland—he again called it Sudetenland, not Bohemia—beautiful but rather sad; he was interested in the future of the graphite and china clay resources of the Upper Moldau, but he was no longer concerned with linking the industry of former Czechoslovakia with that of the Reich, so he had turned this question over to another member of the Reich Industrial Association for Rock and Minerals. He ordered another bottle of wine. After it had been opened and set in the bucket, and the wine steward had left them, Hainstock said: "So you had me released because you are looking for a quarry technician who will apparently have nothing to do."

Arimond did not take issue with this. He glanced around the dining room of the Kaiserhof, where there were not many guests this evening, and in a voice that was not even especially low, said: "Look here, Hainstock, you know perfectly well that we're going to lose this war."

"I know nothing," Hainstock answered quickly. "I've been away for seven years."

"Bravo!" Arimond said. "You're nobody's fool. Do you know, all along I was worried that you would turn out to be one of these politically naïve fellows. Or what would be worse, a broken man with whom I wouldn't be able to do a thing."

"Do what?" Hainstock asked.

"Oh, nothing special," Arimond said, "nothing at all, actually. One of these days it will be to my advantage to point to a few people I was able to help. You see, I'm completely frank with you. I don't want you to think me unselfish."

If Hainstock could have seen himself at that moment he would have been struck by the fact that his eyes—whose pupils were narrowing—looked even more sharply porcelain blue than usual. With those narrowed blue eyes he studied Herr Arimond sharply,

99

cheerfully. Later he would tell Käthe that for the first time that day he felt relieved.

"Whatever your reasons for getting me out of there, Herr Arimond," he said, "I am grateful to you."

"My pleasure," Matthias Arimond said.

"Early in June forty-one," Hainstock said, "it was not at all so obvious that Germany would lose the war. After all, the Russian campaign did not begin until two weeks later."

"And," Käthe asked, "will you come to his rescue some day because he was helpful to you?"

"Of course," Hainstock said. "No question about it. Possibly a few people will survive the camps. But the chances are good that he saved my life."

"Golden Party Badge, Defense Industry Coordinator," Käthe said. "How many has he put in so that he could get one man out?"

"I've kept my ears open. The Golden Party Badge was awarded to him more or less as an honorary matter. He seems to have done nothing vicious."

"He gave money. He helped to finance the whole thing. He must have paid through the nose or otherwise he never would have been given that badge. And that's the kind of man whose hide you want to save later on."

"But he is not a fascist, rather the opposite. He's adjusted, he's played along when he saw which way the wind was blowing. He's a gangster, understand. Basically, capitalism is a system of gangster syndicates, of profiteers who make their little arrangements but they themselves have no ideology at all. They really hate ideologies on the ground that any such doctrines interfere with business affairs."

"I see that your Marxism lets you be so broad-minded," Käthe said. "Sometimes I think Marxism is merely a method for explaining everything."

"Yes, explaining everything but not forgiving everything," Hainstock said. "Arimond isn't going to need my help after all. Since there isn't going to be a revolution and since he has committed no crimes as far as the bourgeois legal code is concerned, he will simply remain in power."

He noticed how the look of dissatisfaction lingered in Käthe's face and then disappeared as her interest in the subject died.

During the night he could not sleep. Around two o'clock in the morning he went to the window, raised the blackout blind, and looked down on unlighted Wilhelmsplatz. He could distinguish the low black mass of the Chancellery opposite, the taller mass of the Propaganda Ministry on the right, the iron monuments like gray shadows under his window. The times were long gone since anyone looking out of a window of the Kaiserhof had thought *Schulenberg Palace* or *Palace of the Order of the Knights of St. John*, or *Schwerin, Anhalt-Dessau, Winterfeldt, Keith, Zieten, Seydlitz*. Hainstock, at any rate—a totally political person to the extent that he was not a quarrier of stone—did not even think *Prussia* these days; his only thought was *fascism*. Or perhaps even that thought did not come to him; rather, on that June 6 at two o'clock in the morning he looked down on Wilhelmsplatz, not yet transformed into a ruin by bombs, as if it were a dark quarry of history wrapped in unlighted night. Then he lay down again, wearing a pair of Herr Arimond's pajamas, upon a bed in the Hotel Kaiserhof, astonished almost to disbelief at the sudden change in his fortunes, but once again political enough to realize that tonight, as on the night before, he was in the very heart of fascism. He lay and stared at the gray rectangle of the window. He had forgotten to lower the blackout blind.

Arimond would drop in to see Hainstock at intervals of about six months. One day in October 1942, which would be curiously repeated in October 1944—the same lovely weather with a mild autumnal mist that made the Winterspelt quarry beneath which they stood look like a bright veil, the difference being that the war was then out of sight in that region, not just seemingly invisible because of the kind of warfare Major Dincklage waged—on one such day Arimond said to Hainstock, embracing the quarry with a broad gesture of his right arm: "Well then, if you like you can have it."

This sentence seemed to be one of Arimond's sudden inspira-
tions. At any rate, it had no direct connection with the argument
about social systems they had earlier been conducting inside the
shack. It had become a habit with them to engage in disputations
about capitalism and communism, in the course of which Hainstock tested Arimond's soft arguments based on practice against
the hardness of theory, and found them wanting.

The many horizontal lines in Hainstock's face shifted slightly
upward, while his mouth remained a line. His eyes, those small
blue stones, became even smaller than they naturally were. He did
not deign to answer Arimond.

"I don't mean to tease you," Arimond said.

"Assuming I would want to have it," Hainstock said, suddenly
feeling that the man meant it seriously and stunned by the tremendous possibilities implicit in this offer, "could you also reveal
to me where I would get the money?"

"From the bank," Arimond said promptly.

Hainstock laughed dryly. "But you know I have no money in
the bank," he said.

"You make me feel as thought I were talking to primitive
man," Arimond said. "All right, this is the way it is: we draw up a
purchase agreement. I estimate that the value of the quarry is
twenty-five thousand Reichsmarks. Tomorrow morning we go together to the district savings bank in Prüm, and on the basis of
this agreement they will pay out the money to you."

"Pay it out just like that!"

"Not just like that, but in return for eight per cent annual interest, payable semiannually. Every six months you'll have to raise
a thousand marks. But you can certainly do that, Hainstock, from
the salary I am paying you, and of course that will continue because you will go on supervising the other quarries, so I hope."

"Are you trying to tell me that the district savings bank in
Prüm will grant me a loan of twenty-five thousand marks on a
shut-down quarry?"

"It will grant it on the understanding that you will reopen the
place within a reasonable time. And in addition I'll guarantee the
loan."

"Aha," Hainstock said, "then the quarry will belong to the

bank in the first place and continue to belong to you in the second place."

"Oh my goodness," Arimond said, "pay a call on any businessman in this country or elsewhere and ask whether he can get along without bank credits and guarantees. And then ask him whether he feels himself any the less a businessman on that account. All that matters is that the enterprise makes a profit. It must make a profit, Hainstock! The more profit your quarry makes later, the more money you'll be able to borrow. So that you can expand it so that it will make more and more of a profit.

"I always knew," he concluded, "that you Communists didn't have the vaguest idea about economics."

He began criticizing Hainstock. Instead of worrying about the right of ownership, he said, Hainstock should have dickered with him about the price; but he'd foreseen that he wouldn't and had therefore set the price as low as possible, though on the other hand not too low: the Winterspelt quarry was indeed worth twenty-five thousand at the moment. Later, when Hainstock began exploiting it, he'd see that he'd bought it dirt-cheap; in fact, if he, Arimond, started thinking too much about the potentialities of the Winterspelt quarry he would retract his offer to sell. That was not true. They were both aware that the Winterspelt quarry lent itself only to a limited production of quality stone, for windowsills, door embrasures, steps, and the like; it would never provide general building stone, nor would it yield—as the Lauch quarries did—raw materials for large-scale use: crushed rock, cement lime, ordinary wall stone. At full capacity the Winterspelt quarry would employ a dozen workmen. To Herr Arimond it was the smallest of his fish.

At the end they stood, absorbed in technicalities, side by side looking at the stone wall which already lay in shadow, with shadows that reached out for them but did not quite reach them—two men of more or less the same small stature, bathed by the light of this warless October day, for in those days the war stayed (aside from air raids on German cities) in the steppes to the east of the Don, at sea between Iceland and Murmansk, and on the borders of Egypt, not here in this land of somber villages, hamlets, forests, silent under the screeching of the buzzards, where the snow would soon be falling. So that these two men who had become friends, the one with white silky hair that reflected the light, the other with light-absorbing iron-gray hair—it had grown back by now but Hainstock still kept it cropped short—were able to conduct a technical conversation that led them from questions of capital flow and credit balances to problems of working shell limestone from an *ostiolatus* horizon. The future Major Dincklage was at that time a lieutenant in Cyrenaica; Schefold was at Limal Castle writing up a critique of a Flemish minor master of the fourteenth century, had never heard the name *Hemmeres*, and even Käthe Lenk had not yet turned up in Winterspelt; she was still going around Berlin, taking English lessons (every Friday evening) from Fräulein Heseler in Dorotheenstrasse, and frequently meeting her boy-friend, Lorenz Gieding.

The following day Arimond and Hainstock had the purchase contract drawn up by the notary Nösges in Prüm, affixed their signatures, and with the document in hand went to the district savings bank, whose director approved the loan after receiving Arimond's co-signature. Hainstock never saw the money, for it was simply transferred on the books to one of the accounts of the Tufa and Basalt Lava Company in Mayen. That same morning at the land registry they initiated the process of change of ownership, the transfer of a property of approximately five acres, north of the road from Winterspelt to Bleialf, to the name of Wenzel Hainstock.

"Why didn't this man Arimond simply give it to you?" Käthe Lenk had asked when Hainstock described the procedure to her.

"He went into that matter, too," Hainstock said. "He said that giving it to me would be a violation of good business practice. 'Besides,' he said, 'if I gave you the whole works you would not be forced to make something of it.' Probably I wouldn't have accepted on that basis either," Hainstock added.

But he was ready to concede that Arimond had emerged the victor in their disputations on capitalism and communism, victor as a result, moreover, of what the philosophically trained ("intellectual") Käthe called an *inductive conclusion* ("derivation of general principles from specific facts; knowledge from experience"). Arimond had succeeded in making Hainstock, if not a capitalist, at any rate a proprietor of mineral resources.

Could it be that Arimond helped Hainstock become owner of the Winterspelt quarry not because he wanted to expose the *reductio ad absurdum* of Hainstock's Marxism but because he had noticed that this man from Bohemia spoke very differently about this particular limestone deposit from the way he spoke of the other properties he supervised? Had he ever, before coming into sight, observed Hainstock smoking his pipe, leaning on a block of stone that lay in the abandoned workyard below the cliff, studying the bright wall, although there was nothing much to see there, especially for someone who had been living at the foot of it for quite some time? We do not know, cannot judge the mode and operation of Matthias Arimond's sensibility. Since the previous winter he had not put in an appearance in the Prüm district, presumably because he was busy preparing the Reich Industrial Association for Rock and Minerals, as well as his own enterprises and himself, for what he had predicted as far back as June 1941; and we may assume that closeness to the front was a condition not at all to his taste.

Middle Devonian, Couvin Stage, Lauch strata. The sandy formation is limited to the northeast rim of the syncline and extends from Mühlbach to Duppach. It is essentially a light-colored, gray-green shading toward blue, somewhat soft, sandy, thin-leaved, and disintegrating slate. Limestone layers begin only on the roof of the Lauch strata, on the north rim. The fauna are fairly rich; along with brachiopods, chiefly in the sandy strata, the mollusks are numerous and seem restricted to this sandy facies. The limestone evolution is present on the western part of the northern wing . . .

(Winterspelt!?)

. . . and on the southern wing. The light-blue to dark-blue, sandy, partially sparry, fossil-rich limestones are hewn into building

105

stones in the larger quarries (such as Rommersheim, Ellwerath, and Oberlauch). The iron content is very high and can be recognized by the intensity of the blue coloration, which changes to an equally intense reddish-brown in the course of weathering. The rough surface of the rock is due to protruding fragments of shells. The beds, up to thirty centimeters in thickness, show mostly scaly weathering and when hammered open reveal rings of discoloration from outside to inside. Dark, slaty marls are often embedded in them. (Happel and Reuling, *The Geology of the Prüm Syncline*. Proceedings of the Senckenberg Society for Natural History, Frankfurt am Main, 1937)

What was interesting first of all about that was that Ludwig Happel and Hans Theodor Reuling, doctors of philosophy at the Institute of Geology and Paleontology of Frankfurt University (as the title page identified them) during the years in which he, Wenzel Hainstock, had been an inmate of the Oranienburg concentration camp, had peacefully gone about investigating the geology of the Prüm syncline. So a science existed that unfolded alongside politics and in fact completely independently of politics. Moreover, and this was the most incomprehensible aspect of the whole thing, there could not really be any objection to that. It might well be that Ludwig Happel and Hans Theodor Reuling were in addition members of the Nazi Party, or else underground fighters against the rule of that Party; but these would be only their personal concerns, so to speak. Presumably they kept aloof from any political commitments and defined themselves solely by dividing the Devonian of the Prüm syncline into four stages which they located precisely. Hainstock, versed in the doctrine of how dependent science is on social change, was nevertheless infected by the suspicion that work and history existed in separate compartments. For the present he rejected that idea.

He had reason to be grateful to Happel and Reuling. While he was doing hard time in the concentration camp they had investigated the nature of the Couvin Stage of the Middle Devonian, so that he was now able to recognize the nature of the Winterspelt quarry and to justify his spending so much time gazing at it or climbing around it, with the result that he continually replaced the rungs of the ladder leaning against it whenever they showed signs of decay.

Under the conditional form of that sentence *Assuming I would want to have it* Hainstock had scarcely concealed the fact that he was already snapping at Arimond's bait. But why this snapping, this sense of being overwhelmed by a *tremendous possibility*, when he suddenly guessed that Arimond, this feeble theoretician but subtle psychologist and tempter, meant it seriously? Was he not thereby recanting, or rather betraying the principle he had recognized thirty years earlier in the face of a geologically very similar wall of rock? So that Käthe's question, which she asked as soon as he had asserted that he would not have taken the property as a gift, was altogether appropriate: "Why did you take it at all?"

He did not answer this question, merely shrugged; he did not tell Käthe that when he returned from Prüm with the purchase agreement in his pocket he had been so childishly out of his mind with delight that he had patted the wall, saying to himself that now it belonged to him.

E. Süss conjectures that the highest elevations of this ancient mountain chain were in the vicinity of the Ballons of the Vosges, and in what is today Voigtland, the territory of the ancient Variscans, for which reason he has called the entire chain the Variscan Mountains. In the following, immeasurably long periods of geological time these mountains were slowly but incessantly worn away; grain upon grain was blown or washed away. Repeatedly, the sea rose above the mountain chain or part of it, leveling it down to its base, so that the high chain became an almost featureless plain into which, when it rose out of the sea again, the water courses furrowed their valleys and weathering carved the hard rocks out of their soft surroundings, leaving them towering above the plain as more or less distinct ridges. Several times the earth's crust burst open, huge strata sank into the depths and were flooded by the sea which deposited its minerals on them. As a result of these events, we today see only remnants of the base of the former Variscan Alps towering like eyries above the younger elevations around them. Among these remnants are the Sudeten Mountains, the Erzgebirge, the Harz, the ancient rocks of the Black Forest and the Vosges, and the Rhenish Slate Mountains. The Eifel forms a part of the latter. (Professor Holzapfel, *Geological Sketch of the Eifel Mountains*, published by the Eifel Association, Trier, 1914)

And a part of that part, according to the prevailing bourgeois legal standards, belonged to him, Hainstock. A cliff risen up out of the Tethys Sea, a bed formed of petrified crinoids, brachiopods, corals, ammonites, and minute ostracods, a part of sedimental rock millions of years old, set upon a base of still older mountains, was now his property, and in addition several acres of rare limestone pasture flora, stemless thistles and orchids, bergamot and Carthusian pinks, along with several pines at the summit, under whose broad umbrellas he could stand and observe what was going on round about his mountain.

Further reflections on Hainstock's part, which can only be suggested here:

We regard history as a sedimental bed.

Wars, revolutions, as the foldings which have confused the sediments. Everything now depends on beginning a millennium of peaceful deposition not to be disturbed by anything. A pious wish.

His dislike for metamorphic rocks from the earth's interior, also for volcanos. Sediments, stratified rocks, preferably formed by living creatures, rocks of organic origin—that was the thing.

Marxism as a deposit, in the geological sense.

From a geologist's report which Arimond had once commissioned, he gathered that the limestones of the Winterspelt quarry consisted chiefly of calcspar and dolomite; the accessory clayey minerals included in them consisted of quartz, iron oxide, and bitumens. He immediately asked himself which components of Marxism were essential, which accessory.

In spite of his personal decision (to become owner of the Winterspelt quarry), he belonged to the Marxist stratum. The geologists of the future would find him in it ("I am a Communist swine"). However, they would hardly accord him the rank of an index fossil.

The Caledonian orogeny at the boundary between the Silurian and Devonian uplifted the northern continent out of the sea; in the east it extended as far as Bohemia and in the west to Northwest Germany. The Ardennes formed an island much like the so-called Alamannic island which extended from the central plateau across the Black Forest and almost all the way to Bohemia . . . The Sudeten folding initiated the end of the Grauwacken formations and a new large orogenic movement which welded a new ring of mountain chains, the Variscan Mountains, to ancient Caledonian Europe. The Variscan Mountains, interspersed with granite masses, formed vein upon vein along the southern rim of the northern continent that was forged together during the Caledonian disturbance. We find its traces in the southernmost parts of England, in Brittany, in Normandy, in the Rhenish Slate Mountains, and in the Harz . . . Just as the northern trunk came from the north, the southern trunk reaches from the south and southeast around the Bohemian core. (Professor J. von Bülow, *Geology for Everyone,* 9th edition, Stuttgart, 1968)

He found the statements of Happel and Reuling corroborated. The limestones of the Winterspelt quarry were light blue to dark blue. The rough surface of the rock was due to the weathering fragments of shale. Dark, slaty marls were embedded. The fauna were rather numerous; in addition to the brachiopods there were many mollusks, chiefly in the sandy strata. Freshly split rocks tended to be intensely blue because of their iron content in the form of finely distributed iron sulfides. The handsome old stone houses that were still relatively common in the villages of the vicinity had all been made of Winterspelt stone. He had learned that the quarry was being worked as early as the seventeenth century. Since 1932 it had been shut down; the worldwide depression had finished it off. Because it yielded only irregular building blocks that were hard to square off, its fortunes had not been

affected even by the Westwall building boom, as Matthias Arimond had informed him.

When Arimond put him in charge of all his quarries in the
western part of the Prüm district, Hainstock had decided in favor
of this light-gray wall. That is, he chose the workmen's shack at
the Winterspelt quarry for his quarters. The other quarries had
thick beds of dolomites, sheet limestones, or sandstones rich in
quartzite. These were more valuable, and until the winter of
'40–'41, when they also were shut down, had supplied fine building blocks, cement, and road metal. Hainstock decided in favor
of the Winterspelt quarry first because it was situated farthest to
the west, closest to the frontier, secondly because it was both
remote and offered a panoramic view, thirdly because it bore the
greatest resemblance to the limestone quarry near Aussergefild
where he had spent three years learning his trade. He found in the
Winterspelt quarry the same facies of rock that he had worked
with the mallet in Bohemia, and when he climbed to the top of
his wall and contemplated the Schnee-Eifel, which was a chain of
hard quartzite rocks like any of the hills between Winterberg and
Oberplan, when he gazed over the forested lines of the Ardennes,
calmly, spaciously arranged in tilted strata, rising in the same
Devonian slope to the Hoher Venn as the woods of Aussergefild
and Strni rose to the Mittagsberg, he thought he was dreaming.
He was in Bohemia.

Of course there were differences. The Ardennes were more
heavily weathered and consequently flatter than the Bohemian
Forest. The chalk hollows in which the villages lay were longer
than the scattered clearings of the Sumava. The air was damper,
more Atlantean, than the air in which Hainstock had grown up,
which had often seemed to him so still that he would imagine the
planet had stopped moving.

Matthias Arimond paid Hainstock eight hundred marks a
month to look after his closed quarries, in other words, to do
nothing. Hainstock's responsibility was obviously great; consequently he had an old but reliable Adler at his disposal for his inspection tours. He was one of the few civilians in the Prüm district who had permission to drive a car this late in the game—in

the sixth year of the war. And he had used the three years he had
so far spent in this region to assemble a respectable collection of
fossils; its showpieces were a Devonian (therefore very old) am-
monite of the genus *Clymenia*, a *Phacops* with large faceted eye,
and a colony of twenty four-branched corals which he had found
in the iron horizon of one of the quarries near Lauch.

Käthe often stood and admired this collection. But once when
he wanted to give her a particularly beautiful specimen, the petrified chalice of a sea-lily, she refused.

"It's too heavy for me," she said. "You know, I'll want to travel
light when I leave here. I can't very well load myself up with
rocks."

## Readjusting the Main Line of Defense

The view from the crown of Hainstock's quarry more or less
matched the view two kilometers farther to the west from the
Ourberg, a hill on the footpath that leads from Winterspelt to
Auel. The local road from Winterspelt to Bleialf crosses hills and
later on the Ihrental, but there is no hill comparable to the Ourberg anywhere along it. Nor would anything like the quarry be
found there; it is unlikely that the Couvin Stage of the Middle
Devonian extends so far to the west of the Prüm syncline. The
forested valley that Schefold used to travel from Hemmeres to
behind the German lines corresponds approximately to the Ihrental, but the brook known as the Ihrenbach flows into the Our a ki-
lometer above Hemmeres. Moreover, at Hemmeres the Our does
not flow through a distinct ravine; its western bank alone forms a
steep, beetling slope, while to the east of the river high but well-
rounded pastureland rises more gently. The solitude of the (then
Belgian) hamlet is a matter of authentic memory; it has grown
into a smallish village since, and is no longer solitary. The wooden
footbridge and the railroad viaduct have vanished. (Before 1918

Hemmeres was German, from 1918 to 1940 Belgian, from 1940 to
1945 German, from 1945 to 1955 Belgian; in 1955 Belgium ceded
it to the German Federal Republic.) Maspelt and the vicinity,
where Captain Kimbrough commanded, have been described with
a fair degree of accuracy. Winterspelt has undergone the greatest
changes. The village of that name is not at all a village in a limestone syncline; rather it lies exposed on a ridge of the western
slope of the Eifel Mountains, where they join with the outlying
region of the Ardennes. A village in the eastern part of the Prüm
district has been used as a model for Winterspelt. Finally, it must
be confessed that not even the course of the front line has been
reconstructed in exact accordance with historical accuracy. In the
autumn of 1944 Winterspelt was no longer in German hands; it
had been captured by the Americans earlier and had to be seized
from them at the beginning of the Ardennes offensive and
reconquered by them in January 1945. We have shown the Americans still lingering on the western bank of the Our at the beginning of October in order to give Major Dincklage's plan greater
topographical plausibility. Unlike history, storytelling (that sand
table game) can be permitted such little readjustments.

### End of Crow's Nest

October 12, 1944 (a Thursday), shortly after noon. Just as he
was about to descend, he caught sight of Käthe as she came cycling cautiously along on the gravelly shoulder of the road. Whenever she came by day she borrowed Therese Thelen's bicycle so
that she would lose less time on the way out to him, and today of
course there was special need for haste. She had to be careful not
to run the tires over sharp splinters of rock, which meant that she
did not see Hainstock standing up at the top, waving. He quickly
started down so that he would arrive at the shack at the same
time she did.

# Sentry's Report
of an Incident

Although Reidel had been constantly preoccupied this morning thinking over the consequences that would result from Borek's reporting him, he took note of the movement, the hint of a shadow and of some kind of color between the pines at the top of the slope. He noticed it the moment it grazed his retina. His light-brown, almost yellow eyes scarcely narrowed. They were so keen that they seldom needed to narrow when sighting an object. Without moving his shoulders, Reidel drew the carbine from his hip with his right hand. He just had time enough to make sure that the rim of his steel helmet and the edge of the foxhole in which he stood were at the same level; by the time he had checked this, the movement had already vanished because it had become a clear image: a man visible among the pines paused and regarded the terrain before him, the gently sloping pasture, its treeless expanse interrupted only by occasional junipers. The man was a civilian, and so unexpected in appearance that Reidel was simply flabbergasted. But since he hated being surprised and was therefore constantly on the alert to see that he was never caught out by anything or anyone, he promptly began thinking in tactical terms. He had hoped that the movement signaled the appearance of an American patrol, perhaps three men whom he could pick off with three rapid, successive shots in their knees. Then they could be brought in as prisoners. He himself would accompany the medical squad when they delivered the wounded men on their stretchers to the battalion command post in Winterspelt. A soldierly act like that would be mentioned in the divisional order of the day; that would take care of Borek's charge against him. But of course such strokes of luck didn't happen. It might also be that a Winterspelt or Wallmerath farmer, seized by the urge to look at the rye fields he could no longer till because after harvest the region had been declared a battle zone, had wandered over here in front of the first line of sentries. But that wasn't likely. The

114

farmers knew what was what. Nothing about this whole thing was likely. Neither he nor any of his fellows had so far been able to report any incident whatsoever; not the slightest event had taken place during a tour of sentry duty. Only the daily fighter-bomber attack and the artillery fire in the north, the muted thunder of which reached them in the early morning hours (it was said that the Amis were trying to work their way up to the Urft dam), reminded them at all that there was a war on. In the twelve days since he had been back at the front, Reidel had been taking it easier than previously in peaceful Denmark, where the deadening garrison duty imposed by the battalion commander, that game-legged medalist, had finally gotten Reidel down. Those rookies, Borek for example, had not believed him when he told them that service at the front would be a whole lot easier.

It wasn't just not likely, it was altogether inconceivable that in front of Reidel's foxhole there should appear, coming from the enemy direction, a tall and bulky fellow wearing a sports jacket of some soft fabric, grayish-brown, faded slacks, a white shirt, and actually a fiery red tie. He had opened the top button of his shirt and loosened the tie. Over his left shoulder was loosely slung a light-colored raincoat. He had a broad, florid face with a gray close-clipped mustache. Since it was in Reidel's character to regard everything he saw as real, he immediately abandoned the brief thought that he could not trust his own eyes. Nevertheless he decided the size up the unknown before he acted. He permitted the man, who had paused between the pale-gray shadows of the pines that had advanced farthest down the slope, to light a cigarette. Or perhaps it was the other way around—perhaps Reidel let the fellow light a cigarette not because he wanted to size him up, but rather, since the fellow lit a cigarette, Reidel decided he needed sizing up. With his unnarrowed, extremely keen eyes, he followed the movement with which the man thrust his left hand into the pocket of his jacket, took out a pack of cigarettes and a lighter, held the two objects quietly in his hand for a while without looking at them, and after an interval that seemed endless to Reidel took a cigarette from the pack with the fingers of his right hand, thrust it between his lips, rapidly exchanged the position

115

of lighter and pack, and concentrated for a moment on the flame of the small black and silver lighter before looking over the terrain and dropping the articles back into his jacket pocket. Reidel observed that this series of gestures, which he thought were done easily and without any particular intention, sprang from a massive body. Massive was the right word for the man. He was not at all fat, had no belly, but there was a massiveness that pervaded his entire body, yet did not keep him from carrying out ordinary motions in an easy, weightless way. Reidel's feeling for fine movements in men was highly developed, for which reason he could not bring himself to interrupt the stranger.

He came to two conclusions: the unknown was in the first place a stroller, in the second place a guest. He behaved exactly like someone who is taking a stroll and pauses to have a cigarette—consequently, he was a stroller. But by October 12, 1944, there were no strollers in the battle zone on a sector of the Eifel front—not only weren't they allowed, they simply no longer happened. That being the case, there was something fishy about this fellow. Someone who approached the foremost line of sentries and was coming from the enemy direction, no matter how unconcerned he might appear to be, was primarily and under all circumstances to the highest degree suspect.

The idea that the man was a *guest* had a purely personal meaning to Reidel. He was the son of an Elberfeld hotelkeeper. His father had sent him off to learn the hotel business from the ground up, and what was more, in a first-class hotel in Düsseldorf. The result was that Reidel divided the human race into hotel guests and those who waited on them. He had no doubt that the fellow he was now observing belonged to the group of guests in first-class hotels. Not just because he was dressed so unobtrusively well, aside from the fiery red tie. From the very first second he had appeared to Reidel to be a gentleman.

After all these reflections were completed, or to put it another way, after he had satisfied himself about what he was seeing, Reidel raised the carbine, not snapping it into position as he had intended, but very slowly, very cautiously. The man had now folded his arms over his chest and was no longer looking at the slope in front of him, but at the more distant landscape. From time to time he took a puff of his cigarette, let the smoke curl out of his mouth. At last he discarded the butt. When Reidel had brought the weapon as high as his hip, he quickly pushed the bolt upward and forward. The noise of the lever forcing the cartridge into the barrel sounded dry, metallic, and very loud in the still air of this lovely October day. Reidel was sorry that guns could not be cocked noiselessly. He had already paced off the distance between his foxhole and the pines at the top. He knew it was almost exactly thirty meters to where the fellow stood.

Whenever Schefold left the woods in the ravine to the south of Hemmeres—his ordinary route through the German lines, the one Hainstock had recommended—he entered the background of one of the paintings by the Master of the Tiburtine Sibyl. The draftsmanship, the contours of the graceful hills layered one behind the other, the meadows and undergrowth, corresponded with extraordinary closeness to the rather dry manner of the Crucifixion that hung in the Van Reeths' Limal Palace. Even Wenzel Hainstock's limestone quarry was depicted in that painting, white and massive on the right edge of the picture. Every time he saw it, Schefold took delight in the amazing resemblance between reality and image, for it reminded him that among the older works of the Städel Institute his favorite had been the painting in which the Tiburtine Sibyl announces the birth of Christ to Emperor Augustus. He had incidentally collected all the necessary documentation to correct Friedländer's ascription. Since Schefold was familiar with every painting in eastern Belgium and Luxembourg —a degree of learning that, moreover, had so far saved his life— he was convinced that the master in question was a painter named Albrecht van Ouwater, who had collaborated with Dieric Bouts at the end of the fifteenth century in nearby Louvain. But whether or not he was right, the fact that in the course of his first expeditions on German soil he was walking among the landscapes of that master (whom Friedländer had named after a painting in the Städel Institute) struck Schefold as a sign of his already successful homecoming. It was part of his vocation to put faith in

117

signs. Hainstock was in the habit of warning him. As though he could read thoughts, Hainstock had once said: "You have come home too soon, Dr. Schefold. You're running around this area too much. Stay in Hemmeres for a few months longer. You're safe there."

Schefold had enough of being in safety. Some great collectors or owners of collections in Belgium had kept him safely in their palaces or their city residences. They took it for granted that a person like Schefold was to be protected. They passed him on from one to the other—since the occupation of Belgium in 1940 he had lived successively in Antwerp, Tournai, Dinand, and in Walcourt, Comines, finally at Limal Palace. A Belgian passport had even been provided for him; he had no need to fear sudden check-ups by the German Army, and could have gone about freely, but had forborne, not from fear but in order not to endanger his hosts. He catalogued collections and libraries, wrote critiques. Hidden in private archives, surrounded by coats of arms, paintings, and first editions, he had to admit that this shadowy life in old palaces suited him. Broken towers, stepped gables, castellan's quarters, inner courts of gray Bentheim stone—from the viewpoint of Hemmeres his clandestine existence seemed like something done in exquisitely executed grisaille. What is more, the food had been excellent everywhere. Schefold maintained that for a first-class goulash he was capable of killing his brother Abel. He had no brother. He was the only son of a Frankfurt district judge.

In the spring he started moving. The news from Italy and the Ukraine indicated that the war had already been decided. After the Allied landing and the Battle of Minsk he could no longer bear to stay on in Limal. Monsieur van Reeth warned him; just as Hainstock was now doing, he advised him not to leave his cover too soon; but Schefold would not be restrained. He traveled to the eastern border area, stayed in Malmédy with friends of the Van Reeths' for some time, observing the retreat of the German troops, then wandered around in the Ardennes. Like everyone else, he overestimated the speed of the Americans, waited impatiently. Out of impatience he settled down in Hemmeres—an act of incredible folly. He had been in Maspelt and had been tempted by the proximity of the Our to take a look at this border river. When he arrived on the western side above the valley he caught sight of the two white farmsteads on the German shore. A man was chopping wood, a woman was going back and forth between the buildings, a child was driving cows out to the pasture by the river. Perhaps Schefold was attracted by the wooden footbridge that led across the black, shallow stream to the farm buildings. He struck up a conversation with the man who was chopping wood. Since then he had been living at the farm. Probably the arrangement would not have lasted very long; one day fairly soon the man would have asked him to disappear or would simply have reported him. But then everything happened very fast after all; the Americans occupied Maspelt, the Germans withdrew behind the heights east of the Our. From the middle of September on, the hamlet of Hemmeres lay in no-man's-land. Among the hills that surrounded the bottom of the valley, Hemmeres' two white houses formed a parenthetical statement about peace in the midst of war. Schefold congratulated himself. He had chosen blindly but rightly. Besides, it filled him with satisfaction that he had returned to German soil not in the wake of the Allied troops, but far in advance of them. He wondered about this feeling. Since 1937, since his flight from Frankfurt, he had systematically worked at breaking the habit of loving Germany. The words "my country" no longer melted on his tongue; at best they tasted like grains of salt.

In Hemmeres, too, he ate remarkably well. They even allowed him to cook there, and warily tasted the unfamiliar dishes he prepared of meat, eggs, potatoes, and vegetables. Now and then he dropped in at a tavern in Saint-Vith, not for the food, which was bad, but because he had fallen in love with a waitress. Schefold, born in 1900 and thus a man of forty-four, had never yet slept with a woman, was always infatuated with one, and what is more, persistently and passionately, but had made it a rule never to betray his feelings by a single look or a single word. He called himself a radical *Stendhalien*. During the whole of the first half of 1944 he had adored Madame van Reeth in this way—she was a

seventeen-year-old petty-bourgeois wench from Brussels whose
figure obviously awakened in Monsieur van Reeth associations
with Rubens. Schefold had become so attached to her that it had
cost him considerable inner struggle to leave Limal. So now it was
this waitress. Schefold guessed her age at thirty-five. When he
tried to determine wherein lay the curious attraction of her
angular, hollow-cheeked face, he rejected the thought of Memling, although a strong resemblance to the portrait of Marthe
Moreel in Bruges simply could not be denied. But where women
were concerned, Schefold forbade himself to think of paintings.
He merely observed once again how easy it was for him to change
types. There could be no greater difference than that between
Madame van Reeth, a blithe display of pink and gold, and this
dark-haired Walloon who stepped out of the background of the
dimly lit tavern, came over to his table, and mutely waited for his
order. To have a chance to see her—he sometimes doubted
whether his method of concealing his feelings from women actually worked with this one—he hitched rides to Saint-Vith with
the drivers of American jeeps. By now he was going through the
American lines on the heights to the west of Hemmeres like an
old acquaintance. The regiment had instructed Captain Kimbrough in Maspelt to make out a pass for him. He could have returned to Limal at any time. Hainstock called him a fool for not
doing so—though he stopped calling him a fool after involving
him in the Dincklage affair.

On the morning of October 12, Schefold considered which tie
to wear for his call on Major Dincklage. Since he had taken only a
single outfit with him to Hemmeres, his old tweed jacket and a
pair of still older corduroy slacks, his wardrobe problems came
down to the choice of shirt and tie. For the shirt he considered
only a white one. Schefold firmly believed in the magical efficacy
of white shirts in the social game played between citizens of his
and Dincklage's level. The white shirt would immediately unite
him and Dincklage in veneration of the same fetish. Precisely because he was making this concession, he then chose the fiery red
woolen tie. It was essential to show Major Dincklage not only a
consenting white but also a challenging red.

Regarding himself in the shaving mirror—there was no other mirror in Hemmeres—he carefully brushed his close-clipped mustache; it did not bother him that it was gray and made him look older. Once Schefold was finished dressing, he gave no further thought to how he looked. He thought he knew. Going to the open window, he gazed out at the old apple trees, which were already nearly bare. Their leafless branches allowed a view of the dark river glittering in the morning sunlight. At the time of his arrival, in July, the green foliage had cast a pale-green light on the whitewashed walls of the room in the early morning. Later on, in September, that light had been reddish. Lying in bed, observing changes in the light, Schefold regretted every morning that he was not a painter but only a connoisseur of painting; but each morning he also reconciled himself to that fact, and lay for a while dozing, lost in greenish white or reddish white sleepiness and dreams. Until July the watercolor by Klee, hanging on the wall opposite the window, had proved to him that a picture like that could be painted only by a painter. Schefold had left his manuscripts and all the materials for his work back in Limal, but not this painting. Early in July he had taken it to Hainstock; if it were to be preserved anywhere, it would be safe with him. A few months hence, when the war was over, he would fetch *Polyphonically Bounded White* from one of Hainstock's perfect hiding places and carry it to Frankfurt in triumph, to return it to the Städel Institute from which he had stolen it, rescued it, in 1937. He was surprised not to miss the picture but told himself that parting from it had been relatively easy because he knew by heart every square centimeter of that watercolored paper surface.

He left his room, went down to the kitchen, and prepared his breakfast. At this hour the house was empty. He fried two eggs so that the yolk lay golden yellow inside the white framed by a brown crust—it was important to singe the edges. With this he ate two slices of rye bread that he buttered neither too thinly nor too thickly, and drank strong black coffee. The Hemmeres people had everything; the only item that Schefold had to rustle up for them was the coffee. They profited from him in other ways; he paid them in Belgian francs, and recently even in dollars, for in

121

Saint-Vith there were already money-changers who exchanged Belgian francs for dollars, although at fantastic rates. When Hemmeres ceased to be a no-man's-land, its inhabitants would have money that was not entirely worthless. Not much; Schefold was not a rich man. But since he had enjoyed continual free board and room during recent years, he had managed to save up his fees. While he breakfasted he looked out the kitchen window at the brown footbridge whose logs rumbled so pleasantly when you crossed it. Over on the other side, in Belgium, there was a meadow that belonged to the Hemmeres farmer. Schefold sat for a long time, smoking his first cigarette and then, contrary to habit, a second. It was a great pity there were no morning newspapers here. Before he left the room he spent some time with the big gray-striped tomcat who lay on the windowsill. Schefold was crazy about cats.

Later, in the woods, he realized after a glance at his watch that he was still arriving too early. He walked a short distance in the direction he always took until he reached the point at which he must deviate from it today, turning to the right and uphill through beech underbrush, hazel bushes, and other wild growth to the top of the hill. He sat down on the stump of a tree and waited. He would have preferred to go straight on ahead, walking on the level needle-covered floor of the evergreen forest, along the ravine under the dark, tall red spruces to where the wall of Hainstock's limestone quarry gleamed through the tree trunks, and the views familiar from fifteenth-century paintings began. For reasons he did not understand because he had not the slightest knowledge of military matters, the way through the ravine was the surest way through the German lines, for which he had no pass. Hainstock had pointed out this secure way to him on the survey map; what was more, he had actually snipped out the section of the map and given it to him to take along. Sitting on the stump, Schefold looked at the piece of paper and decided it was useless, just as he had decided the day before yesterday; it was as superfluous as this whole premature and pointless visit to Major Dincklage. He needed only to climb up the slope of the eastern height above the Our valley, which turned into the ravine here, and he would be

there. In the silence of the forest he suddenly thought it was unbelievable that two armies were confronting one another here.
The phrase itself struck him as so absurd that he would have
stood up and returned to Hemmeres, even to Limal, if he had not
realized promptly that of course these were not armies. The forces
confronting each other here were nothing but Kimbrough's company and Dincklage's battalion.

The climb was steep, difficult. In other circumstances Schefold
would have felt the light shadows of the pines on the height, and
the pines themselves, as pleasant; but since here he was traversing
the only really dangerous part of his course, he paid no attention
to them, but walked with rapid steps among the tree trunks, coming to a stop only where they stopped and where he could survey
the slope that dropped gently before him. Even Hainstock had admitted that this would be a critical moment—it was always possible that one of the men standing in foxholes halfway down the
slope might fire straightway at Schefold instead of challenging
him. Only after a few seconds, during which he waited in a kind
of daze, was Schefold able to concentrate upon the slope. With
surprise he observed that it was deserted. He could make out two
foxholes, but these were not occupied. Somewhat systematically,
he began noting small irregularities in the terrain, the shadows of
juniper bushes—but there was nothing else. He was perplexed.
The fact that the foremost line of German sentries was not where
it was supposed to be did not fit in with his plan. He wondered
how he was to conduct himself. Simply go on until he was
stopped somewhere? He was not only confused, but also relieved,
already beginning to think of turning back. Something was amiss;
he had to obtain fresh instructions from Hainstock, who for his
part would have to seek new information about Dincklage's tactical dispositions. Schefold lit a cigarette. Relieved, he turned his attention to the remoter landscape. He had never been up here before. The barren slope, grayish-green, gave way to undulating hills
covered with tilled fields and pastures that dropped off toward the
south into the hollow where the village of Winterspelt lay: shapeless white farmyards which distance and the light bundled together into a flat structure of gray and lighter segments. Outlines,

123

planes, curves, were altogether different out here from the way they looked in the paintings by the Master of the Tiburtine Sibyl. Schefold did not seek comparisons, only icons of this reality; he tried the names Pissarro, Monet, abandoned them, finally took a fling at Cézanne. He tossed away the cigarette.

Although he was not prepared for it, he reacted quickly, raised his arms at once when he heard the dry, hard clack, a metallic noise, and almost at the same moment the shout, "Hands up!" likewise hard and piercingly cried out by a high voice whose position Schefold was instantly able to determine because he now saw the steel helmet, the face and shoulders, the gun barrel pointed at him, not at all far, only twenty or thirty paces downslope from the spot where he stood. So someone had been watching him all this time. Invisible. The devil! Almost simultaneously with his fear he felt vexation with himself. Had he been blind?

Reidel had actually been determined to shoot. He had done no shooting since his time in Russia. Target-shooting in Denmark did not count, to his mind; that served only to confirm his status as a marksman first-class. Because of an attack of jaundice he had been withdrawn from the Russian front in March and sent to a hospital in Westphalia, from there to Denmark. He himself had arranged his assignment to the new division that was being formed in Russia—old corporals like himself knew how to organize the right transfers—because he had his belly full of Russia. Russia had had only one advantage for Reidel—he'd been able to shoot there. To him shooting meant aiming his blunderbuss at living, moving objects. The memory of Red Army men collapsing as they ran, or rolling painfully to one side in what they had thought was their cover, could sometimes make him half sick with desire. Of late he had occasionally fallen into peculiar depressions. During such states it seemed to him intolerable that for half a year he had not had a chance to fire. Out of the series of hand movements that resulted in a shot, Reidel most loved the noiseless and trivial motion with which the index finger of his right hand moved the trigger to the firing point. Not that it was any more important to him than its continuation beyond this point; but he took such delight in that final crooking of the finger before the shot that his buddies and superiors often threw glances at him in simulated rifle practice. At any rate, they assumed he was practicing. Once, at target-shooting, an officer who had been standing beside him and observing him for a while said: "Reidel, you're trigger-happy."

Trigger-happiness, and being for so long allowed no chance to exercise it—such simple and natural motives explain why, at the moment he saw the man up there on the slope, Reidel was strongly tempted to let him have it. Make a sieve out of the fellow. Since Corporal Hubert Reidel was a marksman first-class, he had been issued one of the few modern rapid-fire carbines that had been distributed to the division. He had nothing but contempt for the great mass of riflemen. He thrilled at this chance to empty the carbine's entire magazine in a single burst. An opportunity like this would not come again very soon. Nothing was going on in this sector of the front; maybe nothing ever would be going on. What saved Schefold's life was Reidel's other trait, his tendency to think things out in tactical terms. It was not that he was checking up on his instincts, but on the advantages that might accrue to him if he obeyed those instincts. At first he saw his impulse as strategically correct. At any rate, nobody could call him to account for such an act. "The man made a movement that led me to think he was reaching for his weapon." Statements like that were irrefutable, even if it were discovered that the dead man had no weapon in his pocket. "The man did not stop when I shouted, didn't raise his arms." Given the distance of the corpse from Reidel's sentry post, that might prompt some cool looks. Questions would be asked. So the first excuse was better. Fortunately there were no witnesses; the front line was hardly occupied at all today because a training exercise for the rookies had been set for this morning—close-order advance, fall flat, fire, roll away, close-order advance, all under realistic conditions. Contrary to his forecast, that service at the front would be easier than in rear echelon, the battalion was keeping the kids on the go. Fritz Borek would come back sweaty, pale, not even able to drag himself to the chow line. He'd just sit there at the table in quarters. Reidel would have been glad to help out, but instead of accepting a favor from an older buddy, the idiot had gone and reported him.

Ten minutes after the burst of fire at the soonest, Pfc. Dobrin, the lunkhead, would come cautiously up the slope from the left to see what had happened at Reidel's post. Reidel could fire his gun absolutely without risk. Only the man's unusual behavior had made him hesitate; after Reidel had sized him up as, variously, a *gentleman, fellow, suspect,* and *guest,* there was no longer any reason to delay firing. But at the same time Reidel had been considering whether that would help or harm his general situation. The image of the rookie, Fritz Borek, had diverted his thoughts. Reidel could have hit himself over the head when he thought of the foul-up with Borek. That he should flub it that way after years of perfect conduct! In 1939, in a West Wall bunker, he had committed the single slip-up, to now, of his entire military service—an insignificant slip-up, but it had been sufficient for a report; people were all too ready to make reports on the basis of such a slip. He had been punished with two weeks' strict detention, and they must have made some entry in his papers, a notation that apparently went along with him to the office of every unit in which he had served over the years. That was the only explanation for his never having made sergeant. After seven years in the service, a soldier with his qualifications would normally be a master sergeant, a platoon leader. Would Borek's report have reached Battalion yet? At the front there were no long, slow channels from platoon to company, from company to Battalion. The whole pack were all jammed together in Winterspelt. Such words as *court-martial, punishment battalion,* crossed Reidel's mind without really frightening him. But now he began considering whether bringing in a spy might not exert a certain influence on the treatment of the report that would be labeled *Borek v. Reidel.* Probably not much; after all, he was only carrying out his duties if he turned a suspicious bird in at Battalion Command Post. But if there were only the slightest chance that they would let him off with a disciplinary measure—if, for example, the commander and the top sarge couldn't quite agree about passing on the report—a minor incident perfectly handled might just tip the scales in his favor. Especially if that fellow at the top of the hill, at whom he was now shouting the order to come down while keeping his hands up, actually turned out to be a spy.

He had judged him rightly. The man was not fat and old, only heavy, but at the same time strong, muscular. Reidel observed the way he moved down the slope toward him. His face was flushed and healthy; the gray above his lips meant nothing. He wore that close-clipped mustache, the kind that only a very special type of gentleman went in for. He was holding his hands up in a way that suggested he was doing it only for fun. As he approached, smiling, actually smiling, he looked exactly like a good-humored stroller. Reidel came out of his foxhole with one bound. Nothing about his expression changed. He'd soon wipe this spy's smile off his face.

How fast the fellow bolted out of his hole, looking like a gray-green reptile until the movement ceased and he froze into a rather small young man, thin, but tough and tight-knit in his smallness, and as laconic as the short barrel of the carbine. Schefold's first start of fright, which was normal, did not pass away; it became fear that lingered. He had to pull himself together in order not to turn on his heel and simply run away. Then he started moving; there was no escape. Although he could not yet make out Reidel's eyes, he already knew he had stepped into a trap.

So he had been wrong to let himself in for this game of being captured. It had not been enough to express his doubts about this ploy. He should have firmly stipulated that he be allowed to come safely through the ravine to pay a call on Major Dincklage as a private individual and art historian. A walker, incidentally charged with the safety of artistic treasures, provided with adequate papers for that purpose, would introduce himself to an army officer, would be drawn into conversation—such was the scene that Schefold had more or less dimly imagined. But Dincklage had insisted that he must come "through the line"—so Hainstock had learned. The message came through a third person whose name he would not reveal. Through a slip of the tongue on Hainstock's part, Schefold had at any rate found out that this third person was a woman. Hainstock did not even know Dincklage. "Dincklage wishes you to come to him escorted by his soldiers," Hainstock had said. Schefold had protested that this was asking too much, until Hainstock said: "Don't you understand that the major needs proof?"

This quarryman was like the minerals he sometimes showed Schefold, unalterable, undoubtable. But it might well be doubted that the major was entitled to make such a demand as long as the game was still so unsettled. Probably he made it out of impatience, and out of suspicion.

The soldier's eyes, which he could now make out, yellow under the shadow of the steel helmet, seemed more fixed, more unfeeling, than Hainstock's crystals or ammonites. Nevertheless Schefold held the smile that he had forced upon his face as he approached.

In as friendly a tone as he could muster, he said as he stopped: "I am quite harmless."

"Shut up," the soldier said.

If someone declared himself quite harmless, he certainly wasn't. But Reidel did not blame the fellow for trying to put something over on him. People who came sailing in like this guy had something up their sleeve. What annoyed him was the tone the man adopted. That was the way guests spoke when they wanted something from you, clean towels, breakfast in their rooms, a newspaper; they'd use the same friendly, pleasant tone, then turn away with total indifference to talk to their wives or friends, and you could hear the way their intonation changed, the way they put you completely out of their minds the moment they handed over your tip.

"I am quite harmless."

It sounded exactly like the wistful, courteous request that a guest might make: *Would you please draw my bath.*

Full of hatred, Reidel said: "Shut up."

128

He kept the carbine at the ready on his right hip, while with his left hand he frisked Schefold from head to toe. The man was strong, as he had expected; besides, he was a head taller than Reidel. Feeling the pack of cigarettes and the lighter in his jacket pocket, Reidel recalled the fine movement this gentleman had made while smoking. He carried no weapon, nor was there one in the raincoat, which Reidel plucked from his shoulder, then carelessly dropped on the ground. In the back pocket of the fellow's trousers was a wallet. Reidel had just made up his mind to take it out when he heard the singing sound, high, metallic, and still very far away.

He took a step back. "Fibos," he said. "Quick, flat on your face."

Schefold saw him disappear into his hole. The gray-green reptile. Schefold continued to stand. As it happened, he knew that *fibos* meant fighter-bombers. He had once experienced an attack by the American fighter-bombers in Hainstock's shack at the foot of the quarry.

"You asshole, lie down, flat on your face, I said."

Schefold heard not only the hiss of fury in the voice, but also the nervousness. The soldier wanted him to lie flat because he too was in danger if Schefold attracted the attention of the men in the cockpits. He exploited the situation.

"May I lower my arms now?" he asked, talking down in every respect.

He did not await the reply, but threw himself beside the foxhole on the short, hard grass. The grass and earth smelled good, dry and wild. It had not rained since the end of September. Days of a blue and wild melancholy, laced with the fragrance of these slopes. *Asshole. Shut up.* He had not expected words like these, but was already beginning inwardly to parry them, although the sense of having committed a serious error did not depart. Something had gone wrong. A type like this soldier had not fitted into Dincklage's reckoning. But a good reckoning should take in all the factors. The clause about coming "through the line" had proved to be a reckoning with unknown factors. And the most curious factor of all, Schefold thought, is that Dincklage insisted on this visit even though he knows I will be coming with empty hands. He watched as the soldier fished for the light-colored raincoat and drew it into the hole with him before crouching in absolute mimicry. The top of the helmet lay at exactly the same level as the rim of the foxhole. The hole itself was not like ordinary foxholes, surrounded by a circle of lighter earth that had been thrown up during the digging. When a man stood in this hole, nothing betrayed his presence except the top of the helmet, which was only a tiny curvature in the terrain, the remainder of an old mole's mound or an overgrown, decayed juniper stump. For Reidel had smeared the helmet with a mess of earth colors which so exactly matched the prevailing tone of the slope that Schefold decided this dangerous little soldier who had taken him prisoner might have helped a landscape painter mix his colors. Schefold did not know that Reidel's model foxhole had been criticized by his platoon leader, Sergeant Wagner. Wagner, preferring safety in combat to camouflage, had insisted on a rampart of earth around the hole—until Reidel had pulled out the sandbags on which he was standing.

He had dug very deep and shoveled part of the dirt into sacks. With the rest he had reinforced the rampart around Borek's hole. Borek, a student of philosophy, or whatever the crap he was studying, had naturally made no headway with his hole. He stood there helpless, done in from half an hour's digging, with a ridiculous little mound of dirt beside him, until Reidel came along. Reidel had fixed him a perfect foxhole in twenty minutes. So now he'd shown his thanks by informing on him.

In case of an attack the sandbags not only gave better protection than the usual piles of earth; they also made it possible for men taller than Reidel to use the hole when they relieved him. For all he cared they could take out the sandbags and place them in front of the hole. Wagner had gone on, shaking his head, feeling part admiration, part irritation that he could not quarrel with the technique devised by this experienced loner.

Schefold began to feel better about his failure to observe the man on the slope. It wasn't that he was blind; the soldier actually had been invisible.

"May I lower my arms now?"

That's the way they were. They crapped all over you. They didn't say, "The beer is warm," but, "Have you ever heard of refrigeration?" They said: "But my friend, I know we won the Battle of Tannenberg," if you happened to bring them yesterday's newspaper by mistake. They thought they were being funny when they said things like that. They had some word for that kind of talk; at the moment Reidel couldn't remember what it was and didn't care anyhow. What stung worst was when they said "my friend" or "my dear fellow." That made him want to smack them in the face. He'd smack this bastard in the face if he tried anything at all.

The incessant low-grade humiliation, the mockery and the tips. He hadn't run away from the hotel that evening in February 1937 to put up with that stuff ever again. His father's outraged gawk when he announced that he'd punched the guest in Room 23 in the nose. His mother's sorrowful outcry: "Where do you intend to go, Hubert?" Reidel could not help grinning when he thought of that. He knew where he wanted to go: to the army. In the course of one night in the Düsseldorf hotel an officer who had called him to his room had said to him: "You don't belong in a hotel, you belong in a barracks." He spoke the word *barracks* as if it were a synonym of paradise. And Reidel had instantly grasped what he meant. But perhaps the advice had stuck in his memory only because that officer, a captain in the air force, was the only *guest* who had not thrust a banknote into his hand before he left the room toward morning. The barracks had not disappointed Reidel. Although you were sometimes badly treated, they didn't do it to you as a person, as Reidel recognized, and when those times were over, when you did your job, you were left alone, could even keep to yourself; you had your locker, your bunk, your things. Civilians had no idea how you could keep to yourself when you were in the army. The advantage of the barracks was not the fact that you lived exclusively in the company of men. In this respect there was nothing doing; on the contrary, since 1937 Reidel had had to keep a grip on himself, watch like a lynx. He had camouflaged himself so well that his buddies took it for granted he was as interested in women as they were.

On learning that he had a background in hotel work, officers had repeatedly tried to make an orderly out of him. Whereupon he'd snapped to attention, and standing like a ramrod had formally requested not to be used in any such capacity.

Schefold remembered how he had clutched the bench on which he was sitting with both hands and stared at Hainstock when the planes came over the quarry, each for an endless second, the first, the second, the third. "Oh well, it's already over," Hainstock said, concealing his own fear. "They aren't aiming for my shack; probably they can't even see it, it's so overgrown. Anyhow, they only attack moving targets." In the growing stillness Schefold had observed him once more: an iron-gray man sitting at a table and smoking a pipe. The table, half of an old double door resting on sawhorses, was covered with samples of rock, calendars, newspapers, books, a typewriter, ashtrays, pipes, boxes of matches, a kerosene lamp. All motionless targets.

Lying prone—so the airmen would not see his white shirt—Schefold forced himself to turn his head and watch the planes. He resolved not to let himself dissolve in fear as he had that time in Hainstock's shack. But the test he wanted to impose on himself did not take place because the planes did not fly over the slope where he lay; they kept farther to the east, roared above the road from Bleialf to Winterspelt, three light-gray sharks gleaming in the sunlight as they swept through the glistening aquarium of this October day. They did not fire their guns; evidently the road was deserted. Schefold recalled Hainstock's remarks on Major Dincklage's strategy; since Dincklage had taken over the sector, Hainstock had said, the German army seemed to have vanished from the surface of the earth. Next time he saw him Schefold would tell Hainstock how precisely Dincklage's camouflage orders were being carried out by the soldiers. He did not know that Reidel

had merely twisted his lips in brief contempt when the latest battalion orders on conduct in the front line were read aloud at
morning roll call.

While the planes were still flying over the village of Winterspelt, Schefold considered whether he should say something to
the soldier in the foxhole that would make him appear to be a
German, someone who belonged with the Germans. For example,
he could point to the sky and say, "Those swine!" Whereupon
the usual and incidentally true stories about planes firing at plow-
ing farmers and women with baby carriages would follow. Schefold had listened to such stories in the taverns where he stopped.
But suddenly he realized clearly that the man he was dealing with
would not listen to any such stories and that it was pointless to attempt in any way to buddy up to him. There was no need for him
to build up any such false relationship. That was actually a relief
and one which made this enemy—who was once again as invisible
as a person could possibly be, nothing but a steel helmet smeared
with an indefinable wash of colors—briefly likable.

He just had time to reflect that the planes must have passed
over the quarry shortly before they appeared to the east of the
slope. There in the shack, at that table, Hainstock would be sitting now, smoking his pipe and waiting. "When you arrive in
Winterspelt, I'll know it fifteen minutes later," he had said. That
must mean that he would hear about it from the woman with
whom Major Dincklage was connected. Suddenly Schefold no
longer found it reassuring that there were people who were following his course with concern.

As always, the fighter-bombers stuck to the road, but that did
not mean they could not machine-gun the slopes on either side of
it. The road was only three hundred meters away, running
through the cleft between the two chains of hills where the battalion had settled. The gunners knew where the enemy was even
though they did not see any signs of him; they knew because he
simply could not be anywhere else. For this reason they raked the
hills whenever they were in the mood or saw nothing on the road.
If they fired a few rounds at the pasture slope again today, that

fellow, that spy hunkering down outside his foxhole, was as good as dead. Reidel felt annoyance as he considered this possibility because it would rob of any point his own restraint about killing the man.

The man's coat, which he was still holding with his left hand, was crushed, and dirty around the collar, but it was just the kind of coat a guest would have.

Schefold could have informed him that the coat was eight years old, no longer fitted, came from the rack of a ready-made clothier in Frankfurt, and as far as price went was within the means of any member of a hotel staff—

But to Reidel it absolutely smelled of the kind of gentlemen who entered the lobbies of hotels, whose leather suitcases he carried, who distractedly gave him tips. This spy's clothes were worn, but made of expensive fabrics, as Reidel had observed when he frisked him for weapons. The snootiest of them never wore new suits; the lushest tips came from deliberately baggy pockets; but everything they wore was, like this coat, impregnated with a special smell. After-shave lotion? Cigars?

Schefold used no after-shave lotion and smoked no cigars, although recently he had taken to American cigarettes. But his tweed jacket did come from one of the best tailors in Brussels; he'd had it made before the war in a flash of high spirits when he'd received an unusually fat fee for a critique; this was after he himself had become fat. If anyone had told him that he was being labeled as a guest of luxury hotels, he would probably have burst into laughter. He had had to visit such establishments on occasion, to meet wealthy people who were worried about their paintings. But the phrase *grand hotel* had played no part in his upbringing; when the Schefolds traveled, they frequented Swiss and Italian pensions, Bavarian inns. A Frankfurt district magistrate never set foot in the Frankfurter Hof.

134

After the burst of laughter Schefold, recalling his stays in Walcourt, Comines, Limal, might have turned a shade more thoughtful. "But," he would have objected, "in those palaces I was practically a member of the staff, even though I sat at table with the owners."

If they were the way he was, such gentry usually gave him a try. To find out whether he was the way they were, all that was needed was the well-known eye-to-eye contact. That firm, unabashed, looking straight-in-the-eyes, in the elevator, in the room. They would then be surprised, overwhelmed by the hatred with which he let himself go with them, but they enjoyed his eruptions.

Now the planes roared along the road and away. They did not fire. The guy was lucky. He was incidentally not his kind. Before, while frisking him, Reidel had looked briefly into his eyes, but the stranger had not reacted.

After a while Reidel raised himself out of the hole, threw Schefold his raincoat, and in a voice that was as yellow as his eyes said: "Come on, get up, you bastard."

"I will not have you using such language to me," Schefold said. He picked up his coat and stood up slowly and carefully. Then he fell to his knees because Reidel had kicked him in the backside.

There it was again, that tone that Reidel had promised himself he would never listen to again, when he left the hotel and ran away to the army. A military bawling-out was something entirely different. It linked the reprimander with the reprimanded. The bellowing of a sergeant arched like a bell over a company drawn up before him. Whereas the reproofs from guests excluded you. The low-voiced, cold way they lowered the barrier when something did not suit them. "Kindly knock before you enter." "Haven't you learned that the lady is served first?" "I will not have you using such language to me." He took one stride toward the man who was getting to his feet and drove a boot into his backside with such force that he was surprised when Schefold only fell

135

to his knees, not flat on his face. "That's what spies like you get when you shoot your mouth off," Reidel said. He had not wanted to kick the man; the particular sureness in Schefold's voice had warned him against going so far; but he had no longer been capable of controlling himself.

As soon as Schefold was back on his feet, he said: "I have an appointment with your battalion commander, Major Dincklage." He brushed back his cuff and looked at his watch. "At noon. So we no longer have much time. You will kindly bring me to him now. And if you go on insulting me or physically assaulting me, I shall complain to Major Dincklage about you."

He had not planned to give such elaborate explanations to the first sentry he encountered, had meant to speak of his destination only to someone of higher rank because he rightly assumed that the ordinary soldier who captured him would not have the authority to take him directly to Battalion Headquarters. Hainstock had confirmed this idea. "The soldier who receives you will certainly take you to his corporal," he had said, "and he in turn to his platoon leader or, if you're lucky, straight to the company; probably one of the company commanders will deliver you to Dincklage."

"Funny," Schefold had replied, "it would be so much simpler to go to him directly." Hainstock had not answered that. But whatever the case, the way this soldier was treating him had prompted Schefold not to wait until he reached some higher point in the military hierarchy; such behavior could not be endured a moment longer, must be changed instantly, and to do so he had to play the trump that would impose decent conduct on the man.

Moreover, the soldier had used the word *spy?* Had he just been talking loosely? Was this simply a product of the man's own bile, part of his mental system, like kicks and words such as *asshole* and *shut up,* or had he actually been expecting a spy? If he had been ordered to look out for a spy, then the whole game was lost. Schefold had no time to consider what would await him if that were the case, for Reidel's next words put his fears to rest.

The fact that he still held the carbine pointed at Schefold did not matter; he was a member of the staff now and it was his business to address the gentleman respectfully. He made a weak retreat: "Sorry, but why didn't you say so right away?"

"May I remind you that you told me to shut up," Schefold said. But he sensed it was wrong to use that ironic tone with this man.

If what the fellow said was true, if he were not just bluffing, it would have been a serious mistake to knock him off. The commander himself would be interrogating you, and no matter what excuses you offered, it certainly wouldn't help any in regard to Borek's report.

"Can you show any proof that you have been ordered to the commander?" Reidel asked in a last attempt to stand up for himself.

"I have not been ordered to him," Schefold said. "We are having a conference." He took out his wallet and drew from it the letter from the Städel Institute. As he handed it to Reidel he was inwardly praying that the soldier wouldn't demand to see his wallet. He imagined what Hainstock would say—or perhaps he wouldn't say anything at all, only stare at him with narrowed eyes—if he were in a position to observe that Schefold's wallet contained several dollars and a number of Belgian francs. It was sheer idiocy not to have removed these bills before he set out on this mission; he could just hear the way this soldier would whistle between his teeth if he found the foreign money.

In his walks on German territory Schefold had never been stopped and checked by the military police. "You've had enormous luck," Hainstock had said to him. Hainstock's quarry was his landmark. Whenever he caught sight of it, white between the black trunks of the red pines, he knew that he could leave the ravine by way of the woods, because then the German lines were far behind him. Then he walked calmly up the gravel road, stopped by with Hainstock for a while, later took the footpath to Eigelscheid and paid his visits all around the neighborhood. Both Hain-stock and the cattle dealer Hammes sometimes gave him a lift in their cars, the latter without knowing who he was.

If he had been subjected to a search, he would have produced his old but thoroughly legitimate identity card, and the letter from the Städel Institute that Reidel was reading at the moment. It commissioned him to register works of art in the Prüm district and, in cooperation with the local military commanders' offices and the civilian authorities, to take measures for their protection. Only a very experienced eye would have noticed that the umlauts in this letter had been typed with an *e* following the vowel, not with the usual two dots over the vowel itself, indication of a foreign typewriter that had no umlauts. Not even Hainstock had been bothered by that; his commentary on the letter had been merely: "You were certainly foresighted, Herr Doktor."

"Not foresighted," Schefold had replied. "I was forced to leave in something of a hurry and had a few letterheads in my briefcase. For years I thought of them merely as souvenirs."

He was dead sure of the effectiveness of this sheet of paper. No German MP would be aware that the artistic treasures of the Rhine province fell under the authority of the Prussian Ministry of Education in Berlin. Therefore no MP would ask what the devil the Frankfurt Art Museum was trying to do in the western Eifel district.

Reidel's fingers were itching for that wallet. All the time he was reading the letter he considered whether he ought to latch onto it. He must have been nuts to have let the fellow keep it just because the planes were coming over. Earlier, in the foxhole, he would have had time to flip through it at his leisure. Whereas now—if there were nothing important in it, nothing that incriminated this bird, he would only be accumulating one more minus point by grabbing it away from the guy. Dr. Bruno Schefold. Art treasures. Shit. And he'd picked this bird to kick in the ass. This sure was one of his bad days. Reidel blamed the fact that it was one of his bad days on the Borek affair.

"Very good, sir," he said, handing the letter back to Schefold. In one respect he was quite content: the letter gave him his pretext for taking Schefold directly to Battalion. He'd been determined to avoid going through channels in any case; no one was going to do him out of his chance to deliver the prisoner—who wasn't really a prisoner any more—to Battalion in person. At this hour he would be able to get to the battalion office without being stopped; the whole crew would still be taken up with the morning schedule. The company chief, a top sergeant, would bawl him out good and proper when he heard about his acting on his own this way. But he could now craftily refer to papers the man had carried with him. "What the devil does a punk like you know about papers?" "I request you to ask Major Dincklage, sir, whether I have done anything wrong." The top sarge would stalk away, his face white with fury. And that would be the end of the matter. Reidel knew how to handle superiors. But in imagining such an interview Reidel automatically reckoned that the major would cover him; he could not have said why he assumed that the major would hold out the lifesaving pole for him. The letter was unimportant, meant nothing, did not concern the commander at all. But this man Schefold did mean something. He did not lie. It was out of the question that he had lied. He really had an appointment with the commander. Reidel, who did not think in terms of such concepts as *knowledge of human nature*, knew for a certainty when a man lied, and when he spoke the truth.

What did the commander have to discuss with a man who appeared in front of the lines coming from the direction of the enemy, an altogether suspicious type? Reidel at the moment did not waste time reflecting on that. He gave Schefold a sign to follow him and slung the carbine over his shoulder.

Schefold, who had no very great knowledge of human nature, took it for granted that Reidel should sling the carbine over his shoulder and precede him. He did not know that Reidel would have preferred to have driven him along with the weapon at the ready, would have preferred not to have believed him.

Enormously relieved, Schefold had taken the letter back,

slipped it into his wallet. He did not suspect that Reidel hated him for having been forced to say the words *Very good, sir* like a hotel employee handing back a guest's passport, not exactly servilely, but still sedulously respectful.

Reidel was intent on penetrating all the way to Dincklage's ante-room, perhaps even to Dincklage's office itself, for that was the place where Borek's report would be acted on. In carrying through this urge he was violating—and he knew it—the fundamental rule of military life, the rule not to attract attention, but he could not resist the lure. He thought he would get something out of turning up there, of demonstrating that he existed and that in bearing, appearance and achievement he was a model soldier. It was a ridiculous self-deception, born of fear, and quite useless, as Reidel would have realized had he been capable of thinking clearly and without illusions about his case. Unfortunately such phrases as *self-deception, without illusions,* were not at his disposal; since in keeping with the environment in which he grew up his speech had remained crude, his occasional bouts of reflectiveness were not very useful to him. His mind could come up with the word *useless,* but his response to it was crude: "I'll go anyhow!" The word *useless* permitted crude reactions, whereas a word like self-deception would have changed Reidel's entire viewpoint. A command of speech would have saved him; for example, Borek, the philosophy student, would probably have refrained from reporting Reidel if in the course of their encounter Reidel had supplied at least some hints of a plausible explanation for his assault. But to do so Reidel would have had to be a different person, one not so speechless. And if Reidel had been a different person he would not have assaulted Borek, at least not in that way. Conditional sentences!

Reidel, a soldier who in battle did not know what fear was, had since yesterday been thinking about nothing but Borek's report. Not courage but fear drove Reidel into the lion's den. Delivering Schefold at Battalion would probably do him no good. He would even have to expect the battalion topkick to give him the devil for leaving his post. But if Schefold had not lied, Reidel would count on the commander's intervening on his behalf. Reidel could actually hear him saying: "That's enough, Kammerer! The soldier acted correctly."

"Why are you alone up here?" Schefold asked. He wondered at himself; in spite of the kick he was trying to start a friendly conversation.

Reidel did not deign to answer. To a question of that sort the only thing that occurred to him was the word *pumping*. The distillation of hours of barracks lectures on secrecy in service regulations.

Schefold discerned the next sentry at a distance. He appeared between two junipers, emerging from his hole from the chest up and watching them approach.

Dobrin, that idiot. Without a doubt he'd been reading his trash and had put it away in plenty of time because this civilian made as much noise as an elephant. Day and night Dobrin read pulp magazines, stories. Reidel read nothing but the local newspaper his father sent him. He skimmed the political news, the war communiqués, and lingered over the local news from Wuppertal. He had clipped out the picture showing his father's bombed hotel. Hubert Reidel grinned every time he looked at it.
"Who's this you're bringing?" Dobrin called out. Obviously he was flabbergasted.
"Dunno," Reidel said curtly. "Got to take him to Battalion. Chief's orders."

The icy calmness with which he brushed off his buddy! Schefold was irritated. Was it possible that the man had orders after all? He went over the stages of his captivity, this lout's behavior. No, it was not possible.

Dobrin gaped at Schefold.
"Wow," he said.

He was so dumb he didn't even ask how Reidel had come to receive such orders. But perhaps he did not ask because he was afraid of Reidel. Reidel was his group leader and the nastiest sonofabitch in the whole platoon. It was best to steer clear of Reidel. Every time you had dealings with him you were sorry.

Anyhow, there weren't any decent buddies left. *The last buddies were killed at Langemarck*. That was a saying that had been around the army for years, and Dobrin repeated it to himself at every opportunity.

Groaning, he dragged his hundred and eighty pounds out of the foxhole. He wanted to stretch his legs a little.

This second soldier was fat in a way different from Schefold, who saw that the man's bulk weighed him down. His uniform did not conceal the fact that his body was melting. The helmet over his broad, good-natured face looked so martial that you could not help laughing. From his eyebrows and the tiny hairs on his fat hands Schefold could see that he was a flaxen-haired type. Why hadn't Dincklage appointed this man to be his reception committee? Why had he had to run into such an unsympathetic, frightening type as this other fellow?

When Lance Corporal Dobrin unwrapped a sausage sandwich and bit into it, Schefold became aware that he was slowly growing hungry. He would gladly have gone on to Winterspelt with this munching soldier. No lack of subjects for conversation with this fellow—for example, the subject of provisioning.

He wondered whether Major Dincklage would arrange for him to have something to eat. All at once he was no longer so confident that he would be well treated.

"Five minutes out, then back down you go," Reidel said to Dobrin.

From the way he said it, it was apparent to Schefold that Reidel bullied everybody, not just himself. He noticed the way Dobrin's light-blue eyes assumed a cross, offended expression. He did not know that Reidel was throwing his weight around in a

manner not at all usual in the German Army. It was not common
for a corporal to issue orders to a lance corporal.

The stinking fag. That kid Borek had showed up Reidel for the
stinking fag he was. By tomorrow at the latest Battalion would
send Reidel for a ride. Court-martial, no question about it, court-
martial. Fine, a damn good thing to be rid of this firebrand.
Dobrin, who was a peaceable person, wished Reidel to hell and
gone. He himself, the group, and the whole platoon would certainly be a hell of a lot better off when Reidel was gone. The
worst pusher and shover they had in the company. Who would
have thought he'd turn out to be a fag?

Until Reidel disappeared, caution was advisable. In the army
you could never tell what was going to happen till it happened.

Reidel did not know that word of Borek's report had already
made the rounds. On the one hand he was cunning, knew what
was what, seldom deceived himself; on the other hand he was so
much a soldier that he thought channels never leaked.

They reached the road. On the road they walked side by side.
Reidel set a rapid pace, but Schefold kept up with him. Again he
tried to break the silence by gesturing at Reidel's Iron Cross.

"Iron Cross, first class," he said. "My father had one. Where
did you get yours?"

"Russia," Reidel said reluctantly.

"My father got his in Flanders in 1917."

He remembered that his letter written in the fall of 1938, in
which he described to his father a visit to the battlefields of
Flanders, had been his last letter to Frankfurt. In reply his father
had let him know by a clandestine route that it would be advisable to stop the correspondence.

Early in July Schefold had succeeded in reaching his parents by
telephone, from the post office in Prüm.

A recklessness seized him. "After my father came home in
1918," he related, "he always used to say that there would never
be another war."

Just in time he managed to doctor his father's statement. His father had said: "There must never again be a war like this one."

Perhaps he could have quoted the sentence exactly without danger. Schefold had the impression that Reidel was not listening to him at all.

If only he hadn't laid a hand on Borek! If only the incident last night had been just a dream! If only he'd never arranged matters so that Borek's mattress had been placed beside his in their quarters. He must have been nuts when he reached across to Borek.

He loved Borek. For the first time he'd fallen in love with a boy. In the hotels Reidel had always been picked up by men older than he. Then that long interval, and now this. Out of the whole lot he'd had to fall for that squeamish dreamer.

A memory came to him. Some man in the hotel had said to him vindictively, because Reidel got up at once and dressed after he was finished: "Some day you too will be what the straights call a queen."

Why was he trying to chat with this man who'd given him a kick? Just the desire to break his inhuman silence? Or was he afraid of him?

"Your other medals . . ." Schefold meant to say he could not identify them, but thought better of it and instead said: "I can never remember their names."

He meant Reidel's Infantry Assault Badge, Close Combat Clasp, and Marksman's Medal. When he received no reply, he said: "You must be a brave soldier."

When was this fellow going to shut up? A *brave soldier*—the phrase made you want to puke. Where the devil was this creep living? *Brave soldiers* existed only in the newspapers and on the radio. Otherwise not a soul in Greater Germany was still talking about *brave soldiers*.

"Thank you, my dear fellow, that was splendidly done." "Fifi adores you; you obviously have a way with animals." "You must be a brave soldier." The worst of it was that for a moment you felt flattered when things like that were said.

"And your major is a holder of the Knight's Cross. Your battalion must be a crack formation."

If he only knew! Three companies far below rated strength. Kids carrying rifles made in '38. Most of them—except for Borek —so dumb they were still gung-ho about the war. Crazy to sacrifice themselves. Nothing like heavy weapons, no tanks, no antitank guns; it was even rumored that the commander had had trouble getting hold of a couple of heavy machine guns. All in all, the lousiest infantry battalion Reidel had ever seen. It was true that the chief had whipped them into some kind of shape, but it was and remained an outfit from the Stone Age. "They'll be arming us with clubs next," Reidel had remarked to Sergeant Wagner, pointing to a recruit's rifle. "Be careful what you say," Wagner had answered.

Only now did Reidel realize that Schefold had mentioned the commander's decoration. That was to show that he knew him. As though Reidel gave a damn about that. It was of no concern to him that these two gentlemen knew each other; what was bothering him was the question of how they had met. How was it that someone who came from the enemy side knew what medals the chief was wearing? If he lived on the other side, when and where had he seen the chief before?

Reidel asked no questions. In the hotels he had been trained in discretion. His business was to take one gentleman to another gentleman, that was all.

Schefold had no idea that in referring to Dincklage's Knight's Cross he had excited Reidel's suspicions. Tactical military considerations were alien to him; he could not imagine where the gears of Reidel's thinking meshed. If anyone had explained the process to him, he would have exclaimed, thunderstruck: "But that all sounds like boys playing Indians."

Which might have reminded him of the time Hainstock in-

145

formed him—not exactly breaking the news gently—that Dincklage's plan provided for him, Schefold, to cross the lines. "But
my dear Herr Hainstock," he had protested, "that's simply playing
Indians!"

"Of course," Hainstock had replied. "Does that surprise you?
Wars are fought by immature human beings." He followed this up
with a brief Marxist lecture on the origin of wars and the future
society which would solve its problems and differences by
scientific methods.

Hainstock had not been able to brush aside Käthe Lenk's objections so easily.

"This Doktor Schefold does not seem to be at all the right man
for the part," she had said. "From what you tell me, he sounds
lost in the clouds."

"He isn't lost at all." Hainstock tried to correct the picture of
Schefold that he had evidently given Käthe. "His living down
there in Hemmeres implies a lot of courage. And you ought to see
him taking his walks around here, strolling through the villages as
though there were nothing to it."

Käthe never left Winterspelt except to visit Wenzel Hainstock
in his quarry. Since her flight from Prüm she felt safe only in
Winterspelt. She had never met Schefold.

"Maybe it's only because he has no idea what a risk he is running," she said.

"He knows," Hainstock said. "I've warned him repeatedly. But
he just won't lie low. I have the impression that he wants to be in
on it, understand—in on it." He paused before he added: "And
you have to realize he's a tall, strong man. He's very interested in
food, can go on and on about recipes."

He sensed he was not convincing her. The expression in her
eyes rejected all his arguments. She adjusted her glasses. When
Käthe was critically inclined, she adjusted her glasses in a particularly resolute fashion.

"Besides, we just don't have anybody else," Hainstock said.

The chief's medal dated back to the Africa campaign, as everybody knew. (In the imagination of the entire battalion it simply

had to have come from the Africa campaign. A Knight's Cross awarded merely for defensive battles in Sicily would have seriously diminished Dincklage's prestige.) Actually, it was odd that a wearer of the Knight's Cross from the Africa Corps should not have made any kind of career since; his promotions had stopped at major. Why hadn't they at least given him a regiment? It was true that he limped; for some reason he used a cane when he walked; but nowadays that was no reason not to promote an officer. Apparently he wasn't very popular with the top brass. Seemed the chief was no brown-nose. He, Reidel, wasn't one either. Once you realized that you wouldn't be promoted no matter how you knocked yourself out, you could give up all attempts to make yourself popular with your superiors. He was a first-class soldier only because he didn't want to take any guff from anybody. Mainly for that reason, and also just to show them. Let them see the kind of man they were keeping down to corporal. Was it possible that the major kept the battalion so rigidly in line for exactly the same reason?

Reidel was apt to keep worrying an idea if it didn't satisfy him. He decided that maybe he and the major were acting the same way, but for opposite reasons. The difference between him and the chief was that he was no brown-nose because he was not being promoted, but the chief wasn't being promoted because he was no brown-nose.

"They think you're a beaver, a go-getter, a firebrand. But that's not sufficient; you spread acute anxiety all around you." Such was the fancy language Borek had used yesterday, when Reidel tried to keep him from making that report. He already knew he was not popular with the men who ranked below him.

"Unpopular? They hate you!"

"Nuts!"

Secretly, he gloated at hearing what he already knew. After all, he'd done his damndest to make himself hated.

Schefold fell silent. All the way down the slope and along the road he had managed to extract only a single word from this man who was escorting him: the word *Russia*. All right then, no chatting.

By way of Hainstock, or rather by way of the unknown woman who was the liaison between the major and Hainstock, the major had promised him safe-conduct. But safe-conduct with kicks and words like *asshole* was a strange business, and would be embarrassing to Major Dincklage. Schefold resolved to spare him this embarrassment. Some time in the future, if everything worked out, he could tell him—in a humorous way—how he had been treated. Still, it troubled him that such an odd mistake could have occurred in his calculations. Was he reckoning somewhat too carelessly?

This fatass with his disgusting red tie. Suddenly Reidel had to realize that the tie wasn't that disgusting. He caught himself repeatedly glancing at that spot of fiery red.

Large, ugly, single-family houses before him, to either side of the street. The slopes of the hills ran down to them, ending in isolated trees that stood beside the unstuccoed rubblestone barns or in the pastures. A village in a limestone syncline, framed by the verdigris of the hills, as in Lorraine, Wallonia, the Jura, Courbet. But not Courbet's heavy light; no sheen as of ravens' plumage or oil paints. Rather chalkiness, surfaces not bathed by the amber of this October day, but only lightly delineated flat planes, membranes of color laid on the background with the spatula. Thinly painted. So Pissarro after all? Actually Cézanne? Or a light never yet painted?

Since his escort remained so obstinately silent, Schefold wanted to shape the first houses of Winterspelt into a picture, as was his habit. But he could not concentrate; Reidel's silence threw him off. Every second of Reidel's silence reminded him of the danger into which he had stepped. He gave up trying to find comparisons for Winterspelt. If Winterspelt was nothing more than the name of a danger, it could be nothing but Winterspelt.

He had to look out that some superior didn't come by at the last moment. Sergeant Wagner, for instance, or the topkick. They'd give him the devil publicly in the village street. "Since when do you leave your post on your own initiative?" "You should have waited to be relieved and turned the man over to your guard leader." An incredible breach of sentry duty! I'll have you court-martialed, Reidel." Naturally they'd want to take the prisoner from him and bring him to Battalion themselves.

But he knew how to head them off. The same trick he'd used with Dobrin, only snapping it out this time, as a report.

"Corporal Reidel with prisoner on way to Battalion HQ. Major Dincklage's orders."

They wouldn't be as dumb as Dobrin. The top sergeant would say: "Come on, Reidel, cut the comedy. Who is supposed to have given you orders?"

"Request you ask Major Dincklage himself, sir."

He could hear their angry laughter. They would accompany him to the battalion orderly room to check his assertion and to be there when he was exposed as a liar. But they'd be in for a surprise. The major himself would cover him. Since the man walking at his side had not lied, since there was no doubt that the chief expected him, Reidel would be exonerated. "The man acted rightly." He might even draw a moral: "I need soldiers who can show initiative. In 1944 robots who just take orders no longer fill the bill, my friends; kindly take note of that." The commander had already made speeches of this sort, in Denmark after training exercises, to the whole battalion drawn up in formation. "I need thinking soldiers." That statement had inspired many jokes, had become a standard expression. "Aha, I suppose you're one of these thinking soldiers," was the comment when someone did something wrong.

The funny thing about it was that the man at his side hadn't lied and that the chief therefore was really expecting him. That really was crazy.

Of course it was preferable not to meet any superiors. Luckily, Reidel did not have to pass by his company's command post in order to reach the house where Battalion Headquarters had been set up.

The threat of court-martial would leave him cold. He was due for a court-martial anyhow. There was a very, very faint possibility that in delivering Schefold to the commander he might quash that court-martial. It was just a feeling. Reidel felt it in his guts.

Something very odd was happening to Schefold. While he was giving up on his usual practice of converting views into paintings, for instance the first houses of Winterspelt, the street, the hills, into a Pissarro, or into some not yet painted painting, he suddenly and in all seriousness considered whether he should not loosen the bonds he had imposed on himself in his treatment of women.

This was prompted by his beginning to anticipate his next visit to that inn in Saint-Vith. First he had merely thought of his return. He would be back there—an idea that made his growing uneasiness bearable. He would have his interview with Dincklage and would be back in Hemmeres in the afternoon. Toward evening he would meet with Kimbrough in Maspelt.

Strange that the house in Hemmeres, the orchard by the river, the river in the valley, suddenly no longer seemed a refuge to him. The feeling of security came only when he recalled the bar, a low dive out of a genre painting, where plain food was also served. Tables covered with worn brown oilcloth on which beer glasses stood. Small, dirty windows, gray from the gray of the houses opposite. An old enamel plaque advertising Rodenbach beer. The people who entered and sat down at the tables had worn, thin faces, were unassuming. In low voices they talked about the war, discussed whether the Americans would stay or the Germans return. Tonight, this very evening, he'd go to Saint-Vith. Some jeep driver would take him along after he'd talked with Kimbrough. By that hour Saint-Vith would be dark, the bar a cave of spiderweb light. The bitter taste of the beer would confirm his feeling that the tramp to Winterspelt was already becoming a legend, an old experience already weathered.

Out of the darkness she would come over to his table, a fabric of shadows. He would ask her: "When do you have your day off?" He would say to her: "I would like to get to know you." This thought, absolutely monstrous for the sort of person he was, assumed complete form as he walked alongside Reidel on the last section of the road before Winterspelt.

She was dark-haired, sinewy, had a lean face made of topaz that exerted a peculiar charm. She would say: "Lemme alone."

"But I really must get to know you better."

He heard himself saying these words, tossing them off so easily and at the same time with the requisite intensity. He almost murmured the words under his breath, but just in time he remembered that Reidel was marching along beside him.

Maybe this fellow, this agent or whatever he was, would complain about him to Dincklage.

"May I call your attention, sir, to the fact that I had to regard this man as a spy."

That line wouldn't work. "Was that a reason to treat him brutally?" the major would ask.

It would be better to be absolutely frank. "The man behaved in a provocative manner."

The major would turn to his guest, smiling, surprised. "What did you do to provoke the corporal, Herr Doktor?"

At least that way he would gain time, blunt the whole issue. First of all there would be an exchange of charges and countercharges back and forth.

"You shouldn't have tipped him," he heard the woman saying. The door was still open; he held the three-mark piece in his hand.

"Why not?" the man asked.

"You know, he's the owner's son. He gave you an odd look."

"What the hell!" Laughing, the man brushed aside the reproof. Reidel could still hear the way he said it: "He belongs to the class that takes tips."

Behind the desk, the old man's stunned, popeyed stare when he reported that he had slapped the face of the guest in Room 23. His mother's outcry when he turned away to leave: "Where are you going, Hubert?" They had stood in the hotel lobby, which was no lobby at all, just a reception room with a dark-brown wallpaper that looked as if it were made of leather. His mother's high-piled coiffure had blocked his view of the painting, the rutting

151

stag standing in a forest clearing. His mother was a statuesque woman.

His parents' hotel was not first-class, like the one in Düsseldorf where he had trained. It was a family place, solid and respectable. Regular clientele. His father was a short, tenacious type of man. In stature Reidel had taken after him. Whenever he asked himself, as he sometimes did, what he had inherited from his mother, the answer was always: nothing. She was a stranger, a statuesque woman with a high-piled coiffure. He had crawled out of this stranger woman. The stranger had embraced him, kissed him, whispered pet names to him.

Afterward, when he was outside the hotel, he found the three-mark coin in his jacket pocket. He had stuck it there to have his hands free before he slammed the guy right in the puss.

He had struck a yellowish face that felt like leather, first with his right, then with his left, so that the man reeled to either side. Some businessman or other, one of his old man's regular clients. The slob had been so surprised that he had put up no defense. The woman had screamed.

In the morning, the recruiting office. They'd sent him from one desk to the next. Finally an official in civvies had registered him. "Born 1915," the man had said. "Oh well, you would have come up for the draft soon anyhow." He had asked Reidel whether he had any special wishes on where he would like to serve.

"Air Force," Reidel had replied.

Although he would have been just right for the Air Force because of his size and the extraordinary keenness of his eyesight, they inducted him into the infantry at the town of Siegen.

# Appointment of a Courier

When she pedaled the bicycle for a while in the lovely but cool weather of this autumn, Käthe felt overheated, out of breath, but without having perspired. A feeling of dry, insipid heat that she did not consider pleasant.

Even before she leaned the bike against the wall of the shack, she said: "He arrived punctually almost to the minute, accompanied by a soldier. I waited ten minutes; then I started off."

Since she had taken another ten minutes or perhaps a little more to reach Hainstock, Schefold must by now have been in conversation with Major Dincklage for almost half an hour.

After they entered, Käthe waited for the groaning noise the old door made when it closed. In the heat of the room, which came from the iron cookstove, her glasses misted over. She took them off.

"I imagined him altogether different," she said. "You're right, he doesn't look lost in the clouds at all."

After she had cleaned the glasses and replaced them, she noticed the owl, and like Schefold was relieved that the bird had taken to sitting in the topmost crate of his tower and did not begin to flutter his wings the moment she entered the shack.

As long as the owl had been alone, it had fixed its black eyes unswervingly on the door through which Hainstock had left the shack more than an hour ago. When Käthe entered the room, it closed its eyes because it assumed she was watching it. It hated being watched. Behind closed lids it annihilated the idea of being watched.

"Are you sure he was being brought in by an enlisted man?" Hainstock asked.

"Yes," she said. "A corporal. A rather unpleasant type."

154

She forbore to describe to Hainstock the jerk of the head with which the soldier had instructed Schefold to mount the stairs to the house. Hainstock would not accord much importance to such a detail. Perhaps, she hoped, she would be able to explain to Dincklage later what an insult had been inflicted upon Schefold by that single bit of pantomime.

Hainstock did not even respond to the *unpleasant type*. He merely remarked: "That's odd. I would have sworn it would be at least a sergeant."

"Do you realize what impression he makes?" Käthe asked. She did not wait for his answer, but said: "Very much of a gentleman."

She had not thought out this appellation for Schefold beforehand. The term had slipped out of her, that was all. Almost simultaneously she asked herself whether she liked a man who looked *very much of a gentleman*. She decided she did not. Wenzel Hainstock was no gentleman, but neither was Joseph Dincklage in spite of his Knight's Cross and his officer's uniform.

"I wouldn't know what that was," Hainstock countered quickly. He was sorry that Käthe would make use of an expression belonging to the vocabulary of feudal traditions. Schefold was the son of a judge who'd afforded himself the luxury of drifting into the world of art, the descendant of probably any number of generations of fairly high officials, those highly trained servants of the bourgeois state. Naturally that gave him a certain style. Aside from that, he was rather a naïve person. He knew a great deal about paintings and little about life.

But Hainstock decided to make use of Käthe's characterization of Schefold, wrongheaded though he felt it to be.

"I hope it reassured you," he said, "to see that he is not an unworldly professor."

The word *unworldly* startled him the moment he spoke it. He had long been seeking the right word for Schefold.

"On the contrary," Käthe said, "altogether on the contrary. He looked not only very much the gentleman, but a gentleman who is being led to the guillotine. He walked beside that soldier like a fallen monarch. Do you understand what I mean? He looked unusually defenseless."

"I tried to observe the slope that Schefold must have come along," Hainstock said, "but the Elcherath woods were in the way."

"This morning Dincklage withdrew the recruits from the line. 'So that nothing unforeseen will happen,' he said." The shadows in the corners of her mouth deepened as she added: "Both of you are much concerned about Schefold's welfare."

"When did he tell you that?" Hainstock asked.

"Early this morning."

*In bed*, Hainstock silently added.

"Have you eaten yet?" he asked.

She shook her head.

"Would you like to fix up something here?"

"No thanks, I'll be biking right back."

"Wouldn't you like a cup of coffee?"

"The last thing I want," she said. "I'm shook up enough already."

"No reason to be shook up," Hainstock said. "It's all gone according to plan. In an hour Schefold will be on his way back. I'll come by to see you this afternoon and find out when he left."

Indignation overpowered her. "You must have a screw loose," she said. "At this moment Schefold is talking with Dincklage. And you say, 'No reason to be shook up'!"

"As though anything were going to come of it," he said. "I suppose you're still hoping for a miracle to happen and the Americans to turn up tonight. Anyhow, it no longer concerns us. For you and me the matter is already over. For Schefold it will be over in an hour or two. All the rest is an affair between Dincklage and that American officer."

Who must be an idiot like me, because just like me he's fallen in with the idiotic scheme of this German officer, Hainstock thought. He actually believed that the business had to be over for him and Käthe as soon as Schefold successfully met with Dinck-lage. Käthe knew his views about the dangers of the operation. He had spelled them out with the utmost clarity.

She recovered her composure. After all, at this moment Wenzel Hainstock did not know that this was her last visit to his shack. Probably he was right; probably the Americans would not arrive, but whether or not something came of the meeting between Dincklage and Schefold, she had decided that the forthcoming night represented her last chance to continue on her way west. If she knew Joseph Dincklage, he would close the gap in his front line if the Americans did not come.

She sat down on the bed. Hainstock stood back of his table, that old door on sawhorses, tapping out a pipe. The bed was an iron army cot with a thin mattress, the blankets carefully tucked under. It resembled Dincklage's bed. The beds of ascetic and mili-tary men. Hainstock, too, she knew that now, was basically a mili-tary man. He was a solid and iron-gray man. He always wore the same gray suit of hard corduroy. She knew his firm, insufficiently supple body. His gaze turned to tools, stones, meditations, and sometimes to her, Käthe. She fell into a mood of farewell. It did not enter her mind that Hainstock assumed she had come straight from Dincklage's bed.

She owed him a good deal. A measure of protection after she had fled from Prüm to Winterspelt in June. She was safe there be-cause everyone in Winterspelt knew she was having an affair with the inscrutable man from the quarry. And again he had saved her when the two of them hid in the cave in the Apert, during the big roundup after July 20, when the generals' coup miscarried. Intro-duction to a doctrine that struck her as reasonable, and that had the merit of being forbidden. Käthe had been twelve years old when this doctrine was banned. When she heard its first axioms in Hainstock's straightforward language, she instantly understood that the darkness in Germany had something to do with the ban-ning of this doctrine.

157

Within the field of such sympathies, based on protection and counsel—not a bad basis for an affair between a young woman of twenty-four and a man twenty-eight years her senior—and furthermore within the area in which she *liked* Wenzel Hainstock, there were shadows, obscurities, blind spots that disturbed her—for example, the fact that he accepted presents from people who, if events had taken a different course, would even have avoided any connection with him.

When she challenged him about that, he gave her an explanation of this sort: yes, he did have a small stock of coffee, wine, and other things because a few persons in the vicinity imagined that some day he might be useful to them. He accepted these unimportant presents from the bourgeoisie without hesitation and without thanks, he said, because he knew that when it was all over he would be able to render these people, middlemen, small manufacturers, officials, the wealthier farmers, real services. In short, he repeated to her what he had already explained in regard to his future relationship with Arimond, except that he owed gratitude to Arimond—she realized that—but to "these people" none at all.

"Before they forget me in my quarry," he said, "and before they resume talking about me as an undercover Communist—which, incidentally, they're already doing—I shall be for a while the most useful idiot in the entire region."

"So you let yourself be bribed."

"What would you want?" he said. "There's not going to be a revolution. Instead, everybody is going to make a deal."

"So you're going to make a deal with them?"

"It's simply that once again bourgeois arrangements will prevail."

"But," she said, "you don't have to take hush money from them."

"Hush money," he said. "How that sounds! I won't conceal any crimes. Only weaknesses. Since the big criminals are not going to be brought to book, the little opportunists have every right to escape. And I mean to help them."

"For coffee and wine?"

"For coffee and wine," he said. "I've given it careful thought. I shall have to go on living with these people for twenty years or more. Strangely enough, people would rather live with someone who once accepted a quarter of a pound of coffee than with a monument of virtue."

"And why do you have to go on living with them at all?" she asked. "You can go away!" And when she received no reply to this, she added: "At any rate, I won't be around when all of you make your deals with each other."

The assertion that there would be no revolution was one of his standard points. In Käthe's eyes this established a close similarity between Hainstock and Dincklage. After she had met Dincklage she realized that Hainstock spoke of the revolution in exactly the same way that Dincklage spoke of his plan. For Hainstock and Dincklage the revolution and the plan were absolute and unattainable truths. The revolution would take place sometime, but not in Hainstock's lifetime; the plan was doomed to remain an intellectual exercise, an operational study on maps. Except that Dincklage had committed the rash mistake of letting Käthe participate in it. She was an intellectual, but obsessed with the notion of transforming abstract ideas into reality, theory into practice, whenever there was the slightest chance for it.

While they talked she clasped one of her wrists with the other hand, a gesture typical of her when she was resisting something, when she did not like what was going on. Later she released her wrist, not because Hainstock's arguments persuaded her, but because she resigned herself to them, and also, perhaps, just to smoke a cigarette.

This talk took place at a time before Dincklage had appeared on the scene. On that occasion, as on many others, Hainstock showed that he was not prepared to meet the moral demands that a twenty-four-year-old girl makes.

But perhaps in that respect he underestimated Käthe. Since she herself was a teacher, had already taught, though only for a short time, she might have been ready to grant that the purity of the

159

doctrine need not be embodied in the teacher. In accord with
what Hainstock had said about the monument of virtue, it may
be imagined that a man with weaknesses, even a man who lived in
such obvious contradiction to his views as did this Marxist owner
of a quarry, would seem more lovable, more interesting to her
than a rigid and unswerving dogmatist.

It had been only last Saturday, October 7, that Hainstock first
appeared to her in a dubious light, enigmatic in a troubling way.
The previous evening Dincklage had told her about his plan. The
very next morning she went to see Hainstock. His first reaction
was to flatly reject the plan itself as well as her offer to take part
in it. She could accept that, as she could his outrage that
Dincklage would be ready to involve Käthe in such a crazy business. She had also accepted his piling objection upon objection
and finally yielding against his better judgment, clearly only because she, Käthe, wanted it that way. In fact she had expected
nothing different, and his objections all made sense; she came very
close to giving up the whole idea.

But then! She had said: "It will be dangerous for you. As I see
it, you will have to go back and forth between the Americans and
Dincklage at least twice."
She amended that: "Of course I'll handle the part with
Dincklage," she said. "It would attract attention in the village if
you were to call on him."
"Whereas your going to him no longer attracts the slightest at-
tention," he said.
"Wenzel!" she said.
"The village would probably assume that I was seeing him on
your account. You know, that would be excellent camouflage."
She pulled herself together, decided to keep things on a matter-
of-fact basis.
"When I said that, I was thinking only of the political angle,"
she said. "You're known throughout the region; everybody knows
who you are. The question would arise why the major would

confer with you. Villagers would make remarks to men on the major's staff."

She took another tack. "Yes," she said, "I am really in a position to talk to Dincklage privately at any time. I can't help it. For this particular affair that's very useful."

"Good," he said, "I will talk to Schefold."

Up to now he had mentioned this man Schefold only a few times and only as a curiosity. From what he said, Schefold must be an eccentric, an oddly unworldly and imprudent loner. She had seen the painting that Hainstock was keeping safe for him, and when she thought about *Polyphonically Bounded White*, she felt a considerable liking for Schefold and wished she could meet him. She never quite understood why Hainstock kept this dreamer of an art historian from her.

"Schefold?" she asked. "What does he have to do with it?"

"Why, that's obvious," Hainstock said. "He's the logical man to establish the link with the Americans. He goes in and out of their headquarters all the time."

"What?" she asked. "Do you mean to entrust this business to a man like him? It's much too difficult and dangerous for that."

Although the virtues of the idea were now dawning on her, she was tremendously disappointed. For reasons that later she could no longer recall, she had taken it for granted that Wenzel Hainstock would assume the most risky role—as distinct from Dincklage's part. He would not let this opportunity pass, she thought, to come forward once more, one last time before fascism fell, as an underground fighter. That would be his revenge for Oranienburg.

"He speaks English," Hainstock said soberly. "I don't."

She did not give up. "You know the route he always takes," she said. "You told me you were the one who showed it to Schefold, so you must know it. You could meet him in that hamlet where he lives and take him along to the Americans as your interpreter. But you must do all the rest yourself. You've said right along that he is harmless and light-minded. He will mess things up. You won't."

"It won't involve his doing anything more than what he always does. He will come to see me twice by this almost safe route and bring me a message which I'll pass on to you."

"And vice versa," Käthe said.

"And vice versa," Hainstock agreed. "He'll take the messages you transmit to me."

He busied himself with lighting his pipe. "Oh yes," he said between two matches, "I'll be nothing but a letter box."

In this form, the plan satisfied him. And he could have come up with even more effective arguments—for example, that Schefold was already trusted by the Americans. Even though he would not carry out espionage missions for them, their intelligence service must have checked him out. He himself, on the other hand, was entirely unknown to them and they would have to investigate to make sure that he was not a provocateur. He might be leading them into a trap: precious time would be lost while they were finding out. Assuming that they entered into Dincklage's proposal at all. She saw the point. What bothered her was the smug tone in which he spoke of himself as a *letter box*. "I'll be nothing but a letter box"—that came out with an intonation of victorious modesty that she did not at all like.

In a last effort to change his mind, she said: "I'm surprised that you find it so easy to involve this naïve person in such an affair."

He merely shrugged.

She dropped her specific arguments about Schefold.

"All right," she said, "then I'll be the one to go."

He answered this with nothing more than a dry laugh that embittered her.

"If you showed Schefold the way, you can show it to me too," she said.

The hope of being able to continue her journey had arisen in her so suddenly that she felt it showed on her face. In an effort to seem businesslike, she said: "And I speak English."

He had sat down behind his table. Now he looked at her, puffing clouds of smoke, and merely shook his head. She knew it was pointless to argue with this headshake.

Besides, it was to turn out that Hainstock's idea of using

Schefold was the only correct course. That same day Dincklage not only approved of Schefold, but spoke of him as essential to the successful execution of the plan.

Had Hainstock really thought, as Käthe supposed: If she goes back and forth twice, as this plan requires, she will make the trip a third time? And only one way this third time? That is hard to determine. But even if this man whose face was marked with a thousand tiny wrinkles that seemed made with a fine engraving needle actually saw through Käthe's intention, he would probably have entertained little hope of dissuading this girl from anything she had taken into her head, such as a decision to cross over and not return. Theoretically Hainstock accepted equal rights for women—he had never given this thesis much thought; it was simply one of the premises of his ideology. But practically, he probably thought: this is no job for a woman.

As he had expected, Schefold was wildly enthusiastic.
"Wonderful!" he had said. "At last I have a chance to do something." And in the same breath: "This will knock Kimbrough for a loop."
"Do you think the Americans will consider the offer at all?" Hainstock had asked.
"Certainly, why shouldn't they?" Schefold had exclaimed, utterly astounded.

Before Käthe left Hainstock that Saturday (October 7), after disclosing Dincklage's plan and persuading him to take part in it, though only as a *letter box*, Hainstock instructed her to tell Dincklage to cease all patrol activities in the wooded ravine to the east of Hemmeres, so that Schefold's safety would be assured.
It delighted him to be able to issue such an order to an officer of the fascist troops, a major and wearer of the Knight's Cross. He actually used such phrases as *cease all patrol activities* and *safety guaranteed*.

After Käthe's disappointment with Hainstock came the unpleasant turn that Dincklage gave to the whole affair.

She called on him at two o'clock because she knew that the office was empty at this time. They showed no inclination to embrace. They sat opposite each other at his desk. Käthe described Schefold to him. She took pains to describe Schefold accurately; no matter what Dincklage's political attitudes were, as a military man he would inevitably be annoyed to learn that there was a weak spot in his sector of the front, and someone who made use of it. He would not want to collaborate with a spy. She was able to put Schefold's activities into the proper light.

"Fine," Dincklage said. And in a tone that suggested he was making a social apppointment: "From what you've told me it will be a pleasure for me to make Doktor Schefold's acquaintance."

"You will have no opportunity for that," Käthe said.

She explained the arrangement she and Hainstock had worked out: "Schefold will come only to Hainstock; Hainstock will pass Schefold's information on to me; and I will bring it to you."

Two strands of information interlocked on a turntable, she thought. "One would have sufficed. Three persons instead of one. If Hainstock would show me the way I could turn the trick alone."

"Excellent," Dincklage said again. "Splendidly thought out. Hainstock is a specialist in camouflage."

She forbore to tell him that the part of the communications system affecting herself had been her contribution. She also said nothing about her having had in mind a still better solution, one omitting Schefold's dubious aid. Since Dincklage knew the nature of her relationship to Hainstock—she had not concealed it from him—she felt a strong reluctance even to hint that she had some criticisms of Hainstock's conduct.

Dincklage himself swept away all her objections to employing Schefold.

"The best part of it is," she said, "that Hainstock has available someone the Americans trust. I'm afraid I would not have been able to accept negotiations conducted through Hainstock alone."

She fixed her eyes upon him. Although he was looking out of the window at the deserted village street, Dincklage must have felt her gaze, for he offered explanations: "Of course I trust Hainstock. But naturally I would have had to insist that he establish a direct contact. I also insist on that now."

He turned away from the window and looked at Käthe.

"There is one change we will have to make in the plan," he said. "The last message must come through the line."

She did not understand, or at least she thought she should not understand him at once.

"What do you mean by that?" she asked.

Impatiently she waited the few seconds that he let pass before he replied: "I am staking everything in this business." He kept pausing between phrases as he enumerated: "Myself. My battalion." (The first time he has called it his, Käthe thought.) Finally he said: "Even you, Käthe." He spoke as though it were a soliloquy.

"That being the case," he went on, "I must insist that the Americans also stake something. Not much. Just that they send the messenger who brings their ultimate agreement through the line to me."

Now she was the one who looked out the window. The Saturday afternoon and the ever mist-shrouded light of the October sun completed the picture of lifelessness to which Major Dincklage's methods of warfare had reduced the village street. The Thelen farm opposite, a leaden white, lay barricaded behind its noonday nap.

She wrenched her gaze away from the hypnosis of that changeless, hopeless light and said passionately: "That won't do at all. It's too dangerous. You cannot ask that of Schefold."

"I will see to it that nothing happens to him," Dincklage said in the tone of an officer who is taking measures.

She tried what seemed to her a simple and reasonable suggestion: "Very well," she said, "we can arrange for him to come to you by his usual route. Then he'll come from the quarry along the road to Winterspelt. Or how would it be if you were to meet him at Hainstock's? It should be possible to arrange that."

"You don't understand, Käthe," Dincklage said. "His coming through the line will serve me as the only proof that the Americans seriously mean it."

Overwhelmed by a sudden sense of the vanity of her efforts, she gave up recommending other solutions. It wasn't just that he had taken some idea into his head, an idea that he could ultimately be talked out of, no matter how obstinate he might pretend to be. Back of this condition she sensed a conviction, a kind of living and thinking, against which rational arguments slid off like hands on the perfectly smooth surface of a wall.

"A structure," she said to Hainstock that very evening (still October 7, the preceding Saturday) in the darkness outside the Thelen farmyard. "Something that cannot be changed."

"Oh hell," Hainstock said. "It's like that story about the fishing, when he really wanted to radio the Americans to pull their men back. This fellow still imagines that a code of honor among officers exists."

Whether a code of honor or something else was involved, in any case she had been depressed and worried at the end of her conversation with Dincklage. She considered throwing up the thing, telling Dincklage that under these circumstances his plan could not be carried out.

She shuddered when she thought of Schefold, of the consequences it might have for him, and only because she, Käthe, had interfered in an affair that without her would have remained a mere fantasy. Filled with anxiety, with dark forebodings, she stared at Dincklage, who now started talking about a different matter because someone had entered the office. She could not manage to enter into this game, paid no attention, remained mute, so that Dincklage had to get up and close the door. When he placed his hand on her shoulder, she remained unmoving and informed him in a murmur of Hainstock's request that during the next several days he not send any patrols into the ravine east of Hemmeres. She noticed that he hesitated for a moment before he agreed; obviously this reminder of a weak spot in his sector of the front somewhat bothered him.

A few hours later she asked Hainstock: "Shouldn't we call the whole thing off?"

He had been at Weinandy's, had bought provisions and newspapers; she had come across him in the main room of the farm-house, talking with old Thelen. Later she had gone outside the door with him. In the pitch-dark wartime night, behind which the whole village was barricaded, she repeated her conversation with Dincklage. The solid single-family house on the other side of the street, now the Battalion Command Post, was nothing but a gray outline.

Hainstock realized at once that at this moment, probably for the last time, he held the decision on Dincklage's plan in his own hand. If he now answered her question with a resolute *yes*, this, to his mind, wild notion of handing a whole German battalion over to the Americans would be swept off the table. But he did not say, "Yes," or even, "Quite right. Let's quash it before we begin." Instead he said: "It's too late now. I've already spoken with Schefold."

There is an absence of logical reasons for this reaction of Hain-stock's. He himself admitted the weakness, in fact the nullity of his argument. For when Käthe pointed out that it would still be quite possible, without the slightest difficulty, to explain to Schefold that the operation could not take place and why, he said: "Of course I could call Schefold off." The conditional phrasing, the *of course*, and his actual refusal to do so, give rise to a number of hypothetical explanations. As follows:

1. In the interval since this morning when he had first heard the novel idea from Käthe, he might have changed his opinion about Dincklage's plan, might have realized that whether or not it succeeded it would involve an event of the greatest significance in the history of the war.

2. He actually believed that the process had already been started. Since Dincklage had spoken with Käthe, Käthe with him, Hainstock and he with Schefold, Schefold with that American officer in Maspelt, a train of events had been set going which could no longer be rescinded. Whether what was involved was the trivial logic of saying, "In for a penny, in for a pound," or some-hing more, some shred of belief in the unalterability of fate in

this man who subscribed to a doctrine of total rationality—who can say?

3. He viewed the existence of the plan, not the plan itself, as the result of the love affair between Dincklage and Käthe, and sensed that the result was too momentous for the relationship, so that he had only to promote the former in order to put an end to the latter. Käthe's discomfort, her actual alarm at Dincklage's condition for accepting Schefold's participation in the operation, was to Hainstock a first sign of her doubts, her criticism of Dincklage himself. At any rate the possibility cannot be dismissed that even for a character such as Hainstock's, jealousy can lead to surprising actions.

He himself, however, gave none of the above-mentioned reasons for his refusal to call off Schefold, but confined himself to the technical aspects, saying to Käthe: "Oh, you know, if Dincklage is willing to guarantee that Schefold will come through the line safely, it's less risky for Schefold than all the rest."

Was he conscious that in saying this he was accepting the idea he had just contested, of the existence of a code of honor for officers?

With this argument he also succeeded in keeping Schefold on tap, although that was not altogether simple.

When Schefold turned up at his shack next morning (Sunday, October 8), he was visibly depressed.

"Kimbrough was odd," he related. "He listened to me, asked questions, but in the end said nothing more than that he would talk with Regiment. He said he could not imagine that they would accept this offer."

"Ha, didn't I tell you!" Hainstock said, but he concealed the fact that he considered such rejection the best solution. If the Americans did not play along, Dincklage could put his pointless individualistic action back in the desk drawer and Käthe, Schefold, and he himself, Hainstock, could calmly await the end of the war.

"The main thing is that Kimbrough himself showed not the

slightest trace of enthusiasm," Schefold said. "Can you explain that?"

"The officers' International," Hainstock said. "They don't like it when one of them jumps out of line."

Schefold shook his head. "You don't know Kimbrough," he said. "He's anything but a one hundred per cent army officer."

"That's made up for by the fact that Dincklage is a hundred and fifty per cent one," Hainstock said, and he then informed Schefold of the condition Dincklage had thought up to complicate the last phase of Schefold's work as a messenger.

Schefold at first flatly rejected this demand.

Hainstock watched him closely as, perplexed, he exploded: "No! That's an outrageous request, you know." Schefold's florid face was not able to turn pale. But in his eyes, which were blue in a very different way from Hainstock's porcelain-blue eyes, something misty formed, a clouding over.

After he had calmed down he said: "Out of the question. I'll be glad to do my best, but I don't want to fall into the hands of Nazi soldiers."

Hainstock did not like the word *Nazi*, which was in common use by the other side. He had heard it from Schefold for the first time. It struck him as too easygoing for what it signified. In his native German Bohemia, the word *Nazi* had been the nickname for the Catholic given name Ignaz, after Ignatius Loyola. Though he had decided he was not going to cajole Schefold, he said: "Of course I can't understand why this officer isn't willing to receive any messages the Americans may send him in a more or less private fashion, from a woman . . ." He broke off.

Schefold quickly seized on the point. "Oh," he said, "so there's a woman involved. Who is she?"

"That's none of your business," Hainstock said. He was irked with himself for mentioning Käthe, and turned his annoyance into rudeness to Schefold.

Schefold would not be headed off. For the moment his interest in this aspect seemed to distract him from his indignation at

Major Dincklage's request. He began to draw conclusions from Hainstock's slip of the tongue.

"So a woman has instigated the whole thing," he said, ignoring Hainstock's bad humor. "Well I'll be damned! She certainly must be a remarkable person if she simultaneously enjoys your confidence and the major's and can function as messenger between the two of you. I had imagined that you yourself . . ." He broke off. "I've been puzzling and puzzling," he said, "about how you ever got wind of Dincklage's intentions, but I didn't ask because I didn't want to pry into your secrets and because I thought you'd tell me one of these days. At the latest, when it's all over. Incidentally, Kimbrough's first question was how you came by your knowledge of the plan. Now of course I can tell him."

He did not seem to notice that Hainstock was glaring at him.

"Is she good-looking?" he asked. He did not wait for an answer, but forged on: "I'd like to know whether you put her up to sounding out the major or whether . . ."

"For Christ's sake," Hainstock said, "will you shut up!"

Schefold gave no sign of feeling offended. He smiled in a manner that rather suggested embarrassment.

At that moment he must have recalled that in the various talks about Hainstock in the taverns of Eigelscheid or Habscheid—talks that had finally led him to pay a call on the man at his quarry—there had once been some mention of the man's girl-friend. A young schoolteacher who had been evacuated to Winterspelt. Now he felt embarrassed that he had dwelt on this subject. He would not have been Schefold if he had not instantly begun to romanticize the image of a Käthe altogether unknown to him. Visions of mysterious intrepid and beautiful women in the underground movement assailed him. For he was a radical *Stendhalien,* capable of processes of crystallization with almost any woman, even one he had never seen. That his passion at the moment was centered on a waitress in Saint-Vith hardly seemed to matter. Possibly the idea that a woman was taking part in the operation tended to induce him to accept the major's condition, rather than Hainstock's assertion that if the major guaranteed his safety there was nothing to worry about.

Hainstock had no ready answer to Schefold's doubts that such a guarantee was at all possible. Dincklage might take all the precautions possible (issue a general ban on firing, thinning out the line, making sure that only his most experienced and reliable soldiers were out there)—nevertheless, the first moment that Schefold appeared in front of that line was fraught with danger.

"Cannot this lady explain to the major," Schefold asked, "that it would be much simpler if I were to come by road to Winterspelt? I would call at his office, present my letter—you've seen it—and he would be receiving a specialist commissioned to see to the protection of works of art. That would be the most natural thing in the world. I'd be taking only a slight risk, and he none at all."

Hainstock did not feel like explaining why Dincklage would turn down such a proposal. Käthe had already made the proposal to the major, after all, though not in such detail, and in reply had heard something about his needing "proof."

Hainstock decided to table the discussion.

"I don't think we really have to worry our heads about it any more," he said. "The Americans won't cooperate anyhow."

But although out of all the Americans only this Captain Kimbrough was ready to cooperate, that had been enough to make Schefold fall into the hands of Nazi soldiers today, so that he had walked along beside one like a fallen monarch, presenting to Käthe the appearance of a person extraordinarily defenseless. If she had known what he was really like, she would have more firmly resisted the desire of both Dincklage and Hainstock to employ him for this mission.

In the end it had all come down to forcing Schefold into a trial of courage. She knew that Hainstock would not accept this formulation. "He could easily have refused," he would have replied if Käthe had made any such objection. Actually he had said to her only yesterday: "A pity that in the final analysis he didn't refuse."

But when she asked, "Did you suggest that to him? Why didn't you flatly tell him not to do it?" Hainstock had replied: "You and Dincklage want the thing to be arranged. Or don't you? Have you changed your minds all of a sudden?"

While she put off leaving because it repeatedly came to her mind that she would never see this shack again, she reflected on what a chance Wenzel Hainstock had missed (with her) when he did not forbid Schefold's going through the line.

So later on, when she remembered the shack, she would first of all think of the owl. You could see at a glance that he was no migratory bird. Stocky, roundheaded, he perched up there in the semidarkness of the crate, a creature of the night and the winter, an abiding presence. Odd, the way he sometimes twisted his head violently around. Since he had no neck, the movement looked as though a great gray mask were being turned by some invisible spindle. Hainstock had told Käthe that owls had exceptionally keen hearing. The plumage on the bird's underside was a smoky yellow, with dark streaks; she would have liked to touch it but did not dare. The bird was not the kind of creature you could pet, except after long habituation.

There was something in his head that still hurt; besides, he felt dizzy, was half absent. Once, when he noticed a moving shadow, he uttered a piercing cry: "Kyu-veek!" Then came the voices again, alien. He felt the lack of greenery that fluttered, whispered, and the absence of hard bark and a caressing air, water that sounded, hollows, darkness.

Once he remembered snow.

Cycling back to Winterspelt, heated but not perspiring, Käthe thought about courage. There were great differences among the various kinds of courage. Schefold's courage in hiking across the line was entirely different from the kind of courage she would have had to summon up if she had gone to the Americans and then returned to Dincklage. As for those solitary walks through the ravine ("doing the job alone"), probably no courage at all

172

would have been required beyond what she already possessed, which was not courage but a frantic urge to break out, to effect a change of scene (she would do it tonight)—that fierce urge she had noticed in herself ever since her departure from Berlin.

Whereas Schefold . . .

When, why, under what conditions did anyone decide to be courageous? Not even the fact that a trial of courage was being asked of him provided a sufficient reason. Hainstock had been quite right: Schefold could have refused.

At least he should have refused this preliminary passage through the lines this morning, which had nowhere been provided for in the program. No one would have blamed him for such a refusal.

*How One Woman*
*Became a Partisan*

## Plugging in a Lamp

### 1.

The acquaintanceship between Käthe and Major Dincklage came about so quickly—as early as the first day of Dincklage's stay in Winterspelt—because late in the afternoon of October 1 an orderly had appeared at the Thelen farm and, somewhat rattled by the presence of three young women, had asked whether a lamp for the major's night table could be found.

It must be explained that the solid one-family house stuccoed gray and quite without character in the midst of the whitewashed farmhouses and rubblestone barns, had been requisitioned for a headquarters by all the units that had so far settled down in Winterspelt. It lay across the village street from the Thelen farm and belonged to it. Old Thelen had had it built for his brother, a clerical gentleman, but he had died before he entered retirement. Aside from its changing military occupants, it stood empty. Since the 18th Motorized had taken over the sector, a yellow wooden sign had been put up, reading *Battalion Combat Command Post*, which Käthe thought ridiculous, not only because there were no signs of any combat but also because she had discovered that behind this impressive title was nothing more than the usual orderly room. Because the Thelens were both the owners and neighbors of the house, the major had already become accustomed to asking first at the Thelen farm when he needed anything.

The lance corporal who was probably Dincklage's personal orderly—an assumption on Käthe's part that was corroborated at the supper next day—grew visibly more and more embarrassed. For old Thelen—who sat at table over a glass of homemade brandy looking as though he were spun out of rusty wire—did not open his mouth, and the girls too took pleasure in letting the soldier dangle, Käthe chiefly because the tone in which he repeated

176

the major's request betrayed the fact that he hadn't the slightest notion why anyone would want a lamp for his night table.

It was Therese who finally ended the moments of mute, even hostile, staring.

"You have a lamp by your bed," she said to Käthe. "Won't you lend it to the major?"

"But I need it myself," Käthe said. She did not want to dwell even for a moment on the threat of being no longer able to read in bed at night.

After the man had left, Elise recalled that there might be another lamp hanging in the storeroom. All three went upstairs and began to search, and quite in contrast to their hostile, impolite conduct down below, they fell into a mood of laughter and silly jokes. They found the lamp, carried it down, screwed a bulb into the socket, tested it, and brushed the dust from the tattered violet shade.

Käthe found herself stuck with the job of taking it to the house across the way, the "Battalion Combat Command Post." Although old Thelen did not even look at his daughters, but continued to stare into the corner of the room above his glass of brandy, Therese and Elise could not, in his presence, be persuaded to undertake this errand, for which they might have felt some eagerness. Elise alleged barn work, while Therese's face wore an expression which Käthe interpreted as not only embarrassment in her father's presence but absorption in thoughts of Boris Gorbatov, who since today was Sunday had not been at the farm. Her affair with the Russian made it necessary for her to avoid any encounters with German soldiers, as far as that was possible.

As Käthe was crossing the street, lamp in hand, she asked herself why she and the two Thelen daughters had behaved like teenagers in the storeroom, although all three of them had long ago passed out of that age in every respect.

### 2.

It was quiet in the building. When Käthe opened the door to the office, without knocking, she saw Dincklage across the room; he was standing by Staff Sergeant Kammerer's desk, and looked up from some document he had been reading. He was alone; probably he had told the clerks they could take the rest of this late Sunday afternoon off, so they could clean up their quarters.

"Why, that's very nice," he said, at once grasping the point. And glancing at the messenger, he immediately concluded from her appearance that she would understand his remark. "This saves my evenings."

"We dug it up out of the storeroom. I couldn't let you have mine because I simply have to do some reading before falling asleep," Käthe said, while it suddenly seemed no longer so unthinkable to her to give up her night table lamp to this man.

"Why, of course," Dincklage said.

She reluctantly admitted to herself that the dark gleam of his Knight's Cross impressed her, but then attributed the effect of the medal to the fact that he wore it around his neck.

"Come upstairs," he said. "Let's try the lamp out and see whether it works."

Naturally Käthe should have answered this invitation by replying: "It's already been tried out; it works and the voltage at the farm is the same as it is over here." Instead she made no objection and followed the major, who switched on the light in the hall and preceded her up the stairs to the attic, where she had incidentally never been before. She noticed his slight limp. The tone in which he had invited her to come upstairs had been neither offensive nor wholly innocuous; it had sounded like a pretext to be able to spend a little more time with her.

On the stairs he paused, turned, and said: "May I ask your name?"

"Lenk," Käthe said.

"My name is Dincklage, Fräulein Lenk," he said.

She looked at him and involuntarily laughed.

"Why are you laughing?" he asked.

"Because you look so funny with the night table lamp in your hand," she said. "It doesn't go with your Knight's Cross."

"Evidently you have exaggerated notions of dignity," he said. "Or at any rate of medals and decorations." He too laughed; he did not seem in the slightest degree insulted.

The room upstairs was not very large, but it was also not just an attic room, although the window was in the gable end between slanting walls. It contained nothing but an army cot, two chairs, and two crates painted gray, one of which stood beside the bed. The cot resembled Wenzel Hainstock's. Army cots like two peas in a pod. On the crate lay several books. Dincklage moved them slightly to one side; the outlet appeared. He placed the lamp on the crate, plugged it in and switched it on. It lighted.

"Wonderful," he said. "Thank you very much."

While he was fussing with the lamp, Käthe stepped to the window, the window which Major Dincklage habitually opened on the following mornings, after he had swallowed his pills, to watch the American bomber wings, calculating how many squadrons of fighter planes would be needed to break up bomber formations in such strength, and mentally forming fragments of sentences such as *if we still had fighters*, for which he afterward castigated himself because he had involuntarily used the first person plural. Now, on this late afternoon that was already passing into evening, no planes could be heard, and Käthe was not looking at the sky, but down into the garden behind the house. The garden was no more than a rectangular patch of meadow in which a few old apple trees stood, no longer tended, in spite of wartime shortages. Still, someone must have picked the apples. ("Probably the men of the Eighteenth Motorized ate them," Staff Sergeant Kammerer had remarked to Major Dincklage that morning, in a tone that suggested he actually blamed the 18th Motorized for not leaving the apples for the 416th Infantry Division.) The leaves of the apple trees were that reddish brown they become in October. The grass in the meadow already showed a touch of grayness. Beyond the meadow rose the slope of the shallow dip in which the village lay. It was pastureland studded with deciduous trees whose foliage was now rust-colored and yellow, fused into disks of molten metal sealed by the twilight.

She heard Dincklage saying: "Of course I could have managed with candles. But they involve so much fuss, waking up at night and having to grope for the matches. And it takes at least three candles to give enough light for reading."

Käthe turned around toward the semidarkness of the room in which the lit lamp under its shade could already form a spot of violet light. She wondered why Major Dincklage had not chosen better quarters than this almost empty room without even a view of the countryside. As a rule officers took quarters in the homes of the rich farmers. The local commander whom Dincklage had replaced had lived it up at the Merfort place.

Dincklage did not join her by the window, but spoke to her from the wall beside the bed, where he was leaning: "I suppose that you are not from Winterspelt, Fräulein Lenk."

"From Berlin," Käthe replied. "I've been here only since June, since Prüm was evacuated. Until then I taught at the Gymnasium in Prüm."

"Are you teaching here in Winterspelt?"

"No," she said. "The school has been closed. Anyhow, I've been shirking any job work since the summer. I don't have permission to be here."

"Is anyone making trouble for you?"

"At first I had to hide. Now they let me alone. There isn't even a police station here. And the local Party chief probably has other things to worry about at the moment."

"Interesting," he said. Käthe had the impression that he was reflecting thoroughly on the incidental information she had given him before he finally said: "Should you run into any further difficulties, come to me."

"Thank you, but that won't be necessary."

At this first meeting with Major Dincklage Käthe was wearing her usual clothes: a black sweater with a crew neckline, a narrow dark-brown skirt, thin gray woolen stockings, rather solid shoes. She had nothing else to wear, aside from the summer dress she had bought in Prüm.

Back at the farm, Käthe was horrified by the way she had impetuously confided in Dincklage, had told him about her flight. Why for heaven's sake had she forgotten in his presence what Hainstock was always bringing home to her—that this was a world in which confidences were followed by denunciations?

3.

People get up early in the country. It had not occurred to Käthe that Major Dincklage would also be up at four, at a time so dark that it definitely still belonged to the night. But at this hour on Monday morning he was standing outside the house leaning on a cane. Sometimes he vanished because he walked a few steps down the village street, but then he would reappear and stay by the stoop that led up to the front door of the house. Käthe stood at one of the windows in the main room of the Thelen farm, an unlighted room so that Dincklage could not see her, although she had raised the blackout blind. From the kitchen came the usual sounds of Elise preparing breakfast for the two Russians, who would be arriving soon. Therese and the old farmer were in the barn. The Thelen compound was, unlike most of the places in Winterspelt, not a rectangular structure but U-shaped, forming a courtyard that stretched between her window and the place where Dincklage was standing. She could observe him well, although there was only the dim light of the street lamp and the diffuse brightness from the white houses to illuminate him. Enclosed by them, he seemed even more compact, more hermetically sealed than by day: a metallic silhouette, the spit and image of a Prussian officer with close-fitting tunic, sharply tailored breeches and gleaming boots—that uniform whose arrogance Käthe hated. He wore a visorless garrison cap. He was a rather short man; Käthe had taken his measure during their talk and knew that he was not much taller than she herself, perhaps five feet seven inches.

She drew down the blind, left the house, and crossed the street to him.

"You are an early riser, Major," she said.

"I have been waiting for you all this while," he said. "You took a long time to come."

He brought out these sentences in a high, somewhat tense voice; it sounded as though he were dressing down a subordinate for some neglect of duty.

Then he became unexpectedly talkative. "I am actually an early

181

riser," he said, "but only because after three hours I can no longer sleep from pain. For the past two years I have been the happy owner of an arthrosis of the right hip joint, if you happen to know what that is." When Käthe said she did not, he explained: "It isn't even a war ailment. Perhaps the war merely activated it. It started on that idiotic expedition to Africa. The medico at Division wants to send me home because of it."

"Good heavens," Käthe said. "I hope you won't have to be told that twice."

The remark simply slipped out, but she also hoped that it would cause him to stick to the subject.

"Six times so far," Dincklage answered. Although Käthe avoided looking at him, she sensed that his gaze was directed at her in the darkness. "That sawbones prescribes excellent pills for me. By day I feel almost nothing." With only the slightest of pauses, he went on: "I hope I haven't offended you, Fräulein Lenk. In wartime things sometimes have to be speeded up."

Käthe felt that this observation was quite true, and considered that fact one of the few positive elements of the war. But she said: "Oh, I see, the warrior is in the habit of speeding things up."

"During the entire war I haven't said anything remotely resembling that to any woman," Dincklage said. "If that is what you mean."

Käthe was still looking in the direction of the Thelen farmhouse.

"The night is reflected in your glasses," Dincklage said. "Your glasses become you."

She took that for what it was worth. It was something of a challenge on his part to address directly the sore point in her appearance. A sentence like that called for no reply. She also had no desire to contradict him, for example by saying something like: "I think my glasses are horrible." But she was relieved when at this moment the Russians appeared.

Around noon, yesterday's orderly brought her a letter from the major inviting her to dinner that evening. "Unfortunately only in the orderly room," Dincklage wrote, "and unfortunately only the field kitchen's cuisine. But do give me the pleasure of your company." His handwriting was coherent, orderly, not very large, without thin upstrokes. Below his name he had written: "No reply necessary."

### "Good Lord, Käthe!"

This was the second time that the messenger had arrived just when she was returning from a visit to Wenzel Hainstock; the same thing had happened yesterday afternoon, after she had told Wenzel about the new unit, the quartering of the men. Today . . . Come to think of it, what had she really wanted to report to him today?

For lack of any new information she had said: "It's oddly still in the village. Hardly a soldier to be seen."

He had mentioned what he himself had noticed about the new unit's camouflage measures.

"Obviously there's a fresh wind blowing," he said. "The commander of these new men apparently knows his job."

Käthe was carried away, let herself say: "I think he's a decent man."

Agitated, she considered how she should parry if Wenzel took her up on that, if he asked how she knew or why she thought so. She was already preparing a phrase: "Why, he just looks decent." But it turned out that he had a poor nose for that sort of thing, or none at all, or else he was slow to catch on; maybe he was just catching on at this very moment, this moment while she was reading Dincklage's letter.

"All these decent officers," was all he had said. "They've served their master loyally."

He had pointed to his chest as an allusion to Dincklage's Knight's Cross, which Käthe had told him about yesterday.

"He limps," she reported. "He uses a cane when he walks."

"Like Frederick the Great," Hainstock said.

He did not seem to notice that his sarcasm annoyed her. Käthe forbore to tell him that she had brought Major Dincklage a lamp last night and had talked to him in the predawn hour this morning.

It was not until four days later, on the evening of October 5 (the week before the Thursday on which Schefold passed through the line), that she told Wenzel Hainstock what was up in the phrase: "Something has happened between him and me." And it appeared that this rock crusher actually had been unable to conceive up to this point that Käthe Lenk would be capable to going over to the enemy camp, as he immediately characterized the event. On that morning, even after Käthe had left, no suspicion entered his mind that anything might be amiss. He merely wondered that Käthe was not in the mood for caresses, but that was something that came over her every so often. Then he had only to let her alone, which he did not find hard, because he himself was aroused only when he noticed that Käthe wanted it. He had plenty of self-control.

### Tirade on Love

In what follows the love between Joseph Dincklage and Käthe Lenk will be discussed in a highly limited way, only insofar as a private concern affects an event in the history of the war. Love had been adequately dealt with in literature; nothing new can be added here to existing descriptions. Its mechanism is always the same, a kind of conveyor belt on which the product is assembled from the first glance through stages of acquaintanceship to the embrace. There are variations that result from differences in character, political, social, and religious factors that affect these characters, obstacles that are placed in the way; the experimental conditions are always different, and in addition, of course, there are varying degrees of poetic density. But aside from all that, it does not matter whether we describe the relationship between Dinck-

lage and Käthe or between Hainstock and Käthe, between
Therese Thelen and Boris Gorbatov, between Reidel and Borek.
It's all one. Not even Schefold's multiple forms of worshipfulness,
those Stendhalian crystallizations which had become an art for
art's sake, constitute an exception to the rule. Because this is so,
that is, because literature has treated the subject exhaustively, we
nowadays no longer wait with breathless suspense to find out
whether boy gets girl.

The mysterious thing about love, after all, isn't how it func-
tions, but that it exists at all, and that those affected by it regard
it as a thing of rarest newness, even though their intellects tell
them that they are merely experiencing what has been experienced billions of times since the genesis of the world (or, let us
say, of an earth habitable by men). They may rightly regard this
feeling of absolute newness as something more than an illusion,
for in their short life it is new (even though it is often repeated
several times in the course of a life) and is expressed in extraordinary physical and psychic states whose reality can be medically
demonstrated. Reference to the mating and reproductive instinct
explains nothing; in its highest forms love rejects this biological
urge. Moreover, it has been demonstrated that at the moment of
most intense emotion the sperm does not enter the vas deferens.
But what causes these states (widened pupils, expanded arteries,
accelerated nerve impulses, daydreams) when there is an encounter between two particular persons who have previously encountered other persons without the slightest exceptional event?
Therein lies the miracle. Of course there is a series of reasons for
every single case of love, and these reasons may be worth com-
menting on. But for the fact that Major Dincklage fell head over
heels in love with Käthe at the moment she entered the orderly
room with the lamp in her hand—for that there is not the shadow
of an explanation. He fell in love with her, that's all, and she,
though with some reluctance, with him.

The latter circumstance also forbids our regarding the event
solely as the result of Käthe's erotic aura, for in that case it would
have remained a fairly one-sided affair, Dincklage's passion for
Käthe. Such one-sidedness had probably marked her relations with

Lorenz Gieding, Ludwig Thelen, and even Wenzel Hainstock. She had put these affairs behind her—and within half a year—not without a measure of pity, but without pain. Old Thelen, who was aware of his son's infatuation with Käthe and of her affair with Hainstock, put it in a nutshell on one of the following days, as he watched Käthe preparing to leave the farmhouse to go across to Dincklage. In an appreciative tone he remarked: "Girl, you can wind men around your little finger." (In the case of Dincklage this wasn't true.) The old farmer thus freely accorded Käthe a freedom he did not accord his own daughters—the three young women jointly, and with all the craftiness at their command, concealed from him Therese's affair with the Russian. In fact, the old tyrant did not even mind when Käthe contradicted him. He liked having her in the house. So much for the strength of the sympathies that Käthe stirred. End of the tirade on love.

## Biogram

Käthe Lenk, born in Berlin in 1920, only child of a businessman (sales agent for a machine-tool factory), Eduard Lenk, and his wife Klara, née Reimarus. Käthe was baptized a Protestant, graduated in 1938 from the Schiller Gymnasium in Lichterfelde, attended the University of Berlin, studying philosophy and languages from 1939 to 1942 (that is, during the first years of the war), did not complete her course of study. From the beginning of 1943 on she attended the Normal School in Lankwitz and served as a substitute teacher at a secondary school in Friedenau. When she left Berlin in the spring of 1944 she was in possession of a certificate entitling her to teach in secondary schools throughout the territory of the Reich, and was in line for a permanent post. From the middle of May to the beginning of July, she taught at the Regino Gymnasium in Prüm (German and geography). When the civilian population of Prüm was evacuated, she was assigned a teaching position in Cologne, but avoided going there. With the aid of one of her pupils, a senior named Ludwig Thelen, she went into hiding in the village of Winterspelt on the frontier of the Reich.

Although even in her own days in Gymnasium Käthe already formed the center of many "movements" involving bicycles, sailboats on the Havel, movies, and the supply of cribs for classmates (Käthe rated high in almost all subjects), she waited until she was twenty and a student at the university before having her first affair, with Lorenz Gieding, art student and painter. This lasted until 1944.

She was nearsighted and consequently had always to wear glasses of minus nine diopters; she used frames of thin, translucent horn because she hoped these would look the least obtrusive. No one had ever told her that with her almost permanently tanned skin, glasses with strong, dark-brown frames would have been more becoming. Her eyes, too, were brown, with splinters of green. She was slender, five feet four, long-legged, but not of feeble constitution, rather vigorous, firm, physically well organized. Her walk was springy, athletic, inhibited (hunched shoulders) only when she felt she was being observed. In Berlin she had played tennis and been the best high-jumper (five feet) in the Schiller Gymnasium. Her head was small, her face both winsome and—in spite of her youth—fully modeled. A pretty nose. Perhaps this head would have been no more than a nut, a bronze oval, a spheroid, or whatever other image for a rounded hollow body might occur to one, had it not contained the penetrating intelligence, the warmth and glow, of Käthe's eyes, which the glasses did not diminish. Life became livelier when Käthe's glance struck it—all who had anything to do with her felt that. Her hair was brown, perhaps shading toward the blond side, smooth, long; she usually wore it tied in a ponytail that fell down her back. To her grief she had neither lipstick nor perfume—she had no idea how to obtain these things in the sixth year of the war. Her wardrobe consisted of two dresses, some underclothing, and a raincoat; Elise and Therese Thelen lent her woolens or aprons for the housework. At the Thelen farm she had taken over the cleaning, after having declared herself incompetent to perform agricultural tasks.

### The Journey to the West

With Dincklage, she recounted the story in more detail. To Hainstock she had said simply that on the evening of March 8 she had been having a language lesson in the city, not at home in Lankwitz, whereas to Dincklage she described precisely how she had read aloud to her teacher the beginning of the seventh chapter of *Bleak House*, with no suspicion that this English lesson would be the last she would have with the old spinster on Dorotheenstrasse.

"I thought those Tuesday evenings on Dorotheenstrasse would be going on for a long time," she said. "First part conversation, second part grammar, third part reading."

She remembered, and told Dincklage, how whenever she would come upon a particularly fine sentence, Fräulein Heseler would first take a sip of tea before she began correcting her pronunciation. *And solitude, with dusty wings, sits brooding upon Chesney wold*, followed by that delicate old hand reaching out for the teacup.

It was Dincklage's fault that she told the story at all. He had asked her—as Hainstock had done earlier—why she left Berlin. This was after the supper on Monday, October 2—orderly room, army rations, but at any rate red wine. The orderly, who had served them, had vanished. Käthe was smoking; the major too smoked one of his strictly limited cigarettes.

"I found a copy of the book in the library of the Prüm Gymnasium."

"You mean *Bleak House?*" Dincklage asked.

"Yes," she said. "But I did not go on with it. I only turned to the beginning of the seventh chapter and reminded myself of how I had intended, when I came home on the evening of March 8, to look in my father's atlas and find Lincolnshire."

Dincklage was acute enough not to interrupt her by describing his own outing in Lincolnshire. He did that later. Now he remained silent, waiting for the point.

In the darkness of the street the blue-gray of Lorenz Gieding's uniform, as every Tuesday evening at nine o'clock when she left the house. (She had spoken of this to neither Dincklage nor Hainstock. No doubt it was none of their business.)

She said to Lorenz: "Some day I should like to meet you on a street at night with the light in your face."

"You can have that," he said, taking from his pocket the flashlight he always carried and shining the beam into his face. She saw his dark-blue eyes behind the glasses with black tortoiseshell frames.

"No," she said, "that isn't the effect I mean. I mean a street lamp." But already someone was shouting at them out of the darkness: "Light out!"

Lorenz accompanied her to Potsdamer Platz; then he had to leave to reach his quarters. Pauses for embraces, kisses, especially on the way through the Tiergarten. Käthe liked everything about Lorenz except the half moldy, half metallic smell of his uniform.

"As I was walking down Saarlandstrasse the sirens howled," Käthe related. "I sat out the raid in the railroad tunnel under Saarlandstrasse. It went on until long after midnight, a good three hours before the all clear sounded. There in the center of Berlin, though, hardly anything of the raid could be heard. Do you know Berlin?" she asked Dincklage.

"I've been there two or three times," Dincklage said. "But I hardly know the city at all."

She concealed from him, as she had concealed from Hainstock, that all the while she sat in the rail tunnel that had been proclaimed an air raid shelter she thought about her friend Lorenz Gieding, a former art student now an air force corporal, who with the aid of a case of TB—long since arrested—plus connections, had succeeded until the spring of 1944 in holding on to a safe post in the army library. He had to live in barracks, however, and Käthe refused to leave her parents' house in order to rent a furnished room where the landlady would not look askance at male visitors. They solved the problem by going out to an inn in Sakrow when Lorenz had a night's furlough. Käthe's parents raised no objection to her staying away for a night on occasion; after all, she was twenty-four, already teaching, and would soon hold the title of instructor. They preferred that to Lorenz's staying the night in Käthe's room, although they liked him. "If we were to marry I would probably be given permission to live outside the barracks," Lorenz once remarked. "That's a reason!" Käthe said, not even taking the trouble to add: *to marry*.

"After the all clear I went to the Anhalter Station; the elevated line was already running and I made a train to Marienfelde without a wait. The area of the freight yards at Marienfelde was all in flames, but everything seemed normal in the quarter to the right of Marienfelder Allee, where we lived."

She recalled how relieved she had been because the sky above the quarter where she lived was as dark as it possibly could be. Under that dark sky reddish and brownish clouds rushed along, smoke rising from the fires in the freight yards. She could already see herself turning into Hanielweg, approaching with slowing footsteps the crowd gathered around the place where her home had stood, the house in which she had lived with her parents.

"There was no need for questions," she said to Dincklage. "When there was nothing more to see but a shallow heap of smashed brick, there was no need for questions, you see. What had happened? Parents had suddenly vanished. Were gone, just like that. Father gone, mother gone. That's what had happened. That's all that happened, you see."

Not for a moment did Dincklage imagine that in this insistently repeated "you see" Käthe was really addressing him, appealing to his understanding. She had been talking to herself, had been calling on herself to understand because she did not understand, would never understand what had happened, because no one was capable of understanding why such things happened, for there was no explanation for them, nothing that could possibly give the thing a meaning, not even something so old and stale as the word *fate*, that stinker of a word that was always invoked to prettify the rottenest crap; the word ought to be deleted from the dictionaries, because fate didn't exist, only chaos and chance. But scientific morons thought they were introducing order when they extracted statistics from chaos and chance. Käthe's parents formed part of the accident statistics of chaos, Dincklage thought.

Were among the victims of the imperialist war, Hainstock had thought, and he once said so to Käthe, what is more at a moment and in a manner (dry, matter-of-fact) such that she could bear it.

Whereas Dincklage could not express his thought about chaos. He could not say a single word of comfort to this girl with whom he had fallen madly in love, and consequently he had to keep his mouth shut. But he was so painfully aware of his failure to speak that he stood up and began pacing back and forth in the orderly room, limping slightly. Or no, not in the orderly room itself, for the supper had taken place in the adjacent room, the room on whose door Staff Sergeant Kammerer had tacked the sign bearing the word: *Chief*. From time to time he cast a glance at Käthe, fearing that she would begin to cry; but there was no question of that.

This has to stop now, once and for all, Käthe thought. I must stop telling people about the liquidation of my parents.

As a quarryman and therefore an explosives expert, Hainstock knew all about the effects of the impact of even a middle-sized bomb on a small brick house, but he kept his knowledge to himself.

She had told Hainstock—not Dincklage, with whom she now desperately tried to change the subject—what had happened to her afterward.

"A neighbor woman spoke to me, told me to come to her house, said I could stay with her as long as I liked. I turned around and went back to the Marienfelde station of the elevated line. I spent the rest of the night on a bench in the waiting room of the Anhalter Station."

The most unbearable thing to realize, she said to Hainstock, was that Father and Mother were not entirely gone, that in all probability they formed a shapeless mass of flesh and bones under the bricks, which because of the danger of contagion would be dug out next morning and scraped off the bricks.

"Father and Mother were now a danger of contagion, you see."

She reported that when she had come to this point in her reflections she had uttered a scream, but that none of the people sitting around in the waiting room of the station had heard her.

"I actually screamed, and they didn't just pretend not to hear my scream, they really didn't hear it."

Hainstock said: "Certainly you screamed, but you didn't open your mouth."

She shook her head, refusing to accept this explanation.

Käthe Lenk never again set foot in Hanielweg. The school board immediately obtained a room for her. She took only one day off from her teaching. From the furnished room in Steglitz she arranged everything: the burial of her parents' remains in the City Cemetery on Alboinplatz, the replacement of ration cards and identification papers, the notification of the property losses to the Office for War Damage, the legal process of determining that she, as the only child, was the sole heir, the transfer of her father's account at the Bank of Commerce to her name—there was something over twenty-five thousand marks—and her resignation from the school in Friedenau. On April 15, 1944, ten days after Easter, she left Berlin.

On the day after her parents' death she delayed a long while before telephoning Lorenz at the army library. He asked only for a summary of the details; but that evening as they sat in an almost deserted café on Mollendorfplatz he said, looking over her head at the rest of the café: "It's tough for you." Only then did she begin to cry; it seemed to her that she went on crying for hours. She would never cease being grateful to Lorenz that he quietly endured her "hours of bawling"—her expression for it—that evening and made no attempt to comfort her. He simply sat there, fended off the waitress when she wanted to talk to the weeping girl, drank ersatz coffee, and saw to it that Käthe could cry her eyes out. When she was finished, he cleaned her glasses, which she had had to take off, and handed them to her.

Some time later, during a walk by Lake Sakrow, she asked him: "Do you happen to know where Lincolnshire is?"

"No," he said after pondering a while. "Not exactly. About all I know is that one of the finest English cathedrals is in the city of Lincoln. Why?"

Käthe had written Fräulein Heseler that she would not be coming for any more lessons.

"A house," she said, "is a place where there's an atlas."

"Oh, I see," he said. He paused before he said: "When the war is over we'll go to Lincolnshire, Käthe. And to London and Paris and New York."

Major Dincklage once said almost these same words to her, and wondered why she rebuffed him.

"After the war you and I will be God knows where," Käthe then replied. And making her rebuff even colder because she wanted to protect her memory of Lorenz: "I shall never wait for a man to take me anywhere."

She watched Lorenz sketching the lake with charcoal on a large pad of white paper; he did the reeds in a succession of harsh, furious lines. His face was, as always, dark-skinned, his nose prominent under a helmet of smooth black thick hair, a face from a Roman coin. His dark-blue eyes behind the black horn-rimmed glasses observed the lake, the reeds.

They were sitting on the trunk of a felled pine, and Käthe told him that she would be leaving Berlin in a few days.

He clapped the pad shut, pressed it against his side, and continued to look at the lake.

"Fly away, ladybug," he said, "fly away from home. Your house is on fire, your children are gone."

193

Three days later he telephoned Käthe at the school to tell her that he was being transferred to active service, detailed to an air force field division located in the west somewhere north of Paris. His marching orders were for the very next day; there was just time for them to meet once more, in Käthe's room in Steglitz.

"At least it gives me a chance for a short visit to my family," Lorenz said, and Käthe could detect that he was immediately sorry he had said that because it reminded her that he still had his parents. Münster, where he came from, would be on his way. They arranged that Käthe would make an attempt to meet him some time, perhaps in Cologne, if he had a furlough. Much talk back and forth about how she could receive mail from him during her journey, how she would find out his army post office number. It seemed to Käthe that he was glad, though perhaps unconscious of it, that he would not be the one to remain behind in Berlin. He was excited, found it hard to conceal the fact that he was looking forward eagerly to France.

When Käthe came away from her last English lesson she was wearing a brown woolen suit, thin woolen stockings, fairly solid shoes, a raincoat. She was given a clothing ration card, but bought nothing but underwear and a black sweater. For months she was quite content with not having to consider what to wear. On her journey she carried a small brown suitcase given her by friends of her parents. It weighed almost nothing.

In Prüm, when summer came, she finally bought a lightweight dress. A few sleeveless dresses of striped linen had been distributed to a shop on Hahnstrasse, and she succeeded in getting hold of one of them. Her seniors were noticeably quiet the first time she came to class in the new dress. Käthe was glad that she had tanned arms and legs; she needed only to lie down in the sun for an hour somewhere and she would turn as brown as a board. ("Board is good," Wenzel Hainstock said, clasping her arm in his hand the time she used this image for the color of her skin.) She sat down behind her desk, removing her glasses so that she would not be able to see the kind of looks that were being directed at her on this day. Her vision was just good enough for her to see that only Ludwig Thelen was gazing out the window.

Therese had insisted that Käthe wear one of her knitted jackets when she saw that Käthe was going to supper with the major in this dress.

"You're crazy," she had said. "It's already good and cold. That's no dress for October."

But Dincklage's orderly had fired the stove in the room so that she was able to remove the knitted jacket. Her arms stuck thinly out of the dress. Käthe thought them skinny; Lorenz the artist had said that the flesh of her upper arms was slightly concave.

Further notes on that supper:

His asking her first name, requesting permission to use it. Of course she had nothing against that.

Not only was he not wearing a wedding ring; he actually was unmarried.

Once or twice there was a sudden long silence—an angel passed through the room, as some people say. When she became aware of the pause, she asked him to describe Africa, Sicily, Paris, Denmark.

He said that at such and such a time they entered the Sahara.

"That doesn't interest me," she said. "Describe the Sahara."

He looked at her, and to his own astonishment began describing the Sahara.

She enjoyed being served at table. Somehow, she had expected to be spooning her food out of a mess kit, but the orderly served them on plates.

"Let us regard this as Irish stew," Dincklage said.

Since she did not know what Irish stew was, she regarded the indefinable stuff on the plate as such. They drank the wine out of water glasses. She had imagined that officers did not eat the same food as their soldiers. She did not know that doing so was one of Major Dincklage's crotchets. He was allowing himself the one extra of wine tonight because of her visit. Something about him—

she could not have said what—confirmed the words he had
spoken early in the morning: "During the entire war I haven't
said anything remotely resembling that to any woman." He did
not seem awkward or inhibited, but yet like a man who had not
had a woman for years.

For some reason, she could not have said what it was, this did
not strike her as quite all right.

On the other hand she asked herself what would have happened if Elise or Therese had brought the lamp instead of herself.
Elise and Therese were pretty girls, each in her own fashion. But
the major would not have waited for either in the predawn darkness, only to say in his high, somewhat tense voice, as though he
were dressing down a subordinate: "You took a long time to
come."

She did not like this "eh-eh" tone in him. As a rule he spoke
quite normally, in a calm, rather low-pitched voice; but every so
often that other tone broke out. She would wean him from this
bad habit.

Wean him from this bad habit, she thought, dismayed. As
though I intended to make a habit of him.

2.

Before they went upstairs—for after all it was clear that they
would go upstairs; in those words he had spoken in the predawn
darkness he had indicated that she would have to reject his invitation if it seemed impossible to her to go to bed with him, but it
seemed to her not in the least impossible—before they went upstairs, then, because in wartime—and not only in wartime, by the
way—things sometimes have to be speeded up—they felt the necessity to make some kind of interval between bed and Käthe's
story about the bomb, an interval that had to be filled with something, although not exactly with conversation. It had already
grown too late for conversation.

"But then what rhyme or reason led you from Berlin to this godforsaken hole?" Dincklage asked.

"There wasn't any rhyme or reason to it," Käthe replied. "I took a train to Hanover. Why I went west from Berlin, I don't know. It didn't even enter my head that I might also travel to the east. Or the south. But the only direction that seemed at all possible was the west, though I've never been able to find any good reason for my choosing this direction. I didn't even choose it—not in the real sense of the word. Funny, isn't it?"

Dincklage did not answer this question. The migrations of birds, directions chosen by instinct, were not "funny."

Hanover had been fairly heavily bombed. She walked around a few streets, decided the city was finished. The heavy façades, whether empty or still occupied, looked like bulging leather. They ignored Käthe. She returned to the railroad station, a dark-red horror under a gray sky, and was grateful to be swallowed up by it. The war had conjured up railroad stations like this one.

"I went to Hameln because I didn't want to stay in Hanover. I liked the name. It was already dark when I arrived in Hameln; I asked my way to the heart of the city, walked down a long street with old houses . . ."

The stepped gables stood out blackly against the night sky.

"There were many small hotels. I found a room."

In the restaurant—possibly it had a rather cheerful air—she ate meatballs made mostly of vegetables, read a newspaper, felt afraid to face her room. At one table sat some citizens, perhaps notables of the town.

"The room was a long narrow tube. A washbowl and a jug of water stood on a table. I didn't dare to open the wardrobe."

When she put out the light and opened the window, the wall of the adjacent building stood almost within reach outside, gray cracks running through it. Käthe looked at that wall as she lay in bed.

"Imagine, I had taken nothing with me to read. No, you cannot imagine that. I forced myself to spend a second night in that room because I did not want to give up so quickly, wanted to find out whether Hameln might not be right for me. Actually it is a fine town."

She listened for a long time to the chimes from the town hall. Leafless trees were mirrored in the waters of the Weser.

"Back to Hanover and then on to East Frisia by way of Bremen. It had suddenly occurred to me that there was such a thing as the sea. All the trains were jammed and crept along; it took a whole night to get from Bremen to Norddeich."

No lights were on in the railroad cars. There was compensation for that: she could look out of the dark compartment at the nocturnal landscape. She had a window seat. Clouds, moonlight over level plains, treetops, glittering water. Once she saw a town in flames; people said it was Jever. In the early morning she stood shivering on the deserted quay in Norddeich. So the sea existed, and the islands out there. Between the quay where she shivered and the islands the sea was gray, with mud flats that did not even glisten because the sky was also gray. Between islands there was a darker, rather slaty gleam.

"At high tide the steamer came over from Juist. I was the only passenger. I stayed a week on Juist. The woman I stayed with was sixty years old; she wove rugs of locally grown wool and wanted to keep me there."

She had come to Käthe's room one evening, sat down on the edge of the bed, and said: "Do stay here, Käthe. Wait here for the end of the war."

"I've studied your atlas," Käthe said. "Peace will arrive here last of all."

"Peace is already here," the woman said.

She had a distinguished and avaricious face. Käthe did not leave the island because of this woman; she would have had nothing to fear from her. But because she realized that from these broad expanses of sand, from the dunes among which she took endless lonely walks, it was meaningless to attempt to draw an imaginary line to Lincolnshire.

"The atlas showed me that Lincolnshire lay directly opposite, on the other side of the North Sea. But in reality it was farther away than from any point on the mainland. I don't know much about your profession, of course, Major, but I had the feeling that on Juist the news of the end of the war would remain a rumor for a long time."

"Do drop the 'Major,' Käthe," Dincklage said. "Otherwise I'll start calling you Miss Schoolmarm. As for that, though, you're not so wrong. I imagine that when the British and Americans occupy Northwest Germany they'll ignore the East Frisian islands. From the military point of view they're totally without interest."

This was the second remark in which Major Dincklage conveyed to Käthe that he regarded the defeat of Germany as a forgone conclusion. He had made the first such remark in the morning. Watching the Russian prisoners of war, whose appearance had interrupted his forming statements of fact directed at Käthe ("You took a long time to come." "Your glasses are becoming to you."), he had said: "There come the victors." And it is quite possible that this sentence, which was likewise a statement of fact, was what decided the issue and led Käthe to accept the invitation for that evening.

This time, too, at the second mention of Lincolnshire, he forbore to weave himself into the fabric of symbols that made up her trauma. It took him until Tuesday or Wednesday to grasp the series of signals, whereupon he then made an (unconscious) attempt to fit himself in ("I should have settled down in Lincolnshire and waited for you there; you would have come") but received no reply. Evidently she did not regard him as a father substitute. After all, if she wanted one she had one in Hainstock.

Incidentally, in her conversation with the woman who offered her security she had used the word *peace* with considerable reluctance. Peace did not interest her. She could not imagine what it would be like. What interested her was the end of the war.

She began to travel at random, drifted to Emsland, then to the Lower Rhine. Since she now had a map with her, she visited the regions where she imagined that war would end soonest. She tramped around the Bourtanger Moor and Bentheim County like a person who wets his finger and holds it up to test which way the wind is blowing. She did not find the wind she was seeking. Moreover, she also did not wet her finger, but acted on her premonitions and intuitions.

It was at the mention of the Bourtanger Moor that Dincklage had interrupted, had asked whether she'd been in Meppen, whether she'd noticed the Dincklage brick factory, had made that unconscious marriage proposal of which she had immediately been very conscious ("You could have visited my parents, could have stayed with them")—that was the proposal that came too soon; he made the second, wholly explicit one that came too late on the day Schefold went through the lines—and finally, steered to this subject by Käthe, concluded his litany of the concentration camps of Emsland with an *amen* that for a second hung like a curse in the dimly lit "chief's room" adjacent to the orderly room where in celebration of this evening all the papers had been cleared away from the desk; only the wine bottle and the two water glasses stood on it.

She spared him the essence of her memory of towns like Meppen, Lingen and Papenburg, Kleve, Emmerich and Kevelaer. She merely said: "Anyhow, I could not read in bed; the woman in Juist had given me some books. Actually, I soon got used to this vagabond life. I didn't mind at all sitting in the parlor of a pension in the evenings listening to the news on the radio, chatting with the proprietress. Perhaps my father, the machine-tools sales-man, led a similar life, who knows?"

She learned to portion out the cigarettes she received on her to-bacco ration card. Formerly she had rarely smoked. The cigarettes were poor, but they dispelled the taste of the food, the smell of the rooms.

Dincklage was given no account of the rest of Käthe's journey to the west up to the point at which she arrived in this "god-forsaken hole"; aside from brief bits of factual information he did not learn anything more during the following days either—for ex-ample, he never heard a word about the entire Lorenz Gieding story—because at this point he suddenly resolved to stake every-thing on one card and to say: "Come, let's go up to my room." Was he surprised that Käthe made no objection? Hardly. From the start there was a large measure of understanding between Joseph Dincklage and Käthe Lenk. Of course they embraced and kissed before they went up. The conveyor belt. The assembly line. The product was being manufactured.

Upstairs he said, indicating his bed: "That is one of the few ad-vantages an officer enjoys: you always have your bed made for you."

So the difference between his and Wenzel's bed is only that Wenzel makes his own, Käthe thought.

She had noted that the lamp was already on when they entered the room: a violet spot in a darkness.

In bed Käthe had to realize at once that her worry about Dincklage's years of continence was unfounded. It is difficult to analyze the source of Dincklage's erotic talent, his aptitude for ex-pressing his feelings naturally. Could it by any chance be traced to his relationship at seventeen to that young farm woman five years his senior in Bentheim County? Or was it something innate which therefore pressed so insistently toward early development? We shall leave the question open, just mentioning Dincklage's talent for nonchalance, tenderness, intensity, only because with-out it the manner in which a private concern affects an event in the history of the war cannot be explained.

3.

Vagabonding. When she had had enough of it, she went to Cologne. The date, May 15, had remained in her mind. At the post
office she was handed a bundle of letters from Lorenz. There was
also a letter from his father, Friedrich Gieding, M.D., Münster.
Käthe had never met him. She wondered how he knew the address she had agreed on with Lorenz, and opened his letter first,
read: "My dear Fräulein Lenk: Our son Lorenz was killed in Italy
at the beginning of May. He spoke of you a great deal when he
was here, and gave me this address just in case, as he put it. My
wife and I would be happy if you would come to visit us some
time."

She left the post office, the bundle of letters in her hand. Outside a May morning, warm and blue. At eleven o'clock there was
an air raid, but a short one; she sat in the shelter for an hour. She
tried to imagine a dead Lorenz, but could not; the only thing she
could grasp was that he was gone, that he no longer existed. This
too, she thought; and later: now I am more free than I have ever
been. Even on the way to the railroad station she acknowledged
that her first two reactions to the news of Lorenz's death had
been egotistic; they referred not to Lorenz but to herself.

On the train she read his letters. The division to which he had
been transferred had been shipped from France to Italy after he
joined it. He described Italian landscapes. The censor had blacked
out the place names he mentioned. He complained that Käthe
never wrote. She realized that it had been irresponsible of her to
dally so long before proceeding to Cologne. Instead of at least
going there directly from Juist, she had drifted into vagabondage.
Actually she had seldom thought of Lorenz. Now she had his
army post office number. From their parting in Berlin until his
death he had not received any sign of life from her, whereas he
had written two dozen letters. Italian landscapes and muted or
blatant declarations of love, on account of which she could not
send the letters to his father in Münster.

Beet fields, the village of Euskirchen, beet fields. She read and

read. When she was finished, she noted that the landscape had
changed. She smoked for a while, then placed the letters carefully
in her suitcase and locked it. This was the first train for a long
time that was not overcrowded. In fact, it was almost empty. In
the Cologne station she had looked once more at her map, this
time rather hopelessly. Not for a moment did she feel any desire
to go to Münster. Finally she bought a ticket for Prüm in the
West Eifel. Going to Münster would have meant traveling toward the interior. Käthe did not want to travel deeper into Germany; she wanted to reach the farthest fringes. Like the victim of
an obsession she had tested out the margins: the island, the Bourtanger Moor, the banks of the Lower Rhine, forever hoping she
would sometime draft into an open zone, a mystery land of vague
transitions, some outermost and already transparent fringe. She
had not succeeded. Beyond the dike of sleep lay not the open
ocean but still more mainland, the geometrical meadowlands beneath the banks of the high dams, the walls enclosing brackish
waters.

Looking out of the train window into the changing landscape,
Käthe saw grand lines of hills, not high, but dipped in deep
colors, with paths like bright ropes through the hollows, low farmhouses of white or gray random stone in which she instantly felt
she would like to live, trees like clustered clouds. Once a tumble-
down castle, vast compared to the neighboring farm buildings, a
ring of walls, unkempt. To Käthe these scenes did not denote a
kind of prison, but a refuge. Not idyls; the cool light of old apple
orchards, forgotten springs.

Käthe thought: no pictures for Lorenz. As a painter he was partial to different effects. She was convinced he would have become
a great painter. He was capable of pointing to a drawing that
represented anything but Lake Sakrow and saying: "Lake Sakrow
is really terrific," though it was only this drawing—which had
taken wing from the Brandenburg lake and from everything the
lake meant—that was terrific. Sometimes that look of his, in
which physical realities were burned to ashes, depressed her; she
caught herself wondering whether it would be the right thing for
her to spend her life at a great painter's side.

203

She had also not been able to make herself go to Münster because she did not want to tell Dr. Gieding and his wife anything about their son's potential as an artist. That would only have made them feel worse. But then again perhaps it would not have done so; possibly it would have stimulated them, given their grief a direction. Lorenz would then no longer have lived in their memory as just another soldier killed in action, but as an unrealized artist. Consequently, in Münster Käthe would have fallen into the role of a survivor, which would have been extremely embarrassing to her. By conferring genius on Lorenz she would be obligated virtually to play his widow for a few days. Anything but that, she thought. She could not imagine herself taking part in the kind of talk that went on after a funeral.

During the summer and the autumn in the Eifel she had stopped thinking very often of Lorenz. But when she did think of him, she did not think of the great painter he might have been but of the dead soldier he had actually become. Of the man nobody would ever hear about. Then she grew sad and depressed; a feeling of tragedy overpowered her and she felt she had to take some action on Lorenz's behalf. From Prüm she wrote to Dr. Gieding advising him to track down and collect Lorenz's drawings and paintings for an exhibition after the war; she gave him addresses where he might possibly find some of his son's works. He thanked her, agreed with her. Some of Lorenz's best sketches had been destroyed along with her room in Hanielweg. She possessed nothing to remind her of him, not even a photo. Lorenz had hated photos, had never asked for one of her either.

Käthe had talked about Lorenz only with Wenzel Hainstock. As far as Käthe's actual involvement was concerned—Hainstock proved he had no nose for these matters. On the other hand it was he who once said to Käthe: "You certainly must have had a young man in Berlin," whereas it never occurred to Dincklage to make such surmises. Or if he did surmise such things, he considered it indiscreet to voice them. Or inconsequential, simply because his love for Käthe, Käthe's love for him, was something so incredible and unique that all pasts were burned to ashes in it, like Lake Sakrow in Lorenz's drawing.

4.

The Prüm phase from the middle of May to the middle of July. For two months she taught German and geography to the senior class at Regino Gymnasium—"I certainly should be able to entrust our seniors to a colleague from Berlin," the principal had said—but from the end of June on, not much schoolwork was done because the students spent most of their time standing at the windows or in the broad square down below. Käthe did not stop them, in fact joined them; she herself wanted to watch an army in flight. But this army was not fleeing at all; the columns moved slowly, pedantically. It rained a great deal in June, and the army marched in a steady downpour, perpetually disgruntled, but simply headed somewhere else from where it had been. Boredom. Käthe persuaded the students to return to the classroom, discussed Berlin, talked about hummingbirds and coffee. She almost let herself be fooled regarding the army's eastward march as just another troop movement; but then it came out that the population would have to leave the city. Even before the principal announced the closing of the school, the seniors received their call-up notices. For a few days the town was full of a confused liveliness; Käthe watched people surrounded by baggage looking dubiously at their houses after they had closed the shutters and put new locks on the door. Soon the town would be a watchamay-callit, a stone object for nocturnal scouting expeditions, pillaging and cannonading. Alone in the classroom after the last day of school, Käthe felt a vacuum beginning to envelope her. The army was not just marching somewhere else; it was evacuating areas, leaving deserted land, no-man's-land, behind it. At such moments Käthe Lenk could also feel intense hope. She had received instructions to report to the school authorities in Cologne "for further assignment."

Prüm was a city in a wooded valley, entirely enclosed. Immediately after her arrival Käthe had decided to stay there. It was impossible to go farther to the west. In a spacious square stood a church far too big for a town this size, with two towers. It was a baroque building, but sheathed with gray stucco. Students streamed into the rambling, equally gray building beside it through an ancient portal bearing coats of arms.

Käthe had rather fond memories of Regino Gymnasium. There had been only two or three Nazi teachers at the school; many were Catholic, several liberal. Once when she sat alone in the faculty room correcting notebooks, the biology teacher, an elderly man, came in and sat down beside her. "Do you really hate the British?" he asked.

"Should I?" she retorted mockingly.

"I just wondered," he said.

"What makes you think that?"

"Perhaps because of your parents."

"I hate the war."

"Then that's all right," he said.

It was Wenzel Hainstock who first convinced her that it did not suffice to hate the war.

As a favor to the elderly biology teacher she once went along on a botanical outing. Her friendship with Ludwig Thelen dated from that occasion. They went hiking along a ravine through which a brook flowed. Dr. Mohr pointed out to the seniors where mezereon and cowbells, violets and lily of the valley, grew. Käthe lingered behind in a lane of sunlight; when she continued on, she noticed that Ludwig Thelen was waiting for her.

"Are you also sick to death of these flowers?" he asked.

"No," she said. "They are objectively beautiful. But perhaps this year they really do not matter to us."

They started to talk about the reasons flowers failed to affect them in this late spring of 1944. Käthe took care that they caught up with the others after a few minutes. Two days later Ludwig Thelen put his composition notebook on her desk. When she opened it, she found a note inside: "Three o'clock this afternoon at the Rommersheimer Held." Letting her eyes fill with coldness, she looked over toward his seat; but as always he was gazing out the window. After a few minutes she realized that there was actually no reason not to meet him.

The Rommersheimer Held is a lonely hill on the highway leading southward from Prüm. Once you have climbed out of the wooded valley in which the town is situated, you come to an area of plateaus, of peaks, of forested horizons or deserted ridges, of mesas, rocky hillocks, and slate-roofed villages. Perhaps Käthe would not have hung on in Prüm if she had not during the first few days of her stay here scouted out the land beyond the beechwood slopes that almost buried the town. She discovered countryside that marched in endless billows of hills toward the west. In this landscape she went on several long tramps with Ludwig Thelen.

He came from a farm in Winterspelt, had been sent on for higher schooling because of his gift for mathematics. His face had a calm, concentrated expression. Käthe never heard him raise his voice; he always spoke quietly, with even-tempered firmness. She sometimes asked herself whether he was altogether passionless.

When he discovered Käthe's liking for the limestone slopes with sparse vegetation, he arranged their hikes so they were over these mountain pastures where the terrain was firm and springy. They talked about books and mathematics, about the war and his impending call-up. Ludwig Thelen regarded the war as his future; in this respect he was a typical eighteen-year-old.

"When the war is over you'll be just as old as I was when it began," Käthe said. "You are lucky."

"Next year?" he asked. "Do you really believe it will be over next year?"

"At the latest," Käthe said.

He seemed so surprised that he could not think of a reply. However, on the day this conversation took place the army had not yet reached Prüm in its flight. The region was still calm, still formed a motionless circle; it marched in endless billows of hills toward the west only in Käthe's imagination.

"That boy is unpolitical, like everybody else here," Wenzel Hainstock once said to Käthe when she—later—talked with him about Ludwig Thelen. "They're all raised as Catholics, instinctively dislike fascism, and regard politics as a natural disaster."

"So do I," Käthe said quickly. "I regard politics as a natural disaster too."

"And nothing can be done about natural disasters, is that it?" he asked. He intended this to sound sardonic, but it merely sounded bitter.

"It ought to be possible to calculate the war," Ludwig Thelen said. "To calculate it precisely. What I don't like about mathematics is that it deals only with abstract objects. Right-angled triangles. Prime numbers. Why not with irregular triangles? It ought to be possible to deduce axioms from concrete prime numbers too."

Since Käthe was an excellent mathematician, she understood his meaning.

"I think it's wonderful," she said, "that mathematics is restricted to structures and consequently produces abstractions. And in the end they aren't abstractions at all, but concrete laws. What does a structure consist of, when you look at it closely? Of rectangularity. Of indivisibility."

"The prime number seventeen is indivisible," he said quietly, in his measured way, "but from that it follows that it consists of a remainder that is unpredictable."

"And you are unwilling to accept that?"

"Yes, I am unwilling to accept that."

They lay on the short, dry grass of a sloping pasture beside a juniper bush; clouds paraded across a vast sky. Käthe saw the clouds indistinctly because she had removed her glasses. On their walks they had never met anybody. After their third rendezvous, Käthe wore her striped sleeveless linen dress. Ludwig Thelen never tried to touch her.

"Prüm is a damnable small town," he said; "I could never dare to come up to your room some evening. And I simply have no desire to lie in a meadow with you."

Käthe had a furnished room in the quarter near the old tanneries. Ludwig Thelen lived with relatives.

"But you are already lying in a meadow with me," Käthe said.

He shook his head in his decisive fashion. She needed only to recall the note in his composition book to realize that he was not shy. To her the meadow would not have been absolutely unpleasant.

"Perhaps we might spend a weekend in Cologne or Trier sometime," she said. "Of course we'd have to go separately, but we could meet there, take rooms in the same hotel."

"Say," he said swiftly and softly, "that's a swell idea. Let's do it!"

She sat up and put on her glasses. "Next Saturday I can't," she said. For two more Saturdays she found plausible excuses; after that he already had his call-up and she her order to proceed to Cologne. She told him she did not intend to obey that order.

"What do you intend to do?" he asked.

"I don't know," she said. "Dissolve into thin air."

She had the vague idea of going to Trier or Aachen, cities that lay close to the western frontier and had also already been abandoned by their populations, so it was said. Perhaps it would be possible to live in a deserted city if it were large enough. If you were lucky enough to reach it, and then once there, you could avoid the patrols. Käthe imagined streets soundless but for her own footsteps. She would break into an apartment, a grocery store. In Prüm she had observed grocers closing the shutters of shops that were still full of wares. Romantic ideas of solitude and robbery. For the first time she tried to calculate exactly when the war would be over.

"I'll take you to my sisters in Winterspelt," Ludwig Thelen said.

She knew that the farm he came from was run by his two sisters and his very old father. During one of their walks he had once pointed westward and said: "Winterspelt is twenty kilometers from here. I must show it to you sometime."

"Your sisters would say no thanks," Käthe said. "Besides, it's simply impossible."

"My sisters will be delighted to have you there." The way he said it sounded convincing. "And not only because they can use every extra hand. Why is it impossible?"

"For example, because I would not receive any more ration

cards. Read the posters. Anyone who fails to obey the evacuation order will no longer receive ration cards."

He shrugged. "At the farm you'll eat better than you've ever eaten here."

"They'll look for me," she said. "It will be dangerous for your family to have me in the house."

He considered. Then he said: "Johannes Näckel is the local Party leader. He's been very quiet lately. Besides, I'll go to see him and tell him where to get off."

It was still pitch dark when Käthe left Prüm next morning and climbed up through the woods to the top of the hill. Her suitcase was still light. By the edge of the road, not far from Rommersheimer Held, she waited for Ludwig Thelen. He still had one day left, would have to report to Koblenz next day. Käthe, on the other hand, was supposed to have been at Hahnplatz the previous evening; she had been assigned to a group of two hundred residents who were to be taken to Cologne in trucks. She imagined the roll call, the names being called out. She had considered where she would be safest for the few hours, and had decided on the school. And in fact no one was there, not even the janitor; perhaps he had left with the transport from which she had dispensed herself. The faculty room was locked, but the classrooms were open; she spread her coat on the linoleum floor of the senior classroom, lay down, and listened to the commotion of an army in flight through the small town. Around two o'clock she set out, and met not a soul all the way to the woods. The noise grew steadily fainter after she entered them; the beeches posed an ever denser barrier between her and the noise; and on the top, on the open plateau where there were only the road and the night sky, nothing more could be heard.

## 5.

Young Thelen came along in a car with Wenzel Hainstock at the wheel. (For a trip like this you appealed to Hainstock with his old Adler.) Käthe was introduced to the driver, barely made out his name, sat down in the back seat. During the half hour to Winterspelt there was hardly any talk.

When they recalled this drive later on, Käthe habitually said to Hainstock: "Don't think I didn't notice the way you looked at me in the rear-view mirror, Wenzel."

He did not deny that on the drive to Winterspelt he had repeatedly looked in the mirror, and not because of the traffic. Käthe's head and shoulders blocked his rear vision anyhow; he really should have said to her: "Please move a bit to one side."

Usually he gave no answer to her question: "What were you thinking then?" But once he said: "What I thought was that the old saying isn't true."

"What old saying?"

"It's the unexpected that usually happens. It happens only rarely."

She let a few moments pass before going on with her teasing. "But you simply dumped Ludwig Thelen and me in front of the door, didn't even get out, drove right off again."

"I knew well enough why you'd come to Winterspelt. Young Thelen had asked me to drive his teacher to a safe refuge. So I knew I'd be seeing more of you."

"The great trapper," Käthe said mockingly. "He can sit and bide his time."

At the Thelen farm she was given much the same sort of reception as that orderly who asked for a lamp for Dincklage. Ludwig Thelen had been acutely embarrassed and had said to her: "They're always that way at the beginning. You'll see, it will all straighten out." He proved to be right; after he left that noon because he had to report to the army next morning in Koblenz, Therese and Elise, who were bursting with curiosity, immediately organized a full-scale Kaffeeklatsch. Later, when they found out that they could count on Käthe in the matter of Gorbatov, the three became a tight-knit clique. It was a help that the letters Ludwig sent her were of such a nature that they could be passed on to the family to read. And it proved fortunate that she had always used the formal pronoun of address with Ludwig. Moreover, he took the precaution to write—first from a garrison in Saxony, later from the eastern front—weekly to the family, to Käthe only every two weeks.

But that first morning had been bad. She had sat down on the stove bench in the main room of the farmhouse and stared at the scoured tabletop, at the chairs with their chipped brown paint. Tacked to the door of a closet were yellowed postcards and photos. Cheap, cracked dishes on a sideboard. Alongside that, a crucifix, china-white on brown wood. The buzz of flies. How and why had she come here? What kept her from asking Ludwig Thelen whether the man who had brought her here could not take her away again immediately was, in the first place, the sheer impossibility of thinking any further goal, and secondly her obstinacy. Shit, she thought—for her glance had fallen on the huge Thelen manure heap outside the window, then on the gray-stuccoed, characterless single-family house across the street, the Battalion Command Post, where there was still bustling military activity—all that slovenly activity of the 18th Motorized—shit, but I'll stay here, I have no choice.

Ludwig Thelen sought an opportunity to be alone with her before he departed. She refused what he perhaps hoped for from her, a kiss; but recalling the so-called fate of Lorenz Gieding, for the first time she was candid with him.

"Get out from under whenever you can, Ludwig," she said. "Pretend illness, and if that doesn't work and you're sent to the front anyhow, try to be taken prisoner. It's essential to survive, understand, to survive!"

She was glad to see that there was no protest in his eyes, only astonishment.

"Will I find you here when I come back?" he asked.

"No," she said. "It's quite certain you won't."

A few days later Therese came to her room in the early morning and said: "You have to disappear from the village for a while."

Last night, she said, Johannes Näckel, the innkeeper and local Party leader, had dropped a hint to her father: in the next few days Winterspelt would be combed for people who were illegally staying in the village.

"And where should I go?" Käthe asked.

"To Herr Hainstock," Therese said. When she saw that the name meant nothing to Käthe, she added: "He's the man who drove you here." She told Käthe what she knew about Hainstock and described the way to the quarry.

"Will you have any trouble on my account?" Käthe asked.

"You mean, will anyone denounce us? Not a chance. Anyone who did would have a tough time in this village. Especially now when the war is almost over."

Käthe thought of her own reception. She could vividly imagine what would happen to the search squad when it entered the Thelen farm. And the Thelen farm was one of the friendliest in this Eifel village.

That was the way Käthe came to Hainstock. What she did not know, never found out, was that on one of his visits to the village he had taken Therese Thelen aside, sworn her to silence, and then told her: "If this schoolteacher you have with you should ever have any trouble, send her to me."

So he hadn't merely sat there biding his time, as Käthe thought.

*Notes for an Essay on Political Consciousness*

Käthe's father has been characterized as a (liberal?) opponent of Hitler. Had he been a follower of the dictator and a member of the Party—would Käthe have grown up to be a young Nazi?

But she had felt very much at ease in that home, with those parents, and had not wanted to leave.

Her consumption of literature. Intellectuality as behavior.

For her first boy-friend she chose an artist with a strong antiwar bent.

During the night of March 8, and later as well, it did not occur to her to hate the British fliers who had dropped the bomb. She said to Dr. Mohr that what she hated was the war, but it may be assumed that she meant those who had started the war. Her father and Lorenz Gieding had no doubt about the identity of the persons in question. But it is significant that Käthe accepted these opinions without opposition.

She had been lucky in her parents.

Her advice to young Thelen (that compound of mathematics and Catholic upbringing) to become a deserter was really her first active step of political opposition.

Then she fell under Hainstock's tutelage. She declared herself willing to accept the following components of the system: History as a history of class struggle. The origin of alienation. Labor power as a commodity, its sale and purchase, surplus value. Bourgeois democracy as providing a mere fiction of political equality. The accumulation of capital. The origin of crises. The origin of fascism and imperialist wars. Socialism.

That was, after all, a great deal.

She could not make herself believe in the coming of a classless society. She found she had no desire to think about utopias. She had doubts about dialectics; this hop-skip-and-jump law struck her as somewhat mechanical; she could conceive different laws of movement. That ideas were not substances in themselves but only reflections of the conditions of production at any given time might apply to many ideas, but not to all. Since everything was labor, she said to Hainstock, there could not be any contradiction between the base and the superstructure.

Such debates were built into the system. She shook the Marxist stereotype only when she suddenly exclaimed that she too, like young Thelen, regarded politics as a natural disaster, or when she refused to discuss the "ifs" of history, history's conditional clauses.

Her journey to the west, that *instinctual resultant of a directional movement*, or *migration*, as Dincklage called it, in no way represented a dialectical process.

But aside from all this, in the summer of 1944, thanks to Wenzel Hainstock's tutelage, Käthe Lenk possessed a clear political consciousness.

Hainstock's linguistic influence: the way he quite naturally talked about the *fascist gang*. His view of politics as crime. Accounts of the concentration camp.

Although she fell in love with Major Dincklage, it is inconceivable that she would have started an affair with him if he had been an adherent of the fascist gang, or even just a snappy soldier and nothing more.

Dincklage's antipathy to the cause he was serving constituted his military existence. That made him acceptable to Käthe.

"It is not man's consciousness that determines his existence but his social existence that determines his consciousness."

Considering the course Käthe Lenk had taken, one might be tempted to say it was not a social but a personal existence that determined her consciousness.

She did not live within any social pattern, was not governed by any conditions of production whose nature she could grasp.

It is true that all her experiences and actions had reference to the war, but she rejected the theory of the war's economic causation. If the war was "the adventure of the German fascist gang"

(Hainstock), it was also a natural disaster, a disaster of human nature.

Her parents were heritage. Lorenz Gieding was already her own choice. The journey to the west, then Hainstock, then Dincklage, likewise. Actually, there was nothing to observe but a meager network of relationships with people. But within this network she invariably made political decisions in the same manner.

Instinctively. Out of personal existence.

On the role of instinct in the formation of political consciousness.

Decisions out of personal likes and dislikes.

A partisan without a party.

*Conditions of Production, Nature Grasped*

By the beginning of August the danger was over. Käthe returned to the Thelen farm, once again took over the housework. Every morning she wet-mopped the bedrooms and the big all-purpose room. Therese and Elise said that really wasn't necessary, but she would not be dissuaded. She changed the water in the pail after having wrung out the mop three times, established a rational system of dividing up the space, worked hard, although she did not scrub on her hands and knees. What she produced was not high polish but a kind of obscure and constant cleanliness. Dusting. Cooking the midday dinner. Washing dishes, three times a day. Once a week washing and ironing the laundry. She undertook all these tasks with determined care, although they were all—with the exception of the last two—repugnant to her. She undertook them because, as she said, they were the lot of all women, and just once in her life she wanted to experience it. As an "educated girl" she had, in her mother's home, needed to experience only a little of it. So this was what awaited all women, what was expected of them, even those who practiced a profession or were rich, for even if they did not have to carry out all household tasks themselves, it was nevertheless assumed that such work was to constitute the real content of their lives: overseeing the inventory of houses, cleaning and maintaining. The life of all women revolved around this special form of exploitation, unpaid drudgery lasting from the time they got up in the morning until they went to bed. It could be alleviated by technology, but not abolished. The life of all women, but not hers. She would be the one solitary and absolute exception. She could no more shape a definite picture of her future life than she could bring herself to think about utopias, but she was determined never again to mop floors, peel potatoes, or iron sheets. The Winterspelt phase would be over in the near future. She was using the interval to have an experience.

"If you don't want to keep your household up to snuff, someone else will have to do it for you," the Marxist Hainstock said; with regard to women and to housekeeping he was rather a reactionary.

"Certainly," Käthe replied, unmoved by this sermon on the iron laws of the division of labor. "Your shack is always marvelously clean. Anyone could eat off your floor. You do your bed perfectly. And you can also cook quite tolerably. For me those would be the strongest reasons to marry you."

Hainstock was not the man to take her up on this and ask whether she had other, possibly feebler but still sufficient reasons for such a decision.

The two Thelen sisters taught her how to bake bread.

She, for her part, instituted the custom of a daily instead of Saturday bath. For this purpose the stove that stood in the laundry at the Thelen farm had to be stoked with beechwood logs, a huge kettle placed on it and filled with water; when the water was hot it was dipped out with a pail and poured into a large wooden tub. All in all, it was the devil of a job, but fun when the steam became so thick that it acted like a mild photographic filter. Their flesh was diffused by the mist, nearly Tahitian brown (Käthe while the effect of her sunbaths in front of the cave on the Apert lasted), softly powdered with brick dust (Therese), of an indeterminate light color (Elise). They scrubbed each other's backs. Käthe thought that Elise, who was two years younger than Therese and herself, was the prettiest of them. She had long, graceful legs and a neck that rose proudly out of her shoulders. Käthe said she should wear her hair up so that the lovely diagonal that marked her neck off from her head would show to advantage. But Elise did not take her advice.

Afternoons, Käthe sometimes relieved the sisters of looking after the cows. That was light work, really not work at all; she could lie in the pasture and read, need fear no disturbance; the low-flying planes had never yet attacked grazing cows. When she looked up from her reading, she listened for a moment or two to the cannonade in the north; the hollow in which she lay muffled the sounds of remoter rumblings.

## While Käthe Tends Cows

In the sector of Army Group B the American forces intended, as a necessary prerequisite for their attack across the Rhine, to widen the breach in the West Wall which they had made some time earlier at Vossenack (southeast of Aachen), and then to take the two dams on the Roer and the Urft. Over weeks of fighting, this intention was frustrated by counterattacks. In particular the heavy defensive battles fought in this sector from the middle of September to November were wholly related to the preparations for a new offensive. . . . These battles, however, had consumed strong forces on both sides. (General Hasso von Manteuffel, "Die Schlacht in den Ardennen 1944–1945" ["The Battle in the Ardennes, 1944–45"] in: Jacobsen und Rohwer, *Entscheidungsschlachten des Zweiten Weltkriegs* [*Decisive Battles of World War Two*], *Frankfurt am Main*, 1960)

## Involvement

As has already been mentioned, it was four days after that supper in the Battalion Command Post—which took place on Monday, October 2—before Käthe summoned up the courage to tell
Wenzel Hainstock anything about her relations with the major.
She was in more haste with the latter. As early as Tuesday she
said to Dincklage: "I have a friend here."

She described Hainstock, and how it had come about that she
had linked herself with the man in the quarry.

They had agreed to meet late at night, after Dincklage's return
from his nightly inspection of the lines; and Käthe let some time
pass after hearing the command car depart before she entered the
house across the street. She sensed the impatience with which
Dincklage was waiting for her, but first began talking to him
about Hainstock; she wanted him to know about that, before she
shared his bed with him ("the enemy's bed," according to Hainstock).

Although he had other things in mind, Dincklage immediately
realized he would have to discuss the subject. He feigned interest
first of all in Hainstock's Marxism, spoke of his own studies in political economy, said he would like to meet Hainstock, that he
had long wished for the chance to discuss matters with a cultivated Communist. At the phrase "discuss matters with" Käthe
concealed the face she made by straightening her glasses; if anyone had asked her why she made a face, she probably would have
answered much as she later did in regard to Dincklage's statement, which she had passed on to Hainstock, about the military
structure, halfway rational behavior, and the least he could still do
in this war. "Sounds kinda wishy-washy," she would have said.

Hainstock and the major never met. On the basis of the rules of
political underground work, Hainstock had blamed Käthe for
even giving his name to Dincklage; but he had stopped scolding

when Käthe buried her face in her hands. This scene took place early in the morning of October 7, when Käthe outlined the major's plan and asked for Hainstock's assistance.

Finally, after going on enough about political economy, Dincklage said: "It must be horrible to lose you!"

"Who is saying anything like that?" Käthe replied angrily. "What puts such an idea into your head?"

In this crisis in their relationship—which developed so rapidly, at the beginning of what was merely their third meeting—Dincklage acted in the only right way: he kept silent. He did not even look at Käthe, but began arranging papers on his desk.

"Is one thing supposed to stop just because another begins?" Käthe said. "That's really idiotic."

He looked up from his papers.

"Yes, I suppose you're right," he said. "Try it."

Did he want to demonstrate his tolerance? Hardly. He had no doubts about the outcome of the trial. In those circumstances he could afford to appear generous.

## The Cave in the Apert

### 1.

As an addendum to the account of that moment in which Käthe said to Hainstock, "Tell me how you became a Communist," it must be mentioned that she was wearing nothing when she made this request. She was taking one of her noonday sunbaths, lying on the patch of moss and grass outside the cave in the Apert. Käthe was noted for needing to lie only for an hour in the sun in order to assume the color of chestnuts—of rather translucent chestnut shells, if such existed.

Hainstock, for his part, a worker who had labored in the open air all his life and who therefore never dreamed of taking sunbaths, was standing dressed in the entrance to the cave, looking down at Käthe—presumably she provided him with a vision of an Indian squaw, though one with glasses—and smoking his pipe. Before she undressed for the first time because the sun was shining so gloriously, Käthe had asked him whether he had any objection. He had said no, but secretly he was surprised by Käthe's openness. By now he was enjoying living with so free-spirited and natural a girl.

The Apert is the rather arbitrary name we have chosen for a height, a hill, a knoll, a volcanic formation. At its foot an abortive tunnel had been started during the building of the railroad line from Prüm through Bleialf to Saint-Vith. Let us situate it in, say, the region on the southwest fringe of the Schnee-Eifel, an area in which as far as the eye can see—and from the high ridges it can see far—there are no villages, no hamlets, not even a solitary farmhouse here and there, nothing but patches of forest and junipered slopes. In such a region the knowledge of this cavern in the mountain might easily die out, and not just since the railroad stopped running at the beginning of the war.

Hainstock, that geologist and specialist in hiding places, did not find the cave by chance; he came across a reference to it in Rappel and Reuling's book. When he set out to hunt for it—he had to hunt because the two authors gave no more than two cursory lines to the description of its position—he found it three hours' walk to the east of Winterspelt. It proved to be perfectly dry, spacious, suitable even for a stay of considerable length. In the course of several hikes—in this case he did not use his car—he brought supplies of food and blankets to the hiding place. For he did not trust the peacefulness of the locale; he counted on situations in which even Matthias Arimond's protection would no longer shield him. A full-fledged fascist system would try to annihilate even its last remaining opponents before it collapsed.

When Käthe turned up in his shack on July 18, he at first gave her his bed and made do himself with a sleeping bag on the floor; but contrary to the generous offer he had made to Therese Thelen ("If this schoolteacher you have with you should ever have any trouble, send her to me") when Käthe arrived in Winterspelt, he was in some embarrassment over what to do with her. He knew several very reliable persons deeper inside the country who at his request would unhesitatingly hide Käthe in their houses. He also thought of Arimond and his house in Koblenz. But when he made these proposals to Käthe, he encountered unexpected and obstinate resistance. She flatly refused to be taken into the hinterland.

"I'm not going back there again," she said. "Why can't I stay here with you? Am I disturbing you?"

He asked himself whether this was already a sign of liking him. In any case it was evidence that it was not unpleasant for her to be living under one roof with him. He did not reply, merely placed his hand on her forearm, and she did not withdraw her arm.

On the same day this conversation took place, July 20, they heard on the army radio station from Calais the first reports of the attempted assassination of Hitler. Since Hainstock had told her about his political past, it was quite clear why he stood up and said: "We must get away at once."

On their way through the darkness to the cave in the Apert— he had loaded up the two of them with more food, his sleeping bag, and all sorts of articles—he explained to her that now there would be huge roundups, mass searches throughout the entire Reich. Everyone known to be an enemy of the dictatorship, including former camp inmates released long ago, could expect to be arrested. (Hainstock's assessment of the general situation was correct; there were mass arrests after July 20, but in his own case no order for his arrest was ever issued. For jurisdictional reasons the Gestapo did not operate within the main battle zone.)

That they slept together in the Apert cave was in the nature of things, resulted inevitably from their dependence on each other, from the basalt walls that closed in around them at night, the darkness, the protection Hainstock was offering Käthe, his enlightened attitude toward the life of the body.

It was only natural that Hainstock regarded the cave in the Apert as a love nest, especially when he remembered moments such as that one: the forested slope opposite, in the southwest, already half in shadow; at its foot the brook from which, as soon as

it was dark enough, he would fetch water; then the rusty rails of
the railroad; and before him on the grass and moss, Indian-brown
Käthe, naked and thin, with legs drawn up and eyes closed (the
glasses now lying beside her in the grass), while he stood dressed
in the black entrance to the cave, smoking his pipe. He told himself later that it had been a romantic idyl, enclosed within but excluded from a world in which people were shot, hanged, tortured;
but he had no conscientious scruples about this because he had already lived for a dozen years in a world in which people were shot,
hanged, tortured, and because this girl came his way unexpectedly
and unhoped for.

Now she was saying to him: "Tell me how you became a Communist."

It may be assumed that Hainstock's thesis that the world of nature could not on principle be subject to ownership thoroughly
appealed to Käthe. Her natural world, too, would never be anyone's property.

Some time later, after they had both returned, she to the
Thelen farm and he to his shack, she had said to him: "I don't
love you at all. I like you."

That was honest and had its value, but Hainstock really would
have preferred to have been loved once more in his life. That was
the way it was: he sometimes had temporary but never lasting
happiness.

Every few nights he went to Winterspelt to ask Arnold Weinandy whether any search was in progress for himself or Käthe, and
even after he had become convinced that there was no longer any
danger he postponed leaving the cave for a few days longer. He
abandoned their cover only at the beginning of August. It was
also beginning to rain and turning damply cold. Käthe sat shivering in the sleeping bag.

2.

Hainstock had also used the cave as a hiding place for the package containing Schefold's painting. Käthe found it, asked what
was in it, and when Hainstock told her she begged until he

yielded and allowed her to open the package, although Schefold had actually sealed it and written on it in black india ink: *Property of the Städel Art Institute, Frankfort am Main.* Käthe had to unwrap the painting from a thick layer of corrugated cardboard and tissue paper. The glass was undamaged. She took it to the entrance of the cave for light. It was in a brown wooden frame, with a narrow mat; the area of the painting itself was small, at most two or three decimeters on a side. In the left corner was the signature, in as strong and neatly executed a hand as the painting itself: *Klee, 1930, Polyphonically Bounded White.*

She recalled having heard the name of this painter once before, from the lips of Lorenz Gieding, of course, but she had never before seen one of his works. She traced the movement of the chromatics that surrounded the white rectangle in the center, although these colors were themselves within horizontal or vertical rectangles. The movement from a dark border to a bright interior actually had the effect of polyphony because the painter had contrived to make the tonal values of the watercolors permeate one another. The transparency, the light coming through the painting, increased toward the center until it vanished in the white rectangle, which was perhaps a light source of maximum intensity, but perhaps also merely something white, a nothing.

Käthe at once recognized that this was an entirely different kind of art from that of Lorenz Gieding, in whose eyes objects were consumed in flames. In this painter, in Klee's work, wholly new objects, objects never seen before, were created.

"A wonderful painting," she said to Hainstock, who was looking over her shoulder. He too had never seen the picture before; he shrugged and said nothing.

She repacked it carefully—though of course the seals remained broken—but during their stay in the cave, unpacked it twice more to look at it. She counted and discovered that the painter had used six successively weakened hues to guide the eye into the center and from there back to the strongest coloristic energy. With the aid of little sticks that she cut to size—she had no ruler—she reckoned out that the rectangles were precisely calculated as to subdivision, arrangement, and measurements; all had reference to the fundamental rectangle but varied its proportions on a mathematical and musical principle.

"The painting is a diagram," she said, but Hainstock did not react to that either.

She had him tell her the story of Schefold, expressed a desire to meet the man, but Hainstock refused for reasons already given.

### 3.

Simple movement strikes us as banal. The temporal element must be eliminated. Yesterday and tomorrow as simultaneities. Polyphony in music met this craving to some degree. And quintets such as that in *Don Giovanni* are closer to us than the epical movement in *Tristan*. Mozart and Bach are more modern than the nineteenth century. If temporality in music could be overcome by a retroactive movement penetrating into our consciousness, a second flowering of the older music would be conceivable. Polyphonic painting is superior to music in that the temporal element has become more spatial. The concept of simultaneity emerges here even more richly. (A note on polyphony by Paul Klee, 1917)

### 4.

"If you know it all so well that you even showed him the way," Käthe said when Hainstock described to her Schefold's trips back and forth between the fronts, "why didn't we use this same route to go to the Americans, instead of to this cave?"

Hainstock could think of no answer to this question. He had at times considered fleeing to the Americans if danger threatened him directly, but had repeatedly rejected this solution because it would have separated him from his quarry. During the very period which he regarded as decisive for himself and the quarry—the months immediately after the end of the war—he would be stuck in an internment camp in Belgium, perhaps even in France, but at any rate altogether out of it. He felt it was important for him to be on the spot when the war ended.

"We're just as safe here," he said. They were sitting inside the cave, and the entrance, in the twilight, was only a gray fabric.

Later on he pursued the idea, reflected that the Americans would have separated Käthe and himself immediately after their arrival, would have sent them to camps divided by sexes. Then they would hardly have come to know each other; later he probably would have had only a vague memory of Käthe. But every evening Käthe swore that sooner or later she would pry out of Hainstock the secret route that Schefold had taken.

### Miscellanies on Käthe's Affairs

Without consultation of any sort, after forty-eight hours Dincklage and Käthe stopped making a secret of their relationship. As major, battalion commander, local commandant, and wearer of the Knight's Cross, Dincklage had no need to play hide-and-seek, and Käthe did not care anyhow; she would soon be leaving Winterspelt for good. From Wednesday on they talked to each other on the village street, took walks together, and met as frequently as Dincklage's duties and Käthe's work permitted. This public behavior compelled Käthe to put an end to the period of guilty conscience toward Hainstock as early as (or as late as) Thursday evening. For she had to forestall his hearing about it first from some villager.

Dincklage had a special reason for not treating their connection with excessive discretion. He told himself that if Käthe went on coming to him only late at night, their affair would become purely an affair of the bed. He did not want that. (Anyhow, in addition to their other meetings, she came to his quarters every night, at least until Friday.)

In talking with Hainstock she realized the intensity of her feelings for Dincklage. There was no question of her taking the freedom she had tried to claim ("Is one thing supposed to stop just because another begins?"), even though Dincklage had given her leave to do so ("Try it"). There were some things that excluded other things.

Besides, Hainstock would certainly not have availed himself of any such possibility.

"Good Lord, Käthe!"

In Hainstock's exclamation she sensed not only lament and despair, but also quick acceptance of something irrevocable. The extinguishing of a light. He was not the man who would want to share her with anyone.

He was a steady and iron-gray man. She realized that it had been wrong of her not to content herself with him, for the short time she would be staying here. It had been quite unnecessary to get involved with Dincklage. She should have pulled herself together.

She concealed her impatience to get away, to return to Winterspelt, to the house where Dincklage awaited her.

To begin with they had talked about the bird, which Käthe was afraid of. Hainstock had described the habits of owls. At twilight and at night they flew through old forests, swooped down on field mice and small birds, gulped down their prey with hair or feathers, and afterward spat out the indigestible portions in the form of pellets.

"Come winter you'll hear its mating call," Hainstock had told her. "There are many of these owls living in the woods."

"I've heard it often," she had replied. "We had a lot of them around Berlin, too."

She recalled from last winter the nightly screeching of the owls in the gardens of Lankwitz, a deep who-who-who followed by a higher-pitched, prolonged, trilling oo-oo-oo. She never would have thought of these cries as love songs.

"In the winter," she had added, "I'll be over the hills and far away."

To that he had not responded.

A while later—they had already begun discussing Major Dinck-lage's measures—he said: "For the first time today I started to doubt that all danger would be over if only I lived in Bleialf."

All day long he had been on the hill above the quarry listening to the silence, observing the immobility—the measures taken by Major Dincklage.

In the case of Hainstock, and in the case of Dincklage as well, Käthe's emotions were complicated by criticism. She had never been "mindlessly" in love. Dincklage provoked her critical sense more strongly than Hainstock. To Hainstock she could say, "I don't love you at all, I like you," whereas in the case of Dincklage it is highly probable that she may not have liked him at all, but only loved him. She was capable of observing herself, of noting how her criticism of Dincklage repeatedly swung round into longing for him.

At such times she did not like herself. Her capacity for self-criticism was, in general, considerable. She was always trying to remind herself that she was no better than those she criticized.

But there were times, moments, in which she liked Dincklage a great deal.

At some point during the following week, while the plan was already in progress, he told her how he had prevented the evacuation of Winterspelt. He did not say why. Yet why not? She would have been pleased.

Then he told her: "At the same time I proposed to Colonel Hoffmann that we blow up the viaduct at Hemmeres. I already had my plan and I knew that it would be much easier to carry it out if this railroad viaduct stood, but still I proposed blowing it up. Can you explain that to me?"

He did not seriously expect her to explain it to him, and Käthe made no comment because she did not want to imperil the plan at the last moment by saying: "That proves that your plan is only something abstract to you, an obsessional idea, something you don't really want to carry out at all."

But she liked him when he asked such questions about himself.

Or when he monologued: "I have never had to detail firing squads, have never been involved in operations against the populace. That's the chief reason I have always refused to go to Russia." And with great satisfaction he patted his right hip.

"But heaven help me," he said, "what nonsense I've sometimes had to go along with. I've carried out attack orders or hold-your-ground orders that were sheer idiocy from a military point of view —orders that everybody all the way up to Division agreed were absolutely wrong from every possible viewpoint. I've seen hundreds, no, thousands of dead and wounded who were dead and wounded because some asshole at some army desk thought he was a great commander. But I obeyed, always."

He added: "I have never defied an order."

If this plan succeeded, Käthe reflected, it would balance out all those orders he had not defied.

Dincklage, that ambivalent and ethical personality, need not have been concerned that his relationship to Käthe would be reduced to a matter of the bed alone. Insofar as it was such, it ended, to his disappointment, as early as the night of Friday the sixth and the morning of Saturday the seventh of October.

That night, at any rate, Käthe slept with him for the last time, and even then she was not fully concentrating on the matter. The plans he had revealed to her in the "chief's" room of the battalion office before they went up to his attic bedroom—those plans were of a kind that diverted her attention from everything else.

We must picture the scene once more! This time she had found him bent over maps under the dim light of the ceiling lamp, and he began to talk of his plans just as naturally and without preliminary as he had remarked six days before, when she entered the orderly room lamp in hand, "That saves my evenings." Several times, when the pain in his hip joint became too acute, he straightened up, then, with the aid of a flashlight, seemed literally to crawl back into the map. Käthe, who stood beside him, did not follow the cone of light from this flashlight. She was only pretending to be interested in the position of the hamlet of Hemmeres and the railroad viaduct that remained there, over which Dincklage's pencil repeatedly circled. She listened to the mathematical tone in which he spoke, waited for his voice to assume a vibrating note, a touch of excitement, perhaps even something of adventurousness; for after all, that too must have entered in if an officer only thirty-four years old were preparing a military coup. But the vibrating note, the excitement and adventurousness, did not come.

She was herself plunged into extraordinary excitement. If the trick could be turned, this would be a real trick. She was tempted to grasp Dincklage's shoulders, to shake him in order to provoke him to at least a semblance of emotion.

The lightness with which she informed him that she knew someone who could get in touch with the Americans, that almost offhand tone of, "Oh, if that's the problem . . ." with which she eliminated Dincklage's chief difficulty, was sheer pretense.

In truth she already realized what she was being dragged into, was already frightened. Dincklage did not protest her transforming his abstract speculations into concrete possibilities, but even as she was engaged in this process by mentioning to him (for the first time) Hainstock's name, by speaking of her acquaintanceship with Hainstock (she did not tell him about its true nature until the following night), she discovered in herself a kind of appreciation of the possible value of abstraction. These thoughts were as yet only dabs of reverie, the Morse code of skepticism, as yet undeciphered.

She certainly had let herself in for something! And when she asked herself: for what, she could only think of that phrase picked up from the boys she taught: a trick. She framed it as they would have done: "Quite a trick, hey?"

Not even she herself would have been able to say when she decided not to sleep with Dincklage any longer—whether it was already this very night in which she could no longer concentrate on tenderness, but kept thinking excitedly about all the things that had to be done from dawn on, or whether she made the decision only during her conversation with Dincklage on the following day, when she was disappointed, distinctly disturbed and filled with forebodings of things going wrong, because Dincklage insisted on his stipulation that Schefold must come through the line, and in fact made a point of honor of this stipulation. It is conceivable that when the operation began—and it began when Dincklage unveiled his plan to her—she unconsciously behaved like a boxer who lives continently for a certain period before the fight. But why would it have to be *unconscious?* A plan such as this, she might very well have consciously told herself, did not permit Dincklage and herself to be continually relaxing.

The rather more likely premise, it must be said, is that their relationship was thrown off course in that conversation of October 7, that it suffered a fracture. As a result of her encounter with his code of honor, her experience with the sum total of his attitudes, the scales of her emotions shifted: from loving to not-liking. The not-liking tipped the balance.

His plan excited her, but she wanted to shake him out of the abstract coldness with which he presented it to her. And she found an easy way to do that when she converted the idea from an intellectual possibility to an act. But when she sat opposite Dincklage at his desk the next day and listened to him setting his condition, she held the wrist of her own hand in the other hand; and she persisted in this gesture which was typical of her when she was offering resistance, when there was something she did not at all like.

They retained all the other modes of their association. They took walks, sat in the orderly room evenings, had long talks, also exchanged embraces and kisses. Käthe spent all her free time with Dincklage, neglected Hainstock, paid only brief visits to the quarry, and really only for the purpose of obtaining news, of finding out how the discussions between Schefold and the Americans were going. She employed the letter box.

Not tenseness but tensions entered into her relationship with Dincklage. If he felt offended, he was not aware of it. Once he told her about his youthful affair with that young farm woman of Bentheim County, who was nevertheless five years older than himself.

"Elise," Käthe said instantly. "Elise Thelen would be the right wife for you."

He looked at her and said: "Now you are being tasteless, Käthe."

He pleaded his case casually, in statements such as that he would, if he were married, be reluctant to use the phrase *my wife*. She repeated these words to Hainstock, hoping he would at least sense that her relationship with Dincklage was not quite so simple as he had imagined. But she was disappointed when Hainstock indicated that he thought Dincklage's remark merely a maneuver.

What impressed her most, of course, was that Dincklage calmly continued his love affair with her. Walks, long talks in the evenings, embraces, kisses. What man can put up with that sort of thing for long? She herself often had difficulty controlling herself.

At any rate, on the morning of October 12, when Käthe came pedaling out to Hainstock to tell him that Schefold had come through the line and arrived in Winterspelt, Hainstock was quite wrong in assuming she was coming straight from Dincklage's bed.

But on the other hand, from Thursday, October 5 (the day Käthe told him she had begun falling in love with an officer of the fascist troops) to the following Thursday, October 12, the day when everything was decided, Hainstock changed his mind in one respect. He was not so obtuse as to cling to his conviction that Käthe had gone over to the enemy camp.

## Pro and Con

By as early as Saturday, October 7, when Käthe unexpectedly
turned up early in the morning with her almost incredible news
about the major's aims, Hainstock could not help having doubts
about his "enemy camp" thesis.

His criticism of the plan coincided with Dincklage's, even
added some elements.

"How does this officer intend to get all his troops together at
one point?" he asked. "A battalion means four companies, something like twelve hundred men, and they're stretched out over the
area from south of Winterspelt to north of Wallmerath and
Elcherath. Those who don't happen to be on duty are loafing in
their quarters; the rest are standing guard in the two lines. What
pretext is he going to use to withdraw the sentries from the lines,
leaving the front unguarded? In a formation that size there is a
certain percentage of fascist noncoms who'll find it very peculiar
for a battalion in the main battle zone to assemble for a night roll
call without arms. Oh well, I don't underestimate the slavish obedience of the German Army; but oddly enough they're very much
on the alert when they smell a rat, anything that's against the
rules, against Führer and Reich. They've got a sixth sense for that
sort of thing, and then they're quite ready to oppose an order,
which otherwise they'd never do. All this officer needs is a single
sergeant who suspects the whole procedure is odd, and he'll be on
the telephone to Regiment the moment his chief lets him out of
sight. After all, he'll have to let at least his top sergeant know
what's up a few hours before the night alarm, otherwise the
topkick will go on strike; there's where a battalion commander's
power ends, and even if the top sergeant doesn't smell anything
fishy he'll have to drop a hint to the company leaders or else the
exercise won't run smoothly; but if he does smell something fishy

233

he'll be right on the telephone to Regiment, as I say. I know how that works."

He dropped off for a few moments into memories of the creaking noises made by the apparatus of the long-defunct army of the Austro-Hungarian Empire. It would sound exactly the same in a so-called modern army. Armies never change, Hainstock thought.

"It will be all right," the major said when Käthe presented Hainstock's objections. "In the first place Kammerer would never act that way. In the second place Herr Hainstock has not considered that I am a wearer of the Knight's Cross, or else he does not know what that means. I can count on each and every one of my company leaders to obey me unconditionally if ordered to arrest Kammerer or anybody else for refusing to obey an order."

"Hainstock thinks it possible," Käthe replied, "that Kammerer or someone else will secretly get in touch with your superiors."

"In that case Colonel Hoffman would telephone me first," Dincklage said. "I would reply that the person in question must have misunderstood something. But then I would know who the troublemaker was.

"As far as gathering the battalion in one place goes," he went on, "I have to admit that Herr Hainstock is right. That actually is technically difficult. And the greatest difficulty of all will be to persuade the Americans to behave correctly during their approach. Everything depends on their being able to follow my instructions exactly and being able to read the map sketches that I'll send them."

It struck Käthe that he did not say "that I'll send them through you" or "through Hainstock" or "through Schefold." (Probably he would have said "through Herr Hainstock" or "through Doktor Schefold.") Was this his way of dodging the fact that his plans were being handled by persons other than himself?

He also avoided discussing the military problems of his project any further with her. She had the impression that it displeased him when she brought up such subjects; each time he cut her off curtly, for example when she felt she had to warn him against dropping even the merest hint about his plan to Kammerer because at such a point the man's disposition for blind obedience would come to an end. Obviously he was unaccustomed to receiving tactical advice from a woman. In such cases he would drop into his high, sharp eh-eh tone.

Which she, in the course of their relationship, had twice quite formally begged him not to use with her.

She had also once asked him in deadly earnest: "Is it really necessary for your trousers to have such a perfect crease all the time?" At first he was staggered. Then he laughed and replied with the same ironical meekness he had once used toward Colonel Hoffmann: "I'll do my best, Fräulein Lenk."

It was only after Hainstock had analyzed the situation in military terms that he came up with his objections on the grounds of Dincklage's virtually nonexistent support among the troops, the lack of a mass base, etc.

"Anything would be possible," he said, "if this person" (for once he did not say *this officer*) "could base his actions on a network of trustworthy men or at least on an intact Party cell in every company. But as things are . . ."

He made a gesture supposed to express hopelessness. Moreover, he told himself, he was committing a serious error in reasoning. The idea that Dincklage could possibly have trustworthy men or Party cells at his disposal assumed that he was more than an officer, a person—was, namely, a comrade. Ridiculous to imagine anything of the sort! The whole thing was merely the pointless act of a lone wolf.

"The foundations are lacking," Wenzel Hainstock said to Käthe Lenk. "And you're asking me to lend my support to this madness."

In Käthe's mind the arrogant idea took root that this affair was really and exclusively hers alone.

She had startled Dincklage out of a theoretical study; but when

she succeeded in translating his theory into practice he had posed
the impossible demand about Schefold's going through the line.

And Hainstock, who had actually refused his collaboration from
the start, finally went along hesitantly and without assuming
much risk; he kept carefully in the background. Why? Merely because someone was violating the rules his party had devised for resistance to fascist dictatorships. To Hainstock, Dincklage was an
outsider, an amateur—he did not abide by the rules and regulations of revolution. With repugnance, Käthe remembered the
false complacency of the expert in conspiracy, the smugness Hainstock had shown when he retreated to his role of letter box.

Moreover, he was altogether wrong even as an expert, Käthe
thought. It would have been simpler, more practical, and less dangerous if I had gone to the Americans.

When she considered the matter rightly, Dincklage and Hainstock were only throwing monkey wrenches into the works.

The American Kimbrough, and Schefold, that wayfarer between the fronts, did not place any reservations on themselves,
did not half back off, not even when Dincklage mysteriously
requested a contact with the courier at a time when nobody yet
knew what there really was to discuss. With Kimbrough's approval Schefold was going through the line although nothing was
as yet ripe for agreement and it had already been shown that the
American army felt not the slightest desire to rake in Dincklage
and his battalion.

On the German side she was the only one who inexorably,
forthrightly, unflinchingly, kept this enterprise moving forward.

Too inexorably, too forthingly, too unflinchingly, it occasionally
occurred to her when she thought about Schefold.

Nevertheless she managed to control herself every time, forbore
to speak her mind to Dincklage or Hainstock. Whenever she was
on the point of telling the men her frank opinion, she recalled in
good time her own irrevocable decision to make use of the night
of the coup to leave by the route that Schefold took, which she
would be getting out of Hainstock sooner or later. She had a full

right to go on pursuing her own plans once the operation reached
its climax, and she could no longer do anything more than wait to
see whether it succeeded or failed. But she could not shake off the
feeling that by leaving just at that point and yielding to her migratory impulse, she was after all engulfing herself in her own private, egotistic affairs. She felt she was being sly; her intention to
clear out on X Day (X Night, rather) was basically no different
from Hainstock's caution, Dincklage's code of honor.

On the day following that unfortunate conversation of October
7, Käthe said to Dincklage: "I've figured out what is wrong in
what you were trying to prove to me yesterday. You said: 'I am
staking everything. So I must insist that the Americans also stake
something.' That is what you said, isn't it?"

Dincklage agreed.

"But that is exactly what's wrong," Käthe said. "You absolutely
must come to the point where you expect nothing more from the
Americans, are not insisting on anything on their part."

She realized at once that in her zeal she had proceeded clumsily. She had phrased what she wanted to say much too bluntly.
Those phrases must have sounded unbearably pedagogical in his
ears. They sounded that way even in her own. She could not free
herself of the damnable schoolteacher within herself.

Helpless with anxiety, she nevertheless hoped he would give in.
The whole background of his plan would change if he gave in and
stopped insisting that Schefold come through the lines.

But he refused to change his mind. Or did he mean to indicate
—with his decision to summon Schefold when it was still much
too soon—that he had given up expecting anything from the
Americans?

Hypothesis concerning the behavior of Major Dinckage during
the period before he made his decision (for reasons which were
perhaps unknown even to himself):

It is established that when Colonel Hoffmann asked him about
the advisability of evacuating the civilian population from Winterspelt, all he could think of was that this procedure would sepa-

rate him from Käthe Lenk. From this it may be concluded that his behavior during the execution of his plan was also influenced by the consideration that he would lose Käthe, and moreover would lose her whether the plan succeeded or whether it failed. In the former case, he would be sent off to an American prisoner-of-war camp, in the latter court-martialed and executed.

But whereas he scotched the evacuation of Winterspelt—to the delight of the Winterspelt farmers—he did not renounce his undertaking.

He placed obstacles in its way, threw monkey wrenches into the works, as Käthe expressed it in her thoughts. Perhaps he brought in what Hainstock scornfully called his code of honor only in order to persuade Käthe to let his plan remain a plan. In that case, he hoped, he would keep her. But he did not clearly frame all this in his mind, and it is by no means sure that such were his motives.

Then, once the plan was in motion, he could only believe it would succeed, wanted to so believe, could not allow himself to believe otherwise. He concluded that after one or two years as a prisoner of war he would return to Käthe who would, all along, have been waiting for him.

Which, given Käthe's character, could not be assumed with any degree of certainty.

### His Word Is His Bond,
### or The Officers' International

Käthe had kept silent when Dincklage asked her to explain to him why he had wanted to blow up the railroad viaduct at Hemmeres. She did not want to endanger the plan at the last moment by getting into discussions of principles. But she spoke out boldly enough once she recognized what was wrong with his argument that the Americans were also obligated to stake something.

238

The Americans were not obligated in any way—if he didn't realize that, he was operating on a completely false premise.

Later on she also ruthlessly reported the remark made by Kimbrough's regimental commander, from which he might deduce how little chance there was that the American higher-ups would even consider Dincklage's offer.

Schefold on Kimbrough, during his last visit to Hainstock (on Tuesday, October 10, at 2 P.M.):

"I have never seen him in such bad humor as this morning in Maspelt. First he snarled at me what the devil did I want again, nothing was arranged yet. Then he apologized, started to explain all sorts of military matters to me, so that I would understand why nothing was arranged yet. You will be annoyed with me, Herr Hainstock, because I simply didn't take in the military arguments. Only what his colonel said to him at the very last: 'Besides, we don't want to have anything to do with a traitor.'

"If he hadn't been so upset," Schefold added, "he surely would have suppressed that remark."

Only an hour later Hainstock passed on to Käthe Colonel R.'s reaction.

When Hainstock was gratified by something, as for example that time in the Hotel Kaiserhof in Berlin when he thanked Matthias Arimond, his eyes could seem even more china blue than ordinarily. When Käthe, returning to him in the course of the afternoon, reported that she had quoted Colonel R.'s use of the word *traitor* to Dincklage, the china blue drained right out of Hainstock's eyes; they became quite dark because the pupils widened so. Aghast, he stared at Käthe.

"Damn it all, Käthe," he burst out, "you shouldn't have mentioned that."

"I absolutely had to tell him," she replied, not even shaken for a moment by the vexation in his voice. "I would have felt like a cheat if I had concealed that from him. After all, he has a right to know *everything*."

"How did he take it?" Hainstock asked.

"I don't know," Käthe said. "He didn't say anything." She added: "You know, he's a master of self-control."

"But by saying that you've endangered the whole operation," Hainstock said.

"You'd be perfectly happy about that," Käthe promptly retorted mockingly. "You never have believed in it anyhow and still think it's foolish."

"He asks you," she said, "to tell Schefold that he will be expecting him day after tomorrow at twelve noon in Battalion Headquarters."

She held out a sheet of paper to Hainstock. "Here. He's made a sketch of the route Schefold should take. Through the line, of course. Without that he simply won't do it."

She watched him as he became absorbed in studying Dincklage's sketch.

"I'll transfer it to a map for Schefold," he said.

Obviously it did not occur to him to crumple the sheet of paper and throw it into the firebox of the shack's small iron stove.

And as for Dincklage: during the entire following day Major Joseph Dincklage, battalion commander, wearer of the Knight's Cross, and traitor, did not call off his operation.

### From Alberic's Treasure

Hainstock watched Käthe as she pedaled back to Winterspelt to be on the scene when Schefold left the house with its ridiculous sign *Battalion Combat Command Post*. Her hair fluttered and the flashing wheels left a small train of dust behind her, for the weather had been continuously dry and fair during this first half of October.

In the afternoon Hainstock would go to Winterspelt to find

out from Käthe when Schefold had left and how his conversation
with Dincklage had gone. Right now he returned to his shack,
fixed himself lunch. He took care that the owl did not feel disturbed, moving in such a way that the bird would have the impression he did not see it. Hainstock felt great sympathy for the
bird's shyness, for what the bird wanted was also his greatest
desire: to observe without being observed. He regretted that
human ingenuity had constructed so many incredible things, but
not the one he wanted: a cap of invisibility.

# Orderly Room Incidents

Approaching Winterspelt, escorted by Reidel, Schefold tried several times to make out the ridge of the hill that dropped off northward into Hainstock's quarry, but he did not manage to spot it, although he could easily have seen it from that part of the road near the barn in which the field kitchen (that unit of the 18th Motorized) had formerly been housed. From there, from the south, the mountain with the limestone cliff looked like no more than an unremarkable barren slope, an autumnally brown hide, inconspicuously stretched between patches of woods and over pastures or harvested, stubbly fields. It would have been reassuring to Schefold to see the point from which a watch could be kept over him.

And Hainstock unfortunately had not thought to use his field glasses to check the short stretch of road leading into the village of Winterspelt; he had given up when he saw what he already knew: that between his observation post and the point at which Schefold crossed the line, the Elcherath woods interposed its dark-red wall. He was obsessed with that point, the only one at which, to his mind, Schefold was threatened by any danger.

After all, Käthe would give him a full report of Schefold's arrival in Winterspelt.

That this character added insult to injury by stopping with hands in trousers pockets and looking all around him—that really was the limit. Reidel was in a hurry. Perhaps the recruits were back already, and the noncoms and platoon leaders with them; in any case, every minute that this fellow lagged he was running the danger of meeting someone who, flabbergasted, would challenge him: "What are you doing here, Reidel? I thought you were on sentry duty!" With that special oily voice those lousy sergeants developed as soon as they posed in front of the nearest mirror to admire their new stripes.

244

Kicking this cluck in the ass again was out of the question now. Until he'd seen the sequel, he had to be polite. Not exactly hotel behavior, though; Reidel already had enough with his "Very good, sir" earlier, when he'd handed the letter back to Schefold as sedulously as a hotel clerk who has checked a guest's identification —an identification that in this case proved nothing at all, Reidel thought—though it had to suffice if he didn't rudely address the man as *asshole*. In his high-pitched, sharp voice he snapped at Schefold: "Come on, keep going! Otherwise we'll be late."

Sighing inaudibly, taking his hands from his trousers pocket, Schefold used his right hand to adjust the raincoat that he had slung over his shoulder—he wouldn't have needed it in this weather, he thought, but on the other hand it would have looked too nonchalant to appear before Makor Dincklage without it, just in his jacket. He turned his mind to the task of entering the village of Winterspelt. He was unfamiliar with it. He knew Eigelscheid, Habscheid, and a few other villages that were situated back of the main battle zone. Winterspelt was a linear village, widening only down below in the hollow to which the street dropped in a shallow descent. At first glance Winterspelt seemed to him larger and wealthier than the flea-bitten places he tramped around in, to Hainstock's displeasure. Wealthier but no prettier. The size of several of the farmhouses had given them no air of comfort or grandness; they merely looked sprawling. Only a few rubblestone houses, whose age Schefold estimated at two hundred, perhaps three hundred years, were handsome in their proportions. Now and then he caught a glimpse—in passing, for Reidel had increased the tempo—of old farmyards enclosed by one-story outbuildings. Once again, as he did on all his walks, Schefold told himself that the landscape of the Eifel region was not beautiful, at most picturesque, but lacking any sense of form, unfriendly. Since he did not want to do Winterspelt an injustice, he fixed his gaze for a while upon the church tower at the end of the village. The tower itself was characterless, dating from the nineteenth century; but below it, as Schefold knew, was a Late Gothic church whose interior, according to the description he had read, must be of some interest. Uninviting though these villages seemed, they were very old; the earliest church of Winterspelt had been consecrated shortly after the year 1000 by the Archbishop of Trier. The later church, the Late Gothic one, was hemmed in by houses. Perhaps he might get a chance to look at it after his conversation with the major; but at this thought he shook his head over his own frivolity. After the conversation no time must be wasted. The talk would surely have some content of which Kimbrough would have to be informed at once.

How would Hainstock learn what was said? That was no longer his, Schefold's, business. This woman could transmit the report, of course, the unknown woman who enjoyed both Hainstock's and the major's confidence.

The emptiness, the lifelessness of the village, was striking. Where the devil were the farmers, the soldiers who populated this large village? Now and again he caught a glimpse of a few uniformed men, behind gateways, in the shadow of a farmhouse. A woman stepped out of a store, the only one he noticed, and vanished down a side alley.

To Reidel, who could read the military signs, Winterspelt was not empty and lifeless. He knew and saw that they were passing first the infirmary, then the clothing room, then the ordnance depot, the field kitchen, the quarters of various groups. Nothing escaped his keen, practiced eye, neither the ambulant sick who were playing cards in the garden outside the infirmary, nor the two supply sergeants who were counting blankets, nor the potato peelers in the yard next to the shed in which the field kitchen had been set up under cover. He knew that he too was not escaping their notice, although their eyes were not so practiced and keen as his. His coming from the line at twelve noon and bringing a civilian, and so striking a type of civilian at that, was an event. Anyhow, he had nothing to fear from this riffraff who'd been detailed to the supply company, not even shouted queries, merely mute gaping which he didn't give a good goddamn about. But in his mind he was preparing answers to idiotic questions from the night shift, some of whom might not be asleep. There were those who couldn't sleep even when they'd stood guard half the night, and who would wander around the village all day like ghosts. When the devil did they sleep? Probably they wouldn't dare to start anything with him. "You spread acute anxiety around you." They were ghosts who feared him.

There was no sign anywhere of the recruit platoons, although the end of the exercise had been set for twelve o'clock. The instructors seemed to be following orders strictly for a change, probably wanted to earn themselves a medal. Reidel thought of Borek's pale, sweating face.

What sleepiness, lethargy, compared to the bustle of Maspelt, where there were always groups lining up or breaking up, marching off in single file to the positions or returning from them, cleaning rifles in the open air outside their quarters, jeeps-full bound for Saint-Vith whenever they were off duty for the day, putting on a show of energy whose chief mark was that alien American style of movement, that loose-limbed sauntering, not at all soldierly, trying rather to give the impression of indifference. They wore uniforms of pliant cloth—not civilian dress, oh no, battle jacket and light walking shoes with thick rubber soles were not by any means civilian dress, but this was a uniform that had abandoned any memory of soldiers as men who had to be put into armor, who had to march stiffly across countries. These men had opted for a careless display of restiveness, for a kinetic spirit; they bounced among the houses of Maspelt, swarmed over Maspelt in olive and khaki, to the musical accompaniment of thick glottal and palatal sounds, that comfortable pronunciation of English that the sight of the Mississippi seemed to engender, with the tongue rolling far back into the palate.

Amazing that they did not use camouflage. When they raised their heads, it was only to watch their own planes darting across the sky, high, far, metallic, and inexorable. These boys from Montana could not imagine a war from the air. Which might also be foolish of them, Schefold considered, thinking of Major Wheeler's pessimistic estimate of the situation.

Hainstock had told him that Major Dincklage was an expert at

247

camouflage. The sight of Winterspelt confirmed that. But there was also something that went far beyond camouflage, hide-and-seek, a catacomb existence. Something like dream and sleep. Something like death, perhaps. In giving that look to the village street of Winterspelt, Major Dincklage had succeeded in producing not an image of desertedness, but of death.

The American forward movement would pass through Maspelt and would one day leave it behind as it had always been, a Belgian village whose farmers spoke German, but in reality neither a Belgian nor a German village, but a border village, a metaphor for smuggling and Catholicism. As such very pretty, prettier than Winterspelt; small, much smaller than Winterspelt, its few houses whitewashed, overshadowed by oaks and elms, crouching behind the cover of hilly pastures over which Kimbrough's infantrymen marched to their positions on the slopes of the Our, in lines like flocks of game fowl.

He could not pass by the two kittens that were playing on the steps of a farmhouse door. Their pelts gleamed in the October sunlight, one of the kittens a gray-black tiger, the other with the same ground colors but with mottlings of russet on its back. The three-colored one must be a female, Schefold thought, for he knew something of cats. The kittens chased each other over the steps, embraced, tumbled over each other, delicately, noiselessly. Schefold guessed their age at two months. He managed to catch the young tom and picked it up; its eyes were as blue as his own. He waited for Reidel's shout, for something unpleasant uttered in that unpleasant tone the man had; but when he turned around, the kitten still in his arms, he saw that Reidel was looking at the little creature with a trancelike expression. Evidently he too was an ailurophile.

Could what overcame him when he saw a kitten like this be called a human emotion? Schefold doubted that even as he set down the little tomcat for whose sake, this one time, he had not been bawled out.

As he walked on he pictured to himself the wintertime and two big, mangy cats, brother and sister, starving, predatory, prowling among the ruins of Winterspelt.

Borek in Denmark. Borek had already been there in the barracks in Mariager when Reidel arrived; Borek was one of that swarm of recruits who made up the core of the 416th, among whom case-hardened old troopers, the backbone of the army, were thinly sprinkled. He wasn't a handsome boy at all; much too tall and skinny for that. A cobra. He stood at the window, arms folded, motionless, watching the rain, while Reidel put his stuff into his locker. He was so thin that Reidel felt as though the rain were raining right through him.

"Idiotic that we have to go out in this weather this afternoon," he said to Reidel after a while.

Naturally Reidel didn't bother to answer. In the first place, he never said anything superfluous; in the second place, the rookie's "cultured" intonation annoyed him; and in the third place, he was struck speechless by the fact that anyone thought war went indoors in rainy weather—and in all seriousness, because Borek had not been trying to joke. He'd sensed that.

But then something else happened to him. After he had watched Borek putting on his boots, he made him take them off again. Borek: "But what for?" Reidel: "I said take them off!" And then he showed the kid how to fix the foot wrappings so they wouldn't rub his feet sore, raise blisters. He actually knelt in front of Borek, set his foot on the piece of cloth, taught him that it had to form a perfectly plane surface under the sole, wrapped the four corners just so around the heel, ankles, and toes, so that there was a thick layer of cloth without wrinkles. He'd never before gone to such lengths with any of the recruits. Several of the others watched him at it. He had Borek repeat the routine; the kid did it the second time as clumsily as the first. Obviously he was all thumbs. Reidel stood up, and to impress respect on the onlookers, to show them what kind of corporal and group leader had been placed in their barracks, he said in his most unpleasant voice; "Besides which this evening you're going to wash those feet for a change, and I mean thoroughly."

He supervised the procedure. Not that Borek had especially dirty feet. At any rate, they were no dirtier than those of most of the others. But it gave Reidel an opportunity, under the pretext of being concerned with hygiene, to enter the washroom and watch as Borek, dressed only in his drawers, raised his immensely long legs and placed his feet in the washbowl. To think that a type like this student could excite him! The kind he liked, or thought he liked—although since joining the army he hadn't touched anyone again, aside from that trivial incident in the West Wall bunker— were handsome boys, preferably no taller than himself, with solid, supple bodies and movements like cats. Instead this kid who was practically a skeleton, nothing but a gangling eighteen-year-old, though with a skin that you could imagine the rain pouring through. Tough, terse, official, saying not a word, he posted himself beside Borek. And then, from this weakling, this long drink of water, there suddenly came that outrageous impudence.

"Clear out!" Borek said to him. "Nobody has to supervise me when I'm washing."

Reidel had been so surprised that he turned on his heel and left the washroom. He had felt caught red-handed. Afterward, considering the possible implications of his conduct—just as he had done an hour ago, when he decided against shooting Schefold, so that this fishy character now stood before him alive and kicking, having no idea what a close call he had had, picking up a kitten and petting it right in the middle of the village street of Winterspelt. Barricaded behind a newspaper at the table in the Mariager barracks he came to the conclusion that he would probably lose out if he allowed this affair to develop into an argument with Borek and reported it to the platoon leader. It was not part of a corporal's duties to supervise the washing habits of the men in his group. There was not a word about it in the army manual.

But how could it be that a lost soul like that, who certainly hadn't the foggiest notion of the army manual, figured it out, knew how to defend himself, knew it to a T? This kid had the nerve to criticize the authority of a superior just the way he criticized exercises in the rain. And the craziest part was that he got away with it, since you walked off. And the way Borek pro-

nounced the word *idiotic* made you see there was actually something to his comment, made you wonder whether there was any
point to sending troops out in the kind of stinking weather they'd
had the day Reidel moved into the 416th in Denmark.

The hinterland of Maspelt was also totally different from the
hinterland of Winterspelt, at least as far as the war was concerned. When Schefold got a ride to Saint-Vith, or when—this
too had already happened—he visited members of the van Reeth
clan or other families who in his mind bore the names of painting
collections, in Malmédy, Stavelot, or deeper in the Ardennes, his
mouth sometimes literally remained wide open with astonishment
because once again he saw a herd of tanks covering an entire
plain. Arranged in rows and incidentally deserted, guarded only by
a few sentries, the war machines dozed, empty and unused. Or
else he saw fields jammed full of artillery, acres covered with clus-
ters of crates (ammunition? rations?), over which nets had been
draped, making landscapes of small gray-green mounds. There
were also airfields on which chunky airplanes (fighters?) stood in
steely packs. These Americans were rich! Every time Schefold
took account of the Americans' wealth he recalled a political joke
he had heard in some tavern in the mountains. It ended with the
question: "Yes, but does the Führer know that?" These Eifel
farmers were amazingly free about telling political jokes, but certain rules had to be observed. The fundamentally annihilating
question, "Yes, but does the Führer know that?" could be asked,
but then it had to hover in the room; no answer was permitted.
For if someone, the teller himself or one of his listeners, was so
humorless as to continue, "I'm afraid somebody will have to tell
him some time," or even, "He doesn't want to know," he would
be violating the rules and in all probability blabbing himself into
the clutches of the Gestapo.

In the places where political jokes made the rounds, military
poverty prevailed, as Schefold naïvely concluded from the condition of the region in which he went walking. Around Eigelscheid,
Habscheid, even as far as Prüm—where he had once ventured,
that time he had been mad enough to telephone his parents in

Frankfurt—he had never noticed anything but small squads of rear-echelon services. These were popular safe jobs, as Hainstock had explained to him. The trucks that supplied the battle zone with provisions came from far away and could use the roads only at night.

"Take all your stuff and finish up the war!" he had said to Major Wheeler. "It's high time."

"Oh, you mean all this matériel you see around here!" Wheeler looked at him with a pitying smile at such ignorance. "This isn't anything at all," he said, snapping his fingers. "Most of the stuff standing around here is discarded matériel, it's just being stored. I regret that I cannot show you a fully equipped American army, let alone a division."

He suddenly turned gloomy and leaned back. "Unfortunately I cannot," he said. "That's just it. You couldn't have picked out a weaker point, Herr Doktor." He said "Herr Doktor" because he spoke German with Schefold, did not simply call him "Doc" as Kimbrough did. "I mean, if you were hoping to find a certain amount of reserve strength here. If the Germans attack in this sector, I won't even have time to write you a farewell postcard."

Schefold looked at him incredulously. "Attack? The Germans?" he exclaimed. "There's nothing on the other side. I assure you, nothing. Behind the front nothing but empty countryside. I've never seen a tank or even a few cannon. And have you seen so much as a single German plane? I haven't."

"As it happens I'm familiar with the figures on recent German airplane production," Wheeler said. "We get them from the Russians. Three thousand units a month. That's quite substantial. And then the Germans have those Tiger tanks, which are superior to any of ours. You know, Doktor Schefold," he said, "you're a layman in military matters."

He stood up and brushed his hand over the map that hung behind his chair—for the conversation was taking place in Wheeler's office at regimental headquarters—indicating the triangle between the Moselle and the Rhine, west of Koblenz.

"In this area," he said, "if the Germans assembled, say, twenty divisions—and you see they can still do that; they need only the necessary mustering time, about four weeks, and we're giving them that, we've already given it—we're so generous—they could crush our front. And right here, moreover, where we're standing. Right here . . . It's more than just a feeling I have," he added. "I'm beginning to know it."

Wheeler was mistaken, at least at that time he was. A short while later he was better informed, as we shall learn from his conversation with Kimbrough. During the period from October 12 to December 16, 1944, Field Marshal von Rundstedt brought into the deployment area against the three American divisions that held the sector of the front between Monschau and Echternach not twenty but forty-one divisions.

"If you ever notice tank formations, even smaller ones—advance detachments, they're called—would you be prepared to inform us of *that*?"

The emphasis on the word *that* in Wheeler's question referred to Schefold's refusal to scout out the German frontline positions. Kimbrough later brought up the matter again with him, but he had already answered Wheeler: "When I think that you would then shell these places with artillery fire or have your airplanes . . ."

Now he took time to reply, reflected for a long time before he said: "Of course. Then I would come to you at once." He added: "But it will never be necessary. You overestimate Germany, Major. She's finished."

Major Robert ("Bob") Wheeler, intelligence officer of the 424th Regiment, half laughing, half furious, signed a pass for Schefold. He watched him as he left the office with much the same feelings as Hainstock watched him stroll off on the road toward Eigelscheid, massive and with a kind of flowing movement; he seemed to be enjoying the beauty of the weather and the emptiness of the road, and the fact that the war had vanished.

Wheeler and Hainstock would have been gratified to learn what Schefold thought as he walked down the deserted village street of Winterspelt: that never had the war been so present. And also: Germany is not finished. For phrases of this sort ran through his head, and calmness would not come, even though he reminded himself that he had already survived the worst and that in a few hours he would be back in Maspelt, although not with a German battalion in his pocket, as he had hoped.

This discussion described above took place on September 20, only three days after the staff of the 424th Regiment had set up headquarters in Saint-Vith. Wheeler had been informed by the Belgian army intelligence service of Schefold's presence in Hemmeres. But it is quite possible he would not have so quickly taken an interest in this bird if Schefold had not turned up at Kimbrough's office shortly after the occupation of Maspelt and asked for permission to pass through the line whenever he wished.

"What sort of person is he?" Wheeler asked on the telephone.

"If this fellow's a spy," Kimbrough said, "I'll eat my hat."

"You must be a real good lawyer, John," Wheeler said. "You seem to know human nature. The Belgians give the man excellent marks. Send him over to me, with one of your men as an escort."

For Schefold had to be screened in any case. The screening went well, but the decisive factor for Wheeler in granting Schefold the pass through the American lines (in Kimbrough's sector) was his refusal to engage in military espionage combined with his agreement to make an exception if really serious information were involved. It was enough for Wheeler if this man would keep him abreast of the mood of the German population. And that he had promised to do.

"It would be better for you," Wheeler had told him, "if you'd take yourself off to Brussels for a while, or somewhere where you'll be in safety."

"Oh, but you know," Schefold replied, "I've seen every painting in Brussels. The place bores me."

And since Wheeler had described himself as a historian, he had asked about recent American developments in certain art-historical fields, and about what had happened to certain German scholars who were exiles in America. Wheeler had been unable to help him. Art history was not his subject.

He telephoned Kimbrough and informed him of the result.

"I'll instruct my men to let him pass," Kimbrough said. "And I'll make it clear that this fellow isn't spying for us."

"Fine," Wheeler said. He too wished Schefold to be treated as decently as possible.

In contrast to Major Dincklage, Captain Kimbough had no inhibitions about referring to the men he commanded (C Company of the 3rd Battalion) as his men.

Because of his height—over six feet—Borek was the right flank man of the company in roll calls. The top sergeant had already begun riding him.

"Can't you stand straight, Private Borek?"

"No."

The company held its breath.

"Say that again!"

"No."

"How do you say it?"

"No, sir."

"Say it again, louder."

"No, sir."

"And you can't stand straight either?"

"No, sir."

"Why not?"

"Because of my psychic makeup, sir."

At this several men laughed. Reidel, who was standing on the left flank (shorty that he was), did not laugh; he admired Borek. Borek was raising a point that the topkick was helpless to do anything about. He could report this recruit, but that would lead to a long inquisition concerning psychic makeups before officers who would listen with interest. Borek was obviously aiming to be pushed off into some safe post, that was clear.

"Quiet!" the topkick bellowed. He turned to Borek again. "Run three times around the company. At the double, hup, hup!"

And while the morning roll call proceeded, Borek ran three times around the company. Every time he passed, Reidel saw the hollows in his face turning paler. So that's the way they'll try to break him, Reidel thought; if they can make him refuse an order, they have him. Reidel noted that the topkick was clever enough to avoid rubbing it in after Borek had completed his rounds and stepped back into line. But he now had Borek on the blacklist; Reidel was sure of that.

To get him out of the direct firing line, Reidel arranged to have him shifted from the first to the third rank at roll call, where he would not attract so much attention.

To achieve this, he turned to Sergeant Wagner, who agreed, but looked at him in astonishment.

"What's got into you, Reidel?" he asked. "Since when are you worried about some half-baked rookie?"

"I don't want my group making a bad showing all the time," Reidel said.

But the following night, lying sleepless on his paillasse, arms at his sides, fists clenched, he thought of the man who had said to him, endless ages ago in that Düsseldorf hotel: "Some day you too will be what the straights call a queen."

Schefold recalled that last Saturday afternoon Maspelt had looked almost exactly as sleepy as this Winterspelt did today, and probably every day. The almost peacetime footing on which the 3rd Regiment of the 106th American Infantry Division operated meant that no duties were assigned on Saturday afternoons, except of course for sentry duty on the heights above the Our. Most of Kimbrough's men spent this time knocking about the taverns in Saint-Vith. The orderly room of C Company of the 3rd Battalion was occupied only by a single Pfc. It nettled Schefold every time, even now, when he recalled the sluggish, bored conduct of this man, who went on lolling in his chair even after Schefold had told him that he had information of the highest military importance for Captain Kimbrough.

"Is it really important?" the Pfc. asked; in civilian life he held a job in the office of a tax consultant in Butte, Montana. He was accustomed to listening to people who always thought everything they had to tell him was tremendously important.

"Do you want to bet," Schefold asked, "that as soon as I've had a word with Captain Kimbrough, he'll drive to Saint-Vith to talk with Regiment?"

To this moment on the village street in Winterspelt Schefold imagined that his use of the word *bet* had induced the soldier to lift his fat ass—Pfc. Foster, the accountant of C Company, actually possessed a massive backside—and make for the door. Schefold did not suspect that he had already convinced Foster, who was a good judge of the pitch of voices, and that the man had let some time pass only because he had to make up his mind to disturb his chief at letter-writing. Kimbrough had reserved Saturday afternoons for taking care of his personal correspondence and had given orders that no one was to bother him unless a war broke out. Schefold, military layman that he was, simply had no inkling of hierarchic considerations of this sort.

The Pfc. locked the orderly room and told Schefold to wait outside the building. Schefold had left Hainstock around one o'clock, had paused only to fix himself a quick snack in Hemmeres, and then had crossed the wooden footbridge to the other bank of the Our. As always the boards of the bridge creaked, and the water was as dark and transparent as ever. He exchanged a few words with the sentry at the top of the ridge. By now he never needed to show his pass; they all knew him. Filled with impatience, he had crossed the hill of open pastures beyond which lay Maspelt. Now it was three o'clock. He saw Kimbrough coming, not slowly, but still sauntering, his air casual, accompanied by Pfc. Foster. Kimbrough, lean and black-haired, wearing a battle jacket and light shoes, carried his cap in his hand so that strands of his black hair fell over his face. Only the two silver bars on the shoulders of the jacket indicated that he was an officer. He looked at Schefold with his violet eyes and said: "Hello, Doc."

Pfc. Foster had been relieved to discover that his report had not come at an awkward time. Captain John Kimbrough was not even annoyed; he was glad to be able to lay aside a letter he had just started. Ever since he had realized that recipients of his letters could not possibly gather what he was feeling during his experiences in Europe, in fact that he could not even properly describe these experiences, he regarded the letter-writing Saturday afternoons to which he had looked forward, which he had meant as opportunities for him to fence off for himself a personal zone, merely as dutiful exercises. Sometimes he considered in all seriousness whether he should not stop completely, simply no longer be heard from. They would survive it. He too would survive not learning what was going on at the moment in Savannah, Georgia. For long centuries there had been wars in which no such institution as the army post office had been known. Bob Wheeler contradicted him and told him that, for example, the knights had written long letters home from the Crusades. All right, so what? To him silence seemed more appropriate for the experience.

He had established himself with his writing materials in the living room of the farmhouse where he had set up his headquarters. It resembled the main room of the Thelen farmhouse in Winterspelt, except that it was smaller. Everything in Maspelt was smaller and consequently darker than in Winterspelt. It did not bother Kimbrough that the farmer and his wife sometimes went in and out of the room, talking to each other. He did not understand their language, a German that, though he did not know it, few Germans would have understood either. What bothered him were the flies. He had just cut short his letter to Dorothy—another duty letter!—with the sentence: "I would like to write to you at greater length, but as I write a fly keeps settling on my right hand."

Foster's reliability was beyond a doubt—Kimbrough had chosen him very carefully for that job as accountant in the orderly room —so that it was really unnecessary to ask him what impression Schefold had made on him.

"Was he worked up?"

From a good many talks with Schefold he knew this big German's tendency to get worked up—for example, when paintings were under discussion.

"He sure was," Foster said. "I figure he has something pretty big on his mind."

That was as positive a judgment as Foster was inclined to make. Kimbrough and Foster exchanged glances. Then Kimbrough grabbed his cap, which lay on the bench beside him, but did not put it on.

The subsequent conversation—which took place in the chief's room beside the orderly room, for Kimbrough, like Major Dincklage, also had such a room at his disposal—bitterly disappointed Schefold, as we already know. Three hours earlier, at around twelve o'clock, he had said to Hainstock that it would knock Kimbrough for a loop when he heard of Dincklage's intentions, and when Hainstock had skeptically asked whether the Americans would even consider the offer, he had exclaimed, utterly astounded: "Certainly, why shouldn't they?"

But Kimbrough behaved *oddly*, as he had had to admit to Hainstock on Sunday morning. Whether he was surprised, let alone knocked for a loop, could not be read either in his expression, nor in what he said.

Perhaps the room was to blame. The room was unbright because a few meters beyond the window the slope of the pasture hill rose up, the hill that sheltered Maspelt. In the nonlight that prevailed there, Kimbrough's face under its strands of black hair looked even paler than it did outside.

"Opposite you there is a German infantry battalion," Schefold said. "You know that. The commandant of this battalion would like to surrender his force to the Americans."

He had resolved to speak as calmly and matter-of-factly as possible in his excellent British English, and to eschew a military vocabulary that he really did not command.

"How do you know that?"

"From my friend Hainstock. I've already told you and Major Wheeler about him. Without Hainstock I couldn't go running around over there."

"How does he know this?"

259

"I don't know. He just knows."

A quick exchange of questions and answers. No interlude allowed for expressions of wonderment or gratification.

"From the intelligence point of view it would be rather important for us to learn how Hainstock obtained this information."

"If you knew Hainstock you would know that everything he says can be relied on."

It was not until the next day that Schefold was able to inform Kimbrough of the source of Hainstock's knowledge, because of Hainstock's slip of the tongue.

"Do you know this officer?"

"No, I've never seen him. A major. His name is Dincklage."

Kimbrough pushed a pad across the desk to him. "Please write the name down."

He read it and said it aloud.

"No," Schefold said. "In German it is pronounced Dinklahga."

"Dinklahga," Kimbrough repeated in the tone of a docile pupil.

"An experienced frontline officer. He fought in Africa and Italy and has received the highest German decoration."

"The Knight's Cross?"

"Yes." (So they knew that!)

For the first time there was a pause in the conversation, marked by a prolonged staring out of the window on Kimbrough's part. Then at last came a question that at least suggested wonderment, although in phraseology it was reduced to the utmost dryness: "What makes him tick?"

This question gave Schefold the feeling that Kimbrough was asking about the mechanism inside Major Dincklage, as if he were something wound up and now running down. Schefold shrugged because he simply had no desire to explain to the young American captain why a German officer would have waited until the last gasp to draw certain conclusions. Undoubtedly he should have gathered up all his patience and explained to Kimbrough what had been wound up inside Dincklage, what was ticking and running down—though it had been running so slowly it could never,

never make up for lost time. Instead he retreated within his exile's sensitiveness, hunched up within the snail's shell of his own proper feelings and timely perceptions which had made it possible for him, as early as 1937, to pack a painting by Klee in wrapping paper and take the express train from Frankfurt to Brussels—in those days a traveler with a valid passport could leave Germany unhindered. Years of exile—and Dincklage would not be beyond implying that he had spent them not exactly in extreme misery. The man who was now returning to them was obviously well nourished.

To Schefold's credit let it be said, however, that he did not altogether pass over Kimbrough's question. To his shrug Schefold added an attempt at an explanation, saying: "Probably he thinks the war is lost."

Kimbrough reflected that Major Dincklage himself, if he were sitting there, would probably give no other justification for his action than this art historian who hadn't the vaguest notion of military thinking. The education of officers—in subjects like theory, logistics, military history—was presumably the same the world over, and if they remembered their Clausewitz—in Fort Benning Kimbrough had heard lectures by a West Pointer on this Prussian military theoretician—most German officers, aside from the greatest blockheads, must know that the war was lost for Germany.

"That is not a sufficient explanation," he said. "I imagine that almost all German officers consider the war lost. But that hasn't made any of them surrender his unit to the enemy."

"Unfortunately," Schefold said.

This heavyweight dreamed about paintings and liked eating well. Kimbrough regarded Schefold's precise accounts of pictures as dreams. Only recently, when he found how hard it was for him to describe the things he himself had seen and convey these impressions in letters, had he begun to feel doubts in this regard. Did you have to dream like Schefold in order to conjure up vivid images of pictures?

261

Besides, Schefold was not a spy, merely a German who had fled
from that monster and was anticipating his homecoming in the
craziest way.

"Wishful thinking, Doc," he said. "Where would we be if every
commander who thought a war was lost were to surrender on his
own initiative?"

Was this really his view, or merely an automatic reflex springing
from his training in discipline? At the moment Kimbrough did
not reflect on the matter. In any case, although he was young in
the legal profession he had already learned to conceal his opinion
when he agreed with a client. Clients did not need to know what
their lawyer really thought about the problem they were presenting to him. Only charlatans in the profession pretended to their
clients to be deeply sympathetic. The good lawyers, even when
they did sympathize, behaved in a matter-of-fact way, were restrained, did not arouse hopes.

"So," he asked, "why this particular man?"

"I don't know," Schefold said irritably. He made a stab at
explaining: "Perhaps he has realized at last that Hitler is a criminal and that one cannot fight for a criminal."

"After having fought for him for years? That strikes me as pre-
posterous," Kimbrough said.

Suddenly the captain became loquacious.

"You see," he said, "there is a very simple psychological law
that prevents the Germans from giving up now: they've missed
the point in time where they could have given up. You can bet on
it that not only this Major Dincklage"—Kimbrough made an
effort to pronounce the name correctly—"but almost every German general has his personal surrender plan in his pocket. He
doesn't pull it out of his pocket because instinctively he knows it's
too late for that. That has nothing at all to do with fear of losing
his honor, but with . . . with . . . yes, with style, with good taste.
It would have been good style if the German generals called the
whole thing off after our invasion and after the Russians' recon-
quest of the Ukraine. Now it's too late for that. There's no longer
any prestige in it. It would be tasteless."

"Is it tasteless to save the lives of hundreds of thousands?" Schefold asked.

"You cannot put yourself into the minds of military men," Kimbrough replied. He leaned forward. He had a knack for dealing with men who were older, more rigid, less flexible than himself. "Don't look at me so disgustedly, Doc," he said. "*I* am not a military man. I would like to make you understand that all this is not a matter of politics, but of psychology. And all I am trying to do is to establish this major's motives. Why is he the one to pull his plan out of his pocket? Is he tasteless, or some blockhead who wants to save himself at the last moment? That's why I asked whether you know him."

Schefold did not answer at once. When he considered it properly, he had only one reason to place a measure of trust in Major Dincklage: that Wenzel Hainstock had let himself be involved in the man's affair. There were also Hainstock's positive judgments concerning Dincklage's military abilities, and some few comments such as the one Hainstock had tossed off, shaking his head: "Like me, he comes from an industry dealing with stone and minerals." (That was the outcome of his mullings on the chancy nature of Käthe Lenk's preferences.) Or there was Hainstock's scornfully quoting Dincklage's statement that he would be glad to meet a "cultivated" Marxist.

"No, I don't know him," Schefold said at last. "From everything I have heard about him he is a cultivated member of the German middle class, if that gives you any notion of him, Captain." He added: "Someone like myself, if you will."

It seemed to him that the American captain passed hastily over this reference.

"Then there must be special reasons for his coming out with his plan just now," Kimbrough said. "Personal reasons, I mean. Maybe someone close to him has been killed by Hitler."

"That would be a political reason."

"A personal political reason."

There was no point playing guessing games about personal political reasons of this sort. Nevertheless, John Kimbrough automatically reacted as he was wont—for young though he was, he

263

was already a respected criminal lawyer—to react in his cases: he looked for motives that might serve to support the defendant. But at this moment he did not as yet fully realize that he had already taken on a case: the Dincklage case.

Something of a bicker followed.

"You don't seem exactly enthusiastic," Schefold said.

"I cannot imagine that the army will accept this offer."

So Hainstock was right.

"What? But surely that's not possible."

Kimbrough began, dryly, methodically, to list the tactical reasons why the army would not accept Dincklage's offer. Schefold did not pay attention. To him this was like the mathematics class at the Gymnasium, where from the outset algebra proved to be beyond his grasp, nor had he wanted to grasp it.

He interrupted Kimbrough to say: "This is a thing that you cannot reject."

Kimbrough was annoyed that Schefold addressed him directly. If he had said *they* instead of *you*, all would have been well. Piqued, he pursued the argument.

"Nonsense," he said. "I don't have to take hopeless cases."

"It's odd," Schefold said. "You talk about Major Dincklage as if he were a criminal."

"So he is. In every army in the world what he wants to do is considered a crime."

"And you would not defend him?"

"Maybe I would defend him. But what you are asking of me is that I participate in his crime."

So Hainstock was always right. Schefold was sorry that this young American, who was after all against this war—though not from pacifism but for reasons derived from American history— seemed unable to rise above the thinking of an International of military men.

"I am participating," he said.

"You are a civilian," Kimbrough said. "And a German patriot. Everything is permissible for you."

The assertion that he was a German patriot struck Schefold like a blow. He had been convinced that in the course of seven years

264

he had systematically cured himself of the habit of loving Germany.

Kimbrough reflected on justice. He realized that in what he was saying to Schefold he was not representing the standards of justice, but merely the rules of a game as played by a certain societal group. In law school it had been pounded into him that ever since the foundation of the Republic the best American jurists had fought the claims of privileged groups.

"Very well," he said, standing up, "I'll drive over to Saint-Vith now and report the matter. This should give them something to think about."

This was his first admission that the proposal could surprise anyone. Aside from that dry and reflective query, "What makes him tick?" he himself had not permitted any sign of astonishment to escape him.

"I really should turn to the battalion commander first," he said. "But I'll go to Bob Wheeler and then accompany him to the colonel. It will let me in for a reprimand, but there's no need to go through channels all the time." It then occurred to him to ask: "Why didn't you take this matter straight to Major Wheeler, Doc? After all, he's in charge of such things and you know that."

"There's no need to go through channels all the time," Schefold said.

Kimbrough laughed. "No," he said. "You were afraid Bob would turn you down right at the start. Whereas the matter has to be sent on through channels because a line officer is advocating it. You see, I'm not going to just report it. I'll advocate it. I'll insist—which you could not do—that Bob inform Colonel R. of the matter. Not because I believe in it, but only because it interests me to see how our brass will react."

The whole thing is interesting enough for me to play it right through, Kimbrough thought. We do not know whether at that very moment he thought or felt that this affair ("which you cannot turn down") would end up sticking like a burr to him.

"Could you take me along to Saint-Vith?" Schefold asked. "I have a visit to pay there."

265

"Gladly," Kimbrough said. "But don't count on my being able to bring you back. As I know the army, they'll spend half the night, maybe all night, chewing on this thing."

It would be wrong to underestimate the army. If it considered the case at all, it would do so thoroughly. Colonel R. would get in touch with Division, and not even the divisional commander would make a decision without having telephoned Army Headquarters.

Whether Colonel R. late that Saturday night routed the divisional commander out of bed, and the latter telephoned Army Headquarters, must remain in the obscurity of history. Major Wheeler merely looked at his friend Kimbrough with amusement when he realized that the young captain in all seriousness expected Alarm Stage VI (and the tempo to match) to be instituted to handle the Dincklage case.

But not even Wheeler foresaw how long the staffs would take before they finally deigned to make a decision.

If, thought Schefold, I had drawn the proper conclusions last Saturday from Kimbrough's half-heartedness, I would not now have to be walking alongside this typical Nazi soldier through a hostile village. I should just have taken that for an answer and let the matter drop. Hainstock wouldn't have given a damn, after all.

He was lying down reading! When he went around to check the sentries, he found Borek right where he had stationed him all right, at the edge of the woods. But Borek was not standing; he was lying in the grass and reading a book.

This breach of the rules for sentry duty was so outrageous that loudly chewing him out was beside the point.

"Come on," Reidel said rather softly, with only that notorious knife-edge in his voice that scared all the others shitless. "On your feet!"

Borek stood up. He pulled his limbs together, whereupon he towered a head over Reidel.

"Put that stinking book away."

The book was small and thin, could fit into the pocket of a tunic.

"Shoulder your rifle."

Then, when Borek once more looked like a sentry: "This will cost you fourteen days in the coop."

With that, the affair was finished; any further words about it were superfluous. But suddenly he heard Borek saying: "What idiocy. I was keeping watch even though I was reading. But there was nothing to watch. The nearest farmers live five kilometers away. Nobody ever comes to this heath. Maybe a lumber truck now and then. But I would have seen and heard anything like that, you can depend on it."

The company was engaged in sharpshooting on Randers heath, and since Borek, who wore glasses, was very nearsighted and consequently unfit for sniping, he had been assigned to the sentries who were supposed to secure the terrain. More precisely, their task was to look out for Danish civilians who might have got a few holes in their vests if they entered the area. Instead of standing guard, Borek had stretched out in the grass to read. There was no two ways about this. But Borek dared to argue about it, and in a way, Reidel thought, that proves he isn't scared just because I switch on the knife blade.

Reidel would have preferred to lay a hand on Borek. But the army manual did not permit a superior to lay a hand on a subordinate. You could smack a civilian, could boot him in the ass—although it must have been a mistake to kick this big shot who was walking beside him through Winterspelt—but never a subordinate in uniform.

"Shut your trap!" he said. "You won't get anywheres with me with that line."

"What do you mean by that?" Borek asked.

"Stop playing dumb." He imitated Borek: "Because of my psychic makeup."

He sensed that the kid was studying him carefully.

"You call that a line?" Borek asked.

"Sure," Reidel said. "You're angling for a safe post, that's all. For that you're even willing to take on fourteen days in the coop. So that they'll examine you and shove you off somewhere where you won't give them a lot of trouble. Then you can read your books in peace."

"Is that what the others think about me?"

"I give you three guesses. They're all pretty sure that's what you've got up your sleeve."

There was a pause of inconclusive silence. They stood face to face. Reidel sensed that Borek was still studying him, but he did not dare to look at Borek. The summer warmth of the Danish heath burned on his skin.

"Those fourteen days in the coop," Borek said. "I'll get those only if you report me, won't I?"

"I've got to report you," Reidel replied, suddenly cross. "Rules is rules and beer is beer."

"My Lord," Borek said, "the sayings you people go by!"

Every time he thought about the fact that from that day on Private Borek made every effort to act like a soldier, Reidel was amazed anew. Less because of his psychic than his physical makeup, Borek naturally never managed to make a model soldier. Marches with packs, together with terrain exercises (such as rolling away after a triple jump), or digging out a foxhole, could reduce him to a state of total exhaustion. But aside from that, he presented to his superiors a pleasing sight of zeal (without toadying), not altogether inept efforts to keep up, discipline, combined with the soldier's highest virtue, the ability not to attract attention.

Even the first sergeant noticed it.

"No," he said one day to Sergeant Wagner, "it's too good to be true."

Wagner mentioned this to Reidel, and added: "I think he's taken Borek off the blacklist."

To avoid confusion, let it be explicitly noted that this is the first sergeant of the third company, not the battalion topkick, Staff Sergeant Kammerer.

She was called Mireille—"Mireille, another couple of beers over this way!"—a name that did not suit her at all, since she wasn't a

girl you might delightedly regard as a little miracle, but rather a
mature woman, a tough woman—but something more than mature, something more than tough, because she had this slanting,
hollow-cheeked face, was so worn by work, by some illness, perhaps had been that way from childhood, that an infatuated man
might even call her slender. Or, if he were Schefold, persuade
himself that she was finely woven of translucent shadows, that she
was the very spot in an etching where the spirit became interlaced
with utmost darkness, although it was probably nothing more
than the effect of someone perpetually in a black dress (was she a
widow? but she wore no rings), of dark hair overshadowing a sallow skin (Memling!) that mingled with the dim light in this dive.

For her sake Schefold made a habit—after Captain Kimbrough
had dropped him in Saint-Vith—of drinking bitter beer from half
past five on, playing the part of a newspaper reader at a table
covered with brown oilcloth in this tavern so low in the scale that
it was off limits to American soldiers, choking down a supper that
consisted of glassy potatoes, beans swimming in water, and a sausage of cotton wool—he shivered himself whenever he thought of
it—and prolonging his stay from the seven-o'clock supper until
nine o'clock before he at last beckoned to this waitress for the last
time, paid, and left. Contrary to his expectations, he found no
one to drive him back to Maspelt, so that he had to tramp the
whole long way to Hemmeres. But it had been a beautiful night.
Beautiful and also instructive, for from the high open road that
ran from Saint-Vith to Luxembourg he had seen and heard the
war, the war that was concealed from him in the valley in which
Hemmeres lay. He saw flares rising and dipping, for a few moments showering bright light over forested mountains, and in the
north the reflection of the battle in the Hürtgenwald illuminated
the sky, a flickery yellow and a distant rumble. A splendid specta-
cle, splendid for a solitary hiker who did not have to fear that
shell splinters would pierce his head or his guts, or at least lop off
the spruces beside his foxhole, cutting them down into stumps
splintered lengthwise, so that their needled branches piled up
above him as he cowered in his hole, mutely pleading with an un-

known being: "Please, God, no direct hit, please, please, no direct hit."

He had switched quickly last Saturday when he asked Kimbrough to take him along to Saint-Vith. During the next few days his life would consist of nothing but visits to Hainstock, then to Kimbrough, finally the visit to Dincklage. No time for anything else, for things that distracted him from the main thing—so Saturday had been the last chance to see this woman once more. Only this evening could he at last grant himself the pleasure of seeing her again.

Odd that she always gave him the feeling that his technique of concealing his feelings from women did not work so very well with her. Although he carefully avoided staring at her, never pursued her with his glances, he considered it possible that some time, arbitrarily and precisely when he least expected it, perhaps after she had mutely taken his order, she would say: "What do you really want from me?"

He feared that moment. He prepared for it, trying out various answers in his mind, and decided to reply: "I would like to get to know you."

How would she react?

He hoped that she would utter an angry, "There's nothing to know about me," before turning on her heel and walking off. But then he would already have half won the game. For who would let slip the opportunity of someone offering to get to know him or her? Certainly not this woman Mireille, of whom some poor parents somewhere had hoped for a small miracle and who had become nothing more than a waitress in a dive, shadowy and emaciated.

But he did not like to think at all about what would happen if she consented to let him get to know her. Getting to know her was not possible without some day spending a night in a room alone with her.

Of course that was out of the question.

Only a short while ago, on the road to Winterspelt, had it suddenly come into question, to his infinite astonishment.

"When do you have your day off? I would like to get to know you."

"Lemme alone."

"But I really must get to know you better."

He recapitulated this dialogue. It was possible, it was even quite simple, that he would begin the conversation on his own initiative.

It was less simple to imagine how he would carry out the business of being alone with her, because all "knowing" came down to was himself and her meeting ultimately in a room between night and darkness, in a chromatic of gray, but even the prominences and eclipses of such rooms could ultimately be viewed with the naked eye, for what was there, really, against someone's having a new experience even at the age of forty-four?

This thought, absolutely monstrous for the sort of person he was, had assumed complete form as he walked alongside Reidel (whose name he did not know) on the last stretch of road before Winterspelt.

He decided to reward himself for this passage through the line by having a new experience.

"No," Kimbrough said when Schefold called on him Sunday afternoon. "I still have no word from Regiment. The staffs are taking their time as usual."

Schefold reported what terms Dincklage was setting for him. Toward Hainstock he had stuck to his refusal ("I'll be glad to do my best but I don't want to fall into the hands of Nazi soldiers"), and although Hainstock had seemed to understand the idea behind Dincklage's terms, he had not pressed Schefold to accept them. At the end of their conversation this morning, he had dodged the issue by asserting that the Americans would not go along, from which it followed that Schefold's going, whether through the line or by some less risky route, would have no point in any case.

Kimbrough's reaction surprised him. He thought Kimbrough would flatly turn down Dincklage's proposal, either starting up in outrage or, still more decisively, responding to the major's condition with a curt, cold laugh.

Instead he said, without reflecting very long: "That shows how serious this kraut is about it."

He took it as if it were a good sign. He too seemed to notice the bewilderment, the unwillingness in Schefold's face, for he at once set about dissipating all possible objections.

"I just have to put myself in his position," he said. "Suppose I had something like this in mind, say, surrendering my company to the Germans. In that case, it wouldn't be enough for me either if some Americans came over to me in the dead of night claiming that they were sent by the Germans and I could rely on them because they were genuine sincere American anti-Roosevelt underground fighters . . ."

He broke off. "Excuse me, Doc," he said, "I don't want to offend you. I know you're a German patriot."

"It's about time you stopped this German patriot business!" Schefold said. "And I'm for Roosevelt too."

"I'm not," Kimbrough said. "We shouldn't ever have gotten into this war. But let's drop that. I'm not going to surrender my company to the Germans on that account. But if I did have that in mind, I would insist that the Germans furnish me with some proof that I really am talking to them. I'd want a sign from them, a sign from army to army. That's what this Major Dincklage is asking for us."

"Of me, you mean," Schefold said.

"Of you, yes, of course," Kimbrough said. "Naturally it's entirely up to you to decide whether or not you want to accept this condition."

He made no attempt to minimize Schefold's difficulties. "As a company commander I would find it easy to arrange such a thing so that it would go smoothly," he said. "For a battalion commander that's harder. He doesn't know the men who are on duty in the first line, the men he has to rely on. You know, even a battalion commander seldom gets up to the very first line."

It was only at the end of a discussion that made the whole thing sound distinctly risky, in which he examined the arguments against Schefold's going through the line, that he said: "But if this German major makes such a demand of you, you can probably depend on his seeing to your safety."

Afterward, Schefold was proud that he had not shown his fear, apart from that one remark he had let slip, that the sign from army to army would necessarily pass through him, Schefold.

He changed the subject.

"I have discovered," he said, "how Hainstock learned about the major's scheme."

And he quoted Hainstock's slip of the tongue. "There's a woman involved."

He very much felt like gossiping a bit now, speculating on some *remarkable person* who simultaneously enjoyed Hainstock's confidence and the major's—those remarks that had thrown Hainstock into a rage in the morning. Or else he would have liked to tell Kimbrough what he had heard in the taverns of Eigelscheid or Habscheid about a young schoolteacher who was said to be the mistress of the man in the quarry. But the American captain gave him no opening; he himself drew the obvious conclusion.

"That must be the major's girl-friend who also knows Hainstock well."

"Evidently," Schefold said.

"Then his decision was forced," Kimbrough said.

"What do you mean by that?"

"Very simple," Kimbrough said. "He made a mistake; one day he told this woman about his scheme. What he hadn't reckoned on was that she would know how it could be carried out. Then he was plumb in the trap. He could have kept his plan in his pocket like all the other German officers with plans in their pockets. But he took it out and showed it. To this woman. Now he has no line of retreat."

"Aren't you pushing your psychology a bit too far?"

I won't answer that question, Kimbrough thought, because otherwise he'll chide me again for comparing this jerry officer with a criminal. Actually, I've never met a criminal who failed to discuss his crime with others beforehand, whether it was a bank robbery or a murder. Aside, of course, from the poor devils who kill somebody in a sudden rage. The silent murderer is a figment of the detective stories. I'm convinced that even Jack the Ripper had people in the know. Somebody talks, and then he can no longer turn back. He talks so that he won't be able to turn back.

Aloud, he said: "I'm almost tempted to ask whether he will introduce a clause into the contract that will make it impossible for us to sign. Will he create artificial difficulties so that you, Hainstock, or this woman will pull out? Or at least it would look that way from the outside. In that case I would be mistaken. Then the condition he is posing would show precisely that he is not serious about it."

But the seriousness of Major Dincklage's plans was really no longer in question. The mysterious unknown woman had informed him that the American army was still behaving indecisively, postponing its decision, but that at any rate one of its company commanders was ready to enter into his plan. Schefold had gone to Hainstock—that was early afternoon on the day before yesterday—and had insisted that this fact be transmitted to Dincklage. He had stuck it out in the construction shack until evening, waiting for Hainstock to return, and had then learned that the major was expecting him the day after tomorrow, Thursday, at twelve noon.

"What for?" Hainstock had growled. "What does he want of you when the business isn't at all ready to be discussed yet?" He tapped his stomach and said: "He ought to have a gut feeling that it's going to be rejected and so he won't need you at all any more."

Schefold replied by quoting Kimbrough's comment, omitting only his careless allusion to Dincklage as a "kraut": "That shows how serious he is about it."

"Oh come on," Hainstock replied, "he's simply a fool. Probably he imagines he can put pressure on the Americans."

It was only after he had calmed down that he said: "I wash my hands of it," and took out the sketch that Dincklage had drawn.

His excessively bad humor, his grumpiness as Schefold privately called it, was due less to Dincklage's incomprehensible condition than to Käthe's casual remark that she had not only informed the major about the Americans' hesitation, but had also reported Colonel R.'s use of the word *traitor*.

Was it right of him to say nothing to Schefold about this? It can be assumed, after all, that if Schefold were aware that this slur had been passed along, he would not have found himself on the village street of Winterspelt today. To confront a man who had been so gravely insulted and who knew it—he would probably have found that too embarrassing to be borne. Not even Kimbrough's appeal would have induced him to go through with it. (Kimbrough had never actually appealed to him, never really asked for his services, but had suggested that he consider whether or not he wanted to perform them. That time Kimbrough visited Schefold in Hemmeres he had not advised against this indubitably premature passage through the lines; but it is likely that he would have strictly forbidden it if Schefold had been in a position to inform him that the slurring remark by his regimental commander had already been passed on to the German major. The scene of profound awkwardness between these two men is easy to imagine—each one ashamed because in a fit of unforgivable loquacity he had brought that remark of Colonel R.'s typical army mentality into the affair. Kimbrough to Schefold, Schefold to Hainstock . . .)

In Hainstock's case it had probably not been loquacity that prompted him to pass on the slur to Käthe. (Schefold had added it as an indignant footnote to his account of the slow motion of American channels.) Why did Hainstock, upon his return from Winterspelt, conceal from Schefold that the major had been informed and that not even this insult had prompted him to withdraw his request that Schefold pay him a visit today? We can only guess about this strange contradiction between his talking (to Käthe) and keeping silent (to Schefold).

Randers. If only I'd handled him that time on the Randers heath, maybe everything would have turned out different.

Handled—not in the sense of the Army Manual.

There's a difference whether you choose a summer day on the

Randers heath to fall on someone, embrace him, try to kiss him, or whether at night in a dormitory that stinks like a monkey house you reach from one paillasse to the other for a sleeper's ass or his prick.

That other time too, at the edge of the forest, Borek would have turned him down, but it would have been a different matter, something Borek would have understood.

Reidel could not find the suitable term, the right word for the thing, so he limited himself to calling it *different*.

All he knew was that at the time, while the Danish summer was burning on his skin, he should have given way, instead of controlling himself and gazing past Borek with iron discipline.

Naturally it would have looked to Borek like exploitation of a situation, like blackmail.

"Aha," he would have said, "I just have to come across and you'll let me off fourteen days' arrest, eh?"

And Reidel would have been able to prove that he was not going to put in that report even though Borek did not respond to his feelings.

Or else they would have been even. Reidel would have overlooked Borek's breach of regulations; Borek would have kept silent about Reidel's overture.

But they would have had a secret together. Borek would have known about his feelings, would have known why the corporal who—as he later expressed it—spread acute anxiety around him was shielding him. He, Reidel, would sometimes have been able to risk a word, a surreptitious remark, which was better than nothing at all, than these years of impeccable behavior.

What had Borek called them yesterday? "Those years you adjusted, did nothing but adjust, you cowardly bastard."

He'd called him a cowardly bastard.

Yesterday, during their furious altercation conducted in whispers—Borek had rushed into the grain room next to the stable where they slept and Reidel had followed him—Reidel had not reminded him of that time he'd abstained from reporting the breach of regulations. There would have been no point in appealing to Borek's gratitude. Borek had seemed adamant, and his report was undoubtedly at Battalion by now.

Borek slipped him a note.

"The power of will," Reidel read, "I define as the desire with which everyone strives to preserve his own being solely according to the dictates of reason. Noblemindedness I define as the desire with which everyone strives, according to the dictates of reason, to support his fellow men and unite with them in friendship."

That was back then in Denmark, after Borek had gathered that Reidel had not informed on him, was letting him off those fourteen days of arrest.

"Rot," Reidel said. "Noblemindedness is cold coffee. It doesn't exist, has never existed."

"You've just shown noblemindedness," Borek said.

That was enough to send you up the wall. If this dope knew why he'd been lenient!

"I just happened to be reading that very sentence when you came along," Borek said.

"Is that philosophy?" Reidel asked.

"Yes. And other things."

"And for that they send people like you to the universities?"

"Not exactly for that. This, for example, is actually banned at the university."

"Banned? Why?"

"Because it was written by a Jew."

"You're reading a book by a Jew?"

"Yes. Does that bother you?"

"Show it to me."

Borek, obviously surprised, fingered at the pocket of his tunic. So he always had the book with him. He took it out and handed it to Reidel with surprise but without thinking any harm, dope that he was, apparently hoping that he, Reidel, would actually take an interest in it. (He had picked up the thin paperback volume in a secondhand bookshop in Breslau, some time after the beginning of the war.) Reidel did not even glance at the philosophical blather but without a second's hesitation ripped the little volume to shreds and with accurate aim tossed the pieces into a refuse bucket that stood nearby.

"You swine!" he heard Borek saying.

When he looked at him, he saw tears in the eyes behind the glasses.

"I don't give a shit about the Jews," Reidel said. "I just don't want anybody to find out that you're reading Jewish books." He counted off the names of members of the company, adding: "They're all in the Party."

He watched Borek as the kid took off his glasses and managed to fight back his tears.

"Damn it," he said, "they'd put you in a camp for that."

But Borek had not uttered another sound; he had merely stared at the wall of the barracks in Mariager, as fixedly as only a dope like him could stare at a wall.


I shall consider human actions and appetites just as if I were considering lines, planes, or bodies.

No one so far as I know has determined the nature and strength of the emotions, and what the mind is able to do toward controlling them, not even the celebrated Descartes and others, for all the excellent things they have written on these subjects.

By good I understand that which we know for a certainty is useful to us.

By evil, on the contrary, I understand that which we know for a certainty hinders us from possessing anything that is good.

The more each person strives for his own profit, that is to say, to preserve his own being, the more virtue does he possess.

Will power I define as the desire with which everyone strives to preserve his own being solely in accordance with the dictates of reason.

Noblemindedness I define as the desire with which everyone strives, in accordance with the dictates of reason, to support his fellow men and join with them in friendship.

Therefore, let the satirists mock at human things, let the theologians denounce them, and let the melancholics extol the uncultivated, rustic life; let them despise men and admire the irrational beasts; yet they will discover that men by mutual aid can much more easily provide for their needs and that only by united forces can they avoid the dangers that threaten them from all quarters. (Baruch de Spinoza [1632–1677], *Ethics*, 1678; banned after publication)

"The Americans are putting on the brakes."

He had blurted out this sentence when he arrived at Hainstock's shack day before yesterday, embittered, upset by the difficulties Kimbrough had reported to him.

"Captain Kimbrough is doing what he can," he said, "but he hasn't come a step further."

Hainstock forbore to point out that he had predicted this very outcome.

"Any idea why they're moving so slowly?" he asked.

"Supposedly for military reasons," Schefold said. "I can't ever remember that sort of thing."

From British officers Colonel R. had picked up the habit of holding a bamboo baton. There was no reason why he should have to explain the thing to Kimbrough. To do so in fact ran counter to all military principles and habits. But Major Wheeler had asked him to, and Colonel R. seldom let slip the opportunity to give inexperienced young officers lessons in operational thinking. "Let's just assume," he said, "that everything is all clear from the intelligence viewpoint—which isn't at all the case—and that we are absolutely sure nobody is setting a trap for us. For the encirclement movement required to round up this German battalion, which occupies the area over here"—the baton described a circular movement on the map that hung behind the colonel, the tip gliding from the Ihrenbach gorge over Winterspelt, along the Our and back to the Ihrenbach gorge—"I would have to start almost my entire regiment marching. In other words, for a single night we would have to sacrifice a strategic situation calculated in terms of the long view in order to undertake a tactical improvisation. Until the regiment returned to its starting positions, the entire southern flank of the division would be exposed for at least twelve hours. In addition, we do not know how the Germans will react to this unheard-of incident. We can assume, of course, that they will immediately close the gap. But in addition, they may be infuriated and in order to cover up such a reverse, and to prevent the example from being imitated, they might go on the offensive in our sector. And I need not tell you what that will mean. Pray to heaven, Captain, that the Germans don't get the notion of attacking us here!"

Replies, objections, were out of the question. The colonel had spoken.

However, Colonel R. decided to cover himself. In the course of his military career he had learned the hard way that you could never be safe from surprises in the tangled network of channels.

"Nevertheless," he said, "I'll report the matter to Division. And from there it will go on to Army. Therefore, Captain, don't count on an overnight decision in this matter."

"Yes, sir," Kimbrough said, thinking what a truly inexperienced young officer he had been when he had assumed that this extraordinary offer might be accepted in the course of a night. Instead, from the Saturday afternoon when Schefold had called on him up to the Monday afternoon when Colonel R. delivered this lecture, a full two days had passed before the matter was even treated on the regimental plane.

Incidentally, it is highly unlikely that Kimbrough repeated the specifics of the colonel's lecture to Schefold. While he could quite well conceive of refusing to obey an order, he would never disobey the rules of secrecy. Probably he had only dropped hints to Schefold, or referred to some farfetched military reasons which would have been so recognized by anyone familiar with military matters—Hainstock, for instance—but which Kimbrough could calmly outline because, as he had noticed, Schefold scarcely listened when he spoke on this theme.

Afterward, released from his status as captive audience at a lecture, Kimbrough could ask Bob Wheeler: "Don't you think my company alone could manage to round up twelve hundred weaponless men?"

"I think you've seen too many westerns," Bob replied.

"I have to disappoint you there," Kimbrough said. "It used to worry my dad that I would stay away from the movies when there was a western showing in Fargo."

We have already seen how Wheeler at this point distracted Kimbrough by enjoining him not to imagine that they, the Americans, were there to free the Germans or anybody else from that monster, and by airing his own views about establishing a *limes*, which so irritated Kimbrough that he spoke to Schefold about it and said: "This gives me one more reason for feeling we shouldn't have come over here."

He brought Wheeler down from the high horse of his historical theories.

"Do you too consider this German major a traitor?" he asked him abruptly.

"No, of course not," Wheeler answered quickly. "But you mustn't blame our people for not understanding the problems of these Germans. Most of them are hundred per cent Americans; they've never been outside the States, know nothing at all about Europe."

"The colonel only voiced what the army thinks."

"That's unimportant," Wheeler said. "Let's assume the thing did work out and Dincklage fell into our hands. You can be sure I'd protect him from all insults. During the first few days, after all, he'd be *my* prisoner; I would interrogate him and afterwards send him on to a special camp in England. The word *traitor* would never reach his ears."

I am a hundred per cent American, Kimbrough thought; I never was outside the States, know nothing about Europe, don't understand the problems of the Germans. What am I really doing here?

Colonel R., emphatically, definitively, when Wheeler and Kimbrough were already at the door, saluting: "Besides, we don't want to have anything to do with a traitor."

Was even a question, the hint of an objection, to his operational lecture—framed with due regard for rank, of course—at all conceivable? Certainly no more than that.

"I simply didn't take in·the military arguments," Schefold said. "Only what his colonel said to him at the very last: 'Besides, we don't want to have anything to do with a traitor.'"

God knows, I've every reason to let this fellow Dincklage run to his own destruction, Hainstock thought. But too much is too much.

"Then we'd best call the whole thing off," he said.

"Oh no," Schefold said. "Kimbrough still thinks that the higher-ups will say yes. His colonel is a blockhead, he said, and there are intelligent men on the divisional and army staffs. That's what I've come about. We have to gain time."

He could see that Hainstock was in a beastly humor, but still he went on and said: "This lady has to preach patience to Major Dincklage. Do you think she can?"

"Goddamnittohell," Hainstock said. "All right, I'll go to Winterspelt now. Wait here till I'm back. Make yourself some coffee. You know where the can is."

Waiting all afternoon for Hainstock's return, he had made coffee, dipped into Hainstock's books on geology, napped for a while in spite of the strong brew. When he awoke he saw the owl sitting on the bookshelves near him, the gray mask observing him. The bird did not stir even after he had opened his eyes. So they looked at each other, immobile.

At five o'clock Hainstock at last came back and declared that he washed his hands of the whole affair; though the Americans were obviously in no hurry, Dincklage was still obstinately insisting that Schefold was expected the day after tomorrow at twelve noon in Battalion Headquarters in Winterspelt. (In speaking with Schefold, Hainstock suppressed the information that Dincklage even knew what an American colonel had called him.)

He explained the directions Dincklage had drawn up for

Schefold and given to Käthe. Then he transferred the drawing to the appropriate section of the survey map, cut out the piece and handed it to Schefold. Schefold studied it, and as had happened that time he sat down on the stump, found he could dispense with it. All he had to do, coming from Hemmeres, after he had entered the forest of red pines, was to climb up the opposite slope, the eastern height of the Our valley, which here turned into the brook gorge. When he reached the top, he was there.

"Up at the top there will be a ticklish moment for you," Hainstock said. "I wouldn't want to keep that from you. Look around once you get up there! Don't just go barging ahead."

"There's still coffee in the pot," Schefold mentioned before he left.

He had walked through the woods to Hemmeres in the last deerhunter's light. Gray dusk; he stumbled over roots but did not have to be on his guard because there were no German reconnaissance troops to fear. In keeping with Hainstock's request, the major had not sent any patrols into the Ihrenbach gorge for days. Since Saturday Schefold could stroll through this wooded valley as if he were a member of the Eifel Outing Club, the discoverer and botanizer of an as yet unexplored biotope. (Schefold's interest in plants and cats was purely aesthetic.)

The white glimmer of the farm in the twilight. The sudden sense that he would have to leave Hemmeres. The Americans would not hold the area east of the Our. Even if they decided after all to press forward as far as Winterspelt during one of the coming nights, they would return as quickly as possible to their starting positions. Kimbrough had called it a raid for the purpose of capturing twelve hundred prisoners, and it was easy to imagine what would follow: new German troops would occupy Winterspelt, Wallmerath, Elcherath, perhaps this time—no, not perhaps, certainly!—place an advance guard in Hemmeres to close the gap in the front represented by the hamlet and the wooded gorge behind it. And there was no need to think even that far ahead. Even if nothing happened because the Americans finally decided to turn Dincklage down and because nothing came of this meeting day after tomorrow, on which Major Dincklage was obstinately and mysteriously insisting, nothing that could change the situation anyhow, the major himself would be the one to occupy Hemmeres, plugging the hole through which the subversion was trickling. Occupying Hemmeres would be the first of a series of acts by which he would bury the memory of his failure to commit treason.

Which meant, therefore, that Schefold had only two nights left in Hemmeres. Returning from Winterspelt on Thursday morning, after his visit with Dincklage, he would see the farm for the last time.

On the village street of Winterspelt he asked himself what he had been repeatedly asking ever since Tuesday: what was it that Dincklage probably had to communicate?

And whatever it might be, it would probably not be advisable to spend the coming night in Hemmeres.

I hope, Schefold thought, that he gives me a different escort for the way back to the top of the hill.

And if I have to come to him a second time, I'll refuse to come through the line. Once will have to be enough for him, he thought grimly, after a glance at Reidel.

But actually he could not imagine paying another visit to Major Dincklage, whether he came through the line or by some other, not so unpleasant route.

Supplement to Hainstock's conduct on Tuesday afternoon in Winterspelt, when he looked up Käthe Lenk so that she could bring Dincklage up to date on the status of affairs. As has been seen, he was aghast, so much so that, as we have reported, his eyes "became quite dark because the pupils widened so," when Käthe upon her return (he had waited for her at the Thelen farm; the big main room was empty in the afternoon on this working day) told him she had not refrained from informing Dincklage about Colonel R.'s use of the word "traitor." This was the first time that Hainstock was ever seized by actual dislike for Käthe. For his sudden sympathy for Major Dincklage, that excess of male solidarity, distinctly contained an element of antagonsim directed at Käthe.

But had he been entirely honest with himself about that? Shouldn't he have asked at that very moment—later he asked himself the question hundreds of times—whether it was not his fault because he surely would have done better to have kept that dreadful statement by the American colonel to himself, at least that afternoon? Why had he not kept his mouth shut? Because he assumed Käthe would not pass on to Dincklage this typically militaristic remark which in the ears of an officer constituted a monstrous insult to his honor? No, but because without reflecting on his own motives he was secretly hoping the opposite: that she—as he had afterward expressed it—would have felt herself a deceiver if she concealed from Dincklage something that he had a right to know. Without consciously admitting it to himself, Hainstock must have been hoping that Dincklage would shrug his shoulders and abandon the project.

Käthe judged him quite rightly when in response to his charge that she had endangered the whole operation, she retorted: "You'd be perfectly happy about that."

"You never have believed in it anyhow and still think it's foolishness," she had said.

"Certainly," Hainstock had replied. "And now more than ever. Now it is absolutely nothing but an isolated incident between two crazy officers. Unhistorical. As a Marxist I do not believe in the value of such individual actions."

She repressed the answer that was on the tip of her tongue: that she preferred an individual action to none at all. The argument came to her much too quickly for her not to mistrust it. And besides, if you had decided, as she had, to use the night in which Major Dincklage's play was to be staged as an opportunity to disappear in the wings, you had no right to recommend actions, individual or otherwise.

Schefold spent forty hours of solitude in Hemmeres, from dusk on Tuesday until today, Thursday morning around ten o'clock,

when he left the farm. The only incident was Kimbrough's visit
on Wednesday morning, just as Schefold was about to set out for
Maspelt to tell the American captain of Dincklage's request for a
rendezvous next day and to ask what he thought about it. After
the talk with Kimbrough he did not visit Hainstock again, but
stayed in Hemmeres, reading, preparing meals, musing, dreaming.
Perhaps Wednesday, October 11, was the most perfect of these
perfect October days of 1944; there are autumn days that can totally engross people who have nothing more to do than wait.

It would have gone against Schefold's grain to tell Hainstock
about Kimbrough's visit: "By the way, he came over to Hemmeres
to see me this morning, before I set out for Maspelt. I thought I
wasn't seeing straight. I had just finished breakfast, was smoking
my morning cigarette and looking out the window, when I saw
him come out of that dense underbrush on the other side, followed by two soldiers. All three had steel helmets on. They didn't
stop, but quickly crossed the meadow over on that side of the
river and started over the footbridge. By the time I came out of
the door Kimbrough was already outside the house, the two soldiers at some distance beside him, their submachine guns raised.
As casual as ever, he grinned, held out his hand, and said: 'Doctor
Schefold, I presume.' I was so dumbfounded I didn't even laugh.
Just think, Herr Hainstock, up to that time no American had ever
crossed the footbridge to the German farm. The anglers who
came down to the Our for a while always stayed in the bushes on
the other side. It was actually a historic moment. The Hemmeres
farmer and his wife stood petrified at the entrance to the barn.
Kimbrough said I should tell them to go on doing whatever they
always did at this time of day, but even after I'd repeated that to
them they didn't dare move. Of course my first thought was that
he wanted to take me away because he and Wheeler had come to
the conclusion that I couldn't stay there any longer; but he only
said he wanted to try out what it felt like to walk on German soil.
For a while he paced back and forth in the area outside the farmhouse, then came back and said: 'It actually feels altogether
different from walking around in Belgium. Or in Georgia. Don't
you think, Doc,' he asked, 'that frontiers are wonderful things? I

love frontiers.' He looked at everything, the solitary farmhouse, the meadow, the apple trees, the river, the wooded slopes, a buzzard hanging in the sky above us, and commented that I couldn't have chosen a better place. 'War all around,' he said, 'but not here. It's like a hole in the ceiling, and nobody will take the trouble to patch it.' Only the viaduct, which crosses the gorge farther to the north, disturbed him. I had led him to the spot where he could get the best view of the viaduct, and he shook his head as he watched that sentry game, the tiny figures emerging from the mouths of the tunnel, in olive from the left, in gray-green from the right, presenting themselves and then like clockwork figures being jerked back into the blackness. Up to that moment he probably hadn't known, just discovered it because I pointed it out to him, that his and Dincklage's men at this spot, on the viaduct of the railroad connecting Saint-Vith and Burgreuland, had come to a tacit agreement to behave as though this war were over for centuries and they were the only reminder of it, like the knights on the clock tower in Lemal. As we were returning to the farm, he said: 'It will be very important for the success of the operation that Major Dincklage withdraw the sentries up there on the viaduct.' Naturally this made me think he had come to tell me his superiors had made up their minds to accept Dincklage's surrender offer. Instead he said: 'Wheeler telephoned me last night and informed me that the army has turned it down.'

"We had sat down on the bench outside the farmhouse. He must have seen how disappointed I was, because before I could reply he said: 'Nothing has been decided definitely yet. It's quite possible that Hodges' chief of staff will reverse Army's decision.'

"General Hodges is the commander of the army corps. I asked Kimbrough: 'How long may it take before we know?'

"He shrugged. 'I don't know; Wheeler doesn't know either. Maybe the thing will go all the way up to Bradley. There's a possibility it might even reach Eisenhower. Wheeler said that what this German major proposes isn't a military operation but high politics. That's why I still have some hope.'

" 'I don't know whether Major Dincklage shares your hope,' I said, 'or what he is planning. He insists that I come to see him to-morrow at twelve o'clock.'

"You can imagine, Herr Hainstock, that this information left him speechless at first. He merely said, 'Oh,' then stood up and paced back and forth for a while. When he sat down beside me again, he said: 'Maybe it's a good idea for you to go. You must coax him into giving us more time.'

"We agreed that he would inform me at once if he received any definite word from his superiors before I went to see Major Dincklage."

But Captain Kimbrough did not receive any such word in time.

"Do you know what he said to me at the very end?" Schefold would have told Hainstock, assuming he had called on him once more in the course of Wednesday. "He said that he would have loved to conduct this raid all alone, just with his company, if the army actually refused to undertake it.

"You must realize, Herr Hainstock, that our conversation, while it wasn't exactly conducted in whispers, was kept very low because of the two guards, who stood around all the while, facing the woods through which I always pass when I come to see you, with leveled tommy guns."

He could imagine how Hainstock would react if he were to go to him and tell him this story.

"But you—on the basis of this you could tell him you're quitting," Hainstock would exclaim in an outraged tone.

So that he would have had to reply: "No, on the basis of this I just have to go through with it. Odd that you don't grasp that."

So it was pointless to bother Hainstock again, one last time. It was too late for bickering.

Perhaps Hainstock really did not grasp why Schefold did not pull out of the business. But he did realize very quickly that it was Kimbrough who would not pull out, who was entertaining illusions, who wittingly or unwittingly was keeping Schefold on the hook. Hainstock grasped that by Tuesday at the latest, when Schefold came to him with the message pleading that the major be patient. Such a plea could never have come from the American army; it had to be Kimbrough's. That realization explains why Hainstock said to Käthe that the affair was now "nothing but an isolated incident between two crazy officers."

Which did not prevent him, Wenzel Hainstock, who understood fascism, who was an experienced strategist of resistance, from saything that he, too, had done nothing to burst that bubble in time.

All Wednesday he hoped that Schefold would turn up and report that Kimbrough had ruled against the visit that this officer in Winterspelt had ordered on his own initiative. When Schefold did not come, he knew that nothing more could be done. He spent a sleepless night, and in the darkness of the shack followed the movements of the owl, whose nature it is to remain wide awake at night.

The implement shed next to the hay barn on any farm in Winterspelt. On such farms everything was under one roof: barn, stable, the family dwelling.

They had stood confronting each other last night, in this shed in which a lighted lantern cast jumbled shadows of harness, wagon shafts, wheels, plows, harrows, ladders, hoes. There was order only along one horizontal beam on which the group's rifles were leaning, with steel helmets, ammunition belts, and mess kits pedantically hanging from it, as ready to hand as the boots which stood beside the guns, polished but sagging and with folds above the insteps.

Borek was wearing only his shirt and long underwear (army issue) to which blades of hay were clinging. Reidel, in the darkness of the shed, had quickly put on his trousers before following Borek. A voice in the darkness, thick with sleep, had protested: "Hey, it isn't time to get up yet."

"You're a swine!"

Recalling his argument with Borek last night, he chiefly remembered that the whole thing had taken place as quickly as possible, in a tone of hate-filled whispering on Borek's part. Borek had not raged, at least not audibly, had not wakened the other ten men who were sleeping side by side to be witnesses of his crime.

"I know that. You told me that once before."

But it had been useless to try to appease him with reminders of earlier matters, to pretend to be the insulted and misunderstood one. The hatred in Borek's voice was all too real.

"You're not a swine because you're a fag. I can understand that part of it. But that a fag tears books to pieces . . ." He had fallen silent, obviously unable to find strong enough words for his feelings. Then he aped him: "'I don't give a shit about the Jews.' A fag says that. And then he tears up the book I cannot live without in this hell."

"I told you it was so they wouldn't put you in a camp."

"I'll get you put into one. Do you happen to know what they do with homosexuals in the concentration camps?"

All at once he was keyed up, was all ears.

"They sew red badges on the Communists, yellow ones on the Jews, black ones on the Jehovah's Witnesses and clergymen, and pink ones on the homosexuals."

Now it was Reidel's turn to glare with hatred. Not that this piece of information was anything new to him; he had heard it somewhere, sometime, or even read it in some newspaper. What rankled him was that someone would say this to him right to his face. But Borek seemed not even to notice that he was choking back his fury. Suddenly absent, he murmured: "I wonder what color they'll assign to me if I'm ever sent there."

Reidel thought: You'll find out. He waited.

Borek went on: "High time for you to be wearing a pink badge. Not because you tried it on me, but because otherwise you'll never find out where you belong. You should have held out, put up a fight for what you are. Instead you adjusted. Probably you're even proud of the years you were adjusting, nothing but adjusting, you cowardly bastard. And what have you turned into? A mad killer. A sharpshooter. How many people have you knocked off anyhow?"

"I haven't kept count."

That was not true. He had kept count.

A silence. There really was no more to say. But he had to make sure.

"So that's the reason you want to report me?"

"Of course. That's the only reason."

Borek had not made a row, had wakened no one. He had no witnesses. But that meant nothing. The item in the file would be stronger than all denials. Nothing counted against such an item in a file. That was why he had never made sergeant. Not even sergeant. That item in the file was sure as hell at Battalion. It would finish him.

Borek seemed suddenly tired, disgusted, as he said: "It was bad enough to be stuck in the army. But to put up with a homosexual assault from a fellow like you . . ."

What followed was that crap about what the others thought of Reidel, climaxing in that sentence about his spreading acute anxiety around him, a sentence that he could only laugh at.

Now only ten steps separated him from the office of their game-legged, bemedaled major.

Not adjust, hold out—easy to say for a kid like that who had done nothing but read books and who had never worked in a hotel, Reidel thought. Yet that was not what he really brooded on, but rather *swine* (so he'd held a grudge against him even in Denmark, since Denmark, because he'd torn up that Jew book, just to protect him), *cowardly bastard, mad killer, sharpshooter* (that eighteen-year-old nitwit couldn't tell the difference), and worst of all that snotty *a fellow like you* (much worse than the direct insults). And maybe I could have spared myself all that, and even being reported, if I'd been able to force myself to say the most ordinary thing in the world. A phrase simpler and shorter than that whole gentle line: that he's a delicate, transparent dreamer, with the kind of skin you can imagine rain pouring through. I could have gotten to him that way, after that short line.

But it's like somebody was standing on my brain, Reidel thought. I'm pretty damn slow on the uptake.

Instead, without any warning, I reach out for his prick. I must have been out of my mind.

The battalion orderly room. Terrific, the way it had worked out. Practically unbelievable that it could go so smoothly. All the way from his foxhole to headquarters nobody'd stopped him, questioned him, chivvied him.

Now there would be a few uncomfortable minutes. But he'd manage to deal with that bunch in there.

Aha, here they were already at their destination. Schefold had barely time to take in the picture of the house (half urban, characterless, gray stucco) before he was mounting the steps to the entrance. He opened the door, followed by Reidel, who had indicated only by a motion of his head that he should precede— an ugly customer to the last. Pausing in the hallway, he heard nothing but the rattle of a typewriter.

The lion's den, he thought. I'm in safety.

So that was what this man Schefold looked like!

But her curiosity about Schefold—tall, heavy, florid face, a gray, clipped mustache—why had Hainstock never told her about the mustache?—with those first impressions, her curiosity about Schefold was distracted by the brutal movement of the soldier's head —the soldier escorting Schefold. A diagonal jerk of the head from lower left to upper right to order his "prisoner" (for he was obviously treating him like one) to precede him. That was the way, exactly the way, that it had been done in Oranienburg, to judge from Hainstock's laconic accounts: mutely, sharply, permitting no resistance, contemptuously. This short, wiry corporal—she could make out the two silver chevrons on his sleeve, but not his face under the shadow cast by the steel helmet—must be a nasty type.

Yet this endangered scholar apparently did not seem to care that someone had reduced intercourse with him to a sign language of contempt and terror. Calmly, majestically, or perhaps only innocently and defenselessly, he walked up the few steps.

She stood back of the window in the main room of the Thelen

farmhouse, the same window from which, in the predawn darkness, she had once watched Major Dincklage waiting for her. Now it was daylight, the noon light of a bright though alternately cloudy and sunny autumn day. At this moment the period between October 2 and October 12 seemed to her an eternity.

It had taken a second, perhaps only half a second, perhaps not even that much—that ever so brief toss of the head that humiliation which had been imposed upon Schefold. That alone has been enough, Käthe thought, to prove that the whole project has been wrong, that I should never have bowed to Joseph Dincklage's demand that Schefold make his way through the line. She resolved, immediately after the interview was over and Schefold had left—not again accompanied by the same soldier, she hoped!—to go across to Dincklage for the sole purpose of explaining to him the importance of a jerk of the head rapidly from lower left to upper right. She must manage to describe that piece of sign language to him. If she did not do it right he would only shrug and say: "Oh well, if all that happened to him is a bit of rudeness on the part of an enlisted man. . . ."

And to think also that Schefold had to endure this rudeness on the part of an enlisted man for nothing, for nothing whatsoever! For his being summoned here today had nothing whatsoever to do with the operation, was only a mysterious whim of the man who had instigated it—no, he had only planned it, I instigated it, Käthe thought. Nothing whatever would come of this visit. There was no chance of the major's changing the situation. It was not his move. His opponents were taking plenty of time; perhaps they had already risen from the board, abandoned the game. One of them had insulted Major Dincklage. If he still had Schefold come, it could only be because he wanted to set a deadline for the Americans, present them with an ultimatum. A reaction of defiance. Käthe adjusted her glasses as she stared at the door that had closed behind the corporal. Really odd, she thought; it doesn't suit Joseph Dincklage's character. It has never occurred to him to present me with an ultimatum.

If he sets a deadline for the Americans through Schefold, she reflected, it could only be for tonight. Why should he wait for to-

morrow or the day after? (For which reason Hainstock was right
when, about fifteen minutes later, he said to Käthe: "I suppose
you're still hoping for a miracle to happen and the Americans to
turn up tonight.") No, Käthe had not really been hoping that,
only occasionally letting her mind play over images of the nocturnal meeting, as if to remind herself of her original hope. Actually
she had already put an end to that hope when she adjusted her
glasses after Reidel closed the door of the battalion orderly room
behind him.

Afterward, once she found out from Dincklage that nothing
had come of his conversation with Schefold, all that would
remain would be for her to ask him not to occupy the Ihrenbach
gorge and the hamlet of Hemmeres until tomorrow morning. He
would grant this request and undoubtedly not even ask her
reasons.

So she would be calling on him for another purpose besides
that of explaining a movement of a head to him, that menace
that had abruptly become visible to her.

She went out, took Therese's bicycle, which was leaning against
the stable wall. On the way to Hainstock she thought of the char-
acterizations of Schefold that later irritated Hainstock. A *gentleman. A fallen monarch. Unusually defenseless.*

Reidel gave one hard knock on the door behind which the rattling of a typewriter could be heard, opened it at once—

so there was no call of "Come in," no such call had to be
waited for—

directed Schefold to go to the right, along the wall beside the
door, noted that the orderly room was full, battalion topkick, the
clerk, the Pfc. who assisted him, the accountant; they turned their
heads toward him as soon as he entered with Schefold, and the
Pfc. at once stopped tapping the typewriter. The whole bunch of
ink pissers were here. Reidel came to attention, fixed his eyes on
the topkick, delivered his report,

while Schefold first of all took in the picture of Hitler that hung on the wall beside Kammerer, showing Hitler as a knight on a charger, holding a sword upright before him, hands clasped around the sword as if in prayer, and from the armor, a hauberk of the twelfth century, rose the face of a deadly earnest postal clerk, a thought that Schefold instantly rejected, for he loved postal clerks; very well then, the face of a morbid butcher of human beings who did his utmost to look like a postal clerk. Some idiot of a painter had hit on the idea of showing this figure in the guise of a knight dedicating himself to the ideals of knighthood: temperance, chivalry, chaste love, loyalty, and Christian compassion; it was the worst joke Schefold had ever seen. Among all the portraits of Hitler that Dincklage might have put there, had he chosen this particular one for his orderly room—for he probably had to hang some portrait of the fellow, couldn't very well get around that!—because it was a bad joke?

Only then did Schefold focus on the four uniformed men who sat in pairs opposite one another along a plank table, their faces turned toward him, then just a second later toward the soldier who now gave his report and whose name Schefold at last learned.

"Corporal Reidel, second company, with a civilian," Reidel reported. "The man appeared in front of the line and asserts that he has an appointment with Major Dincklage at twelve o'clock."

For a while Kammerer said nothing at all, not even after he had leaned back in his chair and taken the time to fix an eye on Reidel.

When he at last condescended to open his mouth, he did so to ask a question.

"Do you mean to say, Reidel," he asked, "that you left your post on your own initiative?"

"I had no other choice," Reidel replied as though fired from a gun. "Request you consider, Sergeant, that no officers can be reached today. Besides"—still standing at attention, he risked the

295

hint of a movement of his head toward Schefold—"the man was able to produce credible identification."

The argument about officers being out of reach today had come to him just in time out there on the village street. It was worth its weight in gold. He noted the vexation in Kammerer's eyes.

Meanwhile Schefold had decided to grant himself an incredible indulgence. He had decided not to remain where he had been placed, at a certain distance from the wall like someone who has been brought before a court, but had instead leaned against the wall, positioning his right leg casually in front of his left. Like the leg bearing the weight and the nonsupporting leg of a statue. Then he removed his pack of cigarettes and lighter from his jacket pocket with his left hand, held both objects briefly without looking at them, and only after a moment reached into the pack with his right hand, took out a cigarette, put it between his lips, and made a lightning exchange of lighter and pack in his hand, concentrated for a second on the flame of the small black and silver lighter, before his attention returned to his surroundings, to this orderly room into which, he felt, a nasty destiny had thrown him. This does not mean that Schefold had not attentively listened to the dialogue between Kammerer and Reidel, but nevertheless he started when Kammerer turned to him. Because Kammerer could not clear things up with Reidel, and because he was irritated by Schefold's cigarette but did not quite know whether he ought to forbid it, he snapped at him: "And you? How did you get in front of our line?"

"Schefold," Schefold said, detaching himself from the wall and giving a short bow. "Dr. Schefold. I live in Hemmeres. Would you please announce me to Major Dincklage. He will certainly give you all the information you desire, as he thinks best."

That was not just thrown out; rather, it had been agreed among the four of them, Hainstock, this lady, and the major. Hainstock, who thought of everything, had foreseen and forecast: "You will first of all fall into the hands of Dincklage's higher subordinates, and you may be placed in a situation in which you will have to answer questions. In that case, don't be afraid to tell the truth: that you come from Hemmeres. The rest you can leave to the major. For his part, he has to maintain that it is an intelligence matter. After all, he would have to keep silent about an assignment given to him by the regimental intelligence officer." "Very clever," Dincklage had remarked when Käthe passed on to him these tactical instructions.

What the four had not taken into their calculations was that someone who was not among the higher subordinates, who was merely listening, might start thinking. Something like this: He didn't tell me he lives in Hemmeres. If he lives in Hemmeres, how come he's met the chief? He acted like he knows him, blabbed about the Knight's Cross. How does he know that the chief has the Knight's Cross if he's never seen him because he lives in Hemmeres? How was he able to make an appointment with him? Hemmeres is cut off, it's in no-man's-land; none of us has ever set foot in it. So how's he worked this?

There's something fishy here, Reidel thought,

but his line of reasoning and the staff sergeant's reluctant decision to go in to Dincklage and announce Schefold were interrupted because the door with the sign reading *chief* had opened and the major, leaning on a cane, stood in the doorway, but only for a moment, for then he limped unceremoniously over to Schefold and extended his hand, saying: "Herr Doktor Schefold, aren't you? I'm delighted to meet you. Come into my office."

The two gentlemen shook hands.

So that proved that they'd never seen each other before. "I have an appointment with your battalion commander, Major Dincklage." Reidel, who did not think in terms of such concepts as *knowledge of human nature*, knew for a certainty when a man lied and when he spoke the truth. So this proved not only that they had never met, but that they had made an appointment. For what purpose and in what way did the chief make an appointment with a civilian who turned up in front of a foxhole coming from the enemy direction? There was a strong smell of rotten fish about this business.

Kammerer, who was not one to worry about what direction the chief's visitors came from, and who could tell himself that he had hitherto always been able to find out why they came from whatever direction, detained Dincklage before he vanished into his room with Schefold.

"Sir," he said, "Corporal Reidel took it upon himself to leave the line to bring this gentleman here."

Dincklage turned on his heel, studied Reidel a moment, and said: "Ah, so this is Reidel!"

Which meant that Borek must have written his report that same night and handed it in at the company orderly room immediately after the day's assignments. Under Winterspelt conditions the company topkick needed only to take a few steps to place it on the staff sergeant's desk. It was fabulous how quickly they worked when they came upon a case like his. When had the commander read Borek's scribblings? At ten, eleven o'clock? At any rate, in plenty of time for him to stare at him now and be able to say not to him but to the whole room (or to himself): "Ah, so this is Reidel!" with the emphasis on the *this*, so that there could be no doubt about there being something in the works concerning him.

Dincklage turned back to the staff sergeant.

"Never mind, Kammerer!" he said. "The man acted correctly for a change. Telephone the company and tell them so."

To the phrase exactly as he had imagined it! "The man acted rightly." The master sarge and Wagner would chew the rug in fury.

Reidel admitted to himself that he hadn't really counted on it's coming off all *that* smoothly. Was it going so smoothly because there were also others who wanted it to go smoothly? What does *others* mean, he asked himself, when the chief is involved?

It was a good sign—Reidel turned his conscious thoughts to this—that the chief hadn't stared at him the way a straight stares at a homo, disgusted and as though he can't imagine that such a thing exists.

How had he looked at him? Like a homo looking at another homo? Certainly not like that. But just looked. Actually rather decently.

But after all he'd been through, that too, the understanding look of officers who were understanding, decent to him because they'd read the item in his file. That was one of the things he couldn't stand at all. Every time such benevolence had been shown toward him, he'd thought in the end: Damn it to hell, kiss my ass! Not one of them had ever promoted him to sergeant. That far their friendliness had never gone. He much preferred tough superiors, officers who couldn't stand him and showed it from across the street, to whom he could oppose his own toughness, so that in the end they capitulated, shrugging, to his snappy soldiering.

Only—in his case and at this moment perhaps everything depended on the chief's having nothing against him just because he was a homo. And maybe understanding that even someone like him went off the rails once in a while. They had all the sympathy in the world for men who were hot for women; anything in that line, no matter how disgusting, was taken as a great big joke.

As though an idea had just come to him, Dincklage paused once more.

"Reidel is to wait here," he said to Kammerer. "Afterwards he will conduct Herr Doktor Schefold back to the precise spot from which he brought him. He knows the spot now."

"Very well, sir," Kammerer said.

Reidel sensed Schefold's movement more than he saw it, for his eyes, like the eyes of all the others, were directed toward Dincklage. But he caught a glimpse of the protesting jerk of the arm, the arm with the hand that held the cigarette, and he braced himself for an objection from the stranger; but Schefold said nothing, seemed to change his mind, and only went up to the desk, murmured, "Permit me," and crushed out the cigarette in Kammerer's ashtray.

"We will be busy for an hour or an hour and a half," Dincklage said to his topkick. "Send in some lunch for the two of us." Then he took Schefold's arm, led him into his room, closed the door.

"Take a chair," Kammerer said.

Reidel removed the carbine from his shoulder, leaned it carefully in the corner formed by the wall and a cupboard, so that it could not slide and fall, pulled over a chair, and sat down close beside his gun, keeping his erect posture even while he sat, looking straight ahead and observing that the four orderly room big shots were going back to their work, but that oddly they spoke not a word to each other. Aside from the clatter of the typewriter and the rustle of the paper, there was not a sound.

After a while Kammerer leaned back, as he had leaned back earlier, after Reidel's report, and fixed his eye on him. At that same moment the clatter of the typewriter stopped. Reidel did not change his posture.

Kammerer said: "You've got yourself into one pretty little mess."

Reidel, ready to react, sprang to his feet at once, clicked his heels, and cawed sharply in his high-pitched voice: "Wish to report, sir, that Private Borek is a traitor!"

We have so far heard nothing about Kammerer except for the fact that he came from Thuringia and was top sergeant of the 4th Battalion of the 3rd Regiment of the 416th Infantry Division and a member of the National Socialist Party. Let us assume that even before the war he had decided on a career as a professional soldier because his garage in Apolda did not really pay off. Let us also give him a family (wife and three children) that meant a great deal to him although he did not consider spending all his time with them as the most desirable of all conditions. (There are, after all, medium positions in the emotional realm.) Presumably he has the frame and face of most top sergeants, that somewhat stocky type of man who radiates authority and reliability, in whose features (were you to take a poll of them) full sensuous lips, unsteady eyes, indecisively soft chins or cheeks, or brows furrowed by thought scarcely ever occur. Instead of such qualities, topkicks have a kind of general and middling solidity. The parts of their faces stick close together. They display a talent for bellowing and for justice.

Granted, we are here undertaking to rescue topkicks from the general calumny. Everybody is familiar with their bellowing. As for justice, every soldier knew he was more likely to get it from the topkicks than from sergeants serving directly in the troop units. For example, on questions of granting furloughs. Moreover, topkicks were corruptible. A good topkick had a subtle feeling for balanced administration. That is what we call justice.

We do not even want to examine here why Hans Kammerer, staff sergeant and garage owner from Apolda, Thuringia, was a member of the Party of that man who hung on the wall behind him, disguised as a knight. Or why he had stopped wearing the badge of that Party—as Major Dincklage had observed—ever since they were in Denmark. At this moment that is entirely without importance, for after Corporal Reidel denounced Private Borek as a traitor and enemy of state, Kammerer did not for a moment think of the Party. That becomes obvious if we note (and all who were present in the orderly room noted it, even Reidel, especially Reidel) the way the look in his eyes changed from initial surprise to vexation to extreme repugnance as he contemplated Reidel. As rule no emotion could be observed in Kammerer's face. Now it could. A flush passed over his face, not of red, but of a dark pigment whose color could not be quite determined, the pigment of disgust. If it had been possible to hear Kammerer thinking, the words which in all probability would have been heard were: What a stinker! This is the worst stench I've ever run into. If he gets away with that, the whole battalion will go to the dogs.

Something like that. Then he got a grip on himself again.

"You have nothing to report to me, Corporal," he said. "You go through channels. But I can tell you one thing right now: if you think any tricks like that are going to get you out of your own stinking mess, you're barking up the wrong tree. Do you understand that?"

"Yes, sir."

"All right, now beat it. Go over and get yourself some chow. And stay away for a while. You poison the air here, Corporal. Do you understand that?"

"Yes, sir."

He took the carbine, slung it over his shoulder, clicked his heels once more so that they gave a loud report, extended his right arm, made a sharp about-face, and left the orderly room.

Since his hat was a steel helmet, he had not removed it all this while. Only fatigue caps had to be removed on a soldier's entering orderly rooms.

Inside, Kammerer said crossly to the Pfc.: "Telephone the company not to make any trouble for the sonofabitch. Say that after mess the man has been ordered back to the chief."

The clerk, a cheeky student, asked: "Can I use the expression sonofabitch, Sarge?"

"Don't you dare," Kammerer said, not even grinning.

First of all, he had acted rightly. The major had confirmed that for all to hear. Secondly, he was now at the commander's special disposition. He wondered whether this stranger would scotch the special assignment by complaining about him, would make a fuss about being escorted back by him. Thirdly, he had delivered his countercharge at once, had struck ruthlessly. He might also have pretended stupidity, might have replied: "Request information, sir, on what mess I've got myself into." That would have been more correct in terms of regulations, but it would have been lame. Now they were all thinking about his report, knowing that a thoroughly unpleasant business would be coming down on them. He'd fired a shot across their bow by informing on Borek. The best defense is attack. By now even the topkick would have seen the point and would begin to figure out that Reidel, driven into a corner, would stop at nothing, would go so far as reporting on him, the topkick, if he treated a case of treason lightly. If he didn't ignore a denunciation of alleged homosexuality because it came from a traitor, an enemy of the state.

Satisfied with himself, Reidel marched off to the field kitchen. As he turned into the carriage shed of the Merfort house, he saw that the recruits had returned. They were standing in the chow line or already spooning the stew up from their mess kits. Today they would have weapon cleaning and clothing repair. That meant that the line would be just as thinly occupied in the afternoon as it had been in the morning.

He immediately had a clash with Wagner, whose buttonhook eyes popped out worse than usual when he caught sight of Reidel, and who poured out all the expected phrases. ("What are you doing here?" "Well now, so you go for walks when you're supposed to be on sentry duty." "Incredible breach . . ." and so on.) Reidel didn't give a damn by now; he did not even bother about the proper forms of address, but said: "If you want anything from me, ask at Battalion!" Wagner: "You dare talk this way to me? I've a good mind to have you arrested on the spot." But at this point a company clerk came up and whispered something into the sergeant's ear, whereupon, shaking his head, he let Reidel alone.

When Wagner bawled him out—a corporal with years of service, in front of all the recruits—it naturally meant that he knew about Borek's report and figured his, Reidel's, goose was cooked. Probably the dope imagined that he was knocked off his feet on account of Borek's report and for that reason had left his post and was running around aimlessly in despair.

303

Reidel looked around. He caught glances that rapidly slid away. Probably they all knew about him, all the men standing around here in this farmyard. I'm a dope too, Reidel thought; I didn't realize that channels leak.

So Fritz Borek had still been able to come to the field kitchen. He wasn't hanging around quarters, exhausted, done in from the terrain exercise. He was sitting on a wagon shaft, another recruit beside him. When Reidel went over to Borek and stood beside him, the other man got up and walked away.

Reidel said: "At Battalion they're very much interested that you read Jewish books. Because without them you can't live in this hell."

Since there was no reply, he went on: "And that I'm some kind of mad killer. And ought to put up a fight instead of adjusting."

Borek looked up. If it were to rain now, Reidel thought, the rain would go right through that face.

"I'm sorry I wrote that report," Borek said. "I really am sorry now. I know you think I'm saying that because I'm afraid of you. But I'm not afraid of anything. I just wanted to tell you that I'm sorry."

Reidel was never mistaken when he felt someone was speaking the truth.

"Too late," he said. "Now it's too late for everything."

He wondered what the others were thinking, seeing him and Borek together like that, in confidential, almost friendly conversation.

Then he went to have his mess kit filled.

At half past twelve, after the orderly had brought lunch for two into the chief's room and left again, there were only the two noncoms remaining in the orderly room, the clerk and the accountant. The top sergeant and the Pfc. had gone to their quarters and were devoting themselves to their midday nap.

The accountant suddenly looked up from his figures.

"Did you see that?" he asked.

"Did I see what?" the clerk asked.

"Earlier. That guy"—he jerked his head toward the door of the room into which the major had withdrawn with Schefold— "That guy was smoking an American cigarette."

The clerk screwed the corners of his mouth down and shrugged his shoulders.

"Don't you realize," the accountant said, "that's wild. A live Ami cigarette. I not only saw it, I smelled it. I worked in the Hamburg Free Port; I know what they smell like."

"Get a grip on yourself," the clerk said. "I don't smoke; I don't know nothing about it."

"But I do," the accountant said, "and I tell you he was smoking an American cigarette. He took it out of the pack. I couldn't read the brand name because of the way he held the pack."

He had an idea, stood up, went over to the staff sergeant's desk and began searching his ashtray. Then he held up the remainder of Schefold's cigarette.

"Here it is," he said. "No question about it, an Ami butt. Too bad he smoked it down so far that you can't read the brand name. But only the Americans have this kind of tobacco. See that—how light it is."

He shredded the butt in his hand and held the tobacco out to the clerk, who glanced at it indifferently.

"How'd a guy like that get hold of one?" the accountant asked.

"Probably from captured stores," the clerk replied, going back to his work.

"Captured stores! Since when do we have captured stores from the Amis? If anything, they'd have stuff from us."

"Careful there!" the clerk said. "Besides, how much do you know? There's nothing can't happen in this war."

The accountant realized that he might be asking for trouble if he pursued the matter. He sniffed at the tobacco on his fingertips. The smell reminded him of those days in the Hamburg Free Port. When he had had enough of it, he let the shreds—from Virginia, he thought—drop into Staff Sergeant Kammerer's ashtray.

305

# Captain Kimbrough

You couldn't blame this German major if he were sick of waiting and so could not be coaxed to wait any longer but wanted to
send an ultimatum by way of Schefold that the operation had to
begin this coming night. This coming night or not at all.
Kimbrough was on his side from the first; for all sorts of reasons
this affair could not be postponed any longer. Would Bob be
proved wrong and the army at the last moment graciously conde-
scend to accept the surrender of a battle-strength German battalion? With this in view, would it bring the reserves of the 424th
Regiment (which was at any rate fully mechanized) up to their
jump-off positions? In a kind of noiseless thunderclap, to be ac-
complished by 2000 hours? By 1700 hours at the latest, Schefold
would be back, supplied with tactical instructions and sketches of
the position from this major, what was his name again, Dincklage,
Dincklage, Dincklage. Damned hard name to pronounce if you
wanted to give it the right German sound.

He had not yet decided what he would do if the army refused,
or simply did not move, continued to cloak itself in silence. But at
any rate he ordered a state of alert for his company for 1300
hours.

"No passes," he said to the master sergeant. "All the men not
on sentry duty are to stay in their quarters from now on. I don't
want to see anybody outside. Tell the platoon leaders to have
them clean their weapons."

Although the weapons must not be used, he thought. If so
much as a single shot is fired, the whole operation is done for.

He sent for Lieutenant Evans, leader of the first platoon, and
told him: "You have some men posted in the tunnel near Hemmeres. They want to watch the opposite end of the tunnel with
special care today. As soon as the Germans withdraw their sentries
from the tunnel, it must be reported to me at once."

Evans was staggered. "Will the jerries do that?"

Eight out of ten superior officers would have replied: "I've given an order!" Or at best: "No explanations called for." That was not Captain Kimbrough's style.

"They may," he said. "I have reason to think they may abandon their advanced positions tonight."

"I wonder whether my men will be able to see," Evans objected. "It's pretty hard to make out what's happening in a tunnel entrance at night."

"You'd better keep tabs on them," Kimbrough said. "Next thing you know your men up there will be playing cards with the Germans. I would strongly recommend, Evans, that you pay some attention to conditions up there on the viaduct."

He called Wheeler. When he had him on the telephone, he said merely: "Kim."

"Kim," Wheeler exclaimed, "I'm beginning to make a damned nuisance of myself around here. I've twice gotten on the nerves of the adjutant to Hodges' staff chief. That's going to cost me a couple of serious, very serious, reprimands. Regiment and Division are going to get their backs up. After all, I'm nothing more than a little intelligence sniffer."

"What am I to do," Kimbrough asked, "if Major Dincklage wants to pull this thing tonight?"

"How come you know that?" Wheeler's voice sounded alarmed.

"From Schefold."

"From Schefold?" Wheeler put all the incredulity and irritated astonishment he could into the name. "But he hasn't even been given the green light."

"At the moment he is talking with Major Dincklage."

After a long pause Kimbrough asked: "Are you still on the line, Bob?"

"Yes," Wheeler said. "The devil you say."

"Dincklage summoned him for today at noon," Kimbrough reported. "I myself heard about it only yesterday."

"When yesterday?" Wheeler asked quickly.

"Yesterday morning. I visited him in Hemmeres and he told me then."

"So you had all day yesterday to report it to me."

Kimbrough's shrug seemed to have been communicated to Wheeler through the wire. He said: "Kim, you knew of course that I would have forbidden this idiocy."

"After the way we've dawdled, it seems to me we aren't in a position to refuse the Germans' request."

"Rot," Wheeler said. "There are unwritten laws of war that this German major is supposed to follow too. According to your own arguments, his job now is to wait till he's blue in the face." He quoted: "The soldier spends most of his life standing around and waiting. But I forget," he went on, "that you're a Southerner. And how! Your ideas about personal honor. Your courtesy. That's why you lost the Civil War. You never counted on a type like Sherman. You did keep slaves, but above the slave level you were the noble knights of the Southland."

"Bob," Kimbrough said, "stick to your twelfth century. You don't know a damn thing about the South."

But Wheeler would not be sidetracked.

"Knight Kimbrough negotiating with Knight Dincklage," he said scornfully. Then he suddenly erupted: "Damn it to hell and gone, I forbid you to act on your own authority, Captain!"

"Yes, sir," Kimbrough said. He wanted to add: "I'm sorry, Bob, but it's too late," but Wheeler had already hung up. While Kimbrough sat there for a while with the receiver in his hand, it occurred to him that Bob had not answered his question about what he should do if word came from Major Dincklage that he was expecting the Americans tonight.

### March to the East

The convoy, forty ships, took twelve days for the crossing from Boston to Le Havre. (The speed was governed by the slowest ship.) The ocean was a mass of gray matter that spilled over in all directions. Boring. Only the ships punctuated the emptiness of the horizons; the sight of them provided some diversion. In the middle were the liberty ships, loaded with the division, surrounded by the pack of destroyers, mine sweepers. The rations consisted of canned food; they tossed the empty cans into the sea. At night, in the holds where they slept, officers and men together, many threw up when the sea grew rough. By day Kimbrough stayed mainly on deck, chatting with members of his company because he wanted to get to know them. In the afternoon he played bridge with Wheeler and two other officers in a corner of the quarter-deck. They did not encounter any German U-boats. Sometimes a man would point out the trail of a dolphin, thinking it the track of a torpedo. So that was the Atlantic Ocean, which his father had warned him against many years ago, when they stood on the beach of St. Simon's Island, looking out to sea. "Keep off the Atlantic Ocean," his father had told him. "What does the Atlantic want with us? Just one thing: for us to go back. But we Americans didn't come to America to go back where we came from, not ever."

Now, contrary to his father's advice, he was in the middle of this ocean. It struck him as just boring. Though that time on the beach at St. Simon's Island he hadn't thought it boring. Odd, he thought, how different the ocean can look depending on whether you see it from land or from on board a ship.

In the port of Le Havre, usable again only in the past few weeks, their heads swiveled around when they noticed the big banner hung between two posts rammed into the ground: GO WEST BOY GO WEST! Obviously tolerated by the Supreme Commander.

There was the army proving its sense of humor again. How well it knew how to take the bull of homesickness by the horns. Who'd be such a sissy as actually to want to turn back after seeing that?

The ruins of Le Havre. Rows of old, uniform French houses that were now transformed into old, uniform French ruins, carefully, methodically burned out behind façades so fire-blackened they looked as if streamers of pitch were hanging from the window openings. Perhaps they looked so startling because the streets were deserted and already cleared.

As soon as he set foot on the continent he was overcome by that malady of not being able to reproduce what he was seeing, thinking, feeling. Reading over his letters to his parents, to Uncle Benjamin, to Dorothy in Oaxaca, before he sealed them, he did not fool himself. The sentences were dead; they rustled like dry branches.

For example, he would have liked to describe what it was like to be standing in the yard of one of these old French or Belgian barracks where they spent the night before riding to the front. Not the shiny white barracks of the American camps, prefabricated, transportable, for folding wars; not the vast fields of tents casually dropped down and gone by the next day; but these walls of stone for standing armies, gray stones, blue stones, red stones, with mortared joints, with morsels of medieval castles, small towers, battlements, which made their dreariness even drearier. On the paved drill yards the companies sat in a square, every man with his rifle held diagonally in his arm, legs drawn up. As is customary in the army, they often had to wait for hours before they were allowed to move into their quarters. (Figure out the reason, if you can.) He, an officer, could while away the time by going around and trying to read the old French and the more recent German announcements and posters that were pasted beside the entrances, but he understood only a smattering of the faded, rain-washed French posters. Later, the echoing corridors. And even the next morning, when the companies lined up again, he told himself that he had never seen anything so dead as these barracks. He must be mistaken; they could not be all that dead, and if he watched closely, listened carefully, he would hear the echo of shouts reverberating from the walls, French shouting, German shouting, now American shouting too. But he heard nothing. Nothing. You couldn't even call it silence. It was the total absence of life. Gray stones, blue stones, red stones. An empty structure made by a child with stone blocks. Nothingness.

He would have liked to describe that to them. But he could not manage to find the right words.

The woods of the Ardennes, through which they rode last, were tuned to a darker tone than the woods around Fort Devens, from which they had come. But apart from the slight difference in the brightness of the two autumns, Europe's and America's, they flamed as endlessly and solemnly as the woods of Massachusetts. Only that they did not end in the sea. When the division was moved from Fort Devens to Boston for embarcation, John Kimbrough thought for a moment that the purpose of this trip was only to see how New England's Indian summer was drowned in the blue trough of the sea.

In the hilly country west of Concord, white toy-box villages perched on the heights, whereas the Ardennes had small gray towns in shadowy valley bottoms, or only stone churches, castles, drop forges.

Wheeler, however, saw this countryside in entirely different terms.

When they met in quarters evenings, he was likely to call out: "Have you seen Castle So-and-so, Kim?"—and he would mention some name that hardly registered on John Kimbrough. "Magnificent, isn't it?" And he would start telling him the history of Castle So-and-so.

Oh well, that was his subject. The army was providing Major Wheeler, professor of medieval German literature at the University of Indiana, with a research trip. Of course he might have to pay for it with his life. But with fair luck, that bill would never come due. The trip ended when they emerged from the forests of the Ardennes. Before them lay not the sea, but gentle mountains singularly deserted-looking, even to Kimbrough, who after all was used to uninhabited regions from Fargo and the Okefenokee Swamp.

## Maspelt 1400 Hours

For studying the region in which he was stationed, and in which some day he would have to operate—unless the 424th Regiment was withdrawn from this sector of the front by some inscrutable decree of the higher army staff and thrown into quite another sector before operations began—Captain Kimbrough referred to the same Belgian survey map (scale: 1:10,000) that Major Dincklage also spread out before him when he wanted to picture the situation of the battalion he commanded. The map showed nearly every tree, every telegraph pole, not to speak of sheep sheds and wood roads.

For the nth time Kimbrough thought through a plan which would not depend on support by the regiment or approval from the division, the army, or the army group.

In the event that Major Dincklage sent him word through Schefold that on the dot of midnight his battalion would be standing in Winterspelt ready to be taken away (giving the exact location on this map), measures could be taken in the following order:

The first platoon would use the Hemmeres tunnel, bypassing the villages of Elcherath and Wallmerath (although by rights these would have been evacuated by the German battalion, but better be on the safe side), and would reach Winterspelt from the north by way of the barren pasture slopes. Distance (from the tunnel), three kilometers; marching time, in the absence of roads, one and a half hours.

The second platoon would start in Auel, cross the Our on a still intact wooden footbridge, and approach Winterspelt directly from the west, on the footpath that led there from Auel. Distance, slightly more than two kilometers; marching time, at most one hour.

The third platoon would proceed across the Our south of Auel.

(The river was shallow enough so that no rubber boats would be necessary, although the men would curse at having to wade up to their hips.) Then through relatively pathless terrain (fields, patches of woods; Major Dincklage would have to guarantee that there would be no minefields along this route) and approach to the edge of Winterspelt from the southwest. Distance, five kilometers; marching time, at least two hours.

At two o'clock in the afternoon on October 12, virtually at the last minute, so to speak, Captain Kimbrough changed his plan. The third platoon could take the same route as the second, only making a detour shortly before reaching Winterspelt and entering the village from the south. That was much simpler.

In this way it would be possible for the three platoons to surround the Germans, who would be assembled for roll call, exactly on the dot of midnight.

The preconditions here were:

1) That the Germans would actually be assembled, all of them, when the Americans arrived. There were always some men so pooped that they stayed behind in their quarters, but these did not count. The majority of the troops would have to be present.

2) That the Germans would not have been standing around long, at the most a quarter of an hour, before the Americans arrived. They must have had time to become distracted, restive, but must stand like walls. Only a completely disciplined military force could be taken completely by surprise. So everything depended on precise timing.

3) That the place for the roll call be so chosen by Major Dincklage that the Americans would be visible when they appeared, but that their numerical inferiority to the Germans would not be evident.

The platoons must carry powerful searchlights with them and at a signal (flare?) switch them on. Then, in the glare of these lights, he would advance across the square to Major Dincklage, salute.

Brief address to his battalion by the major.

The battalion to be marched off in company and platoon formations, with sufficient distances between the units. Best route to take: the road to the north. Through Wallmerath and Elcherath, which would no longer need to be bypassed. Head them into the tunnel. Guarding an unarmed formation of battalion strength on the march by an armed formation of company strength no problem. After emergence from the tunnel assembly on the treeless pasture slope above Maspelt, which for this purpose must be surrounded by four MG nests. End of operation around 2 A.M.

Some time would pass before they realized, at Regiment, what had happened. You couldn't count on the arrival of a column of trucks from Saint-Vith before dawn.

But otherwise everything would go slick as a whistle.

Of course it was absolutely criminal to imagine that all this would go slick as a whistle.

The following possible incidents would have to be reckoned with:
1) After the first few phrases of Dincklage's address ("Fellow soldiers of the third battalion, the war is lost! I have therefore decided . . .") one of his subordinates would draw his pistol and fire at the major. (The enlisted men would be lining up without their rifles, but the sergeants and lieutenants would be wearing their side arms; they would have been highly disturbed if they had been told to come without them—that was unthinkable.)
2) Carried along by the subordinate commanders, a few groups would try to make a quick dash to their quarters to get their weapons. The result would be that within a few seconds all order would have broken down completely. The soldiers would become a confused, frantic mob.

In either of these cases he would have to give the signal to open fire, which would mean a massacre.
If his three hundred American tommy guns did not succeed in

decimating the Germans, the next thing would be a house-to-house battle in nocturnal Winterspelt. In such a battle his company would be wiped out. So he would have only the choice between slaughtering the enemy battalion and disaster for his own company.

3a) It was also possible that they would encounter resistance in the outlying terrain, as they approached Winterspelt. Perhaps some elements of the German battalion would not obey the order to appear for a night emergency without weapons. Some company commanders or platoon leaders might give such instructions on their own initiative. Or:

3b) The roll call might be secretly sabotaged by the second level of command. These subordinates might feel that there was something fishy about this sudden assembly of the troops, and after cautiously querying Regiment might recommend, by hints, lax execution of the order. Having taken the precaution of casually mentioning the strange order in the course of a telephone call about munitions supplies, for instance, a subordinate could then feel safe in treating the order carelessly, not letting anyone get stirred up to a real emergency mood. Unlikely that any suspicion of treason would arise—at most the uncomfortable supposition that the major was losing his marbles. A case for the medico rather than the regimental commander.

But in cases 1, 2, and 3a, at any rate, political fanaticism would enter in, and it would seem highly unlikely that fanatics would omit the chance for a big scene.

Although Kimbrough had no German ancestors and knew little about German history, culture or anticulture, in estimating the situation he came to the same conclusions as Hainstock—who had ample experience with the translation of German thought processes into German actions. These were the arguments Hainstock posed to Käthe on Saturday morning when he expostulated on the presence of a certain number of fascists among the subordinates and explained how they would briefly waver between slavish obedience and alertness upon smelling a rat, or even when he fell back on his private memories of the creaking noise that armies made. Of course such concurrence is really not so surprising. Every day Kimbrough read articles in *The Stars and Stripes* about German fanaticism. He also had not forgotten the statement he once heard in a lecture at Fort Benning on the causes of the war. The lecturer, an officer from the Psychological Warfare branch, in civilian life a journalist, had said: "Remember that this is not a world war, but a world civil war."

These Yankees, John Kimbrough had thought at the time, they're always so quick on the trigger with their civil wars.

So Colonel R., bastard though he was, was completely right in saying that for an operation like this one the entire regiment would have to be committed. He had analyzed the situation correctly right off. At least the entire regimental reserves would have to be called in. The Germans would have to be up against a crushingly superior force—only that would provide assurance against some sudden action on their part. In that case it would not even matter how noisy the force was as it approached, provided that the noise was the clank of a few Sherman tanks and the racket the artillery companies made.

Those fading images of a single company stealing up on Winterspelt came from movies. A western with the inevitable massacre at the end.

If a single shot would suffice to transform Winterspelt into an inferno and blow the whole operation to high heaven, then it followed with absolute logic that the company had to carry out its mission unarmed. An unarmed company would capture an unarmed battalion.

If word of this idea ever got around, every man in the army would split his sides laughing.

Not that this need bother him. But the affair presupposed a contract, even if an unwritten one. Yet such a contract would be worthless, would be legally null and void, Attorney Kimbrough reflected, because the only German who was putting his verbal signature to it was not entitled to sign.

## On Realism in Art

"Don't you take some interest in our history?" Uncle Benjamin used to ask when his nephew again refused to see a western that was running in a movie theater on Broughton Street.

Teenager John Kimbrough did not dodge the question. But before answering he would look off for a while, depending on where they were—sometimes he would look at the colonial-style pieces in Uncle Benjamin's furniture store, sometimes at the steamers on the Savannah River. Then he would say: "I don't like it when so many people are always falling down and pretending they're dead."

"Would you rather have them really dead?" Uncle Benjamin asked in surprise the first time he heard this explanation.

"The landscape and the houses and the way they ride and the clothes they wear are all genuine," John said. "Or at least pretty much so. But when they fall off their horses or die some other way, you know it's fake. I think it's stupid."

Uncle Benjamin looked at him over his glasses. "The historical situation is authentic," he said. "And there was a lot of killing. The movie has to find a way to show that."

"But I just don't believe those people are being killed, Uncle Ben," John countered. "I know perfectly well there isn't any blood running from their foreheads or their chests. If it were real blood I couldn't go on sitting in my seat at the movies."

"You're a funny kid," Uncle Benjamin said.

The fact that he was a funny kid meant that at least one student at Oglethorpe High School in Savannah missed out on several attacks by the Oglala, on the Battle of Fort Apache, on the

319

deeds of the Texas Rangers, on the exciting throb of drums on
the Mohawk, and on the heroic defense of the Alamo; but at least
he missed no scenes from the War Between the States, because
the Hollywood movie industry was noticeably reluctant to portray
the battles of that war. It was considerate of the feelings of its au-
diences in the South.


## The Biggest Painting in the World

The biggest painting in the world (total length: 400 feet) was
to be found in the cyclorama building of Grant Park in Atlanta.
It depicted the first battle of Atlanta, which had been fought on
July 22, 1864, and won by the South; the Confederacy had lost
the other battles of Atlanta. Naturally John Kimbrough couldn't
avoid having a look at it during his student years in the state capital. And while he studied it he asked himself whether battles
might actually be as they were represented in this painting, done
by German artists in 1886. So pretty. Perhaps the puffs of smoke
from guns actually looked blue-gray and delicate. Perhaps—there
was no reason to dismiss the idea out of hand—fallen men, at
least immediately after they had fallen—lay in by no means horri-
fying positions, but rather looked as acceptable as did General
McPherson, who lay struck by a Confederate bullet beside his
likewise outstretched black charger, clearly a thoroughbred from
one of the noblest Kentucky stables. Even if there were no longer
horses rearing up all over a battlefield, a battle—the immanent
*idea* of a battle—came down to the notion of gallant (Southern)
*platoons* waging an assault against superior (Northern) forces.
John examined this notion in all seriousness and decided that it
was not wrong, merely incomplete. It lacked—as did the film
scenes and the biggest painting in the world—the fact that bullets
and bayonets had penetrated into the bodies of men who a moment before had been alive. Beautiful death overpowered someone
who had just drunk coffee. It was already bad enough that there

was nothing to be done about ordinary death. When he had come to this point in his thinking, John hurried to get out of the cyclorama building.

Years later, during the crossing from Boston to Le Havre, he told Major Wheeler about his distaste for those representations of war.

"Then I'd like to know why you volunteered for the army," Wheeler said, laughing.

"That's why," Kimbrough said. "It's clear enough."

"Excuse me, Kim, but it isn't all that clear," Wheeler said.

"Oh well, I saw the war coming," Kimbrough said. "That wasn't hard. You must have seen it coming too."

He stopped there. Wheeler persisted.

"So?" he asked.

"It was a real war. Naturally I wanted to see what real war was like."

*Maspelt 1500 Hours*

His room in the company command post did not have a window on the village street, but toward the pasture slope in the rear, so that Kimbrough could not tell whose jeep noise was breaking the silence of his alert until Major Wheeler wrenched open the door, closed it carefully behind him, and said so softly that his words could not possibly have been heard in the anteroom: "I came to stop you from committing a folly."

He removed his cap and battle jacket and sat down at the desk facing Kimbrough.

"I'm glad to see you," Kimbrough said. "But of course you didn't have to bother on that account. What you call a folly won't be taking place."

"All the same you've put your boys on alert," Wheeler said. "I talked with Lieutenant Evans earlier, on the outskirts of the village."

"I ordered the alert just in case Regiment does go along with it after all," Kimbrough said. "There is the possibility, isn't there," he asked, slyly, mockingly, "that Regiment may at the last moment pull itself together?"

"No," Wheeler said, "this possibility doesn't exist. Get that idea out of your head, Kim."

Kimbrough looked at the survey map that still lay spread out before him. He said: "Besides, we don't know what-all this Major Dinckledge . . ."

"Dinklahga," Wheeler corrected him. "An old Westphalian family name. The root has nothing to do with the German *Ding* in our sense of *thing*, but with *thing* in the Old Norse and Old German sense of a legal assembly. In Middle High German *dincflühtic* is a man who flees the jurisdiction of a court. So *dinclage* would be someone whose case is in court. Or perhaps Dincklage's people were judges. But so far I can make only a guess. I'll have to wait until I'm back in Bloomington and can consult the right dictionaries. Or in a German university, a few weeks from now."

"Very interesting, Professor," Kimbrough said. "Many thanks."

Wheeler ignored the sarcasm. "I can hardly wait to see what condition the German universities are in," he said. "It would be wonderful if we got to Heidelberg or Göttingen and I could have a go at the Grimm Dictionary there. Although I really hope they've stowed the libraries in bombproof hiding places and will have to shelve them all again."

Kimbrough left him to his academic reveries for a few moments before reminding him: "What I wanted to say was—we cannot know what news Schefold is going to bring back. Maybe this German major has thought of something . . ."

"That's just it," Wheeler interrupted, snapping back at once. "I don't trust you across the street, Kim. You're capable of plunging ahead if this guy so much as makes a suggestion that strikes you as plausible. Or if he gives you his grand word of honor that everything will work out."

"You forget that I'm a lawyer."

"You mean coolheaded, I suppose. I know a good many lawyers who are anything but coolheaded. Most politicians were lawyers before they became politicians."

"I'll never go into politics."

"Jesus," Wheeler said, "you're only thirty. From all you've told me, you joined the army in '41 because you couldn't stand watching what a character like Gene Talmadge was making of your Georgia. And now at this moment you can't stand watching the army behave the way armies always do behave. You're just the stuff politicians are made of."

Kimbrough shook his head, but did not reply. Bob Wheeler didn't know Old Okefenok, so he couldn't know there was a swamper hidden behind the mask of captain and lawyer. The swamper in him would never put up with financing election campaigns, attending meetings, shaking hands. He was able to make a pitch to jurymen when it was a matter of life and death all right, or to behave like an idiot in the matter of this German major, but what did anything like that have to do with politics? It was rather the very opposite of politics.

## Wheeler's Coat of Arms

Lean but not scrawny, rather taut, elastically self-contained, of medium height, sparse mustache, strong glasses—in uniform Major Wheeler looked the way every professional officer in the services would have liked to look: virile, aloof, competent. His effectiveness was based on the fact that a man who looked as aloof as he did could without a trace of condescension sit down beside a student, a younger officer, a scout, or a prisoner of war and talk with him quietly, objectively, but interested to the point of probing curiosity. A contrast effect. Wheeler even succeeded in giving a wary interlocutor—and he was constantly running into that kind—the illusion that he had picked out Wheeler to talk to, although of course Wheeler had picked him out. People liked Wheeler; he gave them the sense—not of being understood, but the sense that someone, unemphatically, casually, was making an effort to understand.

This was the manner of John Kimbrough's acquaintance with him. John was extremely surprised when this man, whose appearance suggested academic and military arrogance, a tendency to look down on people, rather courted him during the twelve days of the crossing from Boston to Le Havre. Wheeler sat on with him after the bridge game was over and, as they looked out at the boring circular horizon of water, drew him into serious conversations. At first John had the impression that Professor Wheeler was conducting a seminar with him on the South, Georgia, and the historical and social causes of what he had promptly called John's isolationism. Toward the end of the voyage Kimbrough realized that he had made a friend, and not just because Wheeler, once again addressed as "Major," exclaimed: "For heaven's sake, call me Bob!"

To understand Major or Professor Wheeler, we must imagine him at the University of Indiana in Bloomington. The town is situated in the midst of the dreary expanses of the northern Middle West (which, who knows, may have its hidden charms), an hour by prop plane south of Chicago, where there is no spring and no fall, only a gray winter and a summer of unbearably humid heat. Main Street in the town of Bloomington is a colorless, down-at-heels wasteland of store fronts and shop signs. At the eastern end of this street—you are already out of the town—a park with old trees begins. The university is hidden within this, a shapeless but spacious and pleasant place with the sprawling quality of a luxury hotel or spa of the twenties (perhaps it once was). The park and the buildings are in every respect an island, among other things an island full of music, for the glory of the Bloomington campus is its institute of musicology. It is obvious that universities amid waving fields of grain, whether they are situated in Indiana or Turkestan, must develop their own pride, their own modesties. Scholars exposed on the bleak prairie, desperately dreaming of landscapes that are soaked in history, would sooner bite off their tongues than let on to a rare guest from the east who has strayed into Bloomington that the university could fully compete in research and learning with the guest's famous old cultural center. (Ah, we would recommend to gentlemen from Bologna or the Sorbonne not to introduce the slightest note of patronage into the brief scenario of their visits!) Wheeler was no exception: his constant understatement with regard to Bloomington was accompanied, at least until the mid-thirties, by uncritical faith in the superiority of European education, nostalgia for his four semesters in Heidelberg (1925–26).

We do not know the reasons Wheeler became a specialist in Germanic linguistics and a medievalist besides. That is what he became, period. His monumental work on Heinrich von Veldeke, the father of the German courtly epic, was considered by specialists (along with the studies of Frings) to be *the* book tracing the route from a classical subject (Aeneas) through a French intermediary to Middle High German poetry. Since that publication he had made no stir in scholarly circles, but had devoted himself more and more to his teaching and the pursuit of manuscripts for the Bloomington Collection (the latter an especially anonymous activity because at most ten experts in the whole world knew that a manuscript collection of such incomparable importance had been assembled in the American Midwest).

So much for the pride, the modesty, of Major Professor Robert (Bob) Wheeler. He was the same age as Hainstock, fifty-two, married, two sons, the oldest of whom was with the marines in the Pacific. The army which had assigned him according to Category F (German teachers to be used as intelligence officers) had struck gold. Someone with such a gift for listening was priceless in the intelligence service.

## Statement on Comradeship

The relationship between Major Wheeler and Captain Kimbrough was comradeship: not a collective (mythic) happening, but the rapport between two, sometimes three, in rare cases

several—at most four to six—individualities (psyches). Comradeship exists only while two soldiers belong to the same unit; if one
of them is transferred to another formation, comradeship dies. A
comrade is the fellow with whom you have conspired against the
collective, often unconsciously. The idea that comradeship arises
from mutual aid in armed struggle against the "enemy," that is
from what are normal acts in the mechanics of warfare, will not
hold water. Proof: most of the acts and feelings of comradeship
arise independently of any system of reference to the "enemy."
The "enemy" is not the enemy, but the jailhouse, the iron discipline, of the military collective in which the comrades are
confined.


### More on: Maspelt 1500 Hours

Together, they went through the maps, checking all the arguments for and against the action. Together they came to the same
conclusions that Kimbrough had come to by himself. Wheeler
said: "I don't know why the devil you called me for advice. Even
this damned Major Dincklage should be able to see how hopeless
it is."

"Oh, I was just talking," Kimbrough said.

"You weren't just talking," Wheeler said. "I know you better
than that, Kim."

He assumed a strictly official tone. "Because you informed me
about this premature visit of Schefold to Major Dincklage, it was
my duty as your ranking officer to come to Maspelt and make sure
nothing is done that Army might not like. So I'm going to stay
here until Schefold returns. If at that point you mean to make
any reckless decisions, I'll temporarily relieve you of your command and assume command of C Company myself . . . I'm sorry,
Kim," he went on, reverting to his friendly tone, "but when you
telephoned, you must have been glad that from this moment on
the responsibility lay with me."

Kimbrough folded the map and laid it aside.

"Nobody would ever learn that I informed you," he said. "Not from me, anyhow. So you could have just let me go ahead."

"If you mean that, you're fooling yourself," Wheeler said. "If you had been one hundred per cent resolved to pull this thing off behind Army's back, you wouldn't have telephoned me."

He brooded a while in silence before he said: "You called me because you wanted me to come."

## *Biogram*

John D. (for Dillon, after his mother's maiden name) Kimbrough, born in Fargo, County Clinch, Georgia, in 1914, the son (he had a sister five years older than himself) of poor farmers Isaac Kimbrough and his wife Nancy. On his father's side Kimbrough was descended from Scottish immigrants (his father had traced his name to a Kimbrough who was among the Scots who came over in 1736 and settled on St. Simon's Island), on his mother's side from Puritans who in 1752 immigrated into Georgia, not at all from England but from South Carolina. (In countries where the historical processes are no older than seven generations, people are still keenly interested in genealogy and can even prove their descent. The possibility of extramarital love affairs and their consequences—for example, the fact that a woman of the Kimbrough clan could be swept off her feet by a foreign soldier during the occupation of St. Simon's Island by the Spaniards in 1742 would have been puritanically repented by the lady but also strictly concealed; the child could easily have been foisted upon her husband—this possibility is simply ignored by racist genealogists.) John D. Kimbrough could therefore call himself an American of old stock. The proud past, or at least the past imagined as proud, was long since gone. How John's father became poor, like most of the farmers in Fargo, cannot be related here. There exist voluminous studies of the decline of agriculture in the

South since the Civil War (and before). As a young man Isaac Kimbrough had participated in the populist movement, had remained loyal to Tom Watson until 1908. Now, aged sixty-five, he was still living in his more and more decaying farmhouse between Fargo and the edge of Okefenokee Swamp. He had been able to hang on to the farm at all only because of the supports and credits provided by Roosevelt's New Deal, and because of John's being able to contribute a monthly sum after he became a lawyer, and later an army officer.

Uncle Benjamin Dillon had intervened when John reached the age of twelve. After looking through the boy's school notebooks and talking with Miss Tibbett, the village schoolteacher, he had taken John into his home in Savannah. Uncle and Aunt Dillon, who were childless ran a used furniture and antique shop, Ye Olde Shoppe, in their home on Quai Street. In addition Uncle Benjamin permitted himself the luxury of putting out a small magazine called *The Hermitage* which dealt with local history. John's high school years went on until 1932. Homework in a room that looked out over the river and its traffic. Freshman and sophomore years at the state university in Athens; then, when he decided on law, four years at the Lamar Law School of Emory University. "Tom Watson learned his trade in a law office and just hung out his shingle when he was twenty," Isaac Kimbrough would say when his son spoke about his studies.

John was twenty-five when he joined a law firm in Savannah. Civil suits did not interest him. Outraged by the operations of Georgia's penal code, he took the criminal cases, defended murderers and robbers, paying visits to them in the notorious Milledgeville Prison. He had the bad luck to be a young lawyer in Georgia during the years Eugene Talmadge was governor. At the time the whole country was reading books like *I Am a Fugitive from a Georgia Chain Gang* and *Georgia Nigger*. John D. Kimbrough quickly became famous for the way he would go at a jury, but he made himself unpopular when he attacked the jury system itself—in a series of articles in the Atlanta *Journal* he called it the sacred cow of American jurisprudence.

In the summer of 1941, six months before Pearl Harbor, he threw up everything—to Uncle Benjamin's consternation—and enlisted in the army. After basic training he was invited to become an officer candidate, and since he had no objection was transferred to the infantry school in Fort Benning. He advanced rapidly, was a first lieutenant by 1943, and early in 1944 was sent as a captain to the 424th Regiment which was being formed at Fort Devens, Massachusetts. The army made a practice of sending officers from the South to lily-white formations. That was how John Kimbrough came to head a company of men from Montana who were destined for the European theater of war. He would rather have been sent to the Pacific. Though he had a pretty good idea of the roughness of the war against "the Japs," he sometimes still dreamed about palm trees and coral reefs.

Up to that time he had hardly ever left Georgia, aside from three trips to New York in 1940 when he went up North to visit Dorothy Du Bois, the daughter of a murderer whom he had defended, incidentally without success. He had met her in Milledgeville Prison when she was visiting her father shortly before his execution. When Kimbrough went to New York for the third time, he found her no longer there. Later she wrote to him from Oaxaca, Mexico. Various girls in Savannah, Athens, Atlanta, Savannah. He was easygoing in a gravely friendly way that juries and girls liked. As for his appearance, this is how Schefold saw it on the village street in Maspelt: lean, with straight black hair that fell over his lean face, violet eyes. Was this face truly the legacy of that Spanish soldier on St. Simon's Island in 1742?

Kimbrough liked to live quietly—for example, he did not take part in university sports, did not join a fraternity; but he was not so inclined to keep his thoughts to himself. In fact, he was in the habit of speaking out on significant matters.

### Maspelt and Fargo

The country around here could not be compared to the South. For example, the oaks and beeches, on October 12, were virtually stripped of their leaves, whereas the willow oaks along the streets

329

of Savannah would still be bearing their burden of golden and pointed leaves.

Or Fargo? There the goldenrod would only now be fading along the sides of the road, and the air would still be fragrant with honeysuckle. Only now would the sumacs have kindled the red flames of their leaves. Red oaks, yellow, pink, and dark-red maples against the pines. The cry of the crickets still. In the sky the long wedges of Canada geese.

Or the groundsel with yellow blossoms, the sweet gums, the Carolina poplars. The balsam trees, the cinnamon bushes, the blue ring-doves.
Here the air was cool and crisp; there it was warm, soft, sleepy.

The Our was dark and glittering. The Suwannee was a dark river also, but dull, motionless silk, its shores imperceptibly merging with lotus leaves and water-lily pads. From the boat you could watch the wood ibises, coppery red, feeding in the dim light beneath the tupelo trees.

Not much wind, the evening light fluffy, but sometimes a hurricane coming up from Florida or from the ocean.

The smoke of wood fires was the same, here and there.


### Real Estate and Blues Notes

The poverty was the same too, the poverty of too small agricultural units, except that here the walls were of rubblestone, packed under slate roofs, whereas there the walls were boards that dried in the sun, the paint flaking off, cracks gaping, nails springing. The windows were kept in repair and well screened because of the mosquitoes. But one of the treads on the porch steps was missing; it had been that way for ten years.

2 cotton fields
2 tobacco fields
1 mowing
1 vegetable garden
2 cows
2 dogs (always setters, not quite thoroughbred)
1 pig
chickens
cats (sometimes 2, sometimes 3)
1 house (one story, with a porch)
1 barn (near to collapse and almost always empty because nowadays the dealers came with their trucks right after picking time and took the stuff away)

But from his boyhood he still remembered the smell of the markets in Homerville, tobacco in July, cotton in October, when farmers stood by the hundreds next to their brown and white bales tied with yellow hemp.

In those days, in the twenties, his father had a small black Ford, like all the rest of the farmers. The only cars you saw on the rough highways of Georgia in those days were those small, high-wheeled automobiles. Later, when the Depression got bad, Isaac Kimbrough had to sell his car.

Rufus Magwood's and Joe Proctor's shacks also stood on the Kimbrough farm. (If Captain Kimbrough had ever seen Wenzel Hainstock's shack in the quarry, he would have exclaimed: This reminds me of Rufus's place.) No electric light, and the water had to be fetched from a standpipe by the road. Rufus and Joe were now nearly seventy, but they and their wives were still John's father's farmhands. Joe could prove that his ancestors hailed from Bonoua on the Ivory Coast. (Slaves went in for genealogical research too.) Rufus was skilled at making baskets out of palmetto stalks which he cut in the swamp. His baskets were in demand all over Fargo and the vicinity. He was a small, taciturn man, with a gray beard and glasses, who never removed his gray felt hat. They don't have them here, Kimbrough thought: Negroes. He wondered what the farming here would be like if they had Negroes, and heard Joe Proctor's fine baritone voice, accompanied by a guitar, singing "See See Rider" and other songs of the lost paradise. The diminished thirds, the diminished sevenths, drifted across the cotton field all the way to the farmhouse.

"Animals! They're animals!" he once heard a visitor say; the man had been talking with his father about the Negroes.

After he left, John—he was sitting on the floor in front of the stove with the two setters—said: "Dad, didn't you once say that when we live with dogs, when we get to know them real well, we realize they're the same as people?"

His father, who had already reached out for one of his books, answered: "That's right, son. Only a lot less ornery than most people are."

He would take up his heritage. If he survived the war and set up as a hole-in-the-wall lawyer in Savannah—which was exactly what he'd made up his mind to be: the pettiest of lawyers, renting an office on one of the side streets off Broughton Street and fighting hopeless criminal cases—his income would still be sufficient for him to take over the farm after his father's death. Naturally he'd give up the farming end of it, putting in some kind of orchard in the tobacco and cotton fields. Rufus and Joe would have enough strength left to plant trees and sow grass. He himself would be in Fargo only on weekends, and of course also the whole long, unbearably hot summer, patching up the house, maybe having a new one built. His mother would not object to such changes; she'd had enough of farming. He'd make arrangements with his sister; she had married and she and her husband, who owned a grocery, now lived in Columbus, Ohio. John Kimbrough smiled whenever he pictured himself as a lawyer with a country place, if he survived the war.

The most important item would be buying a new canoe. Last time he'd been home—during a furlough from Fort Devens in August—he'd found the old one quite water-logged, lying sunk beside the gray landing, that by now was rotted through, ready to collapse, pilings and boards over half a century old, half a century on the edge of the swamp.

## Populist Movement, Civil War

From Uncle Benjamin's critical but well-meant comments on John's father:

"All that reading your Dad does won't bring Populism back from the grave."

"The story goes that Tom Watson, pale as a corpse, used to sit on his porch all day long reading poetry before he descended on the countryside like Jeremiah. Story goes that he could say a great many poems by heart."

"But Dad doesn't read poetry."

"I should think not. Still and all."

"Tom Watson made one big mistake. He wanted to coax the poor whites into letting the blacks take part in the revolt. But when he said that the blacks would get some of the benefits too, the whites deserted him."

"Maybe Rufus and Joe stuck with your Dad only because he was known to have sided with Tom Watson on this question too. That probably saved the farm for your Dad. Without Rufus and Joe he couldn't have made it through the early thirties."

"But what a bad loser Tom Watson was. When Populism was done for, in the elections of 1908, he turned bitter and became a demagogue. He took back all the things he used to preach and started writing articles against Eugene Debs and the Socialists, accusing them of the same things he'd been accused of. He ranted against the Jews, the Catholics, and even the Negroes, though he'd formerly been their friend. I could hunt up the issues of *Watson's Magazine* and show you."

"Never mind, Uncle. I'd rather hear what you have to say about it."

"Debs came right back at him, pointing out how petty-bourgeois and small-farmer revolts always ended in fascism. Such explanations don't mean a thing to me. Fascism is just a word to me. Populism too, by the way—I've often argued with your Dad about that."

"Well, how do you look at it, Uncle Ben?"

"To me the main thing is character. If people have good character, everything they do will be good, no matter what they call it. If they have bad character, everything will be bad, no matter how they dress it up in words."

"But in politics it's the bad characters who always win out."

"You can't say that, John." Uncle Ben was truly shocked. "That's pessimism, John. We can't let ourselves get pessimistic."

In his field headquarters in Maspelt, reflecting on the fact that President Roosevelt was on the point of winning out over Hitler, Captain Kimbrough sometimes asked himself whether Uncle Ben had not been right to warn him against pessimism. President Roosevelt, though no doubt obsessed with power and dedicated to the goal of spreading Yankeeism over the entire world, was nevertheless a "good" and probably even a "great" character. Whereas there was no use talking about the insane evil of the German Führer, which went so far that his officers, men like this Major Dincklage, were driven to veritable acts of madness. Still and all, the question remained whether in the long run the things that would vanish with Hitler might not triumphantly return once he was gone. But at the moment, Kimbrough had to concede, these were useless speculations, a backwoodsman's broodings. The good

334

was winning out over the bad, and the world climate was consequently optimistic.

"I've known your dad since 1908 and back in those days it really hurt him to talk about Tom Watson. It was like he'd been hit by something—the life knocked out of him—even if he did go ahead and marry my sister and start a family. It was back then that he began reading, doing nothing much besides. I know there's lots to be learned from books. Only he was letting the farm go down. I might as well tell you that I wasn't too pleased for my sister to marry him."

"He didn't just read. Sometimes he'd take me on camping trips."

"What business does a farmer have going on camping trips?"

"You wouldn't understand about that, Uncle. You're no swamper."

There were in fact other things in the life of Isaac Kimbrough besides his reading of Arnett's *Populist Movement in Georgia*, Brooks's *The Agrarian Revolution in Georgia, 1865–1912*, Mrs. Pelton's *Memoirs*, and a whole library of other works dealing with this theme. For instance, there were the evenings when one or another farmer from the neighborhood, sometimes several at a time, without prearrangement, purely by chance, forgathered on his porch.

John, perhaps ten years old at the time, listened to them as they talked incessantly about the war. The war they were discussing was not the World War that had ended only six years ago, but the War Between the States of more than sixty years ago. It was fantastic. They did not speak of Verdun and the tank battles of Cambrai, but they explored, with the expertise of armchair strategists, the surrender of Fort Sumter, Sherman's march to the sea, the suicide of the Confederate elite troops in the famous frontal attack at Gettysburg, or the battle in the wilderness. The names that came up were not the names of Hindenburg, Foch, or Pershing, but of Lee and Stonewall Jackson, Grant and McClellan. Even if they quarreled over the merits of certain generals, for example arguing expertly and angrily whether the war would have been won if General Pemberton had not surrendered in Vicksburg on July 4, 1863, they would always agree before parting for the evening that in this war the North had destroyed the foundations of the South. When that moment came, a dull hopelessness overwhelmed them. In the darkness their voices would fall into a cadence of self-pity that John instinctively despised. He thought it idiotic of them to be sitting there—in the rocking chairs or on the steps (there was no missing tread in those days), now and then taking a sip of their moonshine and filling the night with talk about this war of long ago. Ridiculous that his father would counter this by urging that they had only to adhere to the populist movement to overcome the consequences of the War Between the States. They disagreed. They insisted that they were poor because "the North" had made them poor. That, John felt, was not altogether wrong historically, but like everything that is regarded as unalterable, it really meant no more than that they were poor because they were poor.

The march to the sea, like Sheridan's campaign in the Valley, was one of deliberate and disciplined destruction. Sherman's army cut a swath sixty miles wide through central Georgia, destroying stores of provisions, standing crops and cattle, cotton gins and mills, railways beyond all possibility of repair, in fact everything that could be useful to the Confederacy and much that was not. The looting of houses, although forbidden by orders, could not altogether be prevented, and many a Georgia family was stripped of its possessions; but outrages on persons were surprisingly few; on white women, none. "No army ever enjoyed such freedom and kept within such bounds." It was the sort of campaign that soldiers really love—maximum of looting and destruction, minimum of discipline and fighting: splendid weather, few impediments: broiled turkey for breakfast, roast lamb for dinner, and fried chicken for supper.

(Samuel Eliot Morison and Henry Steele Commager, *The*

336

*Growth of the American Republic* [Oxford University Press, 1937], p. 621f.)

"After *this* war those farmers in Fargo will stop talking about the Civil War," Major Wheeler said when John had described one such evening to him.

It was clear enough why the Second World War, in contrast to the first, would blot out some things from the memories of Southerners. John would have been ready to agree if the major had not fetched up arguments that went against John's grain.

"Before this war all we were was the richest country in the world," Wheeler said. "After it we'll be the most powerful country. Aside from us, only the Russians will count. Imagine that, we'll rule the world. I'll bet you that will shake every American swamper out of his provincial mud."

"Not me," Kimbrough said. "I don't give a damn about America's ruling the world."

"Neither do I, really," Wheeler said. "Only we can't avoid it."

"America ought to stay in her own backyard."

"That would be nice. If only they'd let us. Or should we have stayed in our own backyard with this Hitler around?"


## Continued: Maspelt 1500 Hours

A damned strong argument, Kimbrough thought when he recalled this discussion. Stronger, at any rate, than that subtle professorial blither about a *limes* the Americans had to erect against the Russians, the stuff Wheeler had spouted after that lecture on Major Dincklage from Colonel R. The *limes* theory linked with the question of whether Kim thought they were there to free the Germans or anybody else from that monster. That had been a terrific job, a brilliant performance in the art of self-contradiction, explainable only on the assumption that Bob merely wanted to stop him from doing anything foolish—the beginning of that strategy that was ending today with his turning up in Maspelt and announcing that he would temporarily relieve him of his command if . . .

Which on the other hand was significantly more than what he might have done: staying in Saint-Vith and washing his hands of the whole matter after C Company had got itself into an unimaginable mess. (No, into one that could be imagined quite precisely.)

*Segregation*

When their conduct once more had left something to be desired, Miss Tibbett would exclaim: "I'd as soon be teaching the nigger kids as you." (This remark would be reported back home, and a good many parents took it amiss.)

The school for the blacks in Fargo had been built by the blacks in the same way that the school for the whites had been built by the whites—with their own hands. In its outward appearance it much resembled the white school—both being one-room affairs, and no more than large cabins. Only the black school was not in Fargo itself, but on the western edge of town, down by the Suwannee, where a few unpaved, gray clay streets ran down to the river. This was the colored section with its row houses of horizontally laid board, blank triangular gables, overhanging eaves supported by narrow posts, beneath which washing hung and old rocking chairs stood among pots of geraniums and tubs of aloe shrubs. Rufus Magwood's and Joe Proctor's children—they'd migrated north long ago, leaving their parents behind on the Kimbrough farm—used to tell John that from the windows of their school they could watch the otter and see the heron standing tall and blue in the reeds. Sometimes they lied and boasted of seeing an alligator, although no alligators ever came that close to Fargo.

338

The children of Rufus and Joe were picked up in a bus every morning, just like John, and taken to school in Fargo, only it was a different bus.

Sometimes when John, alone or with friends, wandered along the Suwannee at hours when the black children were in school, he would hear peals of laughter and shouting from the black schoolhouse, a level of noise that would have driven Miss Tibbett clear out of her mind. It would start with some one child's calling out; other voices chimed in; it sounded like a recitation until a storm of merriment seemed to carry them all along. John and his friends would listen in silence, would even refrain from shaking their heads, while the shrill uproar floated across the slow-moving river.

By day the music of laughter, of rhythmic handclapping; evenings the circle of black faces around the kerosene lamp. (As a child he was free to come into the shack.)

Or at night when he was returning with his father from the market in Homerville or from somewhere else:

then we would pass in the dark some old truck grudging and clanking down the concrete, and catch, in the split-second flick of our headlamps, a glimpse of the black faces and the staring eyes. Or the figure, sudden in our headlight, would rise from the roadside, dark and shapeless against the soaked blackness of the cotton land: the man humping along with the croker sack on his shoulders (containing what?), the woman with a piece of sacking or paper over her head against the drizzle now, at her bosom a bundle that must be a small child, the big children following with the same slow, mud-lifting stride in the darkness. (Robert Penn Warren, *Segregation*, New York, 1956)

He could never have enough of looking at their graves. Sometimes he wasted hours at the cemetery around the old Baptist church. The graves were untended, the ground around the sunken stone tablets and cement crosses was covered with leaves and withered brown pine branches. The Negroes did not place fresh

339

flowers on the graves, but seashells, salt and pepper shakers, jam jars, shaving mugs, the intestines of radios, old alarm clocks, automobile headlights, burned-out electric bulbs, combs, plates, cups, ashtrays, milk bottles, dolls' heads, plaster figures. (He discovered statuettes of Jackie Coogan and Abraham Lincoln.)

All these offerings were broken.

"The life is broken, the cup is broken," Rufus said one time when John asked why they did that.

Besides, he explained to the boy, those broken things kept the ghosts—"the ha'nts," he said—from tramping around on the dead people.

That made sense. Nights, before going to sleep, John could imagine the ghosts swearing in pain when they stepped barefooted on the sharp edge of a grave offering.

### Maspelt 1600 Hours

To while away the time for Bob and himself, John talked. "Yesterday I had a letter from my uncle. He writes that they're in the midst of a boom such as Savannah has never seen. You know, the city was dead for years, on account of the U-boats that were lying off the coast. They completely blockaded the harbor, and that just about finished the city. Now they're gone, my uncle writes, and there's more life in that port than I can possibly imagine. Twice as much activity as before the war. On the streets leading to the waterfront trucks are lined up for miles and miles, loaded with war materials for the ships sailing for Europe."

"They'll arrive too late," Wheeler said. "By the time they're here we'll be finished with the jerries."

"Well, well," Kimbrough said, surprised because Wheeler's forecasts of the duration of the war usually tended to be on the long side. But he made no further objection. Bob was talking that way today only to bring him around to thinking that the surrender of a German battalion was no longer all that important. If they were going to be finished with the jerries just like that, Dincklage's offer could best be taken care of by letting it ride, since it wouldn't have to ride very long.

"In addition," he continued, changing the subject, "my uncle writes it's a pity I haven't had a chance to see the way the new governor of Georgia is cleaning things up. You see, we've had a new governor since last year," he explained. "Arnall. He's only thirty-seven, the youngest governor in the country, and according to my uncle there's a new wind blowing. No more whipping of prisoners, and Milledgeville Prison, that disgrace to the state, has been closed down. Bribery has stopped—under Talmadge you could buy and sell a pardon for a convicted criminal. Things have changed at the schools and universities, too. Talmadge—you must have heard about this in Bloomington—used to dismiss or appoint university presidents as he pleased. Georgia is now spending more, relatively, on education than any other state—the greater part of every tax dollar goes to the schools. I wouldn't have thought it possible but they've even set up pensions for teachers. And now Arnall is taking on twenty railroads, going to the Supreme Court and invoking the Sherman Anti-trust Act. He charges that the railroads' common pricing policies constitute a conspiracy against the South. I suppose only a lawyer can appreciate how exciting that is. I wonder whether he can put it across."

"What was Arnall before he was elected governor?"

"A lawyer," Kimbrough said. "His last public office was attorney general of Georgia," he added to take some of the wind out of Bob's sails, because he knew what would follow—Bob's invariable lecture on the connections between lawyers and politics.

But Wheeler's thoughts took a sidetrack today. He merely asked: "Are you sorry now that you joined the army too soon?"

There would have been no point in explaining to him (for the nth time) that he had not volunteered for the army because of conditions in Georgia. The difficulty was that he could never explain to anyone, even to himself, precisely why he had not waited to be drafted. And so he evaded the question, replying: "I don't really believe there'll be such a great change. They elected Arnall so he can put across a few long overdue reforms. Afterwards everything will go on pretty much as usual."

"You're mightily mistaken," Wheeler said. "There are developments that simply cannot be undone once they've gotten started."

But he did not seem all that interested, refrained—though on similar occasions he had never refrained—from elaborating, from plunging into a grand debate on democracy in America, from expatiating on the swings between progressive and conservative thinking.

Instead, he looked at his wristwatch and said: "Schefold ought to be back very soon now."

## Another Schoolmarm

He could not have reproduced for Bob any of the contents of Dorothy's letters, although they were certainly not love letters and in fact contained little that was personal. When Dorothy became personal she confined herself to sentences like: "A pity you cannot come over here just once," or, "If you were here it would dawn on you that your World War Two is a pretty unimportant business," or—at most!—"Give some thought to the possibility of coming here once the war is over and you're free again. You could help us a lot." (Dorothy worked in an American group that was trying to rescue the culture, the language, and the mode of life of some Mexican Indians. From her accounts John had the impression that the Mexican government was not exactly feverishly eager to preserve the Indian languages. In the government schools the Indian children were taught Spanish; the government was not pleased when North Americans came along and founded schools in which the instruction was given in the Indian languages. Proba-

342

bly this was some maneuver on the part of the U.S. imperialists, calculated to prevent the development of a unified Mexican culture.)

Dorothy wrote: "Spent a few days in Oaxaca and am now back in my mountain hamlet. It is 7,000 feet high and I rode for three days—I can only guess when you will receive this letter. But it will reach you, at any rate, as long as that is up to us Zapoteks. You must imagine how I give it to an Indian woman to mail when she takes her crate of lilies to market in Oaxaca, tramping barefoot down the path up which I rode. She carries the flowers with her forehead; I mean, she ties an embroidered sling around the crate and then fastens the sling across her forehead. Then she sets out, small, bowed, walking very fast, wearing a *huipil*. Every village has its own *huipil*; ours is nothing more than a wide, ankle-length white shirt, but wonderfully embroidered with birds and stars. I wear one too when I'm here in the village, but it does little good because I can't bring myself to go without shoes, for fear of snakes. When I say it does me little good to wear it, I mean that I will never become a Zapotek woman. They don't accept me. My shoes, the glass windows in my shack, the books on my table, my toothpaste, my soap—all this is what separates me from them. Or that I borrow a horse and ride—a woman who rides! I also write letters, though only the monthly reports to my superiors and now and then a letter to you. But the worst of it is not that I remain a white woman, but that they are changing while I live among them. I feel that. Something happens inside them when they sit with me and I write down the words of their language, show them their language as written—written in our alphabet!—show them Zapotek as a script. They've never seen anything like that before. Besides, it's not easy to set down their phonetic system in our alphabet. They catch on at once—but while they alternately read the script and stare at the things all around me, something comes and goes in their eyes, so alien, so morose, that I ask myself whether it would not be better for the Zapotek language to remain unwritten. Maybe the Mexican government official was right, the one who recently said to me in the Hotel Victoria in

Oaxaca: 'What do you really want, Señora? We are not stopping any of the Indians from developing freely. Mexico was liberated and founded by a full-blooded Zapotek.' He's right about that— Benito Juárez was born not very far from the village where I'm living. And then I again think of Julia Tamayo who will be carrying this letter for me, and the way some dealer in Oaxaca will relieve her of her crate of lilies and give her five—that's right, five! —pesos for it. Oh, it's ghastly!

"All the same—you would like our Zapotek country. There's a feeling of liberty in the air such as you cannot imagine. You would stand beside your horse like all the men here, your face in the blue shadow of the sombrero. Imagine riding through mountainous jungles with the red flowers of the tree orchids brushing you; they hang long as swords from the giant pines. You would spend the nights in the huts of people so poor that it is a visible sacrifice for them to offer a guest a few of their tortillas. Next day there would be river canyons, sandbanks, agave wildernesses that would hold you up for hours . . . You'd like that, don't you think?"

His first reaction to a letter like this was, of course, to try to picture Dorothy in one of those long white shirts embroidered with birds and stars. She was a tall, slender girl. A dark flow of hair above a face that tanned slowly, at most to a light cornbread color, if he remembered rightly. He came to the conclusion that this thing called a *huipil* probably became her. Both at their first encounter in Milledgeville Prison and the two times he had met her in New York, she had worn the same gray suit. A considerable change must have come over her if she now went about adobe villages in this artlessly shaped but perhaps highly artistic garment, a fair-skinned phantom.

But as far as his eagerness for Zapotek country was concerned, she was badly mistaken. He had been born on a farm at the edge of Old Okefenok and the one thing in the world he wanted was to return there. (No Benito Juárez, not me!) She did not understand that he needed no Indians because he himself was one. At-

344

torney-at-law, captain U. S. Army—okay, but besides that no, above all!—he was what the Fargo people meant when they called themselves swampers. Dorothy could not know what a swamper was because she had never seen Old Okefenok. He had once tried to explain that to her, four years ago, in October 1940—he'd kept the dates of his visits to New York well in mind. They had sat on a bench in Fort Tryon Park, looking down at the Hudson, the old river of the Iroquois. It flowed between its high wooded banks like some stream straight out of a novel by James Fenimore Cooper until it reached the boundaries of the fabulous city. But from where they were seated they could see nothing of the city. Only the noise it made could be heard, not a composite of many different tones but a single continuous stratum of sound that only occasionally changed its quality.

Dorothy had listened for a while. Then she had said. "I'm sorry, John; I'm willing to believe that your swamp down there is very beautiful, but that's no reason to drop right into regionalism. 'We swampers'—that sounds just like New Yorkers saying 'we New Yorkers.' I'm none too fond of that."

A shower so cold it had been hard to bear. Later he realized that she was right, and each time thereafter that the "we swampers" feeling came over him he'd made a face. Except that to himself he could not deny he was the living evidence against the myth of Americans as forever restless, forever moving on.

And now he could have answered Dorothy (but he did not) by pointing out what a regionalist she had turned into; by mentioning that although she recognized why she could never become a Zapotek woman (for her critical intelligence never deserted her) she could still speak of "us Zapoteks" ("we New Yorkers") and try to seduce him by descriptions of the landscape as well as of the article of clothing called a *huipil* into choosing some region in the south of Mexico as his home (as though he needed a native place at all; what he needed was Dorothy, Dorothy in Fargo, Dorothy whom he could very well imagine sitting in his canoe wrapped in a white shirt, deep in the heart of the Okefenokee), Dorothy who to top it off concealed in a subsidiary clause (touching? clever?) the information that he was the only person to whom she wrote letters.

During his second visit in New York, shortly before Christmas of 1940, he had summoned up the courage to ask her whether she would not come to Georgia some time to at least see Savannah and Fargo. They were sitting in a restaurant on Fifty-seventh Street, had dined, and outside snowflakes were sweeping almost horizontally down the illuminated canyon. Dorothy had not replied, merely shaken her head, and then she had actually cried for a minute. It had been a terrible moment, but after all he couldn't forever beat about the bush; sooner or later he had to find out for certain whether it was altogether out of the question for her to live in the country in which her father had been executed in the electric chair. But if it were impossible for her to live, so to speak, beside the grave in the cemetery of the notorious prison, this meant that he, John Kimbrough, could have Dorothy Du Bois only if he were ready to give up everything and become one of those footloose Americans, those inhabitants of trailers, those displaced persons who were conquering the world. Anything but that! It wasn't that Dorothy wasn't worth such a sacrifice, but rather that it just simply couldn't be done. They could not come together, Dorothy and he; and consequently it was altogether natural for them to remain silent and together watch the swirling flakes on Fifty-seventh Street after Dorothy had had her cry for a full minute, in such a way that none of the other patrons had noticed anything.

There is no reason to linger over George Du Bois. Not an especially tragic case. During the Depression the man had dropped into the underworld, had taken up the all in all not so dishonorable occupation of bank robber, except that he'd had the hard luck, during a holdup of a financial institution in Atlanta, to shoot not one but two cashiers, a circumstance that prompted the judge to listen coldly when John pleaded for a life sentence (basically he liked life sentences no more than he did the electric chair). Let us forget that! Perhaps Dorothy need not have taken the case as hard as she did, but a father is a father; no amount of gentle remonstrance could get around that, and John Kimbrough did not even try.

Was it her father's crime or his execution that made her not only stay out of Georgia but finally leave the country? His third trip to New York (in February 1941), which he took because his letters were returned as undeliverable, proved futile. The people who opened the door when he knocked at her apartment in Clark Street, Brooklyn, had no idea where she might have moved. He considered looking her up in the office near Central Park where she had worked, but decided against that. If she did not arrange to have her letters forwarded and did not get in touch with him, she must have her reasons. And in fact she did not leave him up in the air for long. Soon after he returned to Savannah her first letter from Mexico reached him. Among other things she wrote: "When I think of where the money came from that covered my college expenses!" An argument hard to deal with; and in fact her decision to vanish from the picture was sensible and consistent. It also reminded John of Dorothy's father; one time when the young lawyer was discussing the case with him and kept trying to find extenuating circumstances, Du Bois had nothing to say but: "You know, I'm the kind of fellow who when he does something, does it up brown."

Only it was not consistent that after a while she began to describe the province of Oaxaca, Mexico, in a way that implied it might some day serve him as a substitute for County Clinch, Georgia.

He knew what Bob would say if he told him this story. "Aha, there we have it!" he would exclaim. "So that's why you joined the army." Such stories, stories in general, lent themselves easily to false conclusions.

He had caught a nice case of pneumonia that day he searched vainly for Dorothy in New York. His own fault, because after he found her gone he mindlessly continued on down Clark Street to where it ended in the East River, and so biting a wind was blowing over the river that anyone else would have noticed it and turned around at once. Instead he stood there looking across the river at the clenched fist of skyscrapers, shadowless in the eastern light, the quintessence of power, icily embraced by double winds, double currents. He spent useless and dangerous minutes there asking himself whether he ought to hate or admire Dorothy and the southern tip of Manhattan, before he at last, too late, became aware of the cold and dashed for the nearest subway station. In the express train that shrieked through the night toward the mild, rescuing Southland, his temperature rose, rose steadily from Philadelphia to Washington, from Richmond to Augusta. He arrived in Savannah with a fever of 104 and the certainty that he would never see Dorothy Du Bois again. That was all he could have replied to Bob, and it had nothing, nothing at all to do with the fact that a few months later he stood on a drill ground at Fort Benning and listened with an incredulous grin to the bestial shouting of a sergeant in the Army of the United States.

### Maspelt 1700 Hours

He looked out the window at the pasture slope that blocked the view, though in the twilight it was only a shadow. Major Wheeler had gone out half an hour ago—"have to stretch my legs a little," he had said. Now he returned, sat down, lit a cigarette.

"Well," he said, "Doc Schefold is taking his time."

"I can't figure it out," John said.

"You have to count on these two fellows getting deeply involved in conversation," Wheeler said. "They must have a great deal to say to each other, this German exile and this German officer who'd like to run out on his supreme warlord. I can imagine them talking for hours."

"But that would mean that Major Dincklage has given up on his project," John said, shaking his head incredulously. "If he hasn't given up, if he has something on the calendar for tonight, he would have to send me word of it as quickly as possible."

"You said it. Of course he's given up. I'll bet you fifty dollars, John, that he long ago realized his big coup wouldn't come off."

"I'll take that bet," John said. "Why should he have sent for Doc if he doesn't have anything in mind?"

Wheeler blew the smoke of his cigarette thoughtfully into space.

"Just like that," he said. "He can rehearse the thing up to the point of conferring with Schefold."

"Why should he do that?" John asked. "Endanger a man for absolutely no reason?"

"I don't know." Wheeler stared for a while at the wall behind John Kimbrough, the whitewashed wall of a farmhouse room in Maspelt. The wall was blank except for the C Company schedule that hung on it. "I suppose it's his way of saying goodbye to us. He wants to shame us. By having Schefold go through with it, he's saying to us: You see, I wanted to. Really wanted to. And now goodbye!"

"Damn it all," John said. "It would have been a grand affair, too. Maybe the biggest thing in this whole war."

"What's the sense of thinking about impossibilities?" Wheeler said. "You yourself were just demonstrating to me that it would never work."

"Yes, but only because Regiment isn't going along. With a superior force . . ."

Wheeler did not let him finish. "No," he said, "not even with a superior force. There is absolutely no guarantee that bloodshed could be avoided. And if even a single soldier is killed, one of ours or a German, all Major Dincklage can do is put a bullet through his head. He knows that perfectly well and so do you, Kim."

He reflected a bit, then resumed: "The army could afford casualties well enough, if it were to decide to make a big thing of it. That isn't the problem. But Major Dincklage cannot afford a single casualty. By that I'm not asserting, of course, that the army acts out of any superior wisdom, that it even takes into its thinking the conscience of a German officer. The army certainly has entirely different reasons for not accepting Herr Dincklage's offer. Or maybe it has none at all; maybe it just doesn't like the idea. Armies are unbelievably stiff-necked."

He held his cigarette in his hand much too long, did not crush it out until it was almost burning his fingers.

"Maybe an army that isn't stiff-necked is no army at all," he said.

John said: "I'm worried about Doc, Bob!"

So he wasn't even listening to me, Wheeler thought.

"Serves you right," he said. "You never should have let him go."

To reassure John, he added: "We'll find out sooner or later what's been holding Schefold up. As far as his safety goes, I think we can trust Major Dincklage."

"I won't take that bet after all," John said. "It will be half past five shortly. If Schefold comes this late, there's nothing more to it."

"Fine gambler you are," Wheeler said. "First bet, then pull out. But since I'm fair by nature I'll let you off. You wouldn't have had a chance. There never was anything to it."

"But then I don't understand why he stipulated that Doc had to come see him!" John cried out. "To say goodbye, to shame us, as you said before—all right, but you don't risk a man's life for that. I don't understand it, Bob."

Dincklage asked Doctor Schefold to come and you let him go, Major Wheeler thought, because the codes of honor of Prussian officers and American Southerners are pretty much alike. But he did not express his thought; he contented himself with saying: "It certainly didn't occur to him that he might be risking Schefold's life. This officer is accustomed to having things go exactly as he orders."

*This officer*, he said, not suspecting that he was falling into the same tone as Wenzel Hainstock when in speaking to Käthe Lenk he used the equivalent German term to refer to Dincklage.

Because the pasture slope outside had changed from a shadow to a block of solid darkness, John Kimbrough switched on the lamp on his table and pulled down the black shade. On October 12 between five and six o'clock the illumination prevailing in the Eifel and the Ardennes could at most be called the last deer-hunter's light, and even that only because October 12 of that year had been a bright, sunny day.

There was a knock. Foster opened the door a crack, stuck his head in, and asked whether the major and the captain would care for coffee; they were just making some. When the two said yes, he returned a minute later with cups, which he filled with a pale brown liquid from an enamel pot.

"I would have preferred it black," Wheeler said mockingly, but after Foster had gone out again thus conveying to John that he by no means insisted on black coffee but merely wanted to poke a bit of fun at the mild-mannered coffee habits prevalent in C Company.

"They always overdo the powder," John said. "So it's more digestible with milk."

"Especially for elderly gentlemen from the regimental staff, you mean, don't you? Who are anyhow inclined to get all steamed up for no reason at all about younger frontline officers?"

"Any such thoughts are far from my mind," John said. "As you know, I admire the unshakable calm and wisdom of the higher staff officers."

They teased each other a while longer, but the atmosphere was peaceful and lazy, and after a while they stopped talking and merely listened to noises: the tearing of paper packets of sugar, the rattle of the coffee spoons, the click of the lighter with which John lit the major's cigarette and his own, the murmur of voices, the rattle of typewriters from the adjacent orderly room.

Alerts have their advantages, John thought. Normally I would have to be outside now taking the evening roll call.

Under different circumstances, he thought, it would be very pleasant right now. A pleasant coffee break in a pleasant sort of war.

Major Wheeler was sitting down again.

351

"How long a walk is it?" he asked. "I mean, from Winterspelt to here, by the route Schefold was told to take."

The question reminded John of his visit in Hemmeres yesterday morning. He and Schefold had discussed the time Schefold would need.

"The way back will go quickly," Schefold had said. "Because then I'll know the way, and besides I'll hurry. I estimate that I won't need more than a good hour for the way back. So if I leave Dincklage some time between one and two, I can be in Maspelt by three o'clock at the latest."

They had been sitting on the bench in front of the farmhouse talking about Schefold's rendezvous as if it were a Sunday afternoon outing—this after John Kimbrough had said: "Maybe it's a good idea for you to go. You must coax him into giving us more time."

It was true that after he had spoken these words a pause had ensued, during which John had not dared to look at Schefold. Instead he had gazed past his two sentries at the trees in the wooded valley, imagining those trees swallowing up the bulky man when he undertook his crazy walks in Germany.

Would I have been relieved, he asked himself, if yesterday morning Doc had refused to make this call instead of merely— after that pause during which he didn't even betray whether he was wavering, whether he was apprehensive—discussing the technical arrangements for the mission?

"Two hours at most," he said to Wheeler. "But then he would have to be taking it pretty easy, and he certainly isn't going to do that. He knows that every quarter hour counts."

"Would count, you mean," Wheeler said. "Don't forget that I'm here and therefore it doesn't count."

It was on the tip of John's tongue to say, "Ah yes, Bob Wheeler, the great frustrater!" But he stopped himself in time. Bob was after all still his superior officer, had come here on an official assignment, even though it was one he had assigned himself—a real act of decency on his part, John had to admit, because he could have stayed in Saint-Vith and washed his hands of the whole affair.

He had another thought which kept him from arguing with Bob about fundamental matters.

"Maybe Schefold was held up," he said, "because he's packing his things down there in the hamlet before coming up here to us."

Wheeler looked up.

"Hm," he said.

"Obviously," John said, and once again, more firmly this time: "Obviously." Although the idea that Doc would have to leave Hemmeres had only dawned on him as he said it.

He became uneasy.

"If Dincklage wants to say goodbye to us, as you put it, he will then batten down the hatches. As an officer he can't tolerate a weak spot on his sector of the front. He has to plug that leak. So he'll have Hemmeres occupied tonight. And he will certainly be decent enough to tell Doc so that he can clear out in time, don't you think?"

"You can depend on that," Major Wheeler said.

By now John was sitting on the edge of his chair. He had propped both elbows on the desk and was holding his palms pressed tightly together.

"Good Lord, imagine that I never thought of that up to now," he said. "I must give my sentries instructions. I'll have to send two scouts down there so that they can observe when and whether the jerries turn up. And of course I'll have the farm shelled immediately. I don't want the Germans getting the idea they can just settle down comfortably in Hemmeres."

"I hope you won't do that without querying Battalion first," Wheeler said.

John glared at him.

"Are there any decisions at all that a company commander can make independently?" he asked.

"Cut the comedy!" Wheeler said. "As though you didn't learn the rudiments in your first month at Fort Benning . . . Of course there are situations in which a line officer may decide by himself," he said, and rattled off: "When a unit leader with his unit in the course of combat is completely cut off from the next higher level of command . . ."

"In effect, never!" John exclaimed.

He became shaky when he noticed how Bob was looking at him.

"You have a surprise coming," Wheeler said.

"What do you mean by that?"

"I mean by that," Wheeler said slowly, "that in a few weeks we're going to be right plumb in the middle of the biggest mess of this whole war."

John switched gears rapidly and decided not to take exception to this. If an intelligence man of Bob's ability said something like that, he must have his reasons.

"Wow!" he said, and pretended disbelief in order to make Bob come out with more.

"The Germans are assembling several army corps in the area west of the central Rhine," Wheeler said. "I have ample evidence of that. It coincides with the information that is coming in to all the regiments, and with the results of air reconnaissance."

"What about it?" John asked. "What does the top brass have to say about it?"

"Nothing," Bob said. "No comment."

"You don't believe they'll just look on while several army corps land on us?"

"Haven't the faintest," Wheeler said.

They went on talking shop for a while. It was possible that the wretched three divisions occupying the territory between Monschau and Echternach would be withdrawn in time. Then the Germans would run into the hole between Patton's left and Hodges' right flank and would be caught in the pincers. Or it was possible that the Americans would get moving from the south and the British from the north and would break into the German preparations, defusing the bomb before it could explode.

354

"All theory," Wheeler said. "I have the impression that Bradley is just sitting there and waiting."

"And wants us to get chewed up?" John asked.

Wheeler shrugged.

"Maybe he hopes that we can hold out for a few days," he said.

"Damn it all," John said.

They brooded for a while in the gloomy room, in which the desk lamp shed only a little light.

"When it's all over the story will be that intelligence failed," the major said. "I can just see those official accounts of how the army was taken by surprise. The brass hats will give interviews blaming it all on us, the intelligence people.

"I'll tell you a secret," he said. "There's an order at Regiment that hasn't been sent out to the front yet because Colonel R. foamed at the mouth when he read it. It says the front is to behave so as not to wake up any sleeping dogs! Literally."

"Wow!" John said again, this time not incredulously but merely with puzzlement. Then he grinned involuntarily. He was imagining an army walking on tiptoe in order not to disturb the people next door.

"That's the reason they won't allow you to rake Hemmeres with shellfire," Wheeler said. "And I also think it's one of the reasons Army's only response to Dincklage's proposal is silence. Dincklage is offering it a piece of cake at a moment when the last thing it wants to do is to eat cake."

"Did your intelligence about the German deployment come from Doc?" John asked.

"Him!" Wheeler waved that aside. "Schefold doesn't know a thing. Nothing's happening in his part of the world. The whole region behind the German line is being used for the deception and won't be occupied until the last moment. We even know the code word for the German operation. It's called *Watch on the Rhine*. They're trying to make us think that the build-up is merely intended as preparation for defense of the Rhine. And I've met people at Staff who are swallowing that." He paused a moment, then said: "Oh well, when you consider that probably not even Major Dincklage knows anything about what is going on behind his back . . ."

John Kimbrough's question had incidentally reminded him that all the time he had been in charge of intelligence for the 424th Regiment's sector of the front, he had sidestepped the Hemmeres farm when he sent agents behind the German lines. Why? Only out of consideration for Schefold, who was no agent at all, merely a supplier of reports on morale, and probably unreliable reports at that, for Schefold never had anything to tell but that the farmers and soldiers he talked with thought the war was lost. According to Schefold the Germans were the most commonsensical, most decent people in the world. If you took his word for this, it was a mystery how they had ever happened to come up with their Hitler.

Waiting for Schefold, he reproached himself. He should have used the Hemmeres farm to better purpose!

Even for Schefold himself it would have been best if he had politely but firmly told him to clear out of Hemmeres. Backward march, march! back to Belgium, Dr. Schefold! We cannot have you here. This is no place for art historians, German Romantics, dreamers. Yes, that would have been best. Instead, all this mess today, and it seemed there'd be no end of it as long as Schefold was still out there, somewhere in the dusk at the onset of night, between the lines.

Their conversation began to run down.

"Incidentally, you needn't put on such an act about shelling Hemmeres to hell and gone," Wheeler said. "You're just about the last person to enjoy a thing like that. I can't imagine you wanting to win a decoration that way."

Yes, John thought, he's probably right, and besides I assured Doc yesterday that the war would never come to Hemmeres. When I was standing down there outside that lonely farmhouse, I blathered about a hole in the roof that nobody would mend.

Just because of a few apple trees, a meadow, a river, and a buzzard, I talked nonsense.

"Then kindly suggest a way," he said, "for me to distinguish myself in this war!"

"There's one way," Wheeler said, not entering into his tone. "Capturing a German battalion and being demoted for it by a court-martial—that would have suited you to a T. It would have been your way of winning glory. Yes, you would be demoted and at the same time would become a national hero. Ten years later your story would be in all the schoolbooks."

"And you want to forestall that!" John said, laughing.

Wheeler, who did not laugh, replied: "I'm afraid it's already been forestalled without my interference."

## Of Alligators . . .

He never learned to fish, but he made up for this lack when it came to shooting.

They first shot at empty tin cans that they stood in a row on a porch rail. Then his father threw the cans into the air. After a while John hit every can. He almost always hit them at the apex of their trajectory.

Perhaps, no, certainly, John's outstanding record in target practice contributed to his rapid promotions in the army.

"Good shot!" his father would say every time a can was knocked back at right angles to its trajectory. Then he would look quizzically at his fifteen-year-old son.

"I wouldn't have expected it," he once remarked, "of a boy who's lit out for the city."

The canoe lay in the shade of the cypresses, and the man and boy looked across the reed-grown expanse of flooded "prairie," across to the sandbank off Chesser Island, on which the alligator lay.

"Aim for the eye," Dad said.

John put down his binoculars and took up the rifle. Through the binoculars he had seen that the alligator's eye was closed. The animal's mouth was half open; rigid, it traced those well-known curved lines against the black and red of its maw. The alligator was an adult specimen.

John found the eye in the sight. It lay there in its leathern pouch.

"How far do you estimate?" he asked his father, who was holding the canoe as still as possible by pressing it up against a cypress root.

"A hundred yards," the elder Kimbrough said.

John raised the sight a trifle. If he wanted to hit at this distance, the eye would have to be just a hint below the foresight. Now he no longer saw the eye, just the knob above the eye and the other knobs of the armor, and above that the shimmering heat of the swamp.

He lowered the rifle and said: "I can't."

"What's that mean, 'I can't'?" Dad asked. "Of course you can. That's no shot for you."

"No," John said, "I can't."

Now Kimbrough understood what his son meant.

"Nuts," he said. "Go ahead, shoot! You have to learn!"

John shook his head. He handed Dad the rifle. They changed places and John held the boat fast while Dad stood up and aimed.

The alligator's body doubled up between head and tail after the shot was fired. Then it plopped heavily to the sand and stretched out. Its mouth closed slowly.

It's almost just like the fish, John thought, when Dad takes them off the hook and drops them into the boat: almost the same twitching and doubling up.

They paddled over to the sandbar and looked at the dead alligator. Dad said he would come back in the big boat with Rufus and Joe to fetch the body.

On the way home they did not exchange a word.

### . . . and Swine

The question of whether Captain Kimbrough was as proficient a marksman as Corporal Hubert Reidel must remain open. Probably Reidel was a shade better.

In contrast to Reidel, Kimbrough regarded his shooting skill as mere manual dexterity.

He worried less about the prospect of having to shoot at human beings than that hunting incident in Okefenokee Swamp might suggest. Killing people in wartime would be nothing more than a function of the instinct for self-preservation. In legal terms the situations of war and hunting were altogether different. Animals were defenseless.

In keeping with that view, all the problems presented by the war came down to a single one: the question of courage. Captain Kimbrough was curious, in fact obsessed with the question of whether he would be courageous.

Once, when he hinted something of the sort to Uncle Benjamin, his uncle replied: "Courage? You don't need the army for that. You'll have every chance to prove your courage in life."

John had to smile at the natural way Uncle Benjamin distinguished between the army and life.

"I know all about that," he said. "Moral courage and so on. But I don't mean that. I mean perfectly ordinary physical courage."

The only moments during their class sessions when officer candidates held their breath, John recalled, was when there were discussions of the conduct of officers in battle. The army sent officers with frontline experience from the First World War to Fort Benning, their assignment being to give specific examples, that is, to tell stories of what it was like. During and after such stories silence usually prevailed. The usual banter ceased.

At that moment the preparation barrage stopped. It was time for the attack, but the men refused to move. The valley below Creighton was now crisscrossed by bands of tracers and exploding shells. It was like looking into the bowels of Hell. Since the men would never move into this deathtrap without an example, Creighton stood up and shouted the slogan of Fort Benning, the infantry school, "Follow me!"

He ran down the hill, certain he would never come back alive. Dirt and snow splattered all around him as he ran full speed to the bottom. Here he spotted a stone wall and slid behind it.

"Well, we made it," said someone next to him. It was Sergeant Love. Creighton felt elated. He turned, ready to lead his men on another charge to the next objective, "Cemetery Hill." No one was behind.

"For Christ sake, we're alone!" In his anger he forgot fear. The two turned and climbed back up the hill, ignoring the bullets ripping on all sides. Their men, crouching in foxholes, only stared at Creighton and Love.

"Now listen, you sons of bitches," said Love. "This time you follow the Lieutenant and keep up with him. If you don't *I'm* going to shoot you."

Creighton and Love hurried down the line, pulling the terrified riflemen out of their foxholes. Once more Creighton led the attack. This time the men followed, for Love was behind them with his carbine.

Once started the GI's ran, anxious to get out of the heavy fire— and away from Love. They followed Creighton across the valley and up toward the cemetery on top of the next hill. White figures popped up from nowhere, and retreated to the north. Fox Company followed, too scared to shout or shoot. In five minutes they had taken their objective. "Cemetery Hill" belonged to Fox. (John Toland, *Battle: The Story of the Bulge*, pp. 300f.)

You possessed ordinary physical courage when, for example, during a barrage you were able to keep the peripheral nervous system under control.

The question of courage was in fact an officer's question. The enlisted man, as a rule drafted into the army, should not be blamed if he thought of nothing else but saving his hide.

Attorney Kimbrough had always wondered that conscientious objectors did not claim a lack of ordinary physical courage in explanation for their conduct. They never said: What do you want? We don't have the fundamental trait you demand of soldiers and we don't have any intention of acquiring it.

To John Kimbrough's mind, such an admission would have provided compelling proof of their moral courage. More compelling, at any rate, than invoking the Fifth Commandment or the teachings of Jesus Christ.

"An officer who withdraws before at least fifty per cent of his men are casualties has failed."

Since they were pumped full of this and similar maxims at Fort Benning, John resolved not to let any guilt complexes grow in his psyche, not to be unduly concerned if he should fail according to the army's definition of failure. Whether or not you failed was, so to speak, a purely technical affair, a statement about your constitution, nothing more. (He was unfamiliar with the German phrase, favored by Göring, *innerer Schweinehund*—meaning the character of a wretched little egotist who lacks the "pure" Nazi ideals. He would likewise have rejected that.)

He merely wanted to know.

Conditions in Georgia under the governorship of Eugene Talmadge, the unsatisfying outcome of his relationship to Dorothy Du Bois, a general sense that he would not be able to escape the war and the historical evolution of America, so that it would be better to participate actively in both instead of ducking and dodging his way along—to all these hypotheses about his reasons for volunteering for the army we would add the supposition that he was impelled by a keen desire to learn something about the constitution of his mind and body, something that it seemed to him enormously important to learn.

It may be conjectured here, as an afterthought, that Hainstock's decision—so wrongheaded from the standpoint of underground tactics—to offer his services to the Communist Party as a courier in fascist Germany may have been prompted by similar motives. Hainstock, too, possibly wanted to subject himself to a test. We know that he passed it.

During the past several days Captain Kimbrough had sometimes asked himself whether he was not, in undertaking the coup for which Major Dincklage had issued an invitation, yielding to a secret desire to escape the crucial test. A raid like this one was a bold business, but it was not really a proof of ordinary physical courage such as was needed under a barrage or in an assault.

Wheeler's prediction of what was later called the Battle of the Bulge had greatly excited him. So his joining the army would not prove to have been a flop; his time in the army would culminate in something other than a few lazy weeks on the border followed by spit-and-polish soldiering in an occupied country. Abruptly he felt his interest in Dincklage's operation beginning to fade as he listened to Wheeler, and he asked himself whether there was anything left of it but this unbearable waiting to know what was keeping Schefold.

*Maspelt 1800 Hours*

Now there was nothing left for them to do but suggest reasons for his failure to arrive.

"If something has happened to him," John said, "it must have happened right at the beginning. When he appeared in front of the German lines. Major Dincklage could offer all the guarantees in the world for everything else, but not for that moment. If some German sentry let fly . . ."

He did not finish the sentence because he thought of several soldiers in his company whom he knew to be incurably trigger-happy.

He also told himself that instead of Major Dincklage he could equally well call himself the person responsible for Doc's having to pass through a ticklish moment. Never, he thought, should I have sent Doc into a situation that contained even a single moment for which I could not guarantee his safety. I merely warned him. Warning is not enough.

"Can the men in your advanced line hear if there is firing on the German side?" Wheeler asked.

"Out of the question," John said. "They're not on the Our height, as we are, but beyond it, and the slope in front of them would certainly absorb any sound. I've never heard a peep from over there."

He thought of the hours he had spent on the heights above the Our, peering eastward through his glasses at harvested fields, patches of woods, barren pasture slopes, houses of rubblestone. He had not been able to observe a single position or so much as a movement. Moreover, he had never heard a shot, a sound of wheels, the clank of tank treads. The war had been not only empty; it had also been mute, and he had approved of the aloof silence of this vacuum.

Later it had dawned on him—from stories by Schefold, who had his knowledge from Hainstock—that this emptiness, this silence, was not simply one of the inexplicable characteristics of a mysterious war; that it probably prevailed in the position of the enemy opposite C Company only because Major Dincklage was a genius at camouflage.

"Maybe we ought to go up front and ask," Wheeler said. Apologetically, he added: "Intelligence men are by nature doubting Thomases."

John nodded. It was in any case becoming impossible to stay in this room. He looked at his wristwatch and said: "The men who

had sentry duty this afternoon in the sector above Hemmeres
were relieved from twelve to four o'clock. Now they're back in
their holes up there again."

They stood up, put on their jackets, and donned their caps.

In the orderly room Major Wheeler paused, turned to John and
said: "I think you can call off the alert now."

"You heard it," Captain Kimbrough said to the master sergeant. "Alert ended."

"Yes, sir," the master sergeant said. "I'll pass the order on to
the platoons."

"My theory still is that they've got involved in conversation,"
Wheeler said as they walked along the village street.

"That couldn't be it," John said. "Not for so long."

In the darkness, alleviated only by a last ghostly departing light,
and in the emptiness of the village street—still deserted because
word that the alert was lifted had not yet been passed on—their
voices sounded hollow.

"I have a curious hunch," Wheeler said. "I can conceive of
Schefold's deciding to remain over there. You know he's crazy to
get back home. And then he runs into a type like Dincklage. That
could have thrown him completely off stride."

John did not reply, nor did Wheeler give him time to.

"Two German patriots!" Wheeler went on. "And both of them
left high and dry by us. Yes," he continued in a more subdued
tone, "Schefold, too, must be telling himself that we have only
looked on in boredom while he goes to see Dincklage, nor is it
hard to guess that we will send him back to Belgium, back into
his exile's existence, once he has carried out his mission, which
wasn't even a mission from us. Not a very pretty prospect for him,
the way he is."

"Stay over there?" John asked. "How do you see that practically? He has no ID."

"In the first place he does have an ID," Wheeler said. "Perfectly
usable, in fact—I've seen it. In the second place he's moving
around inside an intact German opposition group. This Commu-

nist, for instance, the one he's always telling us about, who got him into this whole business with Dincklage, could certainly hide him without difficulty. And suppose the major said: "Stay here! I'll take you under my wing . . ."

"Doc is fairly crazy," John said, "but he isn't that crazy."

He recalled how he had quizzed Schefold about Dincklage last Saturday, when the big man brought him the news of Dincklage's intentions, and how visibly disappointed Schefold had been—because I didn't jump on the table in enthusiasm, John thought. Doc vehemently defended Dincklage when I called the major a criminal (only in the legal sense; he didn't understand that at all!). Schefold had replied that Dincklage was a cultivated member of the German middle class. "Someone like myself, if you will." All that argued in favor of Bob's hunch that a deep sympathy could exist between these two Germans, with all that might follow from that. The only real argument against that is the way he remained angrily silent when I asked him what made Major Dincklage tick. He not only had no explanation, he didn't even want to have one; that was obvious.

"It isn't a question of craziness," Wheeler said, "but of feeling for one's country."

Let's assume, John thought, that I'd left America because of an American Hitler—the thought took his breath away for a moment —I too might soften if somebody offered me the opportunity to return to Savannah, to Fargo, to Old Okefenok.

"I have no feeling for my country," he said. "Just for my county."

From the high pasture slope they saw and heard the battle in the north, the lights that circled above the already nocturnal sky, the distant rumble of artillery salvos. The battle in the north did not go to sleep when twilight fell. Rather, it sometimes slept by day in order to be fresh for the time of darkness.

The foxholes of the line lay beneath the shadowy outlines of trees. There were no longer any colors, only various gradations of darkness between the absolute blackness of foliage, the gray of

helmets, the pale faces on the ground which turned up as the soldiers heard their footsteps.

They were told that no one had heard anything that afternoon,
not even the distant echo of a shot.

They walked a few steps farther, to the point where they could
see, through the insubstantial network that by day consisted of
hazel bushes, the Hemmeres farm gleaming, a patch of mold,
vaguely phosphorescent.

John spoke to the man who stood in the holes flanking the footpath that came up from Hemmeres: "Keep a close watch tonight.
I'm counting on Doc's turning up this evening some time. Tell
that to the men who relieve you."

He could count on their knowing whom he meant. Doc was a
familiar apparition to the men of C Company.

It would have been good for the raid that tonight was going to
be unusually dark, John thought. The moon was no more than a
narrow crescent in the east; the new moon would be in the sky in
a few nights.

On the way back he once more dwelt on memories of his talk
with Doc last Saturday. At that time he had not yet fully realized
that he had taken a case: the Dincklage case. He did not realize
that until later, though not long after, at the latest while listening
to Colonel R.'s lecture.

Now it no longer seemed to be a question of the Dincklage
case, but of a Schefold case, and although there might be some
doubt as to whether he had actually taken the Dincklage case,
there was not the slightest doubt that the Schefold case had taken
hold of him. Of course he was not the only person to blame for
there being a Schefold case. But it did not console him that
others—Major Dincklage above all, likewise that Communist, and
the woman who was the intermediary between the major and the
Communist—were also just as responsible for Doc's going
through the German line as he, John Kimbrough. In the final
analysis a word from him would have sufficed to prevent this trip,
from which Doc was apparently not returning.

For the present he refused to assume what would have to be assumed in case Doc did not return; but he suddenly became aware of the difference between the Dincklage and the Schefold cases. He had merely been able to represent Dincklage's case as a (not properly admitted) lawyer before higher courts, whereas in the Schefold case he himself was one of the defendants and should be looking around for a good lawyer himself who would be able to get him off if it came to trial.

## Regionalism

How old had he been when his father took him along on the great trip through the Okefenokee Swamp, across the pine barrens and on to the sea? Eight? Nine? Ten? He no longer knew precisely.

Dad claimed he could identify all the different kinds of warblers. He described for John the golden-winged warbler, the orange-crowned warbler, the magnolia and myrtle warblers. He said: "They're an American bird. You won't find them anywhere else."

Dad also knew where the deep ponds lay to the north of Blackjack Island, on the shores of which the pelicans fished.

They met no other boat. It was forbidden to cross the watery "prairie" that made up the southern part of Old Okefenok. They lived on fish and turtle meat that they roasted over their evening fires. The smoke climbed into the sky above the swamp cypresses.
The noonday heat made the mirror surface of the water opaque. Then only the whiplash movements of the moccasin and indigo snakes shimmered through the dazzling light.

A puma slept in the branches of an amber tree. The very rare Carolina parrakeets were green, red, and yellow.

Dad could point to a flash of crimson far away, against the gray of the cypress woods, and say: "Rhododendron." Or in passing pick a red leaf from a bush and give it a name. "Itea," he said. And: "That one is a variety of Hamamelis."

He did not carry it too far. Sometimes he let the names be names.

At night, lying in their sleeping bags, they heard the bass growl of the big bullfrogs, the low mating call of an alligator, and the bubbles of gas from the muck bursting. The nights were loud. Even the moon hissed through the fog.

In the morning the Virginia deer came up to the fringes of the lagoons, among the flocks of herons and ducks.

After some days Dad found the place where the St. Mary's River leaves Okefenokee Swamp. The river wound among water lilies through the slash-pine country, in which the pines stood here and there amid the prairie grass.

Farther to the east, the plantations, cotton, tobacco, sugar cane. The trees of the avenues that led past old Negro houses of local brick to the white wooden farmhouses were hung with Spanish moss, gray and fluttering.

Then the mud-choked river mouths, the silted coastal strips. Dad showed him the place where the slaves had been landed. A landing stage could still be seen there, and a large boat was rotting in the reeds below the thickets of the shore. Dating from way back then?

They switched from the St. Mary's to the Satilla River, paddled along the quiet coves between the coast and the islands, finally pushed the canoe up on land under the walls of Fort Frederica, walked across the island to the shore of the open sea (which wasn't navigable in a canoe). There, on the beach of St. Simon's

Island, Dad had told him never to worry about the Atlantic because the Atlantic wanted only one thing of Americans: for them to return across it. "But we Americans," he had said, "didn't come to America ever to go back where we came from."

### Maspelt 1900 Hours

"Call me if he comes after all," Major Wheeler said.

He did not return to the orderly room, but went straight to his jeep and sat down at the wheel.

In the village street soldiers were again standing around in groups, dark in the darkness. There were low calls, laughter, gabble among boys. (Some of the soldiers from Montana were very young.)

"Tomorrow I'll try to find out what happened," Wheeler said. "I have a few possible ways to go about it."

They nodded. The major started the jeep and drove off. John watched the red taillights until they disappeared.

There was nothing for him to do but to go on waiting. The Dincklage operation had burst like a bubble, but there was still a chance that Schefold might return.

### Late at night

(he had brought Käthe Lenk to Saint-Vith, turned her over to Major Wheeler, and returned to Maspelt), before going to his quarters he stood by a group of his men listening to one of the fellows singing *John Brown's Body*.

The man was an excellent singer and guitar player. He sang very differently from Joe Proctor. Joe Proctor sang blues, and

*John Brown's Body* was no blues, of course, nothing but a white ballad.

It certainly did not occur to the fellow that he might be provoking his captain by singing the victory song of the Northern states under the starlit sky of Maspelt, and John Kimbrough actually did not care, for the melody was beautiful and the singer sang the words without pathos, as mere statement, intoning them almost as if he were not singing at all, merely saying something to which the guitar was making its shroom-shroom accompaniment.

They haven't an inkling what a hellion that John Brown was, John thought. John Brown already had the massacre in Kansas on his conscience when he set about that senseless slaughter at Harper's Ferry. He was an insane fanatic, nothing more, and we were perfectly right to hang him.

But of course it didn't matter a damn who were the heroes and what were the deeds glorified by the nocturnal songs of all the world's campaigns. *John Brown's Body, Malbrouck s'en va-t-en guerre*, the *Iliad*—in the end they all sounded the same, intoning, shroom-shroom, white ballads.

# Documents, Dreams, and Footnotes on Major Dincklage's Treason

## Document I

Fictional. Letter of Dr. Bruno Schefold to Wenzel Hainstock. It was never written. Schefold did not have a chance to write it.

We shall try, however, to provide him with such a chance. For example, this way: on the late afternoon of October 12 Schefold has arrived in Maspelt. On the way he has stopped off once more in Hemmeres, has packed his bag and said goodbye to the farmer and his wife. On the footbridge across the dark Our, the planks rattling with the same friendly sound as always, he has turned around once more and looked at the hamlet, resolving to return some time after the war to see what might have happened to the two white houses, the meadows, the man, the woman, the child.

In Maspelt he has encountered not only Kimbrough but Major Wheeler also. He has reported to the two officers on his visit with Major Dincklage, delivered the letter Dincklage wrote to Kimbrough. Then he has asked if he might write a letter to Hainstock, and Kimbrough has placed a desk in the orderly room at his disposal—for the orderly room is now, contrary to the conditions described in the preceding chapter, no longer full. At this time only Pfc. Foster is still there, brooding over his accounts. Major Wheeler has promised to have the letter delivered to Hainstock by one of his *stragglers*. When Schefold paused in his writing, he heard from the adjoining room the low, murmuring voices of the two officers discussing Dincklage's letter.

We must rely on conjecture for our knowledge of Schefold's epistolary style. We deduce it from the whole substance of Bruno Schefold as revealed in his various guises as Ph.D. (dissertation on *Depth and Surface in Hercules, Seghers*, published by Wölfflin, 1927), historian of art, Stendhalien, cultivated member of the German middle class, German exile, massive body with flowing movements, on the whole nonchalant personality, wearer of a close-clipped mustache. Let us add that he was rather prematurely gray, blue-eyed, and unworldly. Such a man, when he has an important letter to write, will certainly take his time. Let us grant him this fictional amount of time on the evening of October 12, in the orderly room of C Company, part of a battalion of the 3rd Regiment of the 106th American Infantry Division. After all, he has quite a lot to report.

Maspelt (Belgium, evening of
October 12, 1944)

Dear Herr Hainstock,

I hope very much that the messenger who delivers this letter to you will conduct himself more unobtrusively, lurk more in the shadows, than ever I did. Only since this morning, since I encountered that monster, have I realized that my turning up so nonchalantly at your place in broad daylight and without taking any precautions must often have put you in danger. Belatedly, I ask your pardon. I have asked Major Wheeler to pledge the *straggler* he will be sending with my letter to come to you only under cover of night. I am imagining the man knocking on your door during one of the next few nights, the moment of fear you will feel at that nocturnal knock—I'm sorry to have to put you through that—and how you will then go to the door and a mute unknown will hand you the letter and vanish immediately in the darkness.

It is impossible to provide you, the rightly reluctant and warning *spiritus rector* of our conspiracy, with a final report. You not only have a right to it, but it seems to me the inevitable end of the efforts in which you and I joined that I should report to you how my visit with Major Dincklage turned out. I hope you will not take it amiss if I also regard a lady whom I have unfortunately never met as the co-addressee of my letter; from what I have been able to observe of Dincklage's character—admittedly little—I have the impression that not even she will learn very much from him beyond a few hints, stenographic comments, as it were, which she will be unable to decipher unless she is a psychologist of absolute first rank. Who knows, perhaps she is.

I am not a psychologist, no interpreter of human character. Herr Dincklage has remained an enigma to me.

Incidentally, he is by no means to blame that I was in the

hands of that monster up to the last. Can you recall that I once said I would be glad to do everything I could except one thing, to fall into the hands of Nazi soldiers? That was when you conveyed Dincklage's request—what am I saying? his order!—that I was to come though the line. Well, up there on the slope of the height above the Our I fell into the hands of a man whom the expression *Nazi soldier* may or may not fit. I don't know whether it's even adequate. I observed no sign of political fanaticism in him, but something else: a profound and absolute faculty for arousing acute anxiety. Terror as a human attribute. I imagine you know that well! But in all my life I have never encountered such a person, who from the very first moment on scared me stiff. In the end I could not help thinking of the old fairy-tale and told myself that I had probably set out in order to learn the meaning of fear.

Since Dincklage in his anteroom had already given orders that this person was also to bring me back, our conversation began, even before we sat down, with my urgently requesting him to assign another escort to me for the way home. Naturally he understood immediately, asked questions, and I answered them. I made one mistake: I could not bring myself to tell him that I had been physically maltreated. Addressing you, a man who spent long years in a concentration camp, I have no inhibitions about reporting that this little monster kicked me in the behind with his boot, so hard that I fell over. It will seem to you incredible that I withheld from Dincklage this final evidence of the baseness of that creature, but I did in fact conceal the degree to which he had humiliated me. I simply could not say the words. Of course I did not remain silent because I wanted to spare the fellow anything. For a while I thought I was behaving tactfully, much too tactfully, I rather think, by leaving Major Dincklage in ignorance of the conduct of one of his men. It surely would have been embarrassing to him to find out that this summons of his had started off in such a way. Still later—you must realize that such considerations came to me long after I'd begun talking with the major about altogether different matters—I reflected that perhaps I hadn't wanted to expose myself. Please consider that I was ashamed of being kicked like that. I'd had to put up with it! Out of a sense of shame that was still quite vague during my conversation with this officer I would have found it impossible to confess to him that I'd been propelled into his presence by a kick in the behind.

Finally—excuse this protracted investigation of a moment of physical contact, but I must rid myself of the contamination; I'll get to the point right away—finally I realized that it had been right in every respect to let the incident go unmentioned. Describing it would immediately have introduced a sour note into our meeting. You know how it is when conversations that are founded on a firm basis and are supposed to keep to a certain high plane are suddenly sent off course by intrusions from the realm of utterly trivial reality. What a numbing ill-humor that sort of thing produces. The mind finds itself forced to deal with small specific questions instead . . . Oh, of course I can see the ironic expression in your eyes, the proletarian headshake with which you prepare to listen in on the conversation of two bourgeois gentlemen who regard reality as trivial and specific questions as petty. (But do Dincklage and I really count as bourgeois, since it so happens that the bourgeois and none but the bourgeois are capable of thinking realistically? For so I have learned in working in my profession.)

Of course you are right. It was a mistake to say nothing about the kick. Because aside from that I did not have much to criticize. Because I was incapable of describing the real acute anxiety that this ugly customer aroused. The result was that my complaint sounded rather thin. Dincklage, polite as he is, concealed his shrug. He then explained that the man had a blot on his record, for that very reason was specially suited to accompany me because he could—justifiably—hope to be treated with some leniency if he irreproachably carried out an assignment given him directly by his commander. I tried to find out what the fellow had been up to, but Dincklage refused to tell me; when I pressed him, he said only that it was neither a military nor a political offense. "Aha, then it's criminal," I said, because that was exactly what I would have expected of the fellow. "No, not that either," Dincklage replied. "I certainly am not going to entrust you to a criminal!" I was thunderstruck. Well, no matter, at any rate I now had that weirdo on my back for the return trip, too.

It was only at this point that we sat down. Only at this point did I take the liberty of fixing my eyes on Herr Dincklage. Not that I hadn't made a few notes in my mind from the first moment on, when he appeared in the doorway to the orderly room, approached me, and led me into his room. He limped; he used a cane as he walked—but nevertheless there was a kind of metallic precision about him. Or should I say rather that he looked as if he had been stamped out of some metal, with his rather small, spare figure in the perfectly cut tunic, those trousers that have no touch of the English breeches about them but always remind me of the hieratic form of Far Eastern dress (the Japanese also love Prussian uniforms, you know!). At any rate, at first sight he looked like the image we have of a Prussian officer. Or a tin soldier. Oh, I thought, you're going to have a tough time with him; and on the other hand it was almost a bit funny. So when we were at last seated facing each other at his desk I tried to detect more individual traits. It was hard. I spent precious minutes over the appearance of Major Dincklage's chest before I could finally tear myself away from that and look at his face. I am a person who hasn't landed in his profession by chance. When a picture is placed before me, I can scarcely tame my iconographic lusts. I found myself confronted with a picture. The arrangement of forms and colors on the frontal aspect of a German officer is altogether characteristic, artistically speaking, if we do not fall into aesthetic bigotry and insist on some abstract "purity" in art, but instead concede that art includes the impulse to adornment, the tendency to ornamentation, the fondness for decoration. Whole eras threw their artistic genius into the shaping of façades. You know that from Prague, Herr Hainstock! To be sure, the display aspect of Major Dincklage did not strike me as quite so extraordinary as the façade of the Clam-Gallas Palace, but still it fascinated me. To my utter asonishment I found myself transported into the sphere of problems of modern pictorial thinking, for what was presented to me, ignorant of military matters as I am, that ensemble of a narrow colored ribbon diagonally upper right (I am making these designations from the observer's viewpoint, not from that of the figure), black, silver, and red cross and ribbons, dark green and silver shield shapes, intertwined cord trimmings in ecru, all that on a ground color—unfortunately uninspired!—of gray-green—what was presented to me was exactly what certain modern painters put together in their paintings: abstract signs, optical signals. Don't tell me now that these were simply buckles, decorations, badges, epaulettes, collar, collar insignia. Even I know that all these are objects that can be named, that they carry some meaning. The signs and signals of modern painting also mean something, by the way; they too are not nothing. But in both cases what is involved is no longer imaging, mimesis, but tokens, symbols—translations or untranslatable items, hieroglyphic signs, picture puzzles, abstractions. The world as rebus. Only it's odd—I felt this as a warning—that Major Dincklage's chest in the end did not remind me of a modern painting. Nor of an archaic painting either, unfortunately. Even in the most modern paintings there still remains, though with an oddly alien glow, some recollection of the myths of earlier generations of men. But there was nothing of the kind in this uniform. The painter who could paint it does not exist, will never exist. And if he did exist—where would he find the brush hard enough, the paint dry enough, to do the job? The nature of brushes, the nature of paints, would resist him.

This description of Major Dincklage's emblematical appearance is followed by a sociological digression—which we shall not reprint here—on a "world" (Schefold meant a societal group) in which badges, decorations, ranks, titles are openly displayed. "Childish! Pretentious!" Schefold wrote. "Believe me, it is pure kitsch!" he insisted to Hainstock (as though Hainstock were not already convinced of that). He found the reason to be special traits in men ("women, thank God, have other interests") who everywhere set up hierarchies so that the life of most men revolves around ascents and descents, except that in civilian occupations these are not paraded quite so openly. "The judge's robe, the executive suit—all very well, but not this rooster display, these impressive gestures!"

But he excepted Dincklage. The total lack of vanity, the restraint, the obvious simplicity of the man, did not even permit the thought that he had ever kicked and clawed after promotions. But the phenomenal quality of that uniform did envelope him. And Schefold once again divagated into details, elaborately discussed Dincklage's collar (height, width, stiffness, heraldry of the patches): "Between you and me, Hainstock, I now know why Germany would lose this war even if she had waged it for the most just cause in the world: because of those collar patches!"

Then:

Among all these signs I discovered one to which I cannot concede any character of being a sign. I mean, of course, the swastika. Dincklage wore it no less than three times: black on black at the intersection of the bars of his two principal decorations, the Iron Cross First Class and the Knight's Cross; silver, surrounded by a wreath that was held by an eagle, on the left (from his point of view, right) side of his chest. Of course all German soldiers do wear it in this form, as a kind of national insigne. In view of that, I realized that it is not a sign, I mean that it signifies nothing. It actually signifies nothing. Just try for a change to think out what the swastika could symbolize and you will discover that I am right. It does not even symbolize the exterminations that have been committed in its name, for crimes cannot be symbolized. A murder provokes real horror, and anyone who fails to name it by name, to call it murder, anyone who merely makes a cross or a swastika instead, is a criminal, no matter whether his sign is ever so finely executed in the noblest calligraphy, with india ink on rice paper.

Regarding the swastikas on the uniform of our poor friend Dincklage—it suddenly occurred to me to call him that—I tried to imagine what consequences his wearing them for years would inevitably have for him. The medals could be forgiven—but he's had to wear the swastika insignia for seven years now. Given everything we know about him, I came to a conclusion that isn't so much political, intellectual, as banally medical: that for seven years Dincklage has surely been running around with a constant itch on the right side of his chest! Yes, I am almost certain that there have been times when he could not resist the impulse to scratch himself. Then he took off his tunic, pulled up his shirt, and with his fingernails scratched himself bloody at the spot over which the swastikas rested. And now just imagine, Herr Hainstock, that thousands of German officers (I am not even counting the enlisted men!) are suffering from the same itch. I have no idea how many German officers there are, but a hundred thousand of them, or if you like only fifty thousand for sure, must be scratching themselves like mad from time to time. Of course that isn't the proper treatment for a case of the itch. But it simply never occurs to them to cut out the cause of the disease. Or they don't have the courage to. Yet it would be so easy. I had a chance to look closly at Major Dincklage's national insigne. The swastika is just sewed on.

Depressed, visually overstrained—there are Flemish painters on whose altarpieces you at first notice nothing but jewels and brocade—I asked myself whether this Major Dincklage was really anything but a type. (I don't know, Hainstock, whether you think this question worth going into. Your ideology is as a rule content with noting features typical of classes. In discussions with Marxist art historians I've always noticed that they began to be bored whenever I talked about a typical individual expression in works of art, about the personal *anima* of painting.)

Assuming that this letter had been written and that Hainstock would have received it, we are imagining the monologue, or rather the dialogue with an absent Schefold, into which Hainstock would have fallen faced with this personal attack which, examined closely, constituted a serious objection to the doctrine to which he was attached. He would probably not have engaged in a theoretical argument. "The Communist Party," we can hear him saying, "at least the Communist Party as I knew it, always understood that people are different. All comrades were different, and the Party reckoned with that fact. Even in camp, where they tried to reduce us all to numbers, we were so differentiated you cannot even imagine it. Everyone reacted to the camp in his own individual fashion." He would have paused before saying: "Of course the class enemy exists and we must learn to recognize him. But he too is quite different in all his aspects. There are very different gradations of him, and the Party reckons with that too. You, Herr Doktor Schefold, are not one of the class enemies at all, although you are a bourgeois." And at the very end, almost inaudibly, he would have murmured: "The devil take your Marxist art historians!"

Would his face inform me that he was not just a type? Well, to be candid I found little more in it than a general expression of energy. The only wrinkles were two thin lines running from his nose to the corners of his mouth; otherwise there was nothing but the tautness and tan that obviously come from service in the field. I looked—as discreetly as possible, of course, avoiding any hint of staring—for signs of . . . well, I shall venture to write the words down: signs of a capacity for suffering; but I found none. You know what I mean: personal suffering, or intense sympathy with the sufferings of others, leave traces in a face. Several times I caught him when the look in his eyes became absent; he has gray eyes and suddenly, in the middle of our conversation, and by no means when we were talking of important matters, those eyes became blind, developed cataracts. But those moments were brief.

In addition, he seems likable. Odd that no matter how a person looks he will seem likable or unlikable. I could not discover what there was about this man that struck me as likable—but then, one never can. There is something that goes beyond friendliness, breeding, reticence, intelligence. A pity you have never met Major Dincklage; I'd wager he would also have impressed you as likable.

I am trying to be as objective as possible, in fact I have to be, for all the while I was confronting him I felt different from him in a way that is not to my credit. On the one hand there was I, a rather heavy person who has put on too much weight, a hedonist after my fashion, a lover of good food, basically engaged in nothing more than responding to the beauty of aesthetic processes conceived and carried out by others, a passive admirer of women; and on the other hand there was he, this taut, controlled soldier, a symbol of the war even on the verge of surrender, with the disciplined spirit of the frontline officer. Reasons enough for all kinds of resentments on my part. So first of all I want to register the fact that he aroused feelings of liking in me, and that his eyes clouded over from time to time as though he were suffering from cataracts.

But then again this gives me the right to speak frankly at last of what was on the tip of my tongue all the while: that if I had been able to meet him before the beginning of the affair into which he has drawn us, I would have earnestly advised against it and for my part, at any rate, would have resolutely refused to have anything to do with it.

This will strike you as odd because you sense that my insight has nothing to do with your political and military objections to Dincklage's plan. These remarks sound as though I did not think Dincklage worthy of our trust. Nothing could be further from the truth. Major Dincklage is anything but unreliable. On the contrary, he is a man of rigorous consistency, perhaps too rigorous, I must add when I think of the step he required of me. No—there is something else, something that I have difficulty explaining and for which I can find no other word but: alien. Major Dincklage is alien to me, and I or, rather, we are alien to Major Dincklage. And it is this that makes our connection with him appear to me in hindsight as a mistake, a misunderstanding from the outset.

I will try to explain it to you nonetheless. You see, Herr Hainstock, you and I, and surely this lady whom I unfortunately have never met because of your mania for secrecy—all three of us climbed aboard this business quite as a matter of course, except for our objective reservations, our technical criticisms. We had no inhibitions about it. May I risk going even further and say that we have done so quite cheerfully? From the first moment on, we were in agreement, worked together, formed a gang, to use the American expression—which comes naturally when I consider that even Captain Kimbrough, this Southern anarchist, simply went along in spite of his reservations about the legal aspect, and has risked a good deal to do so. Four persons as different as they could be—but when we were brought together under a particular constellation it turned out that we fitted one another. Only one person did not fit in—Dincklage. Do you know the kind of boy who always stands around stiffly, clumsily, during a game, is always inhibited? Who'd rather withdraw and sit down in some corner of the schoolyard?

Dincklage was very reluctant to play with us—I felt that clearly when I finally met him in person. Yet, you will object, he began the game. I have certain doubts about that; I admire Kimbrough's acuteness on that score. When I told Kimbrough that the un-known lady had informed you of Dincklage's plan, Kimbrough remarked that in that case Dincklage probably had his decision forced on him. (I hope you don't take my indiscretion amiss; after all, Kimbrough was entitled to learn that there was a perfectly normal reason behind Dincklage's action.)

I therefore come to the conclusion that we should not have let ourselves get involved with Dincklage. You would probably sum up the reasons in a formula: that he had not overcome his officer mentality and consequently was not politically mature enough to collaborate fully with a civilian resistance group. Undoubtedly you'd be right to put it that way. The final proof of how right you are is the demand he made of me. Now that I have this ordeal be-hind me, it strikes me as more farfetched, more foolish, than ever. For, Herr Hainstock, if Dincklage had really shared the premises behind our thinking, he would have accepted the techniques of underground resistance without any reservations, without making the rigid attempt to save a shred of military decor for himself and his plan. (And yet, there again I must do him justice: since the Americans turned him down, he would have been forever haunted by the thought that he had shown a lack of military style and seriousness. He offered the surrender from army to army. In almost classical form. It was rejected. Now he's neatly out of the affair.)

But this is only a half truth. The whole truth is that he is the boy who cannot play with the others. Doesn't want to. Feels alienated. Inside tight systems such people are quite useful; they even receive Knight's Crosses and suchlike. But out on the hunt-ing grounds? I understand Major Dincklage very well. I myself was a boy who sat down in a corner of the schoolyard, who read a book when the others played.

Was I still being that, Schefold may have thought, interrupting himself at this point in his imaginary letter, when on that March day in 1937 I wrapped up the Klee, left Germany and took the

train to Brussels? Or on the contrary, have I at this moment left
my corner for the first time, begun to play a game at the end of
which I ran into a rifle pointed at me?

I have just called the behavior of such boys stiff, clumsy; but I
noticed no such qualities in Major Dincklage. After he had dealt
with the precarious question of my escort back to the line—
though unfortunately in such a way that uneasiness seized me
whenever I thought about it—he applied himself to the task of
making conversation. In fact, I have been able to give so detailed
a description of him because up to the meal and during the meal,
which was served punctually at half past twelve, we did nothing
but make conversation. I felt as though we had met one evening
in an officers' casino and retired to a corner to chat quietly with
each other. I am very partial to calmness, what the French call
*désinvolture*, but this simply went too far. Not that our conversation did not move along on a rather high level, as I indicated at
the beginning of my letter. But was this what I'd had to climb up
to that barren pasture slope for, from which I first saw nothing
and then that unholy terror? Considering what I, you, that lady,
Kimbrough, had got ourselves involved in, I longed for reality to
come crashing in—the most trivial aspects of it, for all I cared
upon this cultivated conversation. Or, to put the matter more
plainly, I waited impatiently for Major Dincklage to come to the
point. Had I not occasionally observed a slight temporary clouding in his eyes, a flickering signal of absent-mindedness, I would
have thought the whole business outrageous. Or comical . . . All
right, it *was* comical. Your proletarian headshaking is altogether
justified. You would in fact have made a far better negotiator
than I could be. How much more quickly, decisively, and firmly
than I you would have dealt with Major Dincklage!
    You know, Herr Hainstock, thinking over what has happened,
it seems to me that we have done everything wrong right from the
start.

Once—but he would not have mentioned this to Hainstock—
Schefold caught a trace of disapproval in Dincklage's attitude.

That was when his gaze became fixed on his visitor's red tie. Did he regard it as a political declaration or merely as the distateful whim of a bohemian? Was Schefold a Red or a snob? Was that tie a confirmation that he had been right to preserve the soldierly forms when he embarked on an act of resistance? Apparently it never occurred to him that the tie might be just as much a decorative item as his own, but one that was merely amusing instead of one with a sinister gleam.

And so we chatted about the state of the war (the layman listening to a medical man on the subject of death agonies; he assigned the entire winter for the German throes: "Wars never end in the summer or the winter," he said. "They always end in the spring or fall"), about Hitler (he regards him as the most significant case of paranoia in the history of the world and went on at length about the hypnotic effect of a logically constructed system of delusions; is that supposed to be an excuse for the generals?), about the Americans (he said we would not live to see the end of the era of world powers, but some day they would withdraw, not from Germany and France but from the Emsland and the Auvergne; these ancient regions would prove to be stronger than the world-embracing plans of the Americans and Russians; the Russians, he said, were less to be feared than the Americans because as a pure land power they already knew that they had nothing to gain from being in Britanny and Sicily; in short, he delivered himself of a conservative's fantasies and wishful thinking; I listened with a degree of secret sympathy, for I too, a lover of paintings of many centuries past, do not think in terms of countries but of regions, in terms of differences in the light between Amsterdam and Urbino, although I too, who have always taken an interest not only in the works of art but in the lives of the artists, quickly qualified this by calling to mind that art has had no greater foe than the musty, inturned spirit of the Emsland, the Auvergne—all the Emslands and Auvergnes of the world). What he said was not stupid, but it sounded as if it were coming from another world, a world that is alien to ours, to yours

surely—alien to the world of those who believe in a victory of rationality as one of the goals of world history—but alien to mine
also, for although I speak of a secret sympathy with some of his
ideas I have faith in the worldwide context of art, in the great and
free International of the artists of all times and countries, art serving a high conception of man, constantly reminding him of the
possibility of a free and beautiful life, to such an extent that if art
were ever to cease, man would at once sink to a lower level of existence, where life would scarcely continue to be worth living.
Such convictions should have kept us from entering into an alliance with a man who, speaking of Hitler's paranoia, suddenly
asked me: "Don't you think that all politics is paranoia?" thus betraying that—if only he thinks the idea through to its conclusion
—he regards all human action as meaningless. (I am disregarding
the possibility that he may be right. Perhaps all politics does
spring from obsessions, neuroses, paranoias; perhaps all action, insofar as it is political, is absurd.) But oh, if only we had known
him before! He is a man who is utterly resigned; he never really
wanted to carry out his plan. He is a specialist in death throes.
What has made him that? The infamous system you call fascism?
Or was he inclined that way from the start? When I think of him,
I feel despair.

I shall pass over the meal. If the German Army consumes as
nourishment the kind of fodder that was served up to me, and is
still willing and able to fight, it is performing an act of continual
and supreme heroism. Or of superb idiocy. But whatever it is, heroism or nonsense, in my opinion every German soldier deserves
the Knight's Cross for that alone.

He could have described how, pushing the plate aside, he concealed his loathing for the normal rations of the 416th Infantry
Division by expressing a complaint. "It seems that the walk here
has affected my stomach," he said. Then he took refuge in his
American smokes, first offering the pack of Lucky Strikes to
Dincklage, who took a cigarette and smoked it with interest, lapsing into absent-mindedness as he did so. Schefold was not familiar

with Dincklage's biography and therefore could not guess that in this case the major was only dropping into memories of England.

"Have you anything new to tell me?"

With that question, after the meal was over and the orderly had cleared the table, he ended our chat; and he did this abruptly, unexpectedly, impolitely, in the midst of our each volunteering something about our personal plans for the postwar era—I had already begun desperately seeking fresh subjects of conversation. Moreover, his tone changed so sharply that I gave a start. You ought to have heard that, this sudden change in his voice from a quiet, rather low-pitched conversational level to this high, compressed, incisive tone! For a moment I imagined myself once again standing facing that soldier up there by his foxhole and hearing his "Hands up!" and "Shut up!"

I got a grip on myself, began circumstantially explaining the involved windings of American official channels, and how Kimbrough was trying to fight his way through them. Actually I was sorry, to put it mildly. What right did Dincklage have to ask me whether I had anything new to tell him? He had ordered me to come to him when all of us, including him, knew that matters were not yet ready for discussion. Therefore I had nothing to tell him, he had something to tell me. But I practiced patience. And do you know why? Because I could not help thinking of what Colonel R. had said. Major Dincklage is unaware of this foolish affront, has never heard of it, but I am aware of it, and every time I think of it I tell myself that Major Dincklage deserves every consideration. Therefore I remained expectant, sketching out a rather optimistic view of the situation; I passed on Kimbrough's request that he allow the Americans more time, then became a bit pompous, dropped the names of Hodges, Bradley, and Eisenhower, just as I had heard them mentioned by Kimbrough, said that although Army had turned down the operation . . .

He interrupted me, once again employing that eh-eh tone that I would not have thought possible in such a man.

"That doesn't matter," he said. "I rather prefer it that way."

At this point I thought it appropriate no longer to conceal my amazement. Irritated by a tone that I find altogether repugnant, I also introduced a degree of sharpness into my own voice—unfortunately I'm not capable of very much in that line—and asked: "Then why did you have me come?"

He replied, once more in his normal voice which, as I have said, sounds quiet and low: "So that you could bring Captain Kimbrough a letter."

You will not believe it possible, Herr Hainstock, but that is all there was to it.

I cannot tell you any more—I mean about what was said or what happened after Major Dincklage finally came to the point.

One question, cuttingly spoken, then my explanations, long-winded enough, then two terse sentences, and that was it.

He pulled open a drawer of his desk, took a letter from it, handed it to me. In three minutes it was all over.

So I don't even know why he really had me come, to say nothing of not finding out why he made a proposal and when it turned down declared: "That doesn't matter. I rather prefer it that way."

In that eh-eh tone, which however was followed by a temporary absent-mindedness, as I could gather from the clouding of his gaze—an absence to which I perhaps owed his once again talking to me in a more human fashion.

What makes him tick? I don't know. I'm not a psychologist.

I should not have been angry about his question, "Have you anything new to tell me?" In the nocturnal silence of this American orderly room I have realized that up to the last Major Dincklage hoped for a miracle. Probably he expected, contrary to all probability, that I would come with the news that the Americans would undertake their *raid* in the course of the night.

If so, would he have been a reliable ally after all?

I cannot solve this riddle.

An hour ago Major Wheeler rode back to Saint-Vith. Apparently there is no longer anything in Maspelt that he needs to prevent. We have agreed that tomorrow I shall hand him this letter to you . . .

Incidentally, we continued to sit there for a while, Dincklage and I; we did not part hastily. When I think of the last quarter hour of my visit with Major Dincklage, it reminds me of piano practice, of a lamely performed etude. Someone strikes a few keys at a time; from time to time he manages a chord; in between there are long pauses. Actually we sat in silence for long spells without feeling embarrassment.

I said how much I regretted that our efforts had been in vain.

"It is my fault," he replied. "I would have done better not to have let a word of my intentions slip out."

Keep this remark to yourself, Herr Hainstock. It is not necessary that this person—alas, I have constantly had to limit myself to calling her this lady—should also be reproaching herself. That would top it all off, that she should now feel responsible merely because she believed she had to assist a man's plan by throwing in a little practical feminine common sense.

How stubbornly women continue to believe in the legend that a man's word is his bond. When in fact there are no more vacillating creatures than we are. (Except you, Wenzel Hainstock!)

Major Dincklage asked me about my life in Hemmeres, had me describe the path through the Ihrenbach gorge, commented that I'd been damned lucky not to fall into the hands of one of his patrols. Was I mistaken or did it sound as though he were sorry I had not been caught? Obviously he had for a moment struck a false note, touched the wrong key; he felt that he had, and made amends.

"I advise you to spend no more than tonight in Hemmeres," he said.

I did not tell him that I had already come to that conclusion myself, on Tuesday evening, while I was stumbling home from your quarry in the twilight. I would not sleep in my bed in Hemmeres even this present night, which he still allowed me. Occupying Hemmeres, I had concluded, would be the first of a series of actions that he would take in order to bury the memory of a failed act of treason.

But I wanted to hear this from his own lips, and so I asked: "Why? Because you are going to occupy it?"

To my surprise he said: "No. Not I."

I waited for some explanation, but he remained silent and looked out the window at the place across the road, a handsome old farmhouse, the sight of which had been a comfort to me all this while. It reminded me of the white house in *The Temptation of Saint Anthony* by Hieronymus Bosch, the one with a woman washing linen outside it, in the midst of a world of monsters, chimeras, and the flames of hell.

At last I heard Dincklage saying: "Something is brewing."

Again I waited and again minutes passed before he overcame himself—for that is exactly the phrase I must use if I am to describe the impression Major Dincklage made upon me when he continued to speak, incidentally standing up as he did so and thus putting an end to our conference. Yes, he had to overcome himself; it obviously came hard to him; and to me the proof that he literally had to force the following sentence through his teeth lies in the way he dropped back into that high-pitched, tight tone of command as he said: "You may make use of this information!"

Herr Hainstock, I am really tempted to burst out laughing when I think of all the grand plans for treason on the part of Major Dincklage which in the end came down to nothing more than permission to let the Americans know that a German offensive was impending. A plan which was to revolutionize the history of the war—and then this! The mountain labored and brought forth a mouse. And you could just see how he appeared to himself as he said this—an apostate, a scoundrel, a perjurer, a deserter, and whatever other nasty words there are in his vocabulary for that sort of thing. He actually struggled with himself. But the laughter stuck in my throat. That was what we had taken such risks for!

And yet, then again—he has warned the other side. What contradictions! What a confusion of withdrawals and high-mindedness!

I have made no use of the permission he gave me. No need to inform Major Wheeler of the impending German offensive—the news is new only to me. I must send it to you, however. Now I am the one to utter warnings. Become even more invisible than you already are. Will your shack in the quarry survive the coming battle? I shall come and look when it is over. Do me the favor of still being there!

He forbore to describe to Hainstock his departure from the Battalion Command Post in Winterspelt, the scene between Dincklage and Reidel, whom the major called in when he turned Schefold over to him, and then the forced formalities of departure in the orderly room, in the midst of eyes now observing sharply, ears noting every word, noses scenting American tobacco. Nor did Schefold report anything about the way back through Winterspelt again, along the village street leading northward, until he and Reidel reached the spot where they began climbing the slope they had left that morning . . . We write all this down as though he reported anything at all, writing to Hainstock, during that half of the night which ended October 12, 1944. But since we have conceded to him the possibility of such a letter, we must now grant him fatigue. He has reported what he thinks he had to report. Now he is tired. It is late at night and there is nothing to do but keep the letter short.

That soldier was as detestable on the way back as he had been in the morning. I should have protested against having him for an escort.

At one point I came very close to disconcerting him, but at the last moment I forbore. Perhaps that was a mistake; perhaps I ought to have disconcerted him in order to get at his true nature.

In the end it was I who was disconcerted, so that I let myself be carried away into irresponsible behavior. Into an act of sheer madness. At any rate, Herr Hainstock, you will think everything I did madness. I can just hear you saying, "Are you mad?" if you saw me taking out my wallet, removing a ten-dollar bill from it, and handing it to this soldier. For that is exactly what I did when he threw a last, absolutely unbearable insult at me. "Beat it, spy!" he said when we arrived at his foxhole. And once again made that movement of his head, that mute jerk of the head without the slightest trace of courtesy—ah, how I'd learned to hate it! That was something that could no longer be taken, that "Beat it, spy!" that gesture of ultimate contempt. I ask you to understand that I simply could not take it.

I don't know what put the idea into my head to reach for my wallet. Afterwards it seems to me that I reached for my wallet as if it were a pistol. (I who will never be able to use a weapon!)

"But couldn't you control yourself?" you will ask. "Didn't you think of Dincklage, of what consequences it will have for him when the man makes his report with an American banknote in his hand?"

You will shake your head. I thought of Dincklage. At the end I thought only of Dincklage, not at all of this repulsive creature before me. Of Dincklage who had inflicted this horrible absurdity upon me. For a letter that contained nothing, as it turned out after Captain Kimbrough opened it. All along I knew that it would contain nothing. No, I did not control myself. I was full of rage against Major Dincklage.

"There," I said, "for your not very friendly services."

I gave him a tip. It had become too late to try him again, too late and ultimately foolish. I had made efforts to be friendly with him, let me tell you. Several times in the course of this day I tried!

You should have seen his face. He was so astonished that he took the bill.

Only then did I continue on. I did not turn around again. I climbed the slope until I reached the shadow of the pines. When I was up there, under the trees, I felt the whole nightmare drop away from me. You know, I'd been afraid, Hainstock, and now I was no longer afraid. I was free. Free!

We will not bother to reproduce the final phrases and complimentary close. It may be assumed that Schefold did not conclude the letter without once again urgently recommending Paul Klee's painting to Hainstock's care. He might also have inquired about the owl—a sensitive man, Schefold knew that the bird was at the moment the only living being Hainstock still had to associate with.

After completing the letter Schefold would probably have decided to go to Saint-Vith that very night, in order to look for some kind of quarters. (Had Kimbrough already retired to his, not to speak of Pfc. Foster? But there is always someone on duty in the orderly room of a frontline unit.) Looking at his wristwatch, Schefold would have noted that there was no hope of finding the waitress. All the taverns in Saint-Vith would have closed long ago. But tramping along the road he would probably have enjoyed the night wind, and perhaps, who knows, even the glare of the battle in the north against the nocturnal sky.

## Two of Dincklage's Dreams

On the night of October 11 Major Dincklage had had little sleep. Concise though the two letters sound—we shall copy them in the following pages—they nevertheless, or perhaps for that very reason, occupied him from midnight until two o'clock in the morning of October 12. After that he lay down, but did not fall asleep until about three o'clock, and the pain in his hip joint awoke him again by five. After awakening and gazing into the darkness of his room, he tried to reconstruct the two dreams that had plagued him. He had the impression that they had remained with him all the time he was sleeping.

1.

He had been driving in a car along a river with his wife. Who this woman was, he did not know, only that she was his wife; she did not become visible during the entire dream. The road ended suddenly in a maze of black, muddy tracks amid a landscape of shrubbery such as grows along the banks of rivers. Behind one

392

bush a stocky young man whom he had never seen before stood
up. He was wearing a dark suit. His face was plump, healthy; he
had blond, curly hair combed straight back. Dincklage asked him
whether he knew the way to the *fen*. Together they unfolded a
map of a northern plain, and the young man showed Dincklage
an area marked *The Great Fen Moor*.

Awake, Dincklage reflected for a long time about the meaning
of the word *fen*, until he recalled that it was connected with his
mother. His mother came from East Frisia, from one of the Dutch
farms along a canal in the moors to the south of Aurich. The
name of the canal was the Great Fen Canal.

Dincklage could find no explanation for the dream image of the
stocky young man.

2.

Again he was accompanied by a woman (this time not in a
car), and again she did not appear, but perhaps it was Käthe; he
wanted to show her the street in Meppen where he had gone to
school, where he had spent the greater part of his boyhood. In
order to shorten the way there (as he explicitly stressed), he chose
an underground street crossing which was illuminated and lined
with food stores. He came out on the other side, saw the entrance
to the street he was seeking, but it did not begin in the corner of a
square, as in Meppen, but beyond a meadow; it was no longer the
street he had in mind at all, but an entirely different one. Instead
of the Renaissance town hall and the church, the beginning of the
street was flanked by two gigantic caryatids (which, however, supported nothing). Suddenly he knew that this was not the street of
his school life, but of his birthplace. He did not enter it, but went
into one of the next streets, alone; the woman (Käthe?) had
vanished. This street, which actually did not concern him at all,
was lined with ruined houses, which however had been cleaned up
a long time ago, in fact had actually been burnished. The ruins
stood there like gigantic terra-cotta sculptures. In the wall of the
house at the end of the street there was a hole, through which a

goat had stuck his bearded and horned head; Dincklage saw nothing of the animal except this head, with which he was nodding in all directions. Another buck was trying to climb the wall of the house in order to reach the hole from which the head was nodding, but he could not make it; he repeatedly slid down again.

Dincklage did not know how to interpret this dream.

## Document II

Not fictional. Letter from Joseph Dincklage to Käthe Lenk. Place and date missing. Probably written immediately after the letter (cited here as Document III) to Captain Kimbrough; this may be inferred from the opening phrase ("And now to the two of us!"). Oddly, there is no salutation. We can only conjecture that the salutation *Dear Käthe* struck him as too dry, and that on the other hand he could not make up his mind to such salutations as *Dearest, Beloved Käthe,* or even *My beloved Käthe.* The handwriting is, as always, coherent, neat, not very large, without hairline strokes. On the whole the tails of the letters are somewhat longer than is usual in Dincklage's handwriting.

The letter was delivered at the Thelen farm on Thursday, after 1400 hours, by the orderly whom we already know. Dincklage seems to have calculated very carefully the time at which Käthe would be receiving the letter. Obviously he considered it important that she receive it only after Schefold had left and almost at the same time that he had Staff Sergeant Kammerer issue the order for the battalion's departure, so that, in other words, the deadline would have passed for keeping this divisional order secret.

And now to the two of us!

At the very moment you took my plan into your hands, you likewise took a step away from me.

I cannot stop wondering at myself: that I can understand something and still be unable to accept it.

No, of course I understand nothing. Respecting your incomprehensible reasons, I wear the mask of patience. I find that it doesn't become me.

You should not have left me alone this way.

You have given me too much time for reflection.

*Reflection* is an unsatisfactory word. Nor can I substitute a word like *feeling*. By what word shall I characterize the hours in which I waited for you, while the truth about my plan crept into me?

If you had wanted to show me that it isn't necessary for something to happen, you could have chosen no better example than the step away from me that you took. You wanted to show me how simple it is to act. And then you show me that it is far simpler not to act.

So real things come about anyhow, I thought. There isn't any need to make them happen.

Last night I had one of my fits of meaninglessness. I stared at the lamp, the box of books, the bed, and told myself: this might also not exist.

At such moments I always know that I have experienced them once before. In an earlier life. The darkness that reigns then! The light of the lamp you brought me can do nothing to banish it.

Tonight I canceled my operation.

I do not succeed in canceling the desire to touch you.

J.

P.S. Oh hell—the plan has fallen through for totally different reasons. The division is being relieved. Departure begins tonight. I have known that since Monday. I issued the order to the battalion today at 1400 hours.

Please do not reproach me that I should have informed you of this circumstance on Tuesday instead of concealing it while I listened to your news of the procrastination on the American side and on top of it all demanded that Schefold call on me! But it did not take even that outrageous remark by the American colonel to make me realize that it was absolutely necessary to give the Americans a last signal.

For a while I deceived myself, thought they would have to prove to me that they meant it seriously by sending Schefold through the line. You took issue. You pointed out that I can expect nothing and demand nothing from them. Very well. I realized that. But now I know—and probably I knew it from the beginning that I want to prove to them how serious my intentions are by insisting on Schefold's going through the line. For I have no other way to prove it to them.

And it must be proved to them. Even now. Especially now.

Another P.S. At our Monday conference the regimental and battalion commanders were informed that the division is to be assigned to northern Italy, to fight partisans. Since I do not wish to take part in that, I have asked the regimental medical officer to start the proceedings for my demobilization, which he has repeatedly urged on me. He has assured me that given the nature of my ailment and, as he put it, in consideration of my military deserts, there should be no difficulty. So probably I shall be detached from the battalion in the midst of our move and assigned to the reserve, and from that dismissed within a very short time. As a holder of the Knight's Cross one enjoys certain advantages even in regard to release; one isn't exposed to long, wearing waits in barracks. I count on being back home early in November.

So you may be certain of finding me in Wesuwe if you were to arrive there by about November 5. We could quickly attend to the necessary preliminaries for marriage, and I am almost certain that we could be married before the end of November, or at any rate before the end of this year.

If you should want to choose a different route—and I sense that you have in mind to do so—I want you to know that the Ihrenbach gorge and the hamlet of Hemmeres will lend themselves to that only during this coming night. The division that is replacing ours, a formation of the Waffen-SS far superior to our own division in men and materials, will overlook nothing, not the deepest gorge or the loneliest hamlet.

P.S. I promise that this is the last one. It's just that something always keeps coming to my mind when I think of you. At any rate I would want you to know this: that the Dincklage brick factories are shut down. The furnaces have long been cold, and the last squares of bricks were simply left there. The hunters are out now in the meadows by the Ems, with their small spotted dogs, going after pheasants. The meadows are brown, and if you come in November the trees standing along their margins will be bare. The Ems is a river of dark water flowing slowly in loops through the countryside. On its bank the children fly kites. I remember my first kite—the sky in Wesuwe is more transparent than you can possibly imagine.

## Document III

Not fictional. Communication from Major Dincklage to Captain Kimbrough. On the night of October 11 Dincklage typed it with two fingers on the typewriter and, as we have seen, on October 12 gave it to Schefold to deliver. But it never reached Kimbrough. Dincklage's English, though syntactically correct, would have struck the recipient as slightly comical, for it reflected German government jargon which, with its overuse of substantives, tends to sound somewhat stiff and pompous.

Winterspelt, midnight, October 11, 1944

Dear Captain:

Two days ago I received instructions to the effect that the division to which the battalion under my command belongs is to be relieved tonight and transferred to another theater of war.

Under these circumstances the operation projected by the two of us must be finally canceled.

Regrets that its initiation would in any case not have been possible, as I conclude from the procrastination of your superiors, concerning which you sent me word, are consequently unnecessary.

Irrespective of the present change in the general situation, irrespective of any possible decisions on the part of your superiors, I myself have come to the conclusion that there would have been little sense in carrying out my proposal.

I regard it as my duty to bring this, the result of my thinking, to your attention, Captain Kimbrough.

Please believe me when I say that the term your regimental commander, Colonel R., chose to employ in describing my intentions and my person had no influence whatever upon my decision. Since Hitler would employ the same word for me, I was able to exclude that in my thinking.

I am abandoning my plan for two reasons. (Not my plan, but the idea of carrying it out.)

First, this military episode would no longer change the present status and the further course of the war.

Secondly, carrying it out would be the result of a mere chance. But if an event takes place by chance, it can just as well take place or not take place.*

I accept the fact that this shift in my attitude must appear to you as a sign of a vacillating and inconstant character, and you will regard it as a feeble effort to cover up this irresoluteness when I say that I do not regret having involved you in this affair. But I do say it, and thank you for not having promptly rejected my proposal when it was presented to you.

The development indicated at the beginning of this letter will explain why I had to ask Herr Dr. Schefold to come to see me at a time that could not help striking you as inexplicably premature.

The fact that I asked him to come at all, stipulating that as evidence of military dependable negotiating powers he be sent to me through the line, is due to a single reason: I had to rule out all suspicion that I might not mean my offer seriously. Or my cancellation of it. The cancellation is only the inverse of my offer.

Sincerely yours,
Joseph Dincklage, Major

## Footnote 1

\* Dincklage spent the longest time arriving at the wording of this passage, in the writing of which he recalled Käthe's intervention in his plan ("Oh, if that's the problem"—as though it were the simplest matter in the world to carry out the plan). On a piece of scrap paper he sketched out the phrases in which he wanted to explain to Kimbrough his nonbelief in destiny—for example the phrase "although I hold the view that everything we do is a matter of chance and regard all belief in destiny as a crude illusion, there are still events, situations, constellations which prompt one to say . . ."—here he paused, was incapable of formulating what they prompted one to say because he suddenly realized that the structure of this sentence might lead him to abandon his position. He therefore contented himself with this one sentence that, as he well knew, was philosophically weak, easily disproved. Besides, there is no sense in my sending this American a philosophical treatise, he thought, and tore up the note.

He could guess what Käthe would say to his second reason for canceling the operation.

"If you think," he could hear her saying, "that something can just as well take place as not take place, then let it take place!"\*\*

## Footnote 2

\*\* "Man is primarily a sketch that subjectively experiences itself, instead of being merely foam or rot or a cabbage; nothing exists before this sketch; there is nothing in the observable heavens, and man becomes primarily what he planned to be; not what he wants to be."

399

# *Safe-Conduct*

"This is even lousier than your usual pig's swill!"

The mess sergeant had merely gaped at him, speechless at this brazenness (on which he would file a report); but one of the cooks was not so lame of tongue. "Next time we'll spit in the soup special for you, bellhop," he said, which of course he risked only because he imagined that Hubert Reidel was already out of circulation.

Reidel had not answered; he turned away, called over the Hitler Youth from whom he'd borrowed the mess kit, and loud enough for all those standing around to hear had said to him: "Wash this crap out."

Then he had left, heading toward the battalion orderly room, followed by the eyes of almost the entire company.

Again he took the carbine from his shoulder, leaned it carefully in the corner formed by the wall and a wardrobe, sat down beside his weapon on the same chair on which he had sat previously, this time without waiting for permission, for aside from one clerk who held the rank of Pfc. there was no one else in the orderly room, so he could make himself comfortable without being invited to do so. (But he did not make himself comfortable; he sat bolt upright, sharp even in a sitting posture, looking straight ahead.)

The battalion topkick, this sergeant whose name Reidel did not know (if you weren't assigned to the staff you never came into contact with the battalion personnel)—oh yes, the chief had called him "Kammerer"—this Kammerer had advised him to stay away for a while ("You poison the air here, Corporal!"), but Reidel had not for a moment considered complying. He wasn't such a fool as to let this bastard with the goddamn tinsel on his chest who didn't know his ass from his elbow make him miss the moment when the commander and the stranger were finished with their conference! He was not such a dummy as to risk being absent when the commander wanted him. As though he didn't know that they wouldn't wait for him or waste any time looking him up. The next best corporal would do, could attend to the job and send that queer bird on his way across the line. Then all would be up with his prospects of getting only a disciplinary punishment for the Borek business, maybe even getting away with no more than a warning (because the commander, for some reason that Reidel could not fathom, but literally scented, would protect him if he speeded the unknown—at the moment Reidel couldn't even remember his name—back to the place where he'd appeared in his gunsight). If he missed that chance he'd have reason to be glad that they didn't also hang a charge of leaving his post on his own initiative on his tail.

Schefold was his name. Doctor Schefold—that was what it had said on that scrap of paper the big shot had shown him, up there at his foxhole, and that was the name he had given a while ago in the command post. Reidel was relieved when the name came back to him. Just in case he was questioned some day about the visit of this peculiar customer to the commander, it was good if he could give the name. He did not reflect on how it was the idea came to him that some day he would be interrogated about this business; somehow the word *interrogation* was just there, a sound still at a distance: "Now tell us in order: what happened when you brought this man to Major Dincklage?" He could just *hear* the lingo.

"Doctor Schefold." The way he had said it, a while ago, in exactly the smug tone with which guests introduced themselves in a hotel lobby. "Would you please announce me to Major Dincklage." With a tone not of speaking to an almighty battalion topkick, but to the desk clerk at the Rheinische Hof in Düsseldorf.

Of course Reidel, sitting bolt upright, smartly, staring into space, considered first of all whether this man Schefold would scotch his chance of being allowed to bring him back, thus carrying out irreproachably a direct order from the commander. What was going on behind that door marked *chief*? Had the man already turned the chief against him so thoroughly that anything of the sort was altogether out of the question and he would at most be called in to receive a reprimand, after which all he could do would be to withdraw and wait until they had him up in front of a court-martial? (Remanded to a provost court for investigation, summary proceeding, demotion, penal company, sent on bread and watery soup from one suicide squad to the next till the war was over. It was no consolation that Borek would receive the same treatment if he succeeded in dragging the kid in.)

If that bird came out with the kick in the ass, it was all over. Nothing would count against that. It would also land him in the frying pan in the matter of Borek, would be the final proof that he was violent, aggressive.

He prepared himself for the worst. He'd stay tough as a tank. Not for nothing that saying: What doesn't kill, fattens.

Besides, the war would be over pretty quick. He'd survive those few weeks. In Russia he had learned how you could make life cushy even in suicide squads.

The topkick came in, ignored him as he snapped to his feet, came to attention. Reidel sat down again. He doesn't have the Iron Cross First Class, he thought; I have it. On the other hand he wears aiguillettes, silver ones, almost like the porter's in the Rheinische Hof in Düsseldorf.

Between the two sentences, "Something is brewing" and "You may make use of this information"—sentences that tempted Schefold to burst out laughing, as he wrote to Hainstock (in that letter that was never written)—Dincklage had risen to his feet, thus giving the sign that their meeting was over. Schefold also stood up. He considered various parting remarks. He had to express his thanks for the advice the major had given him about staying, or rather not staying, in Hemmeres.

"One moment," Dincklage said. "I had better speak to that lout."

He reached for his cane, limped to the door, opened it, and said: "Kammerer, send Reidel in."

Schefold involuntarily shook his head. This Reidel was under the major's nose—Schefold could see him through the crack in the door—but Dincklage did not turn to him directly; instead he ordered the next person in lower rank to send him in. Military hierarchy consisted of a system of communications and it did not occur even to an intelligent officer, battalion commander, and medalist to bypass the system.

Reidel was already on his feet, had already slung the carbine over his shoulder, when Kammerer jerked his head at him, precisely the same jerk of the head that had outraged Käthe when she saw Reidel using it to order Schefold to climb the steps to the door of the battalion command post.

How the man stood at attention! Not stiffly, but like a rigid reptile, small, greenish-gray.

"Shut the door!" the major said.

The about-face was performed noiselessly, deliberately so; in this case no clicking heels, Reidel had decided. Then another about-face by the little soldier, sharp eyes under the brim of the steel helmet, which was smeared with a mess of muddy colors.

"Where did you win your Iron Cross, Reidel?" Dincklage asked.

"Russia, sir," Reidel said. "After the fiftieth Russky."

Schefold could not make out the major's reaction.

"Did you count them?" he heard him asking.

"We were instructed to count," Reidel reported. "The count was checked."

For a while the best sharpshooters had their pictures published in the *Berliner Illustrierte*, Reidel recalled. But there too I always had bad luck. I never made the *Illustrierte*. With bitterness he recalled the sergeant who'd had his picture on the front page after his seventy-fifth killing.

"I hear that you behaved very badly toward Doctor Schefold."

So now it was coming.

He said nothing. He was supposed to reply only when asked a direct question.

"Is it correct that you would not let him speak and used abusive language to him?"

Was that all? If no mention was made of his kicking this spy in the backside, it wouldn't be half bad.

"I thought the gentleman was a spy, sir."

That was the trick, not to deny, not even to be evasive, but to admit a mistake that could appear reasonable. Nothing more reasonable than for a soldier in the front line to take for a spy someone who turned up there coming from the direction of the enemy.

Sincerity. The sincere soldier who did not know how to lie to his superior. The cunning aspect is that he still thinks I'm a spy, Schefold thought. "I thought the gentleman was a spy." That didn't sound as though the man were withdrawing his allegation.

Would the major notice the danger?

But Dincklage limited himself to replying: "Apparently you think too much, Reidel."

So there wasn't much to his talk about wanting thinking soldiers, that time in Denmark. Officers' blather, nothing more. Reidel had never taken it seriously.

But that he was supposed to draw no conclusions when somebody turned up in front of his foxhole like that—that was really rich. He must think I'm an idiot, Reidel thought.

He would mull over that later. For the moment the only important thing was that the physical blow he'd allowed himself against the stranger had not yet been mentioned. So it was almost sure that the major had no idea about the biggest damfool thing he'd done, because otherwise that would have been the first thing he'd have rubbed under his nose, not such small potatoes as that he'd told Schefold to shut up and called him *asshole*. Probably he wouldn't be standing here, would have been outside long ago, if the major knew he'd kicked his guest in the ass.

But why doesn't he know, Reidel asked himself. The man peached on me. Why didn't he tell him the one thing that really would have put steam behind his protest?

Reidel kept his eyes fixed on the commander, but that did not prevent him from taking a look at Schefold out of the corners of his eyes. There was a chance the man would bring up his heavy artillery only now. Maybe he was saving his ace of trumps for the last minute.

The soldier must be scared stiff about this report from his squad mate; otherwise he wouldn't have risked trotting up here in person with Schefold. Crazy and brazen as hell; by rights he should have stuck at his post until his sergeant turned up (which, however, would seriously have delayed Schefold's arrival at the battalion command post, so that all in all it was lucky Schefold had run into this fellow. Reidel had corrected the mistake that he, Dincklage, had made: removing the noncoms from the line along with the recruits).

Dincklage took Reidel aside. Reidel is one of my men, he thought—entirely contrary to his habit of avoiding this phrase—and official affairs do not concern an outsider. Of course the precaution was pointless. It was impossible to speak so softly in this room that a third person would not hear. But at least the form had to be preserved. Reidel must not be allowed to have the impression that he was facing anyone but his commander, certainly not a civilian also.

"You want to make up for something," Dincklage said in a low voice. "Isn't that why you left your post in defiance of all regulations and brought Doctor Schefold directly to me? You could not

407

know that for once you acted rightly. Or perhaps you did know. Doctor Schefold turned up most conveniently for you. He offered you the opportunity to call attention to yourself in an advantageous way. That was what you were concerned about, Reidel, weren't you? Of course you had every reason to show yourself to me in a favorable light. In doing so you even broke a fundamental rule of soldiering: the rule of not attracting attention. You'd already attracted attention, in a hopelessly miserable way, Reidel—I have to tell you this bluntly—so it no longer mattered to you that you would attract attention once more if there were a chance of its improving your situation. At any rate, that's what you imagined. Right, Reidel?"

If he only knew, Reidel thought, that I came within a hair of killing his Doctor Schefold.

But otherwise the commander was impressive.

Only he couldn't do him the favor of simply saying, "Yessir," because that would be admitting all the circumstances in the report of *Borek* v. *Reidel*. And that was out of the question. He had to defend himself tooth and nail against the *Borek* v. *Reidel* report. He himself did not know why. He did not even ask himself why. He needed only to say, "Yessir," and it was fairly certain that he'd be out of the whole mess, which probably was just a nuisance to the major. But he couldn't do that.

In the Borek matter he had to lie. Boldly, brazenly. Let the chips fall where they might.

"Request permission to say something, sir."

"That's what I'm waiting for," Dincklage said.

"Borek is lying," Reidel said. "There isn't a word of truth in that report on me. Private Borek is a traitor. He made his report against me just so that I wouldn't report on his treasonous attitudes."

Again, as he had done earlier in the orderly room, he croaked this out. He did not avail himself of the opportunity the major had given him: to let matters rest, at least to all appearances, between himself and the major.

He observed the stranger take a step backward, and the convulsive movement of Dincklage's hand on his cane did not escape him. The knuckles turned white.

So he is not only a frightening individual, Schefold thought, but really a Nazi soldier. I've fallen into the hands of a Nazi soldier.

But what kind of game is being played here, he wondered. Why has this officer with whom I fully sympathize because he is against the government permitted this monster to make a denunciation? The man had something on his record, Dincklage had told him earlier, but it was neither a military nor a criminal offense. (And now a political one seemed out of the question too, from what he had just heard. So what the devil was it about?)

"I certainly am not going to entrust you to a criminal." Was Dincklage so sure about that now?

The hand relaxed again.

"Perhaps, Reidel," Dincklage said, "you are not worth my choosing not to hear what you have just said."

Hoity-toity. Suspiciously hoity-toity. After all, he had reported that Private Borek had shown traitorous attitudes. It remained to be seen whether an army major could afford not to hear such a report. And in his very next sentence the chief took him up on it.

"Reidel," Dincklage asked, "did you by any chance try to blackmail Borek after he made treasonous remarks?"

Nasty. First hoity-toity, then stinking nasty. That's how they were.

Reidel didn't give a damn about Borek's treason. He was only making use of it because he was driven into a corner, in self-defense.

Reidel looked at the major without dropping his eyes. He

would not answer that question. A question like tnat was proper only for a court-martial.

Blackmail? Was money involved? That couldn't be, because then it would be a criminal matter after all, which the major had explicitly denied.

This business was becoming more obscure with every passing minute.

"All right, let us drop that," Dincklage said. "So I am mistaken. You have nothing to make up for. Then kindly explain why you thought it necessary to leave your post and bring Doctor Schefold to me. You wanted to win a citation even though you didn't need to because you have a completely clear conscience, haven't you, Corporal?"

He was right on the track; he really was pretty impressive, this limping medalist, and now the only thing that mattered was to keep your trap shut. While Reidel held his tongue, he realized that he had staked everything. If he'd eaten crow, the mission to take this Schefold back to the line would have been surely his. But now that was no longer so sure.

He decided to make a concession by trying to introduce something like a faint embarrassment into his gaze. He did not succeed. His eyes simply weren't made for that sort of thing. They were light brown, almost yellow, and so keen that he seldom needed to narrow them when sighting at a target. Light brown, yellow, keen and unblinking, they remained fixed on Dincklage's face. Not a trace of embarrassment. Only this lifeless, merciless, hawklike look. Yellow.

"Doctor Schefold is under my personal protection," Dincklage said. "You will now bring him back to the place where you encountered him. I expect that you will treat him with the utmost courtesy on the way. Is that clear?"

So it had worked. Wonderful!

"Yessir!"

If this guy had actually not let out a peep about being kicked and continued to keep his mouth shut about it, he certainly could treat him decently.

"When you have carried out the order to my satisfaction, I will afterwards talk with Private Borek and try to persuade him to withdraw his report about you. Assuming that you want this to be done. Do you want that, Reidel?"

"Yessir!"

It must matter a hell of a lot to him, not only that his guest should get away safely—where to, anyhow? over toward the enemy! funny, very funny!—but that all this reporting back and forth about queers and traitors be dropped.

"Then you do not attach any importance to your report about Borek?"

Careful! He mustn't admit that right out, otherwise he'd be making himself unbelievable and Borek believable.

He said: "I don't have any wish to get Borek involved in any trouble, sir."

Just as he had sensed their tension when he came out with his denunciation of Borek, now he felt their relief. He was prepared to go easy on treasonable attitudes—that gave him a plus. Only a little one, but he could read it in their faces.

Was he mistaken, or was there something actually like pity in their manner toward him? That was enough to make you climb the walls! Pity was just about the last thing he needed.

If it was pity, then it was pity for a rejected queer.

For the first time Reidel asked himself whether the commander's guest knew the charge against him. Had the commander told him in order not to leave him in ignorance of his escort's

411

character? "The man who brought you is a little homo." Followed by a tolerant smile on the part of both gentlemen.

"Aha," Dincklage said. "I thought so. So I was not entirely mistaken."

His voice sounded friendlier now. He refrained from rubbing it in or spelling out the rest. But then he landed a blow that Reidel would never forget.

"Don't imagine, Reidel, that my purpose in speaking to Private Borek will be to do you a favor," the major said. "It's Borek himself I am thinking about. An incident of this sort won't look good on his record."

So that's the way it was. An enemy of the state came in for plenty of protection, but a homo not. He hadn't really wanted to know that quite so clearly. Now he knew it. Major Dincklage had made it plain. He hoped he'd have the chance to pay him back some day.

Still and all and thank God: there'd been no question of pity.

Besides, the major had made a mistake.

If all he wanted was to help Private Borek, it would be enough to send for him and persuade him to take back his report. That wouldn't be hard. ("I'm sorry I wrote that report. I really am sorry now.")

It was impossible to see why it was also necessary for him, Reidel, to win a citation by bringing the stranger back across the line.

But that was exactly what the whole thing was about, and that had nothing to do with Borek.

Rather, for some hidden reason Major Dincklage wanted him, Corporal Reidel, to imagine that he had to earn his forgiveness.

But in that case he shouldn't have made that fuss about helping Borek.

The chief had tripped himself up there.

412

Well, no matter, at the moment Reidel couldn't figure out why
the major was so determined to make him believe he was obligated for God knows what reason. The main thing was, it had all
turned out perfectly. Things had worked out just the way he'd
figured it earlier, up there on the slope and on the way to the village. "The man acted correctly for a change." And he'd been
given the assignment to bring this guy back without having to
budge an inch from his position. They'd sweep Borek's report
under the rug and on top of that be grateful he wasn't raising a
fuss but keeping quiet and watching them do it.

No, he had no interest in getting Borek into trouble. His only
interest was in staying around where Borek was, even though his
chances there were strictly nil.

I've thrown away every single chance to get this frightening person off my neck, every single one. Even while the major was
reprimanding him for the insulting language he'd used to me, I
could have come out with that kick. Or when the viper hissed
that he took me for a spy. After that it was suddenly no longer
possible. From that point on something was being cooked up between the major and this soldier, something I had no right to interfere with. By then it was too late. There are times for taking action. I missed my time.

Oh, the hell, Schefold thought. Excuses. I should have broken
in, at the cost of seeming rude. If something absolutely unbearable is involved, you can't go wishing all kinds of subtleties! I
should have bluntly refused to be escorted by this soldier.

But it also absolutely went against Schefold's grain to bring up
his chief charge against Corporal Reidel at this point. His good
breeding (the breeding of a cultivated member of the German
middle class), his feeling for form (the feeling that had propelled
him into art history), played him a trick. They were stronger than
his fear. Not that they would not have permitted him to show fear.
But not when it was too late for that, not when he'd already
missed the time for action.

413

Dincklage finished. He led the way into the orderly room. Reidel followed him without delay, Schefold only when he realized that there was to be nothing more.

The major was dissatisfied with himself, but in an unclear way. He did not apprehend that Reidel must be telling himself the report would be dropped anyhow, without his having to do anything in return.

He attributed his discontent to the insult he had inflicted on Reidel. It was a needless brutality, he thought, to tell him to his face that I am more concerned with helping Borek out of trouble than him. And it isn't even true. I was quite prepared to help him too. In my command no denunciations for homosexuality will go up through channels.

He turned to Kammerer.

"Corporal Reidel will afterwards return and report to you that he has carried out the order I have given him."

The instructions were directed primarily to the listening Reidel.

"Very well, sir," Kammerer said.

There was not only no need to make mysteries; it would have been wrong. As this fellow Hainstock had understood when he had passed on the advice to mention Hemmeres without a qualm.

"Reidel has the assignment to escort Doctor Schefold back across the line. Doctor Schefold lives in Hemmeres."

"Very well, sir."

Kammerer had meanwhile looked at the map to see where this Hemmeres was. So that was where the man lived. And Reidel on his own initiative had brought the fellow into headquarters, so he said—this now confirmed by the major. Odd. Must be an intelligence matter. Kammerer gave no more thought to it. The major would eventually tell him what it was about.

What the accountant—the one who had noticed the smell of American tobacco (he too was back in the orderly room by now) —thought about what he heard in connection with Schefold's departure must remain likewise hidden in the darkness of history,

414

along with the conclusions that Sergeant Rudolf Dreyer (of the
Operations Section in the headquarters of the Commander-in-
Chief West, now mentioned for the second time) may have
drawn from what he was writing and hearing, contrary to em-
phatic warnings.

Just talking easylike about Hemmeres was the trick, of course.
But it wasn't fooling him, Reidel.

If only he were back in his foxhole so that he could give this
suspicious business a good thinking over.

He hoped that in spite of the sentry relief that had taken place
by now no other man was standing in his hole. If there was, he'd
get him out of there in half a second flat. There were plenty of
empty holes because the line was being thinly guarded even in the
afternoon, on account of the recruits still being freed of sentry
duty.

Big chief here with his chestful of tin had practically sentenced
him to double sentry duty by ordering him to get this bird back
through the lines. He didn't give a damn. The opposite. And he
wouldn't be in any rush to return to the orderly room and report
he'd carried out the assignment. First of all he'd crawl into his
hole for a while and consider what the devil had really been going
on here.

Now I can't even thank him for giving me that advice about
leaving Hemmeres. Now there's no longer time for anything at
all. Why didn't the major take another minute to send the man
out and speak to me privately about him? That would have been
my chance to make a last and extreme protest.

He tossed the raincoat over his shoulder again, as he did so feeling the letter that he had thrust into the breast pocket of his
jacket. The envelope, he recalled, bore no address and was sealed.

"Have a safe journey to Hemmeres, Herr Doktor!" the major
said, shaking hands with him.

Schefold had to pull himself together to frame a reply. He

would rather have left without saying anything. But that couldn't very well be done, with all these eyes on him.

"Goodbye, Herr Major," he said. "And many thanks for your hospitality."

"Don't mention it," Dincklage said. "I must apologize for the meal I inflicted on you."

He turned back to the staff sergeant. "Kammerer," he said, "I think it's high time you paid some attention to the kitchens."

Schefold forced himself to smile. They had staged an innocuous leave-taking.

This Reidel fellow once again yanked the door open in front of him, let him precede again, but with a manner very different from that of their arrival—more or less standing at attention, not quite the same as the posture he assumed in front of the major, but still at attention: a manner suitable for a civilian for whom *most proper treatment* had been prescribed, and before the eyes of the commander who had prescribed it.

The way you yanked open the door for a *guest* and posted your-self alongside it, waiting for a tip.

After they had vanished, Dincklage looked at his watch.

"Half past one," he said. "You can now issue the orders for the move, Kammerer. In twelve hours the battalion can be ready to start. Do we know when the transport vehicles are due?"

"The regiment promised them for eight o'clock, sir."

"Oh well, then don't count on them to arrive before ten. The sentries will remain in the line, of course, until relieved by the new unit. Everything else clear?"

"All clear, sir. It's been a pretty short guest performance we've given here."

"Be glad of that, Kammerer! I suspect it's going to be pretty rough in these parts."

He went to the door.

"Send up my orderly," he said. "He's to help me pack."

After he left, the men in the battalion orderly room exchanged looks of glee. The commander was really a regular guy. Medal or not, he made no secret of the fact that he was as glad as they were to get away from a region where things were probably going to be rough for a while.

Waiting for his orderly, he lay down on the bed and stared up at the ceiling.

Käthe, they had agreed, would come to him at once to hear what had been discussed between himself and Schefold. She was to arrive later, in the course of the afternoon. So he had planned it, on the pretext that it was necessary to cover up, but in reality because he wanted to gain time. He wanted her to have read his letter before she came. He would send the orderly to her with the letter as soon as the packing was done, which would take at most half an hour. From the letter she could gather everything that concerned Schefold and the operation so that all she need tell him when she came was whether she would or would not go to Emsland. If she accepted his suggestion, he had a few lines ready to give her for his parents.

Gazing at the ceiling, he thought: at 2000 hours the trucks, the replacements, the new unit, SS (he would have to give the stiff-armed Hitler salute), the departure in the night. End of the plan. "Oh, if that's the problem!" (Oh, Käthe!) What was left of the plan? Nothing more than a somewhat soft man, a likable sort, art historian, obviously an esthete, who now, accompanied by that nasty customer, that little devil, was going along the road and up the hill.

Käthe. Winterspelt. Käthe.
She would not go to Emsland.

Therese had already taken care of the meal because Käthe returned from the quarry too late; they were already eating and Käthe sat down at the table in such a position that she could

417

keep an eye on the house across the street. Afterward she went out into the yard, busied herself spreading wet towels on the bench that stood beside the entrance, swept the stones outside the threshold with a straw broom. When Schefold and the soldier who had brought him appeared successively in the doorway of the battalion command post and descended the three steps to the street, she quickly drew back into the strip of shade cast by the Thelen farm. The residential wing of the Thelen farm faced east, and by two o'clock in the afternoon it already cast a shadow, narrow, but so dark that it presumably concealed her.

It upset her immediately to see that the soldier whose jerk of the head she had instantly detested, whom she had mentally registered as a rather unpleasant type, was also escorting Schefold on the way back. Joseph Dincklage had asked her to wait an hour before she came to see him, but she had made up her mind to go to him at once as soon as the conversation with Schefold was over and explain to him the meaning of that diagonal jerk of a head from lower left to upper right, and tell him that Schefold should never have been asked to put up with anything of the sort. Was Dincklage so much a captive of his military thinking, of his system of commands and obedience—of his *structure*, Käthe thought —that he did not have enough knowledge of human nature even to notice the dangerous quality of this man? Had he noticed him at all? Perhaps—she could well believe it of the military way—he had not even seen him, just a nameless soldier who sat in the anteroom all that while and waited until a clerk ordered him to bring Schefold back to where he had met him.

But obviously something had changed in the relationship of the two men over there on the sidewalk. For she saw no more of that pantomime of a muleteer, no more of those gestures of mute subjugation, but instead something rather like an adjustment. Yes, it was quite evident that the soldier was now adjusting to Schefold's gait, Schefold's behavior. Schefold did something she would not have thought possible. After he had walked a few steps, he suddenly stood still, nonchalantly to all appearances, fumbled in his jacket pocket, took out a pack of cigarettes, and with a lighter lit a cigarette. And the soldier also stood still, did not reprove him, but waited until Schefold moved on, although without watching him during the process of lighting a cigarette. Turned away, rather. Astonishing. She would have to describe all this to Hainstock when he turned up later to ask her whether everything had gone well.

The Thelen farmyard was enclosed. The two men, the big heavy man with his fluid movements who still looked like a fallen monarch but no longer struck her as so defenseless as he had seemed two hours earlier, and the small, wiry, unpleasant man coerced into politeness, vanished from Käthe's sight at the point where the stable wing of the building met the village street. She removed her glasses and leaned against the whitewashed wall of the house in which she would be living just a few hours more. The farmyard with its manure heap, the village street, the semi-urban, characterless one-family house opposite, a few trees—all this was now merely a composition of white, gray, brown, green, or rust-red spots. It was now necessary to go across to Joseph Dincklage and explain everything to him, head movements and the like. Already Winterspelt no longer existed. Only this shifting composition of merging colors.

He considered whether he ought to offer this, what was his name again, Reidel, that was it, Reidel, a cigarette. The expression *smoke the pipe of peace* occurred to him.

Oh hell, he thought, this isn't playing Indians. He pocketed the pack again. Recalling Hainstock's warnings, he had at any rate, as he had done in the orderly room, concealed the pack in the palm of his hand.

(Schefold did not know that German soldiers, unlike Americans, were not permitted to smoke either on duty or in the street.)

Now to top it off the fellow was standing still and lighting a cigarette. And he couldn't even forbid it! The smallest mistake and this bird would turn on his heel, go back to the orderly room and demand that somebody else escort him. "Come on, come on, no smoking here!" That would be enough to make the pot boil over.

A *guest* would have offered him a cigarette now. But of course not if he'd been treated the way this one had been.

Reidel was an occasional smoker. He used up the ration—that straw that was doled out to them—but he did not suffer if he had nothing to smoke.

He pictured himself extracting the cigarette from the stranger's pack and not tucking it into the breast pocket of his uniform (which would have been allowed; nothing in the rules against that) but letting it drop to the village street right before the man's eyes.

A pity he'd missed out on such a gesture. This guest would give him no chance to do that.

Best to stand still and not even look.

The trick was not to look and nevertheless note that this was some terrific brand the man was smoking. Where did he get *that* stuff. If he was a spy it was easy to explain. If he wasn't one, he must pull a lot of weight.

How did a man who lived in Hemmeres have connections?

Schefold walked on. He decided to walk slowly to irritate his companion, but then he changed his mind. The slower he walked, the longer it would be before he was rid of the soldier. And all afternoon he had looked forward to a single thing: the moment he would be rid of Reidel.

Nevertheless he stopped when they passed by the door of a house where shortly before twelve, on the steps, there had been a tumbling and grappling of gray-black tiger and mottled russet.

He peered all around and said: "What a pity. They're no longer here."

Reidel said nothing to this, but he could see that the soldier also missed the two kittens. The very fact that he was not looking off elsewhere in boredom or impatience but likewise seemed to be looking around for the animals was proof of that.

Two kittens and he becomes human, Schefold thought. Well,
something at any rate.

A few guys from his company were standing outside the Merfort farm. They stopped their jabber when they caught sight of
him coming along the village street with a civilian. Was it beginning to dawn on them that anyone who came straight from Battalion and was carrying out a headquarters assignment couldn't be
written off entirely just yet? None of them dared to give him any
shit. They just stood there and stared at him for all the world like
popeyed morons.

Soldiers in villages. In Maspelt. In Winterspelt. What would
these villages be like when some day they were emptied of soldiers? When nothing was left but Cézannesque aggregates, the
chalky and mossy tessellations of Albrecht van Ouwater, timeless?
Whereas now events passed through them, stories, history. Villages emptied of soldiers managed without words. They were pictures, speechless.

Had to dope out what his position in the platoon would be
when this business was over. (When the major had told Borek to
go fly a kite, when the report was under the rug.) Irreversible fact
was that they all already knew how it was with him. That would
stick. "Reidel? He's a queer." He would no longer spread acute
anxiety. That was over.
Nothing could erase that. Only transfer would help. If the
major was smart, he'd have him transferred. But transfer would
mean he'd lose sight of Borek.

But perhaps Maspelt and Winterspelt would not be paintings
after the soldiers had left, at least not by Cézanne or Ouwater,
but devastated spots, landscapes of ruins in the manner of Alt-
dorfer.
What a miracle that Maspelt and Winterspelt so far presented
themselves virtually unharmed to his gaze! A crater here and

there, a flesh wound, a scar—nothing that cut to the quick. And that despite the fact that two gigantic armies confronted each other here. (No, not armies after all, only Kimbrough's company and Dincklage's battalion.) Hardly credible that instead of Maspelt and Winterspelt the great city of Frankfurt, deep in the hinterland, was said to have vanished from the face of the earth. His father must have exaggerated.

He couldn't slow himself down, wait until he was back in his hole before he started to dope out this whole mess.

So far the only sure thing was that the major was willing to help him out because he was helping out the major.

One hand washed the other.

Why was it so urgently necessary for one hand to wash the other?

This was the question he had to start with.

Let us anticipate the outcome of Reidel's strenuous pondering: right to the last he did not arrive at the reason for Major Dincklage's helpfulness. Dincklage had the welfare of Schefold in mind and he assumed that Reidel was in such a stew that he would do everything, absolutely everything, to carry out his assignment flawlessly. This was a piece of luck, so to speak—Dincklage couldn't understand why Schefold did not realize that. To him it had at once been clear that Schefold was in the safest hands with Reidel.

He was unaware of the error he had made when he told Reidel that he was mostly concerned for Borek.

Reidel had reasoned more sharply than he had: if the major wanted to help Borek, not himself, all that was necessary was to persuade Borek to withdraw his report. Then the whole business ceased to exist and there was no longer any reason to continue to call on Reidel's services. Anybody else could escort Schefold across the line.

That careless remark of Dincklage's, sprung merely from a flash of dislike for Reidel, raised the question of why the major obstinately insisted that he and no one else was the right man for such a discreet task.

Along with the thought of Frankfurt there suddenly sprang to mind, out of the clear, or rather just slightly hazy sky of this autumnal afternoon, the conversation with his parents.

The telephone booth in the post office in Prüm. Somewhere on a road near Habscheid the cattle dealer Hammes had slowed down his car and asked: "Can I give you a ride somewhere, Herr Schefold?" That was before Major Dincklage had transformed the main line of defense into a zone of silence. In those days he'd begun to circulate freely for a while in an area that was at first still under German rule and later became a region of shifting fronts, fluid transitions. Not until September had rigidity settled over the lines; then his meeting with Hainstock and Hainstock's insistence that if he must come across, he must go by the Ihrenbach gorge.

"No thanks, not really," he had answered Hammes.

"I'm on my way to Prüm," Hammes had said. "If you have time, would you like to come along?"

He had got in at once. To go as far as Prüm would mark the crowning glory of his walks in Germany. During the ride the idea had suddenly come to him that he could telephone his parents from Prüm. (He could have called them from any village tavern. But the idea had never occurred to him. He needed Prüm for that, the notion of a post office.)

The small gray town deep in its wooded valley. Only a few people on the streets. Prüm was almost a dead town, but the post office was still operating.

He had gone to the wicket, put in a call to Frankfurt, 27511, in seven years he had not forgotten the number, and it turned out that it was still his family's number.

"Ready on your call to Frankfurt."

He had stepped into the telephone booth, closed the door behind him, lifted the receiver. A small gray telephone booth in a small gray town. In Germany.

July 10, 1944. A date easy to remember, the day on which for the first time in seven years he had talked with his parents on the telephone.

"Who is this?"

"It's me, Bruno."

"Where are you?"

No hesitation betraying astonishment, no sign that he was surprised.

"In Prüm. In the Eifel."

"What are you doing there?"

Dry questions. That was what he was like, his father, district magistrate, reserve officer, Iron Cross in the First World War, never allowed himself to show emotion.

Or perhaps he was only being cautious. Someone might be listening in.

"Nothing in particular, Father."

"Why didn't you stay outside?"

It was as though he were interrogating a defendant.

"How are you, Father? What is Mother up to?"

"Thanks, we're well."

"Father, I'm so happy that I'll soon be with you again."

"Yes, we too are looking forward to a reunion with you."

If only he had added a "Bruno" after that!

"I can't even imagine what it will be like to live in Frankfurt again."

"You needn't come back on account of Frankfurt. Frankfurt no longer exists."

Was that it? That his father was inclined to blot out everything except what had happened to Frankfurt in the course of this war? They must have gone through terrible experiences.

He considered answers. Would it be right to say: "We'll rebuild Frankfurt." No, that would be wrong.

He recalled that his father used to say: "Optimism is only another word for stupidity." His father revered Goethe, but his favorite writer was Schopenhauer. (In regard to literature, too, he was a Frankfurt regionalist.)

Suddenly his father dropped all caution.

"If you're bumming around in the Eifel because you can't wait to come back to Germany, it's very stupid of you, Bruno. You'll never find Germany again. Germany no longer exists."

Ah, at last—Bruno.

He was spared answering that by a brief whispered exchange at the other end of the line and then his mother came on the phone.

"My boy," she said, "don't pay any attention to him. Father is just bitter."

"Mother!"

"I hope you're not being reckless, my boy."

"No, no, Mother. I'm always sensible."

"Oh, how happy I am to hear your voice, Bruno."

"Take good care of yourselves, Mother! I want to find you in good shape a few weeks from now."

"Do you think it will go so quickly, Bruno?"

"Quicker than any of us imagine."

"That would be lovely, Bruno."

He had been smiling when he left the booth. He was a man of forty-four, and so bulky that he suffered from claustrophobia in a telephone booth. But that had turned out to be an error. In reality he was a child.

He can thank his stars that I didn't knock him off.

And so can I. The major would have made hash of me if I had done that.

My bright moment. When I told myself: if it's a spy you can earn yourself a citation, Hubert Reidel! Bring him back alive!

Watch your onions, I thought.

Shit. He hadn't thought *watch your onions* at all. He was just kidding himself. He'd been scared shitless. He'd been thinking about that report *Borek* v. *Reidel*. That there's one more mark against him if he didn't handle an incident on sentry duty like a classy soldier, but simply gave in to his trigger-happiness. And along with that faint hope that he'd wipe out the other mark against him if he acted strictly according to regulations (well, not so strictly at that) and brought in the man who'd emerged from under the trees up there on the slope.

425

Especially if it turned out that he was a spy. That was the most obvious thing, that somebody who turned up in front of the line coming from the enemy direction couldn't be just out for a walk. "Apparently you think too much, Reidel!"

Says who.

But after all that probably was a dopey mistake because the commander just wouldn't be having dealings with spies. That simply couldn't be true. There were supposed to be traitors among the officers, but they certainly didn't carry on so out in the open. The commander would have to be off his rocker if he met an enemy spy in his orderly room. And besides—if Major Dincklage was a traitor, he'd eat his steel helmet.

Or was it by any chance the other way around? Was this man Schefold a German spy? (One of our spies, Reidel thought.) That too seemed fairly unlikely. For civilian agents there was a whole special system of channels, top secret and distinctly separate from the fighting forces. A German spy wouldn't be pumped through his own lines in broad daylight! He didn't go hanging around battalion command posts. Maybe if he were being withdrawn because his cover was blown and they couldn't keep him over there any more. But this man was going right back. In broad daylight through his own lines. Who'd ever heard of that?

So was it just that stuff in the letter the guy had shown him?

Dr. Bruno Schefold. Works of art.

What a laugh!

None of it made sense. All you had to hold on to was a few phrases, and the longer you thought about them the bigger the riddle.

"I have an appointment with your battalion commander, Major Dincklage." "Your major is a holder of the Knight's Cross." "Herr Doktor Schefold, aren't you? I'm delighted to meet you."

How had an appointment between him and the major been set up (if he was neither an enemy nor a German spy)? How come Schefold knew what decoration the chief wore? How come they knew each other's names although a battle line lay between them?

And what would the commander have to discuss with a man who turned up in front of the line coming from the enemy side?

To the topkick this guy Schefold had said: "I live in Hemmeres. Would you please announce me to Major Dincklage."

Hemmeres is cut off, it's in no-man's-land; none of us has ever set foot in it. So what was this?

Watch your step, my boy!

At the Städel Institute he'd had only an assistant's post, although he was already thirty-seven by that time. But the Städel had only five slots for scholars, and the posts of curator and chief curator had long ago been filled.

He had been in Holzinger's good graces ever since the time he proposed doing away with the labels alongside the paintings.

"They just distract from the pictures," he had said. "If people read the title of a picture and the name and dates of the painter, they are no longer looking at the picture but thinking about art history."

Holzinger had looked at him in amusement and asked: "Do you think it's unimportant to find out that a man named Adam Elsheimer existed?"

Elsheimer was Holzinger's favorite painter.

"If I've fallen in love with the way Elsheimer treats night, the way he solves the problem of darkness, then I'll want to know the painter's name," Schefold said. "I may also find out what he borrowed from Caravaggio and how he influenced Claude, and perhaps even Rembrandt. And that his special dusky brilliance results from his painting on copper. But that's what catalogues and books are for. First of all I have to have seen how he lets the light graze one of his tiny figures. Seen it! You know," he went on, "I prefer the visitors who turn up repeatedly and head straight for one or two pictures to those who talk to me knowingly about styles and epochs, make suggestions about hanging the pictures, and try to tell me something about 'historical genre' and 'synchronization.' Horrible! Let's give the pictures nothing but numbers,

Professor Holzinger. Anybody who wants to know more than the picture itself can tell him can always look in the catalogue."

He could see that the idea appealed tremendously to Holzinger. But the director would have run into trouble with the conservative-minded, rather philistine trustees of the Städel Institute of Art. So Holzinger backed off; laughing, he said: "You're leaving out the factor of the artist's vanity. We could do it with the old pictures. But with contemporaries! Beckmann would throw a brush in my face if I walked into his studio and told him we hung his *Iron Footbridge* without that little plaque next to it identifying the painter."

Recalling this conversation, Schefold was very much back in Frankfurt.

Come to think of it, that discussion must have taken place when Max Beckmann was still teaching at the Städel Academy in Frankfurt, before 1933, that is. Later Holzinger could no longer have talked about plaques alongside Beckmann paintings. Not only the plaques but the paintings had been removed. Holzinger had become taciturn, and Beckmann had gone into exile, just as he, Schefold, did three years later.

On that day in April 1937 when Schefold had gone to the storage room to pick out the Klee, he had also seen the Beckmanns in the racks. But there was no possibility of adding a Beckmann to the Klee. That was Beckmann's punishment for working on a large scale—impossible to save his paintings.

A month later Schefold read in a Brussels newspaper that the Beckmanns, the Noldes, the Kirchners, the Kokoschkas, the Feiningers, and incidentally the Klees as well, had been removed from German museums and put up at auction in Switzerland. So that had been the significance of the letter from Berlin in which the Städel was instructed to pack such and such paintings—list enclosed—and have them ready for delivery by such and such a date. And they had thought, taken it for granted, in fact, that the works would be destroyed! Holzinger had not come to the museum for several days, had huddled in his apartment, refused to talk to anyone. But the Nazis had not destroyed the paintings;

they'd auctioned them off! That was pretty bad, but not really sufficient basis for tragic postures, relapses into silence, end-of-the-world thoughts. The German museums would simply have to buy the paintings back some day, and Schefold mentally rubbed his hands maliciously at the thought that the sums demanded would bring many a municipal government to the brink of bankruptcy. They'd have to go begging to donors, to philanthropists, as never before.

But then he had jumped up from his café table on the Boulevard Aspach, had paid hastily and left because he could no longer bear to sit there after he realized what the news meant to him personally. So it had not been necessary at all to save the Klee. By now the Klee would be in some Swiss or American private collection, and out of harm's way.

From which it followed that he, Bruno Schefold, could have remained in Frankfurt, for if it had not been necessary to save the Klee there had been no reason for him to leave Frankfurt. Just living through the time in Frankfurt was in the final analysis not so unlike sitting and waiting in Brussels. The difference was minimal.

He felt robbed of the meaning of his act. It was unnecessary that he should now be walking along the Boulevard Aspach. His exile was based on a misunderstanding.

It took him a long time to free himself from this mood.

If he had remained in Frankfurt, he would have been drafted at the outbreak of the war. Assistant curator in an art museum—that was hardly an occupation that entitled anyone to exemption.

He would now be a soldier like the man walking alongside him.
No, it wasn't likely that he would have turned into that kind.

Instead of staying in Frankfurt he had taken the Klee out of its rack in the storage room, gone upstairs to his office, done up the picture in wrapping paper—it was in a flat frame and so small that he could put it into his briefcase where it looked like just another fascicle among the brochures, catalogues, and stationery he carried home. At the border the customs man had not even asked him to open the briefcase.

He had not so much as taken a last look out the window of his office when he left the Institute. The morning train to Brussels was leaving in half an hour. He would in any case not forget the view from his window. The Main, and on the opposite bank the long façade of white classicistic buildings, only once interrupted by the Leonhard church—in memory those houses seemed to him white, although of course they were light-gray or fading toward buff—and beyond, the towers of churches, the dark-red of the cathedral (which architecturally speaking was not exactly a triumph of sandstone Gothic, but what did that matter?), a river panorama that could match any city's, Florence, Paris, Dresden (no, perhaps not Dresden), and incidentally not just a façade but the edge of something substantial, free, ample, and so dense that a whole series of specific places served only as examples: Römer, Liebfrauenkirche, Katharinenkirche, Karmeliterhof, Weckmarkt, Buchgasse, Grosser Hirschgraben . . .

"Frankfurt no longer exists." His father must have been exaggerating. He was bitter perhaps because some things had been destroyed. The substance of Frankfurt was surely not burned out. The façade along the Main, the Römer, the churches—these would survive the war. Goethe's birthplace a heap of ruins—no, that was inconceivable.

Nonsense, it was conceivable. It was conceivable that he would not return to Frankfurt but to a set of collapsed walls, beams jutting into the air, cavernous window frames, an unrecognizable place whose remaining inhabitants stayed on, though they too were burned out, without complaint, because they could not think where else to go, though this city they clung to was no longer Frankfurt.

He would bring the Klee back to them. (At least that one they would not have to buy back.) Perhaps the basement rooms of the Städel Institute of Art were still intact. He would go into the storeroom in the basement and return the Klee to the rack from which he had taken it. Obsessed as Schefold was with his vocation, he took great comfort from this fantasy. As though the Klee might make up for the loss of Goethe's birthplace (if it were nothing more than a heap of rubble); as if the remaining inhabitants of Frankfurt would see it that way. A watercolor painting 30 by 28 centimeters in size. A seedcorn. Polyphonically bounded white. A new city could grow out of that.

Too bad he had omitted to search that wallet this morning. Missed the moment when he could have searched it. Could be it contained the clue to the whole mystery. For there was something phony there, sure as shooting!

At some point—let us assume: as they were already approaching the end of the village street—Reidel asked himself what he would do if he did catch on to Schefold's (and the major's) tricks. (Although he could not remotely imagine what the answer could possibly be. He was just puzzling about it, sniffing, had a funny feeling, a "suspicion in itself," if there can be such a thing.)

He came to the conclusion—to his own astonishment—that he wouldn't do a damn thing. Whatever it was that came to light— he wouldn't go running to the orderly room and raise an alarm. He had to act exclusively by his own interests, and these told him there must be a direct connection between Major Dincklage's willingness to wipe out the *Borek* v. *Reidel* report and the fact that the major had gone into his room with this Herr Doktor Schefold and closed the door behind them. This mysterious mixing of two different elements had to stay mixed; he must not separate it by making a big hullabaloo about something that suddenly surfaced and had nothing at all to do with his conflict with Borek.

Finding out would be a satisfaction. But only if he could make use of the material for himself. Without any fuss. Secretly, quietly and softly.

Not even if the safety of the troops was endangered—because what if it turned out that the bird was not only suspicious but actually a spy, a secret agent, with whom the commander was in cahoots, with treasonous intentions, but what kind? You just

431

couldn't imagine it—much more likely he had the assignment to spy on the chief, to put something over on him somehow. But even then it would be stupid to charge straight ahead like any idiot, make a big noise about it. He wasn't that dumb. The first thing was to figure out whether a big noise would do him any good. Suppose he did uncover the biggest mess you ever saw—still a stickler for regulations like Staff Sergeant Kammerer wouldn't drop Borek's report into the wastepaper basket on that account. Kammerer would look at him stonily and ask: "What has one thing got to do with the other?" He would receive an official commendation and then the court-martial would start. They were so damned hipped on justice.

No, whatever came out—if anything ever did come out—it would have to stay between him and the chief. If the chief really did have some shit on his shoes, you could do a helluva good business with that. Fat chance you'd be that lucky.

They could stick the safety of the fighting forces . . . The safety of the fighting forces was lost anyhow. Others had endangered it, and for a damn long time. So it was gone now, not just the safety, the fighting forces themselves. He needed only to look around his platoon to know that. The major could strain his gut to keep the troops in form; it was wasted effort. The 416th would simply be chewed up when real soldiers came along; that was as sure as the amen in church.

It would be up the chimney with them, the 416th. Its safety destroyed long since by those . . .

For which reason the only thing that mattered was to find a safe spot for yourself. Old corporals like him knew how you went about withdrawing from forward lines of riflemen, what was more, wrongly placed ones, before things got too hot. Old corporals weren't going to let themselves be sent up the chimney. They dived for cover in plenty of time.

He had no ambition to earn political laurels by smoking out any rats.

432

Had never had. He remembered the soldier whose drunken blabber he'd once listened to, in a bunker on the Westwall at the beginning of the war.

The soldier had waved his bottle of schnapps and shouted: "Heil Churchill!"

Reidel had not reported that.

He didn't meddle with politics. He'd become a model soldier just so that nobody would ever bawl him out for anything.

He didn't give a damn that Borek was a traitor, an enemy of the state. None of his business. If he'd denounced Borek, it was just self-defense. Because the idiot had actually driven him to do it.

"You should have held out, put up a fight for what you are. Instead you adjusted. Probably you're even proud of the years you were adjusting, nothing but adjusting, you cowardly bastard."

Outwardly. Yes, outwardly he had adjusted. Not inwardly. Never.

He had merely camouflaged himself. Neatly camouflaged. People like himself had to use camouflage. As a matter of fact he was fairly proud of his camouflage. Maybe it was his way of putting up a fight. Borek didn't see that.

Borek thought that if you were a queer you had to be an enemy of the state in the bargain, but there he was very much mistaken; in times like these it was not only enough, it was the only right thing to do, to sit behind a well-constructed camouflage so that you could remain the person you were.

(The big camouflage nets colored gray, green, and brown that they had pulled over their positions on the Upper Rhine!)

His camouflage had not been good enough. For instance, his behavior back of the camouflage. Once, just one single time, he hadn't stayed in cover, had showed himself to the enemy. That had been enough. A marked man from then on. The pink badge.

433

Because he wore the pink badge he hadn't even made sergeant in this butcher shop that was now going bankrupt.

Tramping along beside Schefold on the long village street of Winterspelt he may possibly have asked himself, in the moment of a brief breathing spell, whether he could be heading toward a time in which he would be able to drop his camouflage.

A time in which a queer was allowed to be a queer. Still grinned at, sure, but permitted, tolerated. To every son of a gun his own kind of fun.

The devil take their tolerance. Their repressed grin, some day, would be more unbearable than their threats of the penal company now.

In one respect, anyhow, Schefold had been mistaken: in assuming that Corporal Reidel was not only a frightening individual but also a Nazi soldier.

This suspicious bird had not told the major anything about the kick. Funny. The way he'd raised his hand in the orderly room when the major said that he, Reidel, was to bring him back to where he'd found him! Why had he dropped it again, crushed out his cigarette, nothing more?

Probably it had been embarrassing to him. Reidel knew this kind of guest. They'd sooner die than talk about things that were embarrassing to them.

Oh well, in return for that silence he could treat him decently on the way back.

This man Reidel was behaving properly now. Schefold could not make out whether he was still as hostile as he had been this morning, right from the start.

Maybe he was just grumpy now because of having to behave decently.

I wonder who he thinks I am?

The fact that he asked himself this question, perhaps the most

important one he could pose in his situation, only once, and what
is more, casually, then dismissed it from his thoughts as inconsequential, tells one a great deal about Schefold, this person generous to a fault. He should always have had a Hainstock at his side.
Although usually even Hainstock's warnings fell on deaf ears.
When the weather was fine and the street deserted, Schefold
thought the war had vanished—no matter if Hainstock were to
wear his jaws out talking at him. (Which in any case was scarcely
in character for that rock-smasher who limited himself to brief
remarks, dour silences, staring with narrowed eyes.)

He for his part would have been glad to know who Reidel was.
The major had given him an unsolved riddle to take along. Reidel
had a blot on his record—but the major had not deigned to tell
him what kind of offense it referred to. Not a military, not a political, not a criminal misdeed—what in the name of three devils
could it be?

A grumpy soldier. A taciturn officer. Schefold was sick of moving
among these characters who had obviously lost their tongues.
Granted, the major had made conversation, but he had kept his
counsel about the only thing that really would have mattered. The
riddle of Reidel was not the only one he had left hanging.
Not a word about tonight. Both he and Captain Kimbrough
had come to the conclusion that the major was planning something for the coming night. In the final analysis that was why they
were complying with Dincklage's request for him to visit. Marching orders with sketch map: through the line. Certainly there
must be something behind that.
Well, in Maspelt he would find out what was. When Captain
Kimbrough opened the letter. Schefold felt the presence of the
letter, although it was so thin that it made scarcely any bulge in
his breast pocket.
There would not be much in it. What else could the letter contain except, at best, a plea to hurry, some advice, impatience, perhaps reproaches?
Not even that, Schefold thought. When I told him that the

American army was rejecting his proposal, he said: "That doesn't matter. I rather prefer it that way." And later: "I would have done better not to let a word of my intentions slip out."

Moreover, Dincklage had warned him against staying in Hemmeres any longer.

Clear proofs that he had given up.

Mysterious, Schefold thought. He sent for me after he had given up.

And no explanations, but exasperatingly mysterious behavior. At the last a few remarks tossed off, highly informative, certainly, but nothing that could explain the necessity of my coming. Why I had to go through the line, although all of a sudden he would rather nothing came of the whole business.

Between the last houses of Winterspelt, Schefold looked at his watch. A quarter after two. Major Dincklage had merely made conversation with him for some two solid hours.

Some of their talk had been quite interesting, though it had no bearing on the main subject. They had, for instance, speculated on what they would do after the war.

"Can you imagine that I shall spend the rest of my life baking bricks?" the major had asked him. (He had told him about Wesuwe. The usual exchange of information on respective backgrounds. The Emsland. Frankfurt.)

Surely the man was a good ten years younger than he. *Rest of my life.* That sounded as though he already regarded his life as finished. Did he find it unthinkable that after this war he might begin something new? When he laid down his Knight's Cross was he also laying to rest his real life? He tried to imagine Dincklage in civilian clothes. He could not quite visualize him. What did bakers of brick wear? (Those who didn't bake the bricks themselves but had others doing it for them.)

"It must be nice, baking bricks," he said. "I wish I knew how."

"You could drop by and see me when the war is over," Dincklage replied. "I'll show you."

A frivolously friendly phrase that took both of them aback the moment it was spoken. At the same time they realized that if they should ever encounter each other after the war, they could not avoid discussing the subject that the major was today so obstinately avoiding. Baking bricks would certainly be secondary then.

He backed away from that sensitive matter.

"If my museum should give me time for that," he had said.

"I probably know less about a museum than you do about a brick factory." The major was anxious to get away from the subject of postwar lives. "Strangely enough, I've never taken an interest in paintings. Never go to a museum."

A pity. A great pity. At any rate the major had admitted the fact in a tone that contained no self-satisfaction at all.

The defect of the German middle class. Its members were not interested in paintings unless these had been specifically part of their education. Paintings had to be introduced to them "philosophically"; only then were they prepared to "be concerned" with them.

What sort of paintings would be hanging in the Dincklages' home? In the dining room a landscape or a still life, something not too bad from Dutch mass production; in the salon one or two family portraits, Biedermeier at best and only if the Dincklages happened to be counted among the old families. Paintings to Major Dincklage had never been anything but things that by general agreement, the reasons for which were never closely examined, were hung on walls.

He resisted repaying in kind by saying: "You could drop by my museum sometime. I'll show you around."

His museum. He hoped that they would give him a museum when he came home. No, he did not hope; he lived by that thought. He was firmly resolved to seize some museum. Ruthlessly, he would exploit the circumstance that he was a trained museum specialist who was returning from exile. Schooled at home and abroad, he thought fiercely, playing with the idea. The museum they would have to give him already existed. He was entitled to it.

Not the Städel, of course. Institutes like the Städel did not attract him. They were too large. He would only be a successor.

Sometimes he ran down the list of museum directors, savoring them: Swarzenski, Holzinger, Schefold.

What he had in mind was a small provincial museum with a modest collection that could be developed. He would ferret out a few good paintings that hung in the homes of the local Dincklages and talk their owners out of them. He would turn rich men into philanthropists, donors of paintings and money for acquisitions. He could also cultivate several special areas that nobody in the Städel thought of, and which later would prove to be precious rarities. But the most important thing was to hit on the right contemporary figures. To get there before the art dealers demanded fantastic prices for them. A collection in the provinces could anticipate the dealers, could pioneer.

He dreamed of people's saying in ten or twenty years: "Have you seen what this man Schefold is showing out there in whatsitsname? One of the best *small* museums in Germany!"

Schefold had absolutely no patience with the anti-museum school of thought. People needed paintings, and where else were they to find them if not in museums?

He believed that all men needed paintings. (Perhaps not all. There were the Dincklages.)

And why did they need paintings? Not to find out that some painter in such and such a century had expressed "the sensibility of Late Gothic or the Baroque." And not even because painters believed (or did not believe) in God, or expressed the glory of kings or the sufferings of the oppressed, showed trees, houses, bodies (usually women's) as firm or decadent, or, if they worked with abstract forms, permitted the critic to deduce from their manner of working the Platonic or Aristotelian structure of their minds, but

because they placed a specific green against a specific red. Because in the upper right-hand corner they made a blue pass into a gray, a transmutation that was paralleled three centimeters down and somewhat to the left of the middle of the painting by another blue's being graded into a sooty brown. Because in a drawing they made a line break off exactly where the eye was crying out for its continuation. But then made it stand free in a white space.

For that reason.

For that and no other reason men needed paintings; of this Schefold was convinced. And needed them as urgently as they needed bread and wine. Or, as far as he was concerned—he preferred this metaphor—as they needed cigarettes and alcohol.

Consequently, even the Dincklages needed paintings. Only they had not yet found out.

It must have been about the time that Schefold and Reidel left the last houses of Winterspelt behind them that Therese came into the kitchen where Käthe was busy washing up and said: "Käthe, imagine, they're pulling out."

Käthe had not immediately grasped what was being said and she asked thoughtlessly, because her thoughts were elsewhere: "What's that? Who are pulling out?"

"The soldiers quartered on us," Therese said. "The whole battalion. Another bunch are coming tonight. One of the men just told me. They're already packing. 'By tomorrow morning the last of us will be gone,' he said."

Käthe put down the plate she happened to be holding.

"That can't be true," she said.

"I think it is," Therese said. "The man wasn't trying to fool me; I could see that."

For a while they looked mutely at each other.

"Didn't your major say anything about it?" Therese asked.

When she said *your major*, which happened sometimes, she did so without mockery or disapproval. She said it the way Käthe sometimes said *your Boris*—good-naturedly, with an involuntary lowering of her voice and at most in a tone of slight concern.

"No," Käthe said, "he didn't say anything."

"That's odd," Therese said. "And I was going to light into you for being secretive. You're a fine one, I was going to say, knowing for days that they're pulling out and not saying a word. So you really didn't know?"

"No," Käthe said, "I really didn't know."

After passing the big barn at the edge of the village, once again the attempt to make out the site of Hainstock's quarry. Again in

439

vain. Nothing but the gentle line of heights, spreading fields, woods, barren pasture slopes, rising and falling ever so slightly, hazed with blueness, and empty.

Nevertheless, somewhere there, diagonally off to the right, in the north, he must be there, the man with his owl, the philosopher's bird.

He had not kept him back from this insane journey today. Advised against it, yes. But not kept him back. No one had actually forbidden him. They had left it to his discretion.

He should have behaved like the owl. Close his eyes and blot out the thought that he was being observed. Tell himself that he was not a captive, not under observation; not encircled by their looks, but alone and free in his hollow tree, Hemmeres.

The thought of Hainstock reassured him. That solidity with china-blue eyes. The omniscient rock crusher who thought of everything. Nothing could go wrong with him in charge. And after all nothing had gone wrong.

All that had gone wrong was Major Dincklage's plan.

The Americans should have struck while the iron was hot.

Incomprehensible that they hadn't done so.

The only one who had actually taken it up, and right off, was John Kimbrough. Although he had shown no enthusiasm, had brought up nothing but objections. A legal mind, like Father. Determined not to let any emotions show.

A man who even refused to recognize that the Americans had no choice but to enter this war. Who took the view that the Germans ought to solve their problems themselves.

And he of all the American officers had been the only one capable of warming to Dincklage's plan. Not those who could grasp that Germans could not get their Hitler off their backs themselves.

That too was incomprehensible.

A star of ill omen had stood in the night sky above Dincklage's plan from the very beginning.

The red tie would have been the ideal target. Fixing that red tie in the sights, then aiming somewhat lower and taking up the slack on the trigger.

How could anybody go marching around military terrain with such a color. The guy must have a screw loose.

Nevertheless Reidel made up his mind that after the war he would get himself such a tie. Fiery red! A wild signal. Certain people would look at him. It would be his brand.

It hardly occurred to him at the moment that his desire to buy a red tie—the same kind Schefold wore—was the first and only notion he had about his life after the war.

Now there is only the white road through the hills. To the right the low embankments edging the plowlands of the Winterspelt farmers, beyond which were the foxholes and MG nests of Dincklage's second line of defense, the existence of which Schefold did not even suspect. To the left the pastures rising by gentle slopes to the ridge above the Our, through which they had descended to the road that morning. Nothing but their footsteps could be heard. The light had altered, no longer had its morning brightness and sobriety; now it was allowing darkness and shadow to pass through, opened perspectives.

She read Dincklage's letter.
Oh, she thought, so that's it.

Therese had called her. "Käthe, there's someone here with a letter for you."

She was already finished with the dishes, her hands already dry, when she came into the main room of the farmhouse and the major's orderly handed her the letter. He about-faced at once and vanished.

Therese, too, had gone out by the time she opened the letter and began reading.

"You should not have left me alone this way."
She would think that over later.

Reproaches! At the moment she felt she could not muster either the time or the desire to defend herself against them.

"So real things come about anyhow. There isn't any need to make them happen."

Ah, but it had been necessary to make Schefold's going through the line happen! The danger in which Schefold had placed himself was a real thing. It had not come about of itself.

He had sent for Schefold although he knew that he and his battalion were withdrawing. And why? In order to prove to the Americans how serious he had been about his offer. The seriousness and the honor of Joseph Dincklage were so precious that proof of them had to be provided. At Schefold's expense.

Rage swept her.

Of course he knew perfectly well that I would not have let Schefold go, she thought. If he had told me he was leaving, I would have seen to it that Schefold stayed in Hemmeres. Or wandered around where he pleased, only did not cross the line to visit Joseph Dincklage. There would have been time enough to tell me even last night. I would have mobilized Wenzel, made him go to Hemmeres during the night and call off Schefold's visit.

She tried to calm herself. Is it just that I'm offended because he concealed from me his battalion's marching order? But as she thought of it she repeatedly came to the same conclusion: he had no reason to conceal it from her except that he wanted nothing to interfere with his interview with Schefold. There was no other reason for his silence. To arrange to meet her in Wesuwe—if that was his purpose, his chances were better if he put it to her directly immediately after finding out that he would be leaving. He should have spoken to her, and as quickly as possible.

No, she thought, alarmed; now I'm lying to myself. I wouldn't have agreed to that.

Therefore his chances might have been better putting it in writing, this way.

442

He was giving her the choice. Decent. Altogether aside from his unforgivable conduct toward Schefold, a decent letter. Something else about the letter rubbed her the wrong way, but she could not decide what it was.

(Schefold found it out. In his unwritten letter to Hainstock he characterized Dincklage as *alien*. He was predestined to find this word, for he too was alien. Though only in the sense of being alienated from worldly things—unworldly.)

The letter struck her as a bit too pompous. The language was not actually pompous, but not aimed straight to her. It did not fit her. She remembered a Berlin expression. When someone talked pompously, you said: "Aintcha got a smaller size?"

Of course she would not say anything of the sort, later, when she went to see him. She would have to keep herself under control, not be snotty at their last rendezvous.

Suddenly she realized that it was no longer necessary to make that visit. He had left her the choice, and going across the street merely to tell him that she had already decided was superfluous. If she did not come, he would understand.

There would be no last rendezvous. She would never see Joseph Dincklage again.

But this thought hurt so much that she took off her glasses because she was beginning to cry silently. She thought of Dincklage. She thought of herself.

*Your major.* There was something to that.

"Something has happened between him and me." Between her and Joseph Dincklage something had happened that had never happened between her and Lorenz Gieding, Ludwig Thelen, Wenzel Hainstock. No "Good Lord, Käthe!" could ever dispel what had happened.

The house across the street, only dimly visible, veiled by her nearsightedness and tears. Perhaps she would weaken, go across the street again.

443

She had had to keep a tight grip on herself these past few days. He had not realized that.

She stopped crying, reached for her handkerchief, dried her eyes, put on her glasses.
She would mourn Joseph Dincklage for a long time.
It would come hard, giving him up.
I am thinking only of myself, she thought. But if I think about him, I'll give in. Then I'll go across the street and talk to him about Wesuwe.

His desire to be able to touch her went right through her.

Too late. His first proposal had come too soon, his second too late.

Pathetic, this attempt to woo her with Wesuwe. It was not the romance of Emsland she would want to be marrying, but a man with whom she could probably have a very good life.

She tore up the letter. It was too dangerous to keep it, even for the few hours she would still be staying in Winterspelt. She went into the kitchen, lifted the stove ring, and dropped the scraps in. There were still embers in the stove.

She looked for Therese, found her back of the house cutting up green beans into a bowl.
"They really are leaving," Käthe said. "Now I have it officially."
"You've been crying," Therese said.
"I've just had a proposal."
"Are you accepting it?" Therese asked.
Käthe looked at her, smiling, and shook her head.
"Why not?" Therese asked. "He's a fine man. And you're fond of him."

"I say, Herr Reidel, what is your difficulty? I couldn't help hearing what the major said to you before. You tell me what they have against you. I'm interested. Believe me, I am interested."

444

He had come to a stop in the middle of the road, forcing Reidel to stop also. If there were to be any opportunity to clear things up with Reidel, it could only be done here on the road, before they set foot on the pasture slope.

"*You* tell me what they have against you." He had stressed the *you* to make the point that Dincklage had not told him anything. And he had carefully thought out the phraseology of "what they have against you." It left open the question of Reidel's innocence. "What you've got yourself into" would have sounded more casual, but would have implied that the charge was real.

The resultant of complicated considerations.

He was not just curious. It could have been any man who took him in charge, conducted him back. That would have been a purely technical matter; whether more or less dangerous would have been of importance, of course, but really only incidental. Instead he had stumbled into a man's destiny. Underneath this disagreeable person a destiny was hidden, as he had learned. There was no other course—he had at least to make an attempt to find out what was involved here, bad though it was almost certain to be. That it would turn out to be something good, he dared not hope. But as far as possible he wanted to clarify it, meaningfully. It was important for the meaning of the business he had got himself involved in when he undertook Dincklage's (and Hainstock's and Kimbrough's and the unknown woman's) mission. Otherwise the memory of it would plague him all the rest of his life. It was important to illuminate this dark corner into which he had stumbled. A corner that neither he nor any of the others had foreseen.

A fabric of shadows. He needed only to think of the resolution he had come to this morning in regard to that waitress in Saint-Vith to realize the importance this act of his would have for all the rest of his life.

Herr. Herr Reidel. Nobody had addressed him that way for years.

445

"Piss off!" Reidel said. "It's none of your goddamn business!"

In the morning *shut up*, in the afternoon *piss off*.

Was the man still the gray-green reptile of the morning? Or was he nothing more now than an angry little soldier? I've touched him to the quick somehow, Schefold thought. What was it that was none of his goddamn business.
He forced himself to remain gentle.
"But I might be able to help you," he said.

Understanding superiors. He just loved that.

I'm a homo.
Suddenly he realized that he could say such a sentence to this man without any fuss. It wouldn't strike the man as anything special.

It seemed credible that the major had not told him.
Good for the major. He wasn't giving the guy any weapons to use against him, Reidel.
Herr Doktor Schefold. He was interested. In that.
"I don't need any help," Reidel said. "Especially not from a spy."

In saying *especially not* he admits that he does need help, Schefold thought. Which was clear anyhow, when he recalled what Major Dincklage had said to the man.
The last phrase, though, spelled danger.

"I am not a spy," Schefold said. "How dare you say anything like that? I will not have you calling me that!"

My wallet with the Belgian francs, the dollars, he thought. Dincklage's letter. If it occurs to him to search me, I'm sunk. And Dincklage too. Nothing I could do to stop him. I might turn

446

back, invoke Dincklage's anger, but if as a Nazi soldier he stakes everything on one card and searches me here, I'm done for.

"I'll bet that's what you are," Reidel said. "But I don't give a damn one way or the other."

That certainly was the most remarkable thing on this remarkable day. Schefold had expected anything but a statement like this. How come this monster suddenly did not care whether the man he was escorting was or was not a spy? If he didn't care, then was he not a Nazi soldier? Or possibly already a demoralized one?
Schefold did not dare to feel relieved.

I'm a homo. He's a spy. Brothers under the skin. I don't have anything against him.
Besides, I'll cash in on keeping my mouth shut.

But of course he could not simply accept this fellow's suspicion (or certainty). If only for Dincklage's sake he couldn't. It might occur to Reidel to blackmail Dincklage. He was capable of threatening the major with an investigation of the affair. Even when he, Schefold, was already over the hills and far away.
It would serve Dincklage right, Schefold thought. The major hadn't exactly put on a scintillating performance, saddling him with this weirdo for the way back also. A breakdown in the major's reasoning. Maybe not the corporal but his commander sometimes did too much thinking.

Now he would simply have to lie.
"I brought your commander valuable information," he said. "Is that beyond your grasp?"

He could not know that Reidel always had a perfect sense for when someone lied or spoke the truth. "I have an appointment with your battalion commander, Major Dincklage." He had believed that immediately this morning. But Schefold's present assertion he immediately classified as hogwash.

447

Which proved that Schefold could not be a German spy. A German spy, anyone who had to do with intelligence matters, who communicated through channels, who was properly trained for his job, would never have come on with that stuff about *valuable information* or ask whether something was *beyond his grasp.* Instead he would bark: "Don't stick your nose into a classified matter or I'll file a report on you!"

And an Ami agent? An Ami agent would say exactly the same thing! Because a spy would have been carefully instructed by American counterintelligence; he'd have the proper training. He'd know the language and how to behave toward the enemy when he got into a ticklish situation. They would have drilled that into him.

So he was neither a German spy nor an American agent.
Then he recalled that he didn't give a damn who Schefold was.
"One thing I grasp," he said, "is that you'd better move your ass along. Otherwise I'll get you moving."

That was too much; it threw Schefold into a fury. He subtracted just enough from the fury for a temperate rage.
"You will apologize at once," he said, "or I'll not take another step with you!"

That *guest* tone. The tone, and what they said as well. "Where have you learned manners?" "How dare you?" "You will kindly apologize!"
That was how they talked. He had forgotten. He had never forgotten. Now it was all there again, seven years later.
What he had resolved never to put up with again.

He saw that the man meant it. He would turn right around; that was how he looked.

"Oh all right," Reidel said.
"All right what?"
"I apologize."

448

He'd knuckled under. After seven years. Knuckled under to that tone he'd promised himself when he ran away from the hotel and joined the army that he'd never listen to again.

This swine of a spy had made him knuckle under.

Schefold sighed. He was not happy with his victory. He started moving again. Attributed the sudden fatigue that overcame him to the fact that he had eaten almost nothing since breakfast. Major Dincklage's lunch. Best to forget that.

In Hemmeres he would permit himself a small meal before taking the letter to Kimbrough.

Together they left the road, started up the pasture slope.

In what way did Schefold propose to help Reidel? "But I might be able to help you." Was this an empty phrase or did it conceal some specific idea, an offer of practical help? Would Schefold have been greatly embarrassed if Reidel had taken him up on it? What could he do for the man if contrary to all expectation Reidel availed himself of the opportunity that Schefold had casually but not frivolously, with some earnestness in his voice, offered him? Suppose it turned out that Reidel's offense—that neither political nor military nor criminal, hence absolutely mysterious transgression—should be of such nature that it justified help? That someone ought absolutely to rush to his aid?

(Would the monster turn into a human being by revealing his secret? That was Schefold's daring thought. So that helping him would become an inescapable duty? Certainly it was hard to imagine that.)

To find out what Schefold had in mind when he offered help to Reidel, we must hark back to a remark that he had made to Hainstock. In his letter—which we have merely imagined!—to Hainstock he indicated that at one point he had come close to disconcerting Reidel, but at the last moment had refrained. (He considered whether this might not have been a mistake: "Perhaps I ought to have disconcerted him in order to get at his true nature.")

449

(The expression at the corners of Hainstock's mouth as he read this typically bourgeois remark about the "true nature" of Reidel needs no description.)

What did he mean by that? By what means did he think to disconcert Reidel?

Let us put it briefly: on the way home Schefold (let us assume while he was walking along the road, before he halted to ask Reidel what his trouble was) had toyed with the thought of persuading Reidel to desert.

"I'll make you a proposal: come along with me to Hemmeres! Then you'll be free of what bothers you."

He must not suggest right off deserting to the Americans. That certainly would have been too reckless. The idea of Hemmeres contained something open, unclear, vague. Vanishing in no-man's-land was not exactly the same as going over to the enemy. All the rest would work itself out in Hemmeres. (Gruesome to imagine that as the result of his thoughtless generosity he would have to live in Hemmeres with Reidel. But this problem would be settled of its own accord, considering what Dincklage had advised him about staying, or rather not staying, in Hemmeres.)

He could phrase it so that it sounded a good deal more innocent, did not pin him down at all.

"Do accompany me to Hemmeres. You'll see, it will go quite easily."

He rejected this phraseology. After everything that had passed between him and Reidel it was scarcely credible that he wanted his company one step beyond what had to be. He would have to come right out with it one way or another.

It was incredible recklessness in any case. Conceivable only if you started from the assumption that Reidel wanted at all costs to get away from what was troubling him.

He tried imagining replies that Reidel might give.

A completely stunned: "Do you think so?" Followed by a hesitant: "I might at that."

No, impossible. Reidel and stunned; the two ideas simply don't mesh.

The other retort was far more likely: "You're a spy. I knew it right away."

With everything that would follow from that.

Once, very briefly, he imagined Kimbrough's expression if he returned with a German corporal in full war paint.

The idea was so fantastic that it came within a hair of loosening his tongue.

He certainly was a madcap, this fellow Schefold.

Finally he abandoned the idea because he thought of the consequences it would have for Major Dincklage. If Reidel did not return from the assignment, someone would surely want to find out what the connection was between the visit of an unknown person from across the line to Major Dincklage and the total disappearance of a German corporal.

Although on the other hand he wouldn't be all that disinclined to play a trick on Dincklage.

Smoldering within him, under the surface, was his criticism of Dincklage. Now and then he poked at it, stirred up the embers.

In this game inside his head, in which played out the moves that might persuade Reidel to desert, Schefold did not count on a surprise, on a trick on his opponent's part that would utterly startle him. Schefold had no suspicion, was incapable of suspecting, that the proposal to desert would by no means have disconcerted Reidel.

For he had already hit on the same idea of his own accord.

*That* would be the thing, he had told himself (when? as early as the time he was waiting in the orderly room? Or only later when he went tramping through Winterspelt with Schefold?), *that* would be the thing, for me just to take off with this spy! Hop right on over the line and go along with him to Hemmeres. I'd like to see his face if I did it. How would this creep react when I let him know I'll kill him if he don't take me with him to Hemmeres, and by his secret route to the Amis. Because he's got a secret route, that's sure as hell; he knows how to turn a trick or two when things get hot for him.

Man, that would be the trick. The war's just a joke by now anyhow. That would be the best way to end the war.

And they would wipe their asses with Borek's report.

And if it turns out he hasn't got any secret route, if he's actually just a damn fool hanging around in Hemmeres, I can go alone. Wouldn't be all that tough. Just make a bit of noise, stir the bushes loudly, as I go up the hill where they're dug in, so they don't get scared—the Amis.

He summoned up fragments of his hotel English. "Hello, boys" —that was what he had to call out as he climbed the height above the Our on the other side of the river.

The thought that he would have to throw his carbine away into the bushes before he showed himself seemed almost unbearable.

Not for a moment did it enter his head to articulate his idea. As a request. Directed to Schefold. To discuss desertion with Schefold—this possibility did not even have to be excluded because it did not occur to him.

He killed his best idea as quickly as it had come, and without knowing why. Possibly for a man like him the thing itself, surrender, encounters an insurmountable block, no matter in what form it approaches him.

So that he did not, as Schefold assumed, need help when he said: "I don't need any help."

As he had expected, the line was thinly occupied in the afternoon also. All the way up the hill to his foxhole they met only

Pfc. Schulz, who stood in the hole where Pfc. Dobrin had stood that morning. In contrast to Dobrin, Schulz was no idiot. He was, like Reidel, known as someone who kept his lip buttoned. You couldn't pry anything out of him. The story about him was that he saved his army pay, that stinking one mark fifty that a Pfc. received per day, and that he sent home his tobacco ration so that his wife would have something to barter when she went out hunting up grub for the kiddies.

Unlike Dobrin, Schulz did not come out of his foxhole as they approached. He merely turned his head and looked with interest at Reidel and Schefold.

Reidel stopped and said: "Have to bring him across. Classified matter."

"Hm," Schulz said.

He thought: Never happened to me before, classified matter at the front.

Schulz too had plenty of frontline experience: Balkans, Russia.

It cannot be determined whether he thought anything more, for instance in connection with Reidel. Since he was among the few men not afraid of Reidel, in all probability he did not think about Reidel in the terms that Pfc. Dobrin would, not for saying aloud but terms that rumbled around in Dobrin's dim brain ("stinking fag"; "lousy queer").

Looking at Schefold, Schulz thought: Somebody out for a walk who got lost, I'll bet. Reidel is boasting. Let him. None of my business.

Ah, Schefold thought, so that's the phrase. *Classified* matter. That is how I should have said it to make an impression on Reidel.

This war of heads. Even among the Americans he had noticed that it was a war of heads. The bodies were hidden in the earth. Only the heads protruded.

But what bad luck I have had. That sandwich eater this morning would have been better than Reidel. Not to speak of this fellow here. He has the most trustworthy face I've seen in all of today.

But no, I had to encounter this man Reidel!

Schulz doesn't believe it. He'll have to believe it, though, when he goes to the village this evening and asks around. I can't even ask him whether he believes it now because all he said was "Hm." Clever. Schulz can stick it. Don't give a damn what he thinks.

As they moved on, the junipers, behind which Pfc. Schulz's head vanished, that lean, calm face under a steel helmet They were alone again.

Schefold had a magnificent inspiration.
"It really is a classified matter," he said. "To think you didn't realize that!"

He imagined he had to make up for something. Even at this point, when he could already see the tops of the pines under which he had stood at eleven o'clock.

He had no inkling what he had done when he forced Reidel to apologize.

He thought it possible that he could still engage Reidel in conversation.

The stinking spy. The way that came out: classified matter. Enough to make you roll on the ground and laugh till your sides ached.

Or smash him one in his mug.

He had to pull himself together, distract himself.
He could see from a distance that his foxhole was unoccupied. Nobody else had dropped into it. He himself wouldn't need it af-

terward either. No longer necessary to crawl in there and think over the whole business. Now he had it. Or maybe not. Didn't matter a damn what the hell was going on. Once the stinking spy was gone he'd return to Winterspelt without delay and report that the assignment had been carried out.

They arrived at Reidel's foxhole.

"Go on," Reidel said. "Beat it, spy!"

This would not do. This would not do under any circumstances. It did matter even now that it no longer mattered because in a minute he would be up there under the pines. Under the stone pines and away. He must not submit to this. Not submitting cost only a minute more. He must not pass up this minute. Under no circumstances.

He stared blackly at Reidel.

The monster, he thought, the monster.

Then fury at Dincklage overwhelmed him. It was Dincklage who had thrust this monster on him.

He's thinking whether he should beat it or not. Standing there and laughing. I'll give him another kick in the behind if he don't get going this instant.

A day with a monster. And what for? For nothing. For an hour's chat. For a letter containing nothing. That could not contain anything. It was a laugh. It was a laugh.

The poor devil.

Maybe the monster was only a poor devil.

The fire of his indignation was now burning hotly.

In his rage against Dincklage he went so far as to feel pity for Reidel.

What turned a poor devil into a monster?

The training of Dincklages!

He calmed down. I'm exaggerating, he thought. Some things are not produced by training.

455

He had to put this fellow in his place.
He reached back to the rear pocket of his trousers, in which he kept his wallet, took it out.

What's he doing now? What does he want with his wallet?
Suddenly Reidel was filled with agitation.

He looked inside it, found a ten-dollar bill, quite worn out, and held it out to Reidel.
"There!" he said. "For your not very friendly services."
He observed the way the hand moved, automatically.

I don't give a damn whether Dincklage gets into trouble. He thinks he has Reidel tamed. It will be another story when his monster shows him the American currency.

I've taken it.

He had turned away, was abruptly walking as he pocketed the wallet again. He shifted the coat on his shoulder. The short grass of the pasture slope felt good under his footsteps. It crackled pleasantly. He was walking alone. A lovely afternoon.

Reidel held the ten-dollar bill in his hand. Did he read the figures, the English words on it, look at the portrait on it?
He let the scrap of paper drop.

He regretted that he could not turn around, turn around and wave. To the other soldier in his foxhole who had said nothing but "Hm" he would have been able to turn and wave; Schefold was sure of that. A different escort might have made it a pleasant day.
He strode uphill. The way back went somewhat more slowly than in the morning, because it was uphill. Slower, but no harder. The slope up to the stone pines was quite gradual. Schefold did not count his steps; he was not concerned to find out how far it was to the pines.

456

Reidel was concerned to find out. Thirty meters. Forty to fifty steps.

But then he was already under the first tall umbrellas, under the green of those stone pines, providing light shade on so bright an afternoon.

Good Lord, how afraid I was, Schefold thought; all day long I've been afraid. And now I'm no longer afraid. I'm free.

Free!

Schefold's body was brought into Winterspelt about four o'clock. Two medicos carried it on a stretcher. Behind the stretcher Reidel, Pfc. Schulz, and two sergeants followed. Schulz and the two sergeants kept their distance from Reidel.

The few soldiers who were standing outside the houses at this time looked curiously at the group as it came down the village street. They did not dare trail along because they knew the two sergeants would bawl them out if they tried anything of the sort.

The stretcher was put down in front of the steps leading up to the door of the battalion command post, that is, on the unpaved village street. One of the two sergeants went up the steps, vanished inside the house.

Now farmers—men and women—as well as soldiers from the surrounding houses gathered around the body of Schefold lying there on the street. Several Russian prisoners of war joined them. Pfc. Schulz and the remaining sergeant kept saying every so often: "Step back! Come on, step back!" Reidel had posted himself beside the steps.

Käthe did not at once recognize Schefold.

His face was grayish yellow. His suit was everywhere smeared with great splashes and ribbons of already encrusted blood. The right side of his mouth drooped; dark blood had run from it down his throat, over his shirt. His eyes were still half open.

Pfc. Schulz had spread Schefold's raincoat over the corpse, but the coat had slid down while the stretcher was being carried and now covered only his legs. Schulz bent over Schefold and again drew the coat up.

The sergeant who had entered the house came back, followed by Staff Sergeant Kammerer. Kammerer said something to Reidel. Reidel replied something. The bystanders could not hear what was being said because they were kept at a distance. They saw that the staff sergeant looked at Reidel in astonishment, then turned on his heel and went back inside the house.

Shortly afterward a clerk opened the door and beckoned to Reidel. Reidel went up the steps at once. The door closed behind him.

Schefold's body, still covered by his coat, lay on the ground for a while. The coat had about the same color as the dust of the Winterspelt village street. Then the stretcher was lifted by the medicos and carried away, probably to the infirmary.

From somewhere two soldiers appeared, fully equipped, and took up positions as sentries with readied rifles in front of the command post.

The civilians scattered.

We will not linger over a description of Käthe's first reaction to Schefold's unexpected return in an unexpected state.

It can easily be imagined that she thought in such formulas as, "But this isn't possible," or, "This is only a bad dream."

Or perhaps in no formulas at all, but in surges of speechless horror.

Immediately after that she reacted spontaneously.

She had to confront Dincklage. He had to give her an explanation.

One of the guards said to her. "You cannot go in."

"But I must see Major Dincklage at once."

"Sorry," the man said. "We have strict orders to admit no one at all."

An hour later, at five o'clock, Hainstock came.

She went away with him.

Kammerer had said to Reidel: "I hear you shot this man?"

"I must see the major," Reidel had replied.

He had no longer bothered about forms. The prescribed military phrase would have been: "Request permission to see the major, sir."

Estimating the distance was no problem. By the time a man reached the top there, just under the pines, the distance was thirty meters.

He must not release the safety catch and cock the trigger until the last moment, so that the period between the clicks and the firing would be only fractions of a second.

Up to that point he could take up the slack on the trigger.

He could no longer address the red tie as his target. He would have to be content with a point on the moving back.

The ten-dollar bill, a rather worn and limp note, lay at his feet, on the ground beside his foxhole.

I took the tip.

Round about the imaginary line between the barrel of the carbine and a point on Schefold's back stood, motionless, inflexible, the gray of an abstract sociological concept: the class that takes tips.

The noise of the lever that pushed the first cartridge from the carbine's rapid-fire magazine into the barrel sounded dry, metallic, and very loud in the lovely, windless October day.

First he took out the wallet, leafed through it, continued to search the body methodically, and found the letter. One corner of the envelope had been torn by a bullet. He ripped open the envelope. His hotel English did not suffice for him to understand what it was about. Besides, he was in a hurry. It was enough to grasp that Major Dincklage had written a letter to an American officer.

All that blood! He had not imagined there would be such quantities of blood. He wiped his hands off on the grass, pocketed the wallet and the letter.

Schulz came up the hill. Reidel said: "Had to do it. Classified matter. See to it that you locate a sergeant!"

"This can't be," Schulz said. "It just can't have happened. I don't want anything to do with it."

He stood still and looked alternately at Schefold and at Reidel, who was kneeling beside the corpse.

Reidel had to set out himself to find a noncom, while Schulz stood guard beside Schefold. When Reidel returned with a sergeant, Schulz was sent down to the village to fetch medicos.

Later a second sergeant joined them.

The magazine of Reidel's improved carbine K 98k had not been fully loaded; it had contained only twelve cartridges. All we know about the effect of the penetration of twelve steel-clad bullets into a living human body is that if the carbine of a first-class marksman is carefully aimed and fired with an imperceptible downward traverse of the shoulder, the bullets will spray the target from head to abdomen, inducing immediate death.

Thus, as it is customary to say in such cases, Schefold cannot have suffered. Perhaps he experienced a moment of boundless astonishment as he felt twelve fires suddenly beginning to burn in him, but the moment was surely so brief that he would not have had time to become aware of the transformation of astonishment into pain.

And that is all we know for certain about Schefold's last moment. It is not out of the question that something else happened within him, in an act completely suspending all our notions of time. If in the exceptional condition of dying a moment lasts as long as eternity, it would be conceivable that he saw things, paintings, words, not in succession, of course, but in a whirling sphere made of splinters of light, all in an instant. Imagine this construct of past and future rotating before his mind's eye not as a disk, but as something three-dimensional, a whirling round body throwing tangents into infinity!

A hypothesis, no more. Since no one has ever related what went on within him before he gave up the ghost, we content ourselves with saying that Schefold was dead before Reidel put down his carbine. And although his body was still warm and his blood still pouring out when Reidel knelt beside him and searched him, he was by then no more than a piece of inorganic matter.

*Casualty Figures*

### Free as a Bird

At dusk on one of the following days Hainstock released the owl. The bird's concussion had surely mended long ago, and there was no longer any reason to keep it around.

He put on a pair of his stonecutting gloves, held the bird's wings close, and carried it out. The owl attacked the leather gloves with its crooked beak. Hainstock placed it cautiously on the ground, where it remained sitting in confusion for a while. Then it soared up to the right, uttering a piercing "kyoo-veek," and vanished beyond the slanting limestone wall of the quarry. If it flies in that direction, Hainstock thought, it will reach the Elcherath red beech groves. It will have to find something better; there are few hollows in beech trunks.

The screech of the owl had disturbed the jackdaws nesting in the quarry wall. They fluttered up, cracking out their *kyacka-kyacka-kyack* into the early darkness.

Hainstock went back into the shack, took down the crates that had made the owl's towering cave, and carried them outside. When he was finished with this, he looked around the shack. It had recovered its former appearance: the table, the bed, the stove, the shelf of books and fossils.

### What Will Not Be Told

1.

For example, what took place between Dincklage and Reidel. Reidel now had Dincklage's letter to Kimbrough in his pocket.

What crazy luck Hubert Reidel had. So the chief actually did have shit on his shoes. Hubert Reidel could really write his own ticket now.

It is unnecessary to describe what Reidel made of the situation. It can be imagined.

Perhaps he even extracted a promotion to sergeant out of it. Perhaps they compromised: Reidel handed over the letter and in return was promoted to sergeant and transferred.

The promotion would make up for the twinge of losing sight of Borek.

Of course it is possible that Dincklage's second encounter with Reidel took an entirely different course.

Perhaps Dincklage had Reidel arrested on the spot, then went into his room, wrote a brief report for Colonel Hoffmann, and shot himself with his service pistol.

But if that happened, Hainstock would have heard about it when he went to Winterspelt next day. News of the battalion commander's suicide would have spread through all of Winterspelt.

Then again it is conceivable that Dincklage set the pistol to his temple only after leaving Winterspelt. At some time, somewhere during the movement of the 416th Infantry Division to northern Italy, before the order reached him to report to Colonel Hoffmann, he went aside during a halt and made an end of it. In this case Hainstock would not have heard anything.

Conjectures. We do not dare to decide.

Choose whatever solution seems to you the most credible, in the face of so many enigmas and contradictions in the already somewhat obscured image of this problematical character.

2.

We will not reproduce the effect of Schefold's death upon Hainstock.

Or anything of the whole scene between Käthe and Hainstock at five o'clock in the afternoon.

465

The stereotyped language of speechlessness. "But this isn't possible." "This is only a bad dream."

Their total perplexity in regard to the reasons.

A brief quarrel. She ought to wait until she is allowed to see Dincklage, Hainstock argues; it is absolutely necessary. Her refusal. She says she wants to get away. She's had it. She has no more time to lose.

The first shadows, hesitant, still diffuse, of an oncoming night of guilt.

It is obvious that he can no longer refuse to show her Schefold's secret route. He did not even try. And even if he had tried—we can spare ourselves reproducing that dialogue.

### 3.

Käthe's interrogation by Kimbrough and Wheeler was a military routine. Käthe could provide no explanation, could only report the fact that Schefold had been shot.

Afterward they sat together for a while talking about the possible reasons. Major Wheeler reproached neither Käthe nor his friend John Kimbrough. He referred to it as an accident, a mishap.

### The Journey to the West, Last Stretch

Hainstock fixed something to eat for himself and Käthe. They drank coffee. They killed time with silence and with discussions of Reidel's motive for killing Schefold. (They did not know Reidel's name.)

Hainstock returned to his theory about Dincklage's lack of a mass base and hence the acute danger that some Nazi fanatic might smell a rat, might be suspicious of anything against regulations, against the Führer and the government.

"Schefold must have run into one of them," he said. "There is no other explanation."

He reflected for a while before he said: "But Dincklage isn't to be blamed. He couldn't count on there being a a full-fledged fascist around."

Hanielweg for the second time. The unexpected deaths.

Käthe thought: So this afternoon was not the last time I was in Wenzel's shack.

A lamp burned, lighting the table at which Wenzel Hainstock sat smoking his pipe. Otherwise, nothing but shadows. The owl, which probably sat in its cave of the topmost crate, remained invisible.

They set out at eight o'clock. All the while Hainstock had been thinking how they were going to manage in the darkness. The night would be pitch black because the moon was in its last quarter. But there could be no thought of taking along a flashlight.

Käthe was dressed exactly as she had been when she came from her last English lesson: a brown woolen suit, thin gray woolen stockings, practical shoes. When she wanted to put on her light-colored raincoat, Hainstock said: "Better not wear it."

She had left the summer frock from Prüm at the Thelen farm, like everything else.

She had nothing else to carry. In one jacket pocket were a cake of soap, toothpaste, a toothbrush, a comb. Her most precious possession was the case with her extra pair of glasses. That she must not lose.

They entered the forest of red spruce at the very spot where Schefold had always emerged from it. At first there was nothing but blackness, but they found their way better than Hainstock had feared. Among the gray verticals of the spruces stood a gray, permeable substance. Since it had not rained all through October, the floor of needles was dry, crackly. Pleasant to walk on, although they had to walk slowly. Step by step. We'll take an hour to reach Hemmeres, Hainstock thought.

Sometimes Käthe reached out to touch one of the black verticals to make sure it was wood. She felt the bark, rough, corky. Resin stuck to her hand.

Once she stopped and waited until Hainstock also stood still, then went forward the three steps until she reached him.

"Do you think he had him shot?" she asked softly, almost in a whisper.

"Out of the question," Hainstock replied at once, without lowering his voice. "You can put that idea out of your head."

He said it so forcefully that Käthe resolved to dismiss this blackest of her thoughts.

I'd be lost without Wenzel, she thought.

At the bottom of the gorge, where the spruces did not grow, there was a patch of arnica. There had been alders down here until they planted spruces, making the whole gorge monotonous young growth. Because the woods had once been more varied, wherever the ground was not covered with needles you could find violets and solomon's-seal and aaron's-rod.

He turned around and asked: "Do you smell something?"

"Yes," Käthe said. "Strange, this strong flower scent in the woods."

"Those are the lunaries down by the brook," Hainstock said. "They go on blooming until late in the fall. They smell strongest at night."

And he measured his footsteps by herb Robert, starwort, wild pinks, daphne, wild garlic, brownwort, baldrian, monkshood, nightshade, and spurge; nor did he forget the orchids, bee orchis, and wood hyacinth. He left the gorge and strayed over dry lime-

468

stone soils, plucking germander, thyme, bluegrass, geranium, sax-
ifrage, pimpernel, and ground pine until he had gathered a farewell bouquet that he would long remember.

Joseph Dincklage will be packing now, she thought. Perhaps by
tomorrow he will already be on the way to Wesuwe.
Traveling in the direction the curlews are flying.

They sat down on tree stumps, looked at the hamlet of Hemmeres, the farmyard a pale glimmer against the dark wall of the
slope on the other side of the Our. There was no light, certainly
not because of the blackout but because the Hemmeres couple
were already asleep.
"Schefold's things are still in there," Käthe said.
Hainstock shrugged.

"Do you know what they'll do with you once you're across,"
Hainstock said, not in the tone of a question. "They'll put you
into an internment camp. And after the war the Belgians will
send you back to Germany. That is all that will come of it."
"Oh, let that be," Käthe said.
Probably he was right. But it was not necessary for him to ruin
the next half hour for her at the last minute.
"I'll manage something, somehow, so that I'll stay outside,
depend on that," she said. "And if I really have to go back, it will
only be to leave again right away."
"You know where to find me," Hainstock said.
As though she wanted to apologize for leaving, she pointed in
the direction she intended to go and said: "You know, somebody
has to tell them what has happened."

"Go past the farm on the left," he said. "You can't see the
footbridge from here, in this dark, but when you reach the farmyard you'll see it right off. Then run quickly across the bridge and
into the woods there, in case somebody should be awakened by
the sound of your footsteps."

He had played with the idea of taking the Hemmeres farmer into their confidence. The man would know where to reach the American advance sentries. But when Käthe told him what she had learned from Dincklage's letter—that Hemmeres would be occupied early in the morning—he abandoned this plan. He could not depend on the farmer's not blabbing about his nocturnal guests, once the farm stopped being in no-man's-land. And then he, Wenzel Hainstock, would be stuck. That was also the reason they had set out so late. Hainstock wanted to be sure that the Hemmeres people were asleep when Käthe passed the farmhouse.

"When you reach the top you must call out something in English. Or better even before you reach the top."
"Do you think they'll fire?"
"Not very likely when they hear a woman's voice."

It would have been so simple if they'd let me do it all. Instead Schefold had to. Go through the line.

Käthe kissed him on the cheek.
"If I really am sent back, I'll come to visit you."
"Keep well," Hainstock said.

He watched her as she stepped out of the blackness at the edge of the wood and into the lighter darkness of the old clearing, then crossed the meadows to the farm. He noted with satisfaction that she made no noise. She was moving like a ghost across the level stretches of Hemmeres. By the time he heard the boards of the footbridge rumbling, she was only a flying shadow.

He remained sitting there quietly, saw the Hemmeres farmer step outside the house and stare at the footbridge for a while before he went back inside.

Hainstock waited to see whether he would hear anything, shouts, shots, but he heard nothing. Probably an advanced American sentry had caught her halfway up the hill and before she was aware of him.

He stood up and set out for home. For a moment the darkness of the forest blinded him. One ought to be an owl, he thought.

## Phases of a Transition from Fiction to Documentary

### 1.

But then what happened to the 4th Battalion of the 3rd Regiment of the 416th Infantry Division?

While Käthe was going to Hemmeres and through the line (the Americans' line), the battalion prepared for departure.

It is mysterious in itself that the 416th Infantry Division, which was assigned to the Commander-in-Chief West for commitment on a quiet front, is not to be found in the lists of Army Group B. At that time there was only one quiet front, the sector between Monschau and Echternach.
The 416th must have been a ghost division.

Let us then leave it and its 4th Battalion of 3rd Regiment fighting partisans for a while in northern Italy.
It don't matter nohow. To use Reidel's language, the war's nothing but a joke by now. Though not for partisans in northern Italy and for those who are fighting them.

On the night of April 20, after Hitler had spoken to me about the alleged treason of the Fourth Army, I was just about to leave the conference room in the bunker, empty now but for Hitler, when Ambassador Hewel of the Foreign Office stuck his head in through the door and asked: "Mein Führer, have you any more orders for me?" When Hitler indicated he had none, Hewel said: "Mein Führer, it's five seconds to twelve o'clock. If you hope to achieve anything more by political means, it's high time." In a low, completely changed voice, as he started slowly, wearily, and laboriously out of the room, Hitler replied: "Politics? I don't engage in politics any more. All that disgusts me. When I'm dead you'll have more than your fill of politics." (KTB, Document section, Frankfurt, 1961)

Ambassador Hewel of the Foreign Office had misinformed his Führer in regard to the time. In the early morning hours of April 21, 1945, it was no longer five seconds to twelve. Even by the night of October 12, 1944, when the 4th Battalion of the 3rd Regiment of the 416th Infantry Division departed from Winterspelt, midnight was long since past.

2.

And what about C Company of the 4th Battalion of the 3rd Regiment (Regiment 424) of the 106th Infantry Division?

The remnants of the 106th Division—two of its three regiments had been captured in the Schnee-Eifel (as Captain Kimbrough and Major Dincklage had foreseen)—were standing at the end of December in the "goose egg" around Saint-Vith. That is historically certified.

In any comparison between Major Dincklage and Captain Kimbrough it must be repeatedly emphasized that the number of the latter's division can be regarded as authentic whereas the number of Dincklage's is pure assumption.

Ghost divisions are wonderfully suited for sand table games. For *fiction*.

It must be acknowledged that no Captain Kimbrough is listed in the rosters of the 424th Regiment. Hence we do not know whether he succeeded, in the goose egg around Saint-Vith, in finding out something about the makeup of his mind and body which he had thought it so tremendously important to find out about.

But why, if you please, damnitall, must the remnants of the 106th American Infantry Division, and with it John Kimbrough, vanish from our sight in the smoke of the Battle of the Bulge?

*The main obstacle in the Allies' path, once the tide had turned, was a self-raised barrier—their leaders' unwise and shortsighted demand for "unconditional surrender." It was the greatest help to Hitler, in preserving his grip on the German people, and likewise to the War Party in Japan. If the Allied leaders had been wise enough to provide some assurance as to their peace terms, Hitler's grip on the German people would have been loosened long before 1945. Three years earlier, envoys of the widespread anti-Nazi movement in Germany made known to the Allied leaders their plans for overthrowing Hitler, and the names of the many leading soldiers who were prepared to join such a revolt, provided that they were given some assurance about the Allied peace terms. But then, and later, no indication or assurance was given them, so that it naturally became difficult for them to gain support for a "leap in the dark." (Sir Basil Henry Liddell Hart,* History of the Second World War *[New York: Putnam's 1971], pp. 711f.)*

"Is that supposed to be an alibi for the generals?" Schefold, listening to certain of Dincklage's theories.

Yet Dincklage was nevertheless the only person who was prepared to express certain of the principles and insights of military science, on the level of the subordinate leaders, in the form of concrete action.

*Prussian Military Aristocracy
or Dossier on Three Field Marshals
(with notes)*

*When Rundstedt was recalled in September to command the German armies in the West, Hitler told him that new divisions which were being formed in the Reich would be ready to come*

473

*into operation in November . . . By October the 19th, some new
divisions and other reinforcements had already been brought forward for von Rundstedt's defence but his strength had, he said,
fallen by over 80,000 men in the past six weeks; he considered
that, including fortress troops, his armies amounted to the equivalent of only some 27 full infantry and 6½ panzer divisions, less
than half the Allied number at his estimate.*

*But Hitler and his staff had for long been planning a counter-
offensive and on October the 22nd Hitler summoned the Chiefs
of Staff of von Rundstedt (General Westphal) and Model (General Krebs) to his headquarters in East Prussia. There they were
told that the new divisions would be ready for action in November but were not to be tied down in defence, for in the long run
passive defence could not prevent further decisive losses of territory. That could only be achieved by attack. Hitler had therefore
decided that an offensive should be launched from the Eifel "because of the weakness of the enemy forces in that region." The
object was to destroy enemy forces north of the line Antwerp–
Brussels–Luxembourg and thereby bring about a turning point in
the campaign in the West. The recapture of Antwerp would split
the enemy front and separate the British from the Americans.
The Fifth and Sixth SS Panzer Armies were to make the main attack while the Seventh Army covered their southern flank, all
under Army Group B.*

*Ten days later von Rundstedt was sent a letter of instruction on
"basic principles" of the projected operation from Hitler, with a
covering note from Jodl which included a warning that "the gam-
ble of the far-flung objective is unalterable although, from a
strictly technical standpoint, it appears to be disproportionate to
our available forces." Unalternable also was the disposition of armies—on the right Sixth SS Panzer Army: in the centre, Fifth
Panzer Army: on the left Seventh Army. They would attack
abreast and simultaneously. The employment of certain named divisions was also expressly ordered by Hitler.*

*Both von Rundstedt and Model when they learnt of these plans
agreed at once that Hitler's object was unrealisable by the forces*

474

*available and they tried hard to get a more limited plan accepted,
but without any avail. They were told that "The Führer has decided that the operation is* unalterable in every detail" *and
repeated attempts to get a more reasonable plan accepted were
consistently dismissed as "feeble thoughts." (Major L. F. Ellis,*
History of the Second World War: Victory in the West [*London:
H.M. Stationery office, 1962–68*], *pp. 176f.*)

*Note:* See also: KTB, Manteuffel, Westphal, Jung, Eisenhower, Alanbrooke, Bradley, Thompson, Liddell Hart, Cavoressi
and Wint, Elstob, etc.

"Make peace, you fools!" (Telegram from [at that time retired
on pension] Field Marshal von Rundstedt to the High Command
of the Armed Forces after the Battle of Falaise in the summer of
1944)

*On September 28, First Army sent me a handsome bronze bust
of Hitler with the following inscription upon its base: Found in
Nazi Headquarters, Eupen, Germany. With seven units of fire
and one additional division, First U. S. Army will deliver the original in thirty days." Before that 30-day period ended, Hitler had
briefed his senior commanders on plans for the Ardennes counterattack.*

*For a few brief hours one evening First Army thought it might
make delivery sooner than even it dared hope. G-2 had run into
Hodges' van with a radio intercept picked up by its monitoring
detachment. According to a radio broadcast an SS colonel had
delivered to von Rundstedt in Cologne orders from the German
High Command for an immediate counteroffensive. Von Rundstedt rejected the order and protested that he could not obey it
without leading his command to destruction. An altercation followed and the SS colonel was shot. The field marshal, it was reported, had ordered Wehrmacht troops to disarm SS units and at
the same time he proclaimed himself military governor of Cologne. He thereupon appealed to the German people in public*

475

*broadcast, urging them to rally to his side that he might conclude
an honorable peace with the Allies.*

*The bubble broke when G-2 rechecked its monitoring detach-
ment. The report had originated not from Cologne but from
Radio Luxembourg which 12th Army Group used to air its
"black" propaganda in an effort to deceive and confuse the German people.* (Omar N. Bradley, A Soldier's Story [New York:
Henry Holt, 1951], *pp. 426f.*)

*Note:* All in all, a reasonable suggestion by the Americans to
Herr von Runstedt.

The illusions of the Americans! They did not deceive the German
people, but themselves.

In all seriousness they believed that a responsible commander-
in-chief would end a war when it was lost.

*He said that "in general outline he held the same view as the
OKW (High Command of the Armed Forces)," that his suggestion "therefore deviates only in unimportant points from the
Führer's view." "It is clear to me that now everything must be
staked on one card. Therefore I dismiss these reservations
[namely, reservations about the forces being too weak]." (Letter
from [no longer retired] Field Marshal von Rundstedt to General Jodl, Chief of the Armed Forces Operations Staff, dated
November 3, 1944, quoted in Hermann Jung,* Die Ardennen-
Offensive 1944/45, Göttingen, 1971)

*Note:* Major Dincklage: "I have never refused to obey an order."

*Note:* Mitigating circumstance: Just as there was no place in
Reidel's mind for the phrase *knowledge of human nature,* so there
was no place in von Rundstedt's mind for the phrase *refusal
to obey an order.* It is truly a linguistic problem.

*Note:* On the other hand the vocabulary of German field marshals contains the words *Fate* and *Providence.*

*Mein Führer, I believe I may lay claim to have done everything
in my power to master the situation. Both Rommel and I, and*

*probably all the commanders here in the West who have had battle experience against the Anglo-Americans with their material superiority, foresaw the present development. We were not listened to. Our views were not dictated by pessimism, but simply by knowledge of the facts.*

*There must be ways and means to bring about the end and above all to prevent the Reich from falling into the hell of Bolshevism. The conduct of some officers who were taken captive in the East has always been a riddle to me. Mein Führer, I have always admired your greatness and your bearing in this gigantic struggle and your iron will to sustain yourself and National Socialism. When fate is stronger than your will and your genius, that must be ascribed to the will of Providence. You have waged a great and honorable struggle. History willl bear witness to that. Now show your greatness in putting an end to the hopeless struggle, if that is necessary.*

*I take leave of you, mein Führer, as one who with the consciousness of having done his duty to the utmost stood closer to you than you may have recognized.*

> *Heil, mein Führer!*
> *signed: von Kluge, Field Marshall*

*August 18, 1944*
*(KTB, Section 4, Documents. Frankfurt, 1961)*

*Note:* So he wrote, and killed himself.

*Note:* Himself. Not his Führer.

*Note:* Field Marshal von Rundstedt: "You fools!"

*Note:* Telegraphed that and, only two months later, took over command of the Ardennes Offensive as ordered (for a time it was called the Rundstedt offensive).

*Note:* The exception, or a remnant of Prussia's glory.

When you come to Berlin visit Plötzensee.

In Plötzensee, von Witzleben is still holding his trousers up in the presence of the executioner.

Erwin von Witzleben, field marshal, executed on August 4, 1944, for participating in the attempt on Hitler's life.

## Casualties During the Ardennes Offensive

| I. German side | Dead (officers) | Missing | Wounded |
|---|---|---|---|
| 6th Tank Army | 3,818 (146) | 5,940 (149) | 13,693 |
| 5th Tank Army | 4,415 (161) | 8,276 (129) | 10,521 |
| 7th Army | 2,516 (115) | 8,271 (385) | 10,225 |
| | 10,749 (422) | 22,487 (663) | 34,439 |

Irrecoverable losses (dead and missing)

| 6th Tank Army | 9,758 (295) |
|---|---|
| 5th Tank Army | 12,691 (290) |
| 7th Army | 10,787 (500) |
| total | 33,236 (1,085) |

According to American figures, some 16,000 Germans were taken prisoner in the course of the Ardennes Offensive. These should be subtracted from the number of the missing. The remaining missing, approximately 6,500, should be added to the number of the dead. The resulting figures for the casualties therefore are:

|  | 17,200 killed |
|---|---|
|  | 16,000 prisoners |
|  | 34,000 wounded |
| total | 67,200 men |

| II. Allied side | Dead | Missing | Wounded |
|---|---|---|---|
| 1st Amer. Army | 4,629 | 12,176 | 23,152 |
| 3rd Amer. Army | 3,778 | 8,729 | 23,018 |
| XXXth Brit. Corps | 200 | 239 | 969 |
| | 8,607 | 21,144 | 47,139 |

*Irrecoverable losses* (*dead and missing*)

| | |
|---|---|
| 1st Amer. Army | 16,805 |
| 3rd Amer. Army | 12,507 |
| XXXth Brit. Corps | 439 |
| | 29,751 |
| *plus* | 47,129 *wounded* |
| *total* | 76,880 *men* |

(*Hermann Jung,* Die Ardennen-Offensive, *Göttingen, 1971*)

No figures on casualties suffered by the civilian population could be located.

*The fighting soon passed on to the East, into Germany, leaving behind two tiny ravaged countries, destroyed homes and farms, dead cattle, dead people, dead souls and dead minds. The Ardennes was a vast charnel house for over 75,000 bodies.* (John Toland, Battle: the Story of the Bulge [New York: Random House, 1959], *p. 376*)

### Automatons

The Ardennes Offensive began in the morning hours of December 16.

Hainstock observed no more of the preparations than three Tiger tanks which appeared on the morning of December 14 on the narrow road running past his quarry. Snow had fallen from low-hanging clouds; it lay in a thin coating on the road and the meadows as far as the edge of the woods that rose up from the Ihrenbach gorge. From the hill on top of the quarry, standing under the stone pines, Hainstock watched the tanks as they came down the road one after the other, gray and menacing. Their hatches were shut and their long-barreled cannon did not move. After they passed the quarry they left the road and swung out on to the meadows, where the snow and the softer soil muted the clank of their treads, and continued on side by side until they vanished beyond the bend of the valley. They left a fan of black tracks on the snow.

479

## Revenant

The village of Winterspelt changed hands twice during the Battle of the Bulge. What was left of it was finally taken by a division of the VII Corps of the First American Army on January 20.

When it was all over, Hainstock one day went up to the heights east of the Our to see the place where Schefold had been killed. He caught sight of Schefold standing under a stone pine and smoking a cigarette. Schefold did not seem to see him; he smoked and regarded the snow-covered terrain. The only thing changed about him was that he no longer had any colors, only shades of gray. His tie (Hainstock did not know it had been fiery red) was now a deep black.

I'm going off my head, Hainstock thought.

During the following days, having noted that his thinking was as normal as ever, that all his psychological reactions followed their usual pattern, he told himself: all right, now at least I know where I can find Schefold if I feel like seeing him again one of these days.

## Brother and Sister

Anyone passing through Winterspelt in January or February 1945 might have seen the two cats. Gray-black tigers (the female also showing mottlings of russet on its back), emaciated, starving, predatory, mangy, freezing, they prowled through the snow and ashes of the abandoned and shattered village of Winterspelt.

Tender-pawed. Shadowy. Noiseless.